DESTINY

DESTINY

A TRILOGY

by

RANDY WILLIS

Destiny
Copyright 2019 by Randy Willis

Published by:
American Writers Publishing, LLC

PO Box 111
Wimberley, Texas 78676

www.threewindsblowing.com
www.randy-willis-novelist.com
512-565-0161
randywillis@twc.com

ISBN-13: 978-1-7335674-0-4

Library of Congress Control Number: 2019900563

Printed in the United States of America

Dedication

To my three sons
Aaron Joseph Willis
Joshua Randall Willis
Adam Lee Willis

And my four grandchildren
Baylee Coatney Willis
Corbin Randall Willis
Presley Rose Willis
Olivia Grace Willis
And my future grandchildren

With gratitude and love

"Go now, write it on a tablet for them, inscribe it on a scroll, that
for the days to come it may be an everlasting witness."
Isaiah 30:8 (NIV)

TABLE OF CONTENTS

INTRODUCTION

I've read that novels don't need an introduction, but *Destiny* is more than a novel. It is three nonfiction novels. Truman Capote claimed to have invented this genre with his book *In Cold Blood* in 1965.

Destiny depicts real historical figures and actual events woven together with imaginary conversations with the use of the storytelling techniques of fiction.

Destiny was inspired by true stories handed down by my ancestors. In some instances, it is 100% fiction.

The trilogy was revised and expanded, in 2019. *Three Winds Blowing*, for instance, is sixty pages longer than the original.

It is a sweeping family saga that spans four centuries. *Destiny* is the story of two great nations and my ancestor's struggle from tyranny—religious and political.

—*Randy Willis,* 2019

"Hardships often prepare ordinary people for an extraordinary destiny." —*C. S. Lewis*

Beckoning Candle

a nonfiction novel

O N E

"You have enemies? Good. That means you've stood up for something, sometime in your life." —*Winston Churchill*

Prologue

December 25, 1941
The Ole Willis Place
On Barber Creek
Longleaf, Louisiana

Ran Willis arises before sunrise, nestles next to the fireplace, with hot coffee—as alone as the morning star.

The wind whistles through the dogtrot and awakens Julian. He struggles upright, half asleep, and rubs his eyes as he pours a cup of coffee.

"It's our first white Christmas! Grab some firewood—please. And check on the horses, mules, and the dogs too."

"Yes, sir, Daddy. Merry Christmas!" Julian shivers as he chips through the frozen water trough with a horseshoe. He gathers the firewood, now covered in two foot of snow. Icicles adorn the trees overhanging Barber Creek. It is cold and rather barren, but it has the loveliness of a Christmas card. And, like a Christmas card, it will hold that image in Julian's mind for years to come.

Ran's eldest son, Howard, driving his International Harvester truck, can be heard a mile away as it plows through the snow on the red dirt road. The family knows there will be no snowfall that will prevent Howard from delivering a Christmas tree to the homestead—a real tree, and not one of those artificial, awkwardly bent imitation trees that have no texture, no fragrance, no fullness.

"That's a big cedar. Let me help." Julian drags the Christmas tree out of the truck bed.

Howard's wife Zora cries out, "I need help, too." Ran clasps her. "Ah-ha! All my favorites: freshly baked pies, peach preserves, and okra in mason jars. Oh, my, and even your famous buttermilk pie."

Ran's wife Lillie collects each family member's handcrafted decoration for the tree. "Let's hang them." The aroma of cedar, sugared fruit, and gingerbread brings back memories of Christmases past.

Today is Ran and Lillie's grandson Donnie's fourth birthday, to boot. "Can I play with my birthday gifts, Grandpa?"

"Yep, but keep the stick horse at a trot. Let him get used to this colder weather, eh? See what else Santa left you. The new game *Shoot the Moon* and a wooden jigsaw carton puzzle."

Good, long-time neighbors, John and Ruth Duke, along with their two kids, Johnnie Ruth and Jerry, arrive with a pumpkin pie and two fruitcakes.

Miss Ruth always spikes her fruitcakes with a little rum. "It's no different from using cooking sherry and, therefore, is not an affront to the Lord," Ruth says. "It provides moisture and helps preserve the cake."

Ran fidgets. "The better part of valor is not to mention that to Lillie. Her definition of what constitutes a mortal sin may be different from ours. Let me taste-test the cake for moisture." He pinches off a nibble and smacks his lips in approval. "Now, indeed, that's the moistest cake ever! I may have another slice or two later."

Johnnie Ruth and Donnie sit on the floor. Donnie prefers *Conflict*, a military board game—Johnnie Ruth, paper dolls.

Howard reaches and hangs the star of Bethlehem on the tree. "It almost touches the ceiling." His brother Herman carved it from a piece of hickory. Christmas stockings, stuffed with nuts, candy, and fruit, hang on every available nail. Earlier, Lillie had placed books, tablets, pencils, wooden soldiers, and even a-rockin' horse under the tree.

The children's faces glow from the fireplace. Herman stokes the fire with a piece of pine-kindling.

The sunrise colors glisten in the snow. "Who can paint like the Lord of creation?" Lillie proclaims.

Donnie and Johnnie Ruth grab a shovel, off to go sledding from the barn. They slide down the hill to the banks of Barber Creek.

"You kids get back up here," Lillie yells. "That's too dangerous. Ten more feet and you'd both be frozen lollypops!"

Julian blows in his horse's nose to calm him. It's not the first time the animal has experienced snow, but it has been a long time, and any sudden change in the weather makes horses skittish, until they get reassurance from their masters that all is well and everything is still just fine. "The Comanche use to do this in Texas. Helps you bond with the horse."

"I'm going to churn ice cream in my new pewter pot," Lillie promises. She stirs snow, milk, cream, butter, and eggs. She also prepares Ran's favorites, especially dewberry pie, along with a cup of kindness known as Community dark roast coffee.

Ran grins. "I hung some mistletoe."

Lillie looks him in the eyes and kisses him on the cheek. "The kids."

"We have enough to feed Camp Claiborne's 34th Red Bull Infantry," Ran says. The nearby U.S. Army military camp accommodates 30,000 men but does not give Lillie a sense of safety. A world war is still raging, and every American is on alert.

Lillie's eyes sparkle. "Please play my favorite Christmas carol—*O Holy Night*?" Ran's father bought him a fiddle on a cattle drive from East Texas when he was barely twelve. He spent his evenings teaching himself the fingering and bowing techniques.

"How can I refuse a woman of such virtue—and one so beautiful? Our home overflows with your sweet joy."

Lillie hugs him. "Will it be our last Christmas with our sons?"

The snow drifts against the windows and doors, begging entrance into their lives like the events of the previous three weeks.

"There's nothing as peaceful as Louisiana Longleaf pines covered in a fresh layer of snow," Ran muses. "Ah, if only our world were that way."

Ran's eighteen-year-old nephew, Robert Willis, Jr., enlisted July 31, 1940, and reported aboard the battleship *USS Arizona*, on October 8, 1940, at Pearl Harbor. A surprise military strike by the

Japanese Navy Air Service on the morning of December 7, 1941, detonated a bomb in a powder magazine. The battleship exploded and sank. Hundreds of marines and sailors were trapped as the ship went down.

The family held out hope, but those hopes had been vanquished a week ago, like a shadow darkening all elements of light. Rapides Parish Sheriff, U. T. Downs, along with Robert's pastor from First Baptist Church, Pineville, delivered a Western Union telegram to Robert's father.

Downs struggled to speak with tears in his eyes. "It has been confirmed that Robert's entombed in the *USS Arizona* at the bottom of Pearl Harbor. I just can't tell you how grieved I am to have to bring this news to you, and especially so soon after Thanksgiving. This is the part of my job that I dread the most. If there's anything I can do for you folks, just say the word."

Howard and Zora took Donnie to the Pringle Picture Show in Glenmora to see *How Green Was My Valley*. "We need to seem as if nothing has changed for Donnie's sake," Zora insists. "I fear that we will be one of many, many families who will receive telegrams before this war is over. Our hearts are broken, but we must carry on."

Julian now works with the horses and mules—plenty of grain, hay, and water for them. He grooms their coats of hair and checks to see if they are sound and well-shod. He's gentle with horses, the elderly, and children, but as tough as rawhide on men who are no-account. "I wish I could ride you guys into battle, but an airplane will have to do."

Two stray goats, covered with ice, nudge their way into the barn. Julian jumps up to shoo them back outside. "Get out of here. You're going to break Daddy's deer horn hat rack I made. It's his Christmas gift." The goats resist but then yield when Julian gives each a swat.

Herman, quiet and soft-spoken, takes off, without saying a word—impeccably dressed, as always.

Howard and Julian help their father with the firewood. "It's best you two find him—now! Take my Ford," Ran insists.

They pump ten gallons of gas into Ran's '40 Ford Coupe at Bob Johnson's Grocery Store at Shady Nook. "Where do you think he's at?" Howard asks.

"Charlie's Cafe in Glenmora is the closest—let's try there first."

"He just left, but not until he whipped two men for making fun of his khaki pants," the owner tells them when they arrive.

"Did he say anything?" Julian asks.

"He mentioned, he would not be back, ever, and he preferred Boom Town's honky-tonks. Not sure which one, but they're all outside Camp Claiborne's main gate. As long as that base keeps bringing in new boys who are wet behind the ears and willing to waste their pay during a weekend pass, those places will thrive. Check 'em one by one."

This time one man lay on the floor in need of medical attention.

"Let's check the Wigwam, in Forest Hill," Julian says, "before someone kills him or, God forbid, wrinkles his pants."

The sounds from the beer joint known for live music and its jukebox shakes the windows as they drive into the parking lot. Chicken wire fencing wraps around the bandstand to keep the band from getting hit with beer bottles.

As they enter, the bartender yells. "Break 'em up before they destroy the place!" Three men are holding Herman while two others are landing repeated punches and kicks. The jukebox blares Jimmie Davis's hit—*I Hung My Head and Cried*.

Herman, bleeding like a stuck pig, calls out, "Are y'all going to help me or just stand there, whistlin' *Dixie*?"

"I'll take the three holding him, you the other two. Use that chair, Howard."

After a melee of about ten minutes, they settle with the barkeeper for fifty bucks in damages and haul Herman outside to his truck. His lip is busted, his nose is bleeding, and one eye is starting to seal shut. He refuses to show any sign of weakness or pain, although he wheezes when drawing in a breath between bruised ribs.

They arrive home in time for a delayed supper. Ran examines Herman's cuts and bruises. "Save all that anger for the Japs and Hitler."

Lillie brings clean towels. "My three sons fighting in the Devil's playground and on Christmas Day! May the Good Lord find mercy to forgive you for such behavior!"

Ran smiles. "At least they didn't go to the Duck Inn…it provides more than liquor." She does not find the humor in his observation, as her grimace reveals.

Lillie pulls her collar up, tightens her scarf, shoves her hands deep into her pockets, turns her face and walks outside into the biting wind. "I need to gather more snow for the ice cream."

She returns—but with no snow. "It's suppertime." Her words are all that is needed for family and guests to gather around the candle-lit table.

As Ran says grace, a light dispels the darkness in their hearts just as the Star of Bethlehem did long ago. The reflection in Lillie's face, from the beckoning candle, contradicts the devastating news from Hawaii.

Ran bows his head as everyone joins hands. "Lord, we know the world will still turn, the songbirds will again make their joyful sounds, and this too will pass. Keep our sons in the hollow of Your hand. Bless this food—and bless our nation. In the name above all names—Jesus."

American men from coast to coast step forward to retaliate against the attack on U.S. soil. In the days shortly after Thanksgiving, Julian had enlisted in the U.S. Army Air Corps and Herman in the ground forces Army after hearing President Roosevelt's words on the radio: "No matter how long it may take us to overcome this premeditated invasion, the American people in their righteous might will win through to absolute victory."

Howard went with his brothers and did his best also to enlist. However, the recruiter didn't even need to wait for the results of a physical to see that Howard had a deformity that would make him 4-F. Howard had a serious head injury, caused by a blow from a split rim truck wheel. It had exploded while Howard was filling a tire with air in Glenmora. He tried to disguise the injury by pulling a cap down over his hair and forehead, but the recruiter—who was not new to his job—pulled off the cap, surveyed the scar, and motioned a thumb over his shoulder, indicating Howard was "out" of the running. Ran tried to assure Howard he could still be of service to the nation in other ways. For a scrapper and brawler like Howard, those words brought little appeasement.

Now, as they continue to enjoy what will probably be the last Christmas as a united family for perhaps years to come, Howard stokes the flames in the fireplace with a kindling-stick from a busted chiffarobe.

Ran raises his fiddle. "Join me, in the family key." Everyone joins in.

"O holy night, the stars are brightly shining,
It is the night of the dear Savior's birth;
Long lay the world in sin and error pining,
'Till he appeared and the soul felt its worth.
A thrill of hope the weary world rejoices,
For yonder breaks a new and glorious morn."

As the long day ends, Ran leafs through his great-grandfather Joseph Willis's six-inch thick leather-bound journal written long ago.

"What would he do?"

Narrative

{1}

1575
Chettle, Dorsetshire
Southern England

Chettle is known as the loveliest village in England. The Willis family lives in the tiny hamlet in a deep valley dotted with a few limestone cottages and a towering church.

"This is a glorious day," Nathaniel's father proclaims, as the entire Willis clan walks to the Church of St. Mary for three-day-old Nathaniel's baptism. "And I'm not talking just about the weather." He smiles as the approach the huge church.

"How much for his baptism?" Nathaniel's father asks.

"Four shillings," the parish priests replies.

"You've gone up a shilling or two!"

"Salvation is worth four shillings, don't you agree?"

"I'll read my Bible tonight and try to find in the Holy Scriptures were four shillings seals the deal with the Good Lord. If the child lives a long life, even four shillings may prove to be a bargain."

"Would you rather Queen Mary's rule? She would have burned us all on a stake. We can bless Queen Elizabeth that our Parish Church of St. Mary is part of the Church of England."

"God bless the Queen, yes. But I am not sure what that has to do with having to pay for a baptism. What else do I have to pay for—autumn?"

1588
Tilbury Camp, England

Time passes quickly, and before anyone can believe it, it's Nathaniel's thirteenth birthday. Thirty years earlier Elizabeth I succeeded her half-sister, known as Bloody Mary, as Queen of England and Ireland. Mary I was responsible for 300 English Protestants' deaths, burned at the stake for heresy. Elizabeth hates Catholicism. She established the English Protestant church when she became the Supreme Governor of the church.

England's little wealth and many enemies entice Spain. Spain, as the most powerful country in the world, with unparalleled wealth coming from the New World, threatens to destroy this small country. With Spain's military might, endless numbers of soldiers, horses, armor, weapons, and ships, it seems invincible.

The Spanish Armada of 130 ships sets sail in 1588 with the purpose of escorting an army of more than 55,000 men to invade England. The goal is to overthrow Queen Elizabeth I and crush the spread of Protestantism.

Queen Elizabeth prays all day and night. As the sun rises in the dark clouds over the English Channel, the Queen greets her land forces at Tilbury. Dressed in white with armor, a silver cuirass, and mounted on a grey gelding, Elizabeth addresses her army camp.

"Shortly we shall have a famous victory over the enemies of my God."

The queen rallies her troops. "I am come amongst you, as you see, at this time, not for my recreation and disport, but being resolved, in the midst and heat of the battle, to live and die amongst you all; to lay down for my God, and for my kingdom, and my people, my honor and my blood, even in the dust."

Elizabeth rides tall on her grey gelding. "I know I have the body but of a weak and feeble woman, but I have the heart and stomach of a king, and of a king of England too."

The next day her troops observe a public fast for victory. If Queen Elizabeth ever felt nervous about challenging the most enormous power in the known world, she never showed it. Her men draw courage and find determination from their queen's stance.

The Armada drops anchor. While the Armada waits for news from its army, the English mount a surprise attack. The Armada is caught off-guard. Its massive ships are not maneuverable, making them vulnerable to the speedy, fast-turning English warships. The Spanish fall victim to an English fireship attack. The English launch eight burning ships loaded with timber and gunpowder into the midst of the Spanish fleet. Enemy ships start to burn, become greatly damaged, and drift from the protection of their grouping. With time, the Spanish Armada signals for a massive retreat and withdraws north, up the coast. But, a mighty wind begins to blow. The storm blows the bulky, unruly Spanish vessels against the coastline. The Armada's army, blockaded in a harbor, cannot not come to the rescue.

The English celebrate their victory by giving praise to God. Queen Elizabeth calls for a thanksgiving service to be held at St. Paul's Cathedral in honor of the deliverance of the country. A commemorative metal is struck with the inscription, "God blew and they were scattered."

The Spanish Armada was not the only armada sent against England. Others came in 1596 and 1597. However, by God's grace, these fleets too were dispersed by storms. Without these victories, England would have reverted to the Catholic faith.

Nathaniel and the entire Willis clan remain faithful to the English Protestant church all during Elizabeth's reign. She lives until 1603.

1603
Great Britain

In 1603, the King of Scotland, James, becomes King of England and the first monarch to be called King of Great Britain.

The next year King James convenes a conference at Hampton Court for a discussion with representatives of the Church of England, including leading English Puritans. One of the Puritans petitions the king that there might be a new translation of the Bible because others were corrupt. The King jumps on the idea, insisting, "We will name it after me."

In 1607, Nathaniel's son John Willis is born in London. Severe harvest failures had forced the family to move to London.

The King James Bible is completed in 1611 by 47 scholars, all of whom are members of the Church of England.

{4}

August 1620
Plymouth, England

"I must leave London to find employment. I have no choice, Father, with our failing economy," John says. "It falls to me to help support you and our family. I grieve over having to leave all of you, but I see little choice in the matter."

"You're only fourteen. If I were a younger man, I'd go with you. You have limited training and experience. What work do you imagine you will find?"

"A bulletin says there's work to be found 150 miles north of London—near Bawtry," John explains. "There is nothing here. I will explore this option and see if work is available elsewhere. Do I have your blessing?"

"I'll agree if you join a church—first thing once you find employment."

John makes the trip, arduous as it proves to be. Jobs are not as abundant as he had hoped, forcing him to take a lowly position mucking stalls, grooming horses, and feeding animals in a stable. The churches he visits hold no appeal to him, so he does not put forth an offer of membership.

John enquires about a radical church he has heard the locals talk about.

"That church is no longer here," a man on a street corner informs him. "They didn't feel welcome in this community. They pulled up stakes and abandoned this town."

"Where did they go?"

"Holland."

John swallows hard. "This is sad news to hear. From what I've learned, this church held views I could relate to and believe in. I reckon that's God's will for me. I want to join the Separatist William Bradford's church."

The stranger looks aghast. "You know he is a radical, refusing the King's law. You join him, and you will get yourself run through with a sword. Are you willing to risk your life?"

"It's not a pleasant thought, but if needed, I am. The challenge is, how do I find this man and join his followers?"

"In that regard, I have news for you. William Bradford will be in Plymouth in a few weeks. It's a port on the southern coast of England—a hard two-week ride on a good horse."

"I don't have a horse."

"You do now."

"You are a Separatist?"

"Perhaps."

"I know that area. My cousins live in Devonshire. Two of my heroes were born there, Sir Francis Drake and Sir Walter Raleigh. They helped Elizabeth defend England against the Spanish Armada. And both explored the New World—America. One day I dream of going there, too."

"Perhaps you can name a colony like Raleigh did Virginia in honor of our late virgin Queen Elizabeth?"

"Who knows? Anything is possible in a new uncharted, wide open land. Thank you for the use of the horse. It will help me on the first of what will no doubt be many travels in my future."

True to his quest, John arrives in Plymouth on the south coast of Devon in less than two weeks and diligently seeks Bradford.

"Sir, I'm John Willis. Please tell me why you attempted to sail for America last month but then cancelled your plans?"

"Young man, we would have gone the distance if the *Speedwell* had been seaworthy. Her timbers were rotted, her sails were torn, and her ropes were frayed."

"Why are you risking your life to go there now? If you make it, it will be in the middle of winter!"

"We have no choice. The king wants to kill us for our beliefs."

"Why not co-exist with the Church of England like the Puritans?"

"Because the King controls the Church of England. We will have no part of a church headed by a king or a church ruled by a pope. We believe the church should be led by Christ alone. We have no desire to co-exist, but to separate ourselves from any church headed by a man."

"That's why you're called Separatists?"

"I reckon, but followers of Christ is a better name."

"Aye, would that I had the passage and place to join you now. God speed, sir."

The winds that saved England in 1588 blew again, but this time in the sails of a tiny 110-foot ship named the *Mayflower*. It sets sail two weeks after John Willis's encounter with William Bradford.

Bradford's departing words pierce John's heart. "We will be ruled only by Jesus, the Christ—God Incarnate."

As religious persecution increases, Nathaniel and John Willis become Separatists. They, too, have no desire to co-exist. But what options do they have?

July 1635
Plymouth Colony
The New World

Fifteen years after the *Mayflower* voyage and the death of Nathaniel, 29-year-old John Willis sails on the ship *Paul*. John arrives in St. Kitts in the West Indies, on April 3, 1635. Within days he made his way to the New World—America—in Plymouth Colony.

The first thing John does is stop a man on a street corner. "Do you know of a man named William Bradford?"

"You're new here, aren't you?"

"Just arrived."

"He's the Governor of Plymouth Colony. He has been for more than a decade. There're only 400 of us. You will not walk far before you trip over him."

John walks two blocks. He sees a man of erect posture and approaches him.

"Excuse me, sir, do you know where I might find the Governor?"

"You have just done so, young man. How may I be of assistance?"

"Sir, I'm John Willis. We met in England two weeks before you sailed for America. I'm a Separatist now because of your words. It has been my desire to follow you here to this new land, but finances and family circumstances held me back until recently. But, here I am, and as eager as ever to follow your leading."

"Young man, the first thing you need to do is join Plymouth church. We need a deacon—be our guest—my wife has cornmeal pudding and Indian corn on the table by now."

John Willis very soon steps into the role of Deacon John Willis, the first deacon in Plymouth Church. It is the fulfillment of a dream he has had for many, many years.

T W O

"A woman's heart should be so hidden in God that a man has to seek Him to find her." —*Joseph Willis* 1784

{6}

1784
Bladen County
North Carolina

Joseph Willis towers over his friends—six foot, two inches. His slim and muscular build and dark hair and high cheekbones accent his boyish grin.

Despite the fact that he is a recognized Revolutionary War hero—admired by men and women—and the only son of North Carolina's largest plantation owner, he is modest, open, friendly, and patient. He lives out the aspect of gentle in the word gentleman.

In the fall of 1784, Joseph's first-cousin General John Willis begins to plan his annual invitation-only formal debutante ball at his Red Bluff Plantation. As always, it will be the highlight of the year for the Willis family and friends from far and wide. Autumn in North Carolina brings a kaleidoscope of colors for weeks. The bursts of red, yellow, and gold foliage reach their peak then. Nature puts on a display unrivaled by any human artist.

John responds to a request from a beautiful socialite from Virginia to meet Joseph. With wealth, grace, and charm she awes most men.

She arrives with a radiant glow. "Pray, Miss, may I introduce my cousin Joseph Willis," John says, with a slight bow.

"You may, Sir, indeed."

"Miss Cornelia Anne Graham, please meet Joseph Willis."

"Honored, Miss. I'm your humble servant."

"And I am yours, Sir. You're taller than I imaged. I mean, compared to how John described."

Her beribboned black hair in ringlets stands out to him, as does her petite waist.

The two became intrigued with each other. "Would you dance with me, Mr. Willis?"

"Yes, miss, but I have never danced."

"I will teach you—no one will know."

*   *   *

Joseph is most eager to tell his best friend, Rachel Bradford, about his encounter with the intriguing Miss Graham. He has always appreciated Rachel's simple ways and supposes her kind heart and humility came from her great-great-grandfather William Bradford.

"I've met an enchanting woman—a beautiful debutante from Virginia. She taught me to dance. Her waist..." Joseph pauses as he sees Rachel's composure suddenly alter. "Are you ill, Rachel? You're as pale as a sheet. Can I get you a cup of water? Please, sit for a moment."

"No, I must go—now," she insists, turning to make a hasty exit.

"Shy as a schoolgirl, as always," Joseph says, as she rushes away.

Rachel walks a mile to Joseph's mother's home. Ahyoka is sitting on her front porch knitting. She looks up and sees Rachel approaching. She senses some sadness in the younger woman. She holds her arms wide and embraces Rachel, southing her cares.

"Welcome to our home, and thank you for being a loyal friend to my son." Ahyoka's emotion-rich voice gives Rachel a new found confidence.

"That's just it," Rachel confesses, trembling, tears flowing from her eyes. "I want to be more than a friend."

"I know, Dear One."

"How? Miss Ahyoka, how?"

"By the look in your eyes every time you say his name. Do you think I was never young once and in love? I know the stirrings of the heart in matters like this. Truly, I understand."

"I'm so afraid I'll lose him. I do not know how to show I care. I can hardly speak. Do Cherokee women know about such things?

"There's another woman now! He tells me she's beautiful and

has charm, grace, and the smallest waist he's ever seen."

"Do you think he loves her? They have only met. Can love arise so quickly?"

"My dear, men are easily deceived by a glace—a gesture—a smile. It's up to you to show him the difference between a passing fancy and lasting love."

"How? I have no experience in the thoughts and ways of men."

"By realizing you have to tell him."

"I'm not sure I can. I become dizzy and weak in my legs and knees just thinking about it. I know I will become tongue tied and flustered."

"You do not have a choice. I promise Joseph does not know your heart—men never do—tell him. Men like Joseph can plan a battle, organize a plantation, become a master horseman, and speak Latin, but they cannot recognize love when it is staring them in the face."

"Tell me how—tell me now, please do. How can I make my feelings known?"

"Look him straight in his face and tell him the sun and moon rises in his eyes. He will not have a response. Pause a second, and then tenderly and sweetly whisper to him, 'I am in love with you…and only you.' Say nothing more. Just walk away. Give him time to consider your words and behavior."

"But, am I attractive enough to gain Joseph's affection?"

"Attractive enough? There are plenty of pretty ribbons to put in your hair. And, if I know a thing or two, that tiny waist of hers is no doubt the doings of a synched corset imported from Paris. I've heard tell about them. Sounds like a form of torture to me, but it is amazing what some women will do for vanity."

"Can that kind of thing restrict your breathing?"

"We will soon find out!"

Ahyoka smiles with a playful grin. "He will no doubt come to me for advice. Now, the question is, shall we plan the wedding for now or later? I'm thinking a dress of white embroidered organza over rose-colored taffeta and white doeskin moccasins. Oh, but listen to me butting in. This will be your wedding, not mine. As long as it is white, you decide what to wear."

"And this blunt honesty will work? You're convinced of it?" Rachel lets out a huge breath. "I cannot thank you enough."

"Men never know what they want." Ahyoka's eyes sparkle. "They have to be helped along."

"What will happen next?"

"Your hearts will lead your love to where it needs to go—after the wedding."

Afraid that if she thought too long about it she would lose her resolve, Rachel summons up all of her courage and seeks Joseph. She finds him fishing on the banks of the Cape Fear River. Dusk begins to descend, with fireflies and whippoorwills and crickets calling.

Joseph looks up and smiles as he sees Rachel approach. Unlike earlier that day, she is no longer shaking, nor pale. In fact, there seems to be a determination in her step and bearing.

"Hello, Rachel, happy to see you. You look much better than when we last talked. Come closer. I have much to tell you—hold on a moment. I have to see if this is the biggest catfish in North Carolina's history."

Rachel, excitement in her voice and teeth biting on her bottom lip looks him straight in the eyes. "Before you speak, I have something I must tell you. I've hesitated too long. Excuse my bluntness, but this cannot be postponed." She squares her shoulders and leans slightly forward. "Joseph Willis, I love you, and if you're too stupid not to see that, you two deserve each other! And, I'm not wearing any corset, no matter *what*, in this lifetime or the next."

Having said her piece, Rachel pivots and marches off with a downturned face. Joseph is dumbfounded both by her behavior and her words. Absentmindedly, he drops his cane pole and stands there. He stares down at the catfish, whose expression seems to say, "Don't ask me!"

As expected, Joseph goes to his mother for advice. Promptly he is told that to miss a life with someone as devoted and dependable and loving as Rachel would be something he would regret forever. Thus, gaining his mother's approval, and spending time contemplating how he had overlooked the charms and grace of Rachel, he makes a formal call on the young woman and proposes marriage. She eagerly accepts, but never in their entire life together does she ever explain what she had meant by the remark about the corset. "Women...unfathomable," Joseph would simply muse when the remark came to his memory.

Joseph Willis and Rachel Bradford marry on Christmas Day—clandestinely since he is half-Cherokee.

January 1785
Bladen County, North Carolina

Two weeks after her wedding to Joseph, Rachel makes the decision that she should learn more about her new family. Who better to go to for such information than her patient and wise mother-in-law Ahyoka.

Once the two women find a place of privacy, Ahyoka is honored to have Rachel seek knowledge of Joseph's heritage. Rachel eyes fill with an inner glow of joy as she says, "Dearest Ahyoka, I know little of you. Tell me when you first knew you loved Joseph's father?"

"It's a story that delights me, and I'm thankful you ask to hear it. Let me begin by offering you a gift that is part of that story. Where do I begin? It was not love at first sight or second glance, or even after careful consideration." The older woman pauses, squints as she drifts back in time, bringing forth memories of bygone days.

"I trusted no man—none ever gave me a reason why I should. It would take time, lots of it, intertwined with respect and trust for it to grow into love."

Rachel fiddles with her wedding ring to avoid eye contact. "Did you ever consider divorce?"

"Divorce? Never. Murder? Many times! And you will, too, but it's when love seems to fade like the morning dew that respect and trust will bring you through. And, like the dew, love will reappear."

Rachel smiles with both palms pressed to her heart as she notices the twinkle in Ahyoka's eyes.

"Where was I? Oh, when I was about your age, Agerton made his first trip with his brothers to purchase slaves. It was in Charles Towne in the summer of 1756.

"When Agerton arrived in Charles Towne, with his two older brothers, Daniel and Benjamin, he changed his mind after seeing firsthand the torment of slaves. They were treated like beasts—animals controlled with leg irons and neck collars.

"Agerton turned away when someone handed him a handbill advertising a slave auction in Dorchester. Years later he gave it to me. I still have it on my mantle.

"Let me read it to you, 'Just imported in the Hare, directly from Sierra Leone, a cargo of Likely and Healthy Female Injun Slaves. To be sold on the 29th day of June.'"

After a pause, Ahyoka continued. "Agerton dreamed the night before of a beautiful young woman drowning in a river. He jumped in and made a daring rescue.

"He decided all he needed was a woman to cook and clean. She would need to be young enough to serve him a long time but old enough to cook well. No slave fitted that description in Charles Towne.

"He told his brothers, 'No! I can't be a part of this. I'll find a cook somewhere else. I can do without field hands.

"'I'm going to Dorchester. They have an open market on Tuesdays.' Agerton told me all the details. He shook his head and walked away and took the wagon—without their permission.

"Agerton never gave any thought to what slaves faced before they arrived at his brothers' plantations. According to his brothers, they were benevolent-slave owners. Agerton doubted their assessment.

"During the eighteen-mile journey north to Dorchester, the horseflies buzzing around his head and biting his arms irritated him even more. Only the gentle flow of the Ashley River finally calmed him.

"When he arrived in Dorchester, he heard men's loud voices as they bought and sold produce, cattle, merchandise—and slaves.

"A small crowd gathered at the opposite end of the market. Agerton reined in and asked an old man about the commotion.

"'A white man has come to town with a pretty Cherokee slave girl for sale,' he explained. 'Don't normally see Injuns sold around here, especially females. Mostly Negroes. Some men are having a little fun with this.'

"Laughter filled the air as Agerton approached the crowd. Someone had tied up three older Indian women who were held by Indian men, but no one appeared interested. One Indian man tied a young Indian girl to a white man. Many wanted her.

"A fat man with a scraggly beard poked her with a finger. Her eyes were cast down. She would not look at what was happening.

"When she lifted her head, her dark brown eyes and beauty

caused Agerton's heart to race. Agerton's dream flashed through his mind.

"The white man squeezed her shoulders and grinned at the crowd. 'Strong arms and that is not all.' He winked as he rubbed her back. 'Yep, she could light the fire in my chimney.' The crowd laughed as his hand started making its way down her back.

"She cried aloud. 'Lord Jesus, help me!'

"Agerton stepped forward and grabbed the man's arm. 'That's enough.'

"'What ya think ya doing, Mister?'

"'Take your hands off my slave.'

"'What ya mean, your slave? She ain't yours.'

"'She's about to be.' Agerton glared at the white man. 'How much do you want for her?'

"'One rifle. Two knives and three hundred dollars. You got that much?'

"'I do. Come with me. The weapons are in my wagon.'

"As they walked toward his wagon, the girl clenched her jaw—muttering. 'Why, Lord—why?' Agerton led her by a rope tied to his left hand, and asked the white man, 'Does she speak English?'

"'She speaks English. I made sure of that. And, she is Cherokee, so you can work her like a mule.'

"Agerton paid him his due and lifted his rifle and two good hunting knives out of the wagon. He raised his eyebrows. 'Is this what you want?'

"'Yep, that will do.'

"Agerton gently directed the girl into the wagon as the white man returned to the auction. He squatted next to her in the wagon bed and untied her.

"He turned to her. 'We're going to Charles Towne to meet my brothers.'

"He cleared his throat. 'What's your name? I'm sorry about how those men treated you, but I won't treat you that way. I promise. You can trust me.'

"'I am known as Bringer of Joy in your language.'

"Slowly, Agerton looked her in the face in an attempt to comprehend who and what she was. He knew she had no advantages in life.

"But, she had a deep-rooted sense of self-respect, quiet dignity, and personal strength for a slave.

"Agerton smiled politely. 'We're not going to see many folks for the next couple of hours. You might as well sit next to me so we can get to know each other.' Her face became flush when out of nowhere he changed the subject. 'You look very much like the girl in a dream I had.'

"With trembling lips, under her breath, she said, 'Oh, no. He's a crazy one!'

"'How did you become a slave?'

"'That question reminds me of my mother.'

"Agerton reined in the horses and gently touched her arm. 'I shouldn't have asked. I'm sorry.'

"She moved away. 'I've never talked to anyone about it because it makes me cry. She gave me strength. She was my only friend, my only protector, except One other. I am heart-broken over her.'

"Leaning over, Agerton patted her on the shoulder. 'You don't have to talk about it.'

"'Well,' she said, 'maybe he's not crazy,' softly thanking God.

"Urging the horses, he looked her in the eyes as if he could see her soul. 'Go on, please go on.'

"'You're my master. Can I talk like this?'

"'I've never owned a slave,' Agerton said with a shrug. 'If it does not make you uncomfortable—why not?'

"'I was a young girl watching mother wash clothes at the river bank while tending to my baby brother. Without warning the Cherokee warrior, Oconostota, captured us.'

"'Where was your father?'

"'My father, Attakullakulla, was hunting in the mountains." 'Oconostota's warriors took my mother, Nionne Ollie, my infant brother, and me far away to the Little Tennessee River.'

"My mother and brother were adopted by Oconostota's wife. I was sold to a white slave trader because I was young and she was jealous. To increase my value, I was left chaste and was sent to a school to learn English.

"'The school was owned by Christian missionaries. They taught me about Christ, and how He has a plan for each of us. They said that when everything seems hopeless, Jesus will intervene if we have faith. Even though I prayed every day, it all seemed impossible to me as a slave girl with no family or friends.

"'I was treated by my owner's wife as though I was a cursed outsider. I existed only to work and provide food for their family. As I increased in trade-value, his wife, a gloating white woman with twitching hands, insisted I be sold."

"Agerton, teary-eyed, mumbled. 'You—your mother—your brother.' He cleared his throat. 'Did you ever hear what became of them?'

"'Never. Mother was a caring and strong woman. She told me my future would be with white people.

"'I heard tales of my brother, but I knew they were made up stories to try to make me feel not alone."

"Agerton was so taken by the slave girl that he didn't see an enormous mud hole. As the wagon straightened out, they heard a loud thumping. A broken limb with moss and mud had twisted around a wheel.

"The maiden climbed down while Agerton tied the horses to a tree and tried to free the wagon wheel of the limb. He resorted to grabbing a knife from a box in the wagon bed and slicing through the moss to remove the branch.

"He tossed the knife back in the wagon and told her to keep an eye on the horses while he headed to the riverbed to wash his hands.

"'Be careful by the water,' Bringer of Joy called out.

"Agerton laughed, but as he knelt to splash water on his hands, the horses snorted and reared. She screamed. 'Get out! Run! Gator!'

"Agerton saw two enormous eyes atop the water. He only had enough time to yell, 'Oh, God, save me.' The beast lunged and nicked his arm.

"He ran as fast as he could, feeling no pain and seeing no blood until he tripped over a root and found himself on the ground with the gator moving in on him. Agerton screeched in terror when it hissed and roared. Convinced he was about to die, his life flashed before him.

"As the animal edged closer to Agerton, the maiden slipped behind it, her jaw set and eyes ablaze. She lifted her dress to her knees, sprinted, and dove onto its back, forcing its head to the ground. Straddling the alligator in the dirt with her feet pinning its legs, she yelled, 'Run! Now!'

"Agerton scrambled to his feet and took off, shaking uncontrollably, blood running down his arm.

"He spun around to return to help but crashed into her instead. They both tumbled to the ground. They laughed and sobbed as they struggled back to their feet. The gator slithered back into the Ashley.

"Agerton took her into his arms. Amidst tears, panting, and trembling hands he sighed. 'I thought you were a goner. I'm—I'm so thankful! You saved my life.'

"'Let me see your arm,' she insisted, gently pushing him back. 'We have to stop the bleeding.' She tore a sleeve from her dress. 'Lie down.'

"Agerton felt lightheaded as she wrapped the sleeve around his arm. 'You're the girl in my dream,' he whispered and closed his eyes.

"After a long pause, she swallowed. 'Here we go again.'

"When Agerton awoke, she was gone. He eased himself upright. The blood loss had made him weak. He realized he must have been in a state of shock. He had fainted and then gone into a deep sleep.

"Now rested and the blood from his wound stopped, he looked around and realized he was alone. His only vestige of her was the remnant of her torn dress tied tightly around his injury. When he realized the wagon was gone too, he yelled, 'How could you have abandoned me? What about my dream?'

"With no other option, Agerton began trudging toward Charles Towne. Soon he heard a wagon approaching from behind. Desperate for a ride he waved his only good arm, and his heart leaped as she pulled alongside and helped him into the bench beside her.

"'I thought you had left me.'

"'Never! The alligator spooked the horses, and they pulled free of the tree and ran down the road. I had to leave you to find the wagon before dark.'

"Agerton leaned over, closed his eyes, and turned his face toward her. She quickly thrust the reins into his hands. 'We'd better go.'

"Agerton squirmed. 'Yes, it's getting late.'

"Following a lengthy, awkward silence and some wincing, he heard, "The color is returning to your face.' Bringer of Joy assured him he would be all right. 'You're looking better. When we reach your brothers, you should have a doctor look at the gash in your arm. The bleeding has stopped, but he may want to put some stitches there to hasten the healing. It may hurt.'

"Agerton shrugged. 'Not as much as having my arm bitten off.'

"'Yes, well, that is true enough,' she agreed, displaying a wide grin. She bit her lip to keep from laughing.

"'How'd you learn to wrestle an alligator like that? You were amazing.'

"Matter-of-factly, with a crisp nod, she replied, 'My mother was always afraid to be near the water. She said danger hid there and that snakes and alligators lurked nearby. She taught me early about protecting myself from hidden dangers—not only snakes and alligators.'

"'That's why you warned me to be careful?'

"'It was my Mother's words that came out of my mouth.'

"'But it was you who subdued the alligator.'

"'I saw the men of our tribe capture them. It is not as difficult as you think. Once I was on its back, I knew I could control it.'

"'Your mother would have been proud.'

"'Yes, but you and I were fortunate it was not a big one.'

"'It was large enough. You shocked me with your strength and courage.' Agerton touched her hand. She did not move away. 'And thank you for bandaging my wound.'

"'This is my only dress.'

"'I'll buy you a new dress.'

"'With Cherokee colors?'

"'Absolutely.'

"When they reached Charles Towne, Daniel spotted his brothers pulling up to the boarding house. They burst outside and shouted, 'Where have you been? And what happened to your arm?'

"'It's a long story. I'll tell you all about it on the way home, but first I have to buy a dress.'

"Benjamin, pondering why Agerton needed to buy a dress, asked, 'Who is she?'

"'A drowning woman I purchased in Dorchester. We ran into some problems on the way back. She saved my life.'

"Benjamin dared not ask another question.

"Daniel crossed his arms. 'Does she speak English? What's her name?'

"She gazed at him. 'My Cherokee name is Ahyoka.'

"'What does that mean?

"'Bringer of Joy.'

"Agerton whirled around. 'What?' He stared at her for what seemed to be an eternity, completely caught off-guard by her announcement. 'You are a woman of surprises. You told me your name before, but it didn't register with me until now. But, yes, oh, yes, you are Joy—in many ways.'

"He faced his brothers beaming. 'Meet Joy. She will be going home with us.'

"Agerton made good on his word, although he did not buy a dress for me that day. He had one custom made for me. It included a ribbon that wrapped around it from my torn sleeve used as a bandage—with all the Cherokee colors in tack."

*   *   *

"Miss Ahyoka, you were the woman in his dreams?"

"I'm not sure about that. Agerton never saved me—I saved him.

"Precious One, the dress is in that wooden box. Would you take it out for me? I've saved it for this day."

"It is beautiful, Miss Ahyoka!"

"It is yours now. Joseph told me he was called to be a preacher. And, you and he made plans to settle in the Louisiana Territory. Would you wear the dress when you reach your new home?"

With a voice choked with tears, Rachel could only nod—yes.

T　H　R　E　E

"Earth's crammed with heaven, and every common bush afire
with God. But only he who sees takes off his shoes."
—*Elizabeth Barrett Browning*

{8}

1794
Greenville County
South Carolina

Joseph and Rachel enjoyed planning for a family. Rachel first gives birth to Agerton, named after Joseph's father. Mary Willis and Jospeh Willis, Jr. follow in due time.

The family moves to Greenville County, South Carolina, on the south side of the Reedy River.

The delivery of Rachel's namesake does not go well. Proper medical attention is scarce even in developing territories. Many a seemingly strong wife succumbs to infection, blood loss, and delivery complications.

With a warm voice and caring tone, Rachel takes Joseph's hand and says, "Go to the Louisiana Territory. God has called you there. It's my dying wish. It is your destiny."

"Not without you."

She closes her eyes and passes to the other side.

"Why, Lord, why?" Joseph prays aloud. "I will not go without her. If you wanted me to do so, why did you let my helpmate die? Why would you call me on an impossible task?"

The days become months and the months span to four years. At age forty and being of mixed-race, with four children yet to care for and feeling abandoned by God, he finally gives up.

"It was a tragedy," Ahyoka reminds him, "that brought us to this point. God was with me when all seemed hopeless, and He is with us now."

"I'm already forty. I must have misunderstood His call."

"Moses was your age when he decided to choose his Hebrew faith."

"Yes, and he spent the next forty years tending sheep for Jethro. Am I to wait until I'm eighty for a burning bush? God does not appear in that way anymore. And Moses had Zipporah, a wife, to help him. They will not accept me with my dark skin."

"Zipporah was Ethiopian. She was dark. And, yes, Moses's sister Miriam and Moses's brother Aaron spoke against Moses because of it. You have many reasons why not to go. But will you do as Jesus did when He said, 'Not my will but Thine'?"

Joseph mounted his mule and rode to the banks of the Pee Dee River. "Lord, not my will but Thine." He felt older than his years. Depression set in as he wondered about the ups and downs of his fitful life—the death of a loving wife, the joy of four wonderful children, the harsh life of a backwoods preacher, the encouragement of Ahyoka. His pockets lacked gold. His home was humble. His clothes were frayed. His mule was swaybacked. His muscles were sore. He leaned forward, a broken man, sobbing over his failure to have accomplished anything significant. Tears blurred his vision, his breath came is short gasps, his hands began to shake.

"Lord, someone has set darkness in my path," Joseph cried.

Suddenly, as though in a trance, he looked to Heaven. Was it his imagination? Was it a vision? Was it a dream? Of this, he had no judgment, but of one thing he was clear: Christ appeared to him with an outstretched hand.

"It is I who has called you. Go as I have spoken."

"But, Lord, I have nothing."

"I will be with you—I am all that you need. In your weakness will be my strength."

His shaking stopped. His breathing slowed. His vision cleared. No, this had been no nightmare or magician's trick or pipedream or child's make-believe fantasy. He was convinced the Lord Almighty had spoken to him with a directive to spread the Gospel. He would obey.

Slowly, Joseph rides home, meditating on this life changing experience. Upon arriving home, as has always been his practice, he seeks counsel from this mother.

"Mother, the Lord spoke to me. I am not too old, not too poor, not too timid. He has impressed upon me to do His bidding in spreading His holy word. I must depart."

Ahyoka shows no surprise or shock, nor any sign of disbelief in what Joseph tells her. For a fact, it has been her fervent prayer that Joseph would recognize his calling and accept his mission. She smiles and says, "Take the dress I gave Rachel. Keep our Cherokee colors with you always as a reminder of our love for you."

"I need you to go with us."

"I will be a burden—the great *I Am* is all you need."

"It was you who reminded me to pray, 'Not my will but Thine.' Will you do the same?"

"I will, but I will be of no use."

"When you were born, you cried and the world rejoiced. Live your life so that when you die, the world cries and you rejoice." —*Cherokee Proverb*

{9}

1798
Holston, Tennessee, Ohio,
and Mississippi Rivers

Joseph Willis, his children, and his mother decide to leave South Carolina in the spring, traveling by land to the northeastern corner of Tennessee. There, they build a flatboat, and when the Holston River reaches sufficient depth toward the end of the year, they set out for the Louisiana Territory by way of the Holston, Tennessee, Ohio, and Mississippi Rivers.

A month passes before they approach the confluence of the Tennessee and Clinch Rivers. Hostile Indians guard the pass. The Indians captured the family. The children cry out in terror as they are dragged before the preeminent war leader of the Chickamauga Cherokee.

With piercing eyes, a flinty face marked by smallpox, the chief's voice declares, "You do not belong to our nation. We do not allow colonists and settlers. The penalty is death!" The chief turns and gives the orders to his warriors. "Take them to the killing ground."

But then he pauses. "Wait!" He feels intrigued by the look in Joseph's mother's eyes.

"You Cherokee?"

"Ii vv," she replied, in Cherokee for yes.

"What is your Cherokee name?"

"Ahyoka."

"What was your Edoda's name?"

"Attakullakulla was my father."

"What was your Unitsi's name?"

"Nionne Ollie was my mother."

The chief falls to his knees and looks to the sky and cries out, "Unetlanvhi, wah-doh!" meaning in Cherokee, "Creator, thank you."

He slowly rises, becoming unnaturally still, looking back and forth to the heavens and into Ahyoka's face. "I am Tsiyu Gansini— Dragging Canoe—your brother!"

Akyoka embraces and kisses her brother and motions to Joseph and the children to come closer. "He will do you no harm. Dragging Canoe, they are your family too."

"The boys look like me—uhusti. The girls are distoduhi like our mother."

"Yes, I agree, the boys are handsome. And the girls are beautiful, like our mother."

"Who is the man?"

"Joseph, my son—your nephew."

"He is brave and broken, like me. I see it in his face. He looks like our Father, tall with wisdom in his eyes."

Dragging Canoe stands on a stump and announces to the entire tribe, "My sister, who was dead with the white men, is alive again. Let us celebrate."

The next day Dragging Canoe asks Joseph to walk with him to a hill overlooking the Tennessee and Clinch Rivers. Dragging Canoe tightens his fist. "We use this point as a lookout to guard our land. Our ancestors have lived and hunted here for centuries. The white man tries to steal it. I want you to know this. I want your children to understand this and their children one day.

"Whole Indian nations have melted away like snowballs in the sun before the white man's advance. They leave scarcely the names of our people, except those wrongly recorded by their destroyers. We hoped that the white men would not be willing to travel beyond the mountains. Now that hope is gone. They have passed the mountains, and have settled upon Cherokee land.

"When you cross the Mississippi River they will hate you because of your Cherokee blood and the color of your skin. You will need a helper. Take another wife there. Be sure she is not ashamed of our heritage."

"I will, Uncle. I know my Rachel would want that too."

"What does the name Joseph mean?"

"It is from the Bible. Joseph was a man in the first part of the

Bible—called the Old Testament. In the last part, the New Testament, he was Jesus' step-father."

"Jesus. Yes, I've heard of Him. How can you trust a man or a God whose followers say one thing and do another?"

"His Book never asks us to trust His followers, just Him."

"Why?"

"Because...." Before he can finish, Akyoka and the four children arrive.

"Mother, could you have the children sing *Jesus Loves Me*?"

With the voices of angels, the children sing.

"Jesus loves me, this I know,
For the Bible tells me so.
Little ones to him belong;
They are weak, but he is strong.
Yes, Jesus loves me! Yes, Jesus loves me!
 Yes, Jesus loves me! The Bible tells me so."

Dragging Canoe, nods yes with tears in his eyes.

The next day Dragging Canoe's braves load Joseph's flatboat with food and blankets. He instructs young Agerton and Joseph, Jr., "Always carry your canoe."

Joseph, Jr., visibly sweating, lifts one of the canoes over his head. "Like this?"

"That will do. I will call you, Carrying Canoe. I could not lift mine at your age."

Ten Chickamauga Cherokee warriors escort them in their canoes, safely as they travel west on the Tennessee, Ohio, and Mississippi Rivers. They continue with them until they land safely at the mouth of Cole's Creek eighteen miles above Natchez.

Joseph, Jr. insists everyone start calling him Carrying Canoe.

{10}

1798
Natchez District
Mississippi

Joseph Willis decides to cross the Mississippi River alone into Louisiana Territory because of the unknown dangers. He is unable to take the flatboat because his children are too young and his mother too old to navigate the boat back across the treacherous river.

He saddles his mule and walks to the riverbank with the entire family. He eases into the murky waters on his mule Josh. They swim to the other side, albeit arriving two miles downstream.

He returns for his family weeks later and settles in Bayou Chicot, Louisiana. There, in 1798, he preaches the first sermon by an Evangelical west of the Mississippi in the hostile Spanish-controlled Louisiana Territory. Spain's dreaded Code Noir forbids any Protestant minister from preaching Jesus.

Joseph establishes twenty churches, and in 1827, settles in "No Man's Land," the lawless disputed area between Spanish Texas and the Louisiana Territory. He plants two churches there.

In 1853, at age ninety-five, he returns to the mighty river that he swam on his mule more than a half-century before.

June 1853
Steamboat Paul Jones
Two fathoms deep
Mississippi River, near Natchez

Joseph Willis had turned ninety-five in 1853. He decides to see the sights along the Mississippi River one last time. His swimming the mighty river on a mule-days are long since passed. This time he will travel on the Steamboat *Paul Jones* from Natchez to Baton Rouge. A cool breeze breaks up the unrelenting sun. Joseph places a wet towel around his neck to relieve the heat.

The steamboat passes another one loaded with convicts. Joseph sits on the main deck next to a seventeen-year-old boy whom the leadsman called Samuel. They both are watching the colossal paddle wheel churning the muddy waters when the boy turns to Joseph. "How do they navigate in these shallow waters? It looks unsafe!"

Before Joseph can answer, the leadsman throws a knotted rope overboard and yells, "Half twain! Quarter twain! M-a-r-k twain!"

"What does that mean, Mister?" The boy crosses his arms while pushing his glasses up.

Joseph leans forward. "It means it's the second mark on the line, two fathoms—twelve feet deep. That's the safe depth for this steamboat. We're in safe waters now."

Samuel waves an offering of thanks to the leadsman. He also opens up to Joseph, explaining how his father died of pneumonia when Samuel was eleven and how he dreamed of being a steamboatman.

"Tell me more, Samuel."

"I wasn't expected to live when I was born. My brother and sister had already died of childhood diseases. Mother said God spared me because He had plans for me. She made me remember Bible verses. I washed that down with Shakespeare and read everything I could. Mother insisted I never throw a card or drink a drop of liquor, although I did occasionally slip off and smoke my corncob pipe.

"I figured no one was perfect. That is, until a late night

thunderstorm convinced me that God wanted me to mend my ways, so I put my pipe aside. My righteousness did not last long, for I developed an aversion to slavery. Our local pulpit said it was in the Bible that God approved of it. It was a Holy Institution.

"After seeing a dozen men and women chained together to be shipped down the river, I determined that the church and I worshipped a different God. Those slaves had the saddest faces I'd ever seen, and the slave traders were human devils. My Father never laughed, yet he never was as unhappy as those slaves. It all made me want my dream even more."

"Tell me about that dream?"

Samuel's eyes sparkle. "When I was a lad living on the banks of the Mississippi, in Hannibal, I could see the steamboats go up and down the river. I wanted to ride one. One day a big steamer moored up at our little town—this was my chance. After all, I'd already fished away the summer.

"The steamboat advertised it was a 'lifeboat'—I reckoned that meant it was safe and would provide the time of my life. I reckoned wrong—at least about the safe part! It was the kind of lifeboat that wouldn't save anybody.

"I became overjoyed to be on a real sure-enough steamboat, enjoying the motion of the swift-moving craft until it commenced to rain. When it rains in the Mississippi country, it rains. The rain drove me to cover. I realized it was not a lifeboat when the rain was almost my demise. I thought I would die as the red-hot cinders from the big stacks came drifting down and stung my legs and feet. Would I ever see my home again?

"For some reason, Mama's supper came to my mind. I expressed my desire to get off that boat. They put me ashore in Louisiana. I finally made it back home.

"Mister, please excuse me if I was a little edgy when the leadsman yelled mark twain. I thought it meant something bad."

"Just the opposite, son." With a slow smile, Joseph assures him they are safe.

Samuel raises his thick eyebrows. "Where you headed?"

"Only as far as Baton Rouge," Joseph mutters, fanning himself from the heat with one hand. "Seven thousand people have died this year in N'Orleans from the yellow fever epidemic. I want to go to Heaven—but not today. Baton Rouge is far enough."

"Your story of the lifeboat wrongly advertised reminds me of Louisiana's Governor Johnson."

"How's that, Sir?" Samuel asks, scratching his head.

"The good Governor got the great state of Louisiana to build the state prison in Baton Rouge. I'm considering visiting those inmates we passed earlier and tell 'em about a real lifeboat."

"What kind of boat is that, Mister?" Samuel gazes at Joseph.

"One built many years ago by a feller named Noah. His boat was mark twain, too—safe from the dangers that lurked in the murky waters below. That boat had no helm, for it was not guided by human hands."

"I love a good story, Sir. I fancy myself as a storyteller. Would tell me the rest of it?"

"Be glad to. God told Noah He was going to destroy the Earth because of its wickedness. But, God was also going to provide a way of protection from His judgment. The Lord told Noah to build a boat—a boat of safety, if you will. The Good Book says Noah found grace in the eyes of the Lord. That was the first time that word appeared in the Bible. Noah received the unmerited favor of God. Grace provided deliverance from the Lord's judgment.

"Now there was a lot to be done. The Lord told Noah to build the boat out of gopher wood. We call it cypress in Louisiana. It will not rot in our lifetime.

"'Put pitch on the inside and outside too,' the Lord insisted. The word pitch in the Hebrew means atonement. We need to be in Jesus just as Noah needed to be in that boat. As the storms of God's wrath beat upon the ship, the winds of God's wrath would later beat upon the Lord Jesus. If we are on the inside, not one drop of judgment can come through. We are sealed with that atoning pitch—Christ's atoning blood.

"It took Noah more than 100 years to build it. It takes a lot of faith in the Lord's promise to do that. The boat was built like an ancient coffin. There was no steamboat pilot to guide it—only God.

"The Lord gave precise instructions. 'Set the door of the boat in its side.' There was only one door to pass through to escape God's judgment. Jesus is that one door.

"By faith, Noah and his family entered the boat. Once they were all inside, the Lord shut the door. God sealed the door—not Noah.

'Put a window in the top of the boat, Noah, so you can look to Heaven for all your needs.'

"God had Noah build rooms in the boat. There is a room for me. There is room for you—for the asking.

"Noah's boat floated many days. It finally landed on Mount Ararat on the seventeenth day of the seventh month. That's our April 17th—the same day Jesus rose from the grave. Noah went into the boat with little, but when he came out, the entire world was his."

"What is your name, Mister?"

"Joseph Willis."

"You should be a preacher."

Joseph smiles at the irony of that statement. "Grace provides our Salvation. Grace provides our Savior. Grace provides our security—grace keeps us. But, we all must choose to put our trust or not to put our trust in God's ark of salvation—Jesus. There's still room in that ark of safety."

"I reckon Heaven goes by favor." Samuel exhales. "If it went by merit, we would stay out, and our dogs would go in."

"That's a clever way to put it. You should be a writer."

Joseph Willis died in 1854, at age ninety-six in his beloved Louisiana. Forever in the ark of salvation—Christ.

F I V E

"Never let your horse drink water you wouldn't."
—*Daniel Hubbard Willis, Jr.* 1900

{12}

March 10, 1904
On Barber Creek
Near Longleaf, Louisiana

Daniel Hubbard Willis's Narrative

Jeremiah and Jacob Stark are my best friends. They're typical brothers, arguing about almost anything, but Lord help the person who attempts to come between them—and me, too. They are the kind of men you could ride the river with—the river of life that is. I, Daniel Willis, will testify under oath to that fact.

My Grandpa told me when I was only knee-high to a grasshopper, "You have to be present to win." In the cow business that means the stockyards north of Ft. Worth. It's the center of the world for a cowman. It's known as Cowtown.

Names are important. They should have meaning. My eldest son, Henry Elwa Willis, named his son Kit Carson Willis. During the War of Northern Aggression I read every dime novel there was about the great mountain man and Indian scout.

Speaking of the War for Southern Independence, I named my youngest son Randall Lee Willis after my commanding general, Randall Lee Gibson. Hopefully, his descendants will honor him, too, by naming a son Randall.

My sons, Henry Elwa and Robert Kenneth, base their cattle operations near the Lecompte, Louisiana railyards. My son, Daniel Oscar, chose a different path after his brother Eugene died of appendicitis because there were no doctors nearby. Daniel Oscar is the only medical doctor in Vernon Parish, in the town of Leesville.

I became a cowman in 1865, near our home—the Ole Willis Place. The fertile, red dirt hills of Louisiana have been good to us.

We live near Babb's Bridge and Longleaf. It was here, on the banks of Barber Creek, and on cattle drives from East Texas, that I first learned the cattle business. It was on one of these drives I first met Jeremiah and Jacob Stark. I thought I knew everything there was to know about being a cowboy—it would not take long for me to discover just how little I knew.

In December of 1899, the Texas & Pacific passenger depot opened in Ft. Worth. I'd seen a postcard of it. Never had I ever seen a building so grand. I had to see it with my own eyes and perhaps buy a cow or two. But, I would need help.

That help came when the Stark brothers agreed to accompany me to Cowtown.

They said all I had to do was introduce them to my old friend Charlie Goodnight, who had settled 300 miles west of Fort Worth. I agreed. And, of course, I needed to make sure my bride of a half-century was good with it all.

Years before, I met the enterprising Goodnight when we both joined in making the gather, after the War of Northern Aggression. We built our herds from gathering Longhorn cattle that roamed free after the war. He showed me how to build a kitchen on wheels he invented called a chuckwagon. I used it on many a cattle drive from East Texas to Louisiana.

We first met at a Confederate Reunion in Houston. He had been a scout for the Southern cause. Before that he'd trailed cattle to Louisiana. After telling me all about it, he offered me a cigar, which I declined, but I did accept his advice on improving my herd through cross-breeding with Hereford bulls. I knew I needed to buy more high-grade bulls to build a better herd.

Perhaps, he would sell me one of his prized Herford bulls on this trip.

Years before, Goodnight invited me to the JA Ranch in Palo Duro Canyon, but I got word he no longer managed it. A stomach ailment almost proved fatal to him, so I figured if I ever was going to visit him I'd better do it soon. I purposed in my heart if the opportunity ever arose I would do just that. That opportunity came in '87 when the Fort Worth and Denver City Railway was built through the Texas Panhandle. Goodnight was ranching in Armstrong County near the Fort Worth and Denver City line. I got excited to see him again.

My wife, Julia Ann, did not share my excitement. "Wait until your brothers can go with you." Wrinkling her nose always meant no.

She'd read in the *Alexandria Town Talk* that Ft. Worth had dance halls with whiskey and rye and woman of ill repute. That kind of lifestyle does not sit well with her or the ladies at Amiable Baptist Church. That's putting it mildly.

I informed her that the newspaper had failed to mention Alex had those vices, too, not to mention N'Orleans. My observation did not diminish her concerns. "And, remember, don't get above your raisin'. The Good Lord don't like that—neither do I," Julia Ann said.

"I know, pride goes before a fall," I said, trying to assure her of my knowledge of the Bible. My words were of little comfort.

"All I'm saying is, don't let the Stark boys pitch your tents toward the cities of the plains," Julia Ann said.

"Cities of the plains. I thought that was Sodom and Gomorrah."

"Exactly—exactly my point!"

"My dearest, Julia Ann, where are you getting all of this? Was it from that article in the *Town Talk* by Billy Sunday?"

She smiled.

"Mr. Sunday must have had those heathen Yankees in mind. Nevertheless, my wife had a long talk with the Stark brothers. More like the Spanish Inquisition.

She reminded the Stark brothers and me that the Lord loves the Yankees as much as we Rebels.

"My favorite novelist was a Yankee general, Lewis Wallace. He was inspired to write his second novel by the goading of an agnostic," Julia Ann said.

"Wallace conceived the book after sitting on a train, listening to Colonel Robert Ingersoll for two hours," she explained, and she pulled out an article that explained the incident.

I kept that article about it. I'll share here an excerpt. Wallace wrote that Ingersoll poured out "a medley of argument, eloquence, wit, satire, audacity, irreverence, poetry, brilliant antitheses, and pungent excoriation of believers in God, Christ, and Heaven, the like of which I had never heard."

Until then, Wallace had been indifferent to the claims of Jesus. He wrote, "Yet here was I now moved as never before, and by what? The most outright denials of all human knowledge of God, Christ, Heaven... Was the Colonel right? What had I on which to answer yes or no? He had made me ashamed of my ignorance: and then–here is the unexpected of the affair–as I walked on in the cool darkness, I was aroused for the first time in my life to the importance of religion... I thought of the manuscript in my desk. Its closing scene was the child Christ in the cave by Bethlehem: why not go on with the story down to the crucifixion? That would make a book, and compel me to study everything of pertinency; after which, possibly, I would be possessed of opinions of real value."

Wallace subtitled the book, "A tale of the Christ." He later wrote, "It only remains to say that I did as resolved, with results— first, the book *Ben Hur*, and second, a conviction amounting to absolute belief in God and the Divinity of Christ."

The next morning Julia Ann packed enough of her famous dewberry pie, smoked ham, and fresh bread to have fed everyone on the train. She included Daniel's Bible and her copy of *Ben Hur*.

I didn't dare mention to her that Ft. Worth's downtown was known as "Hell's Half Acre." Butch Cassidy and the Sundance Kid were said to have roamed the streets of Hell's Half Acre between robberies. Sam Bass once used the Acre as a hideout, but he was long since dead and Cassidy and Sundance were rumored to have fled to South America three years ago.

I figured, why mention that since I had no intention of venturing into the Acre. The fact that Jeremiah had a reputation as the fastest man with a gun in East Texas would have been of little comfort to her, too—but it was to me. The one thing we all three agreed on was we did not need Mr. Sunday's approval.

As we boarded the Texas & Pacific Railway in Alexandria, her words and Great-Grandpa Joseph Willis's teachings flooded my mind. The trip from Alexandria on the Iron Horse added to the excitement, with continuous speeds up to 20 miles an hour. Within two days we approached the Texas & Pacific Railroad passenger depot in Ft. Worth. A porter pointed to one building that was eight stories in height. We marveled at it. It must be the tallest building in the world. The postcard I'd seen, as a boy, did not do the depot justice.

As we deboarded the train, excitement and anticipation hung in the approaching spring air. Ft. Worth's population had grown to more than 26,000. The railroads made possible the tremendous growth. Drovers had trailed more than four million head of cattle through Fort Worth since The War of Northern Aggression. The railroad and barbed wire had long since ended the great cattle drives north. Northern cattle buyers now established their headquarters in Cowtown. We soon discovered Ft. Worth's slogan, "Where the West Begins," to be true.

Cowtown came of age in 1902 when Armour, Swift, and Libby, McNeill & Libby built their packing houses. It brought a significant influx of new people.

There are horse and mule dealers in abundance too. I needed to replace Father's wagon—an old broken-down wreck—held together with wire, but a good one in its heyday. No doubt about it—this was the place to be for a young cowman trying to better himself in the cattle business.

March 11, 1904
Cowtown, Texas

The train chugged into Ft. Worth. "I think that's Miss Tilly's Steakhouse in the distance," I said.

"It has a reputation as the best eatery in Cowtown, and this brochure says it's a short ride on a mule-drawn streetcar."

The sign on the front door read, "No Dancing On Tables With Spurs." Beef steaks were not the only thing on the menu. The second sign confirmed that. "You Must Be 18 or Older to Enter." The hostess seated us at a table in a courtyard out back.

We discovered that the cost of a 28 ounce T-bone was 35 cents.

"Who can afford that?" I asked the brothers. They both shook their heads in agreement and shared their opinions.

"We've traveled to Cowtown's Union Stockyards to buy Longhorn cows and maybe a Hereford bull or two later from Goodnight to build your herd, Daniel," Jacob said, justifying the extravagance as the high cost of doing business.

Jeremiah agreed. "This is research, if you will, of your future purchase's quality."

That's how the brothers saw it; that is, after I offered to pay for the meals.

As we waited for our meal, Jacob noticed a beautiful stuffed bird on a counter next to a portrait of Robert E. Lee mounted on his horse Traveler. Pointing to the stuffed bird, he inquired of Jeremiah. "What kind of bird is that?"

Jeremiah crossed his arms. "I don't know, but Miss Tilley needs to get a better taxidermist. That's the worst job of stuffing a bird I've ever seen."

"Have you ever known anyone with the gift of criticism? Well, you have it," Jacob said.

Jeremiah smirked. "No, I don't!"

Suddenly, off his perch, the bird flew out a window.

Jacob and I busted out laughing.

"Case settled." Jacob started whistling *Dixie*. I couldn't help but smile in agreement.

As we devoured our research, I asked a feller sitting at the table next to us, "Mister, where's a good place to bed down for the night?"

"The Westbrook Hotel, in the 'hotel block.' It's the most noted boarding house in all of this cow country. Expensive though, at a dollar a day, but I wouldn't go there just yet."

"Why's that?"

"No rooms available, but I heard Frank Fore will be checking out soon. His room should be available within two hours."

"Bless you, Mister. May I be so bold as to ask your name?"

"Jim Miller, but most folks call me Deacon Jim Miller since I'm at the Methodist Church every time the doors are open. I rarely come in here since I don't smoke or drink ardent spirits. I agree with Billy Sunday, they defile the Lord's temple."

"Here we go again," Jeremiah whispered. "Did Julia Ann hire this guy to follow us or was it Billy Sunday?"

Jeremiah, with an inquisitive look, observed Deacon Miller's gun lying under his black frock coat and Stetson. "That's a mighty fancy shotgun you have there."

"Thank you. I plan on squirrel hunting a little later." He glanced at his gold pocket watch.

As we walked out the door of Miss Tilly's, Jeremiah seemed enamored. "I feel fortunate that the first person we met is such a Christian gentleman."

"What a pious and kindhearted soul. He reminds me of your Grandpa," Jacob said.

"Not hardly. There's one big difference. My grandpa never talked about how he lived the Christian life, he just did it. I was taught by him to keep a keen eye on a feller who starts every other sentence with I."

"Ah, Daniel, now you're being a pessimist," Jeremiah said pulling at his ear.

"Do you know what a pessimist is Jeremiah? An optimist with experience."

"Funny, really funny." Jeremiah chuckled.

Two hours later, the room did become available just as Deacon Miller predicted. Miller had killed Mr. Fore in the washroom of the Westbrook Hotel. Rumor was Miller and Fore did some real estate business in Fort Worth that had gone south. Frank Fore was said to be an honest businessman who threatened to tell a grand jury that Miller was selling lots submerged in the Gulf of Mexico.

Deacon Miller failed to tell us he was also a great actor, in the tradition of John Wilkes Booth. According to the newspaper, people rushed to see what happened. Miller fell over Fore's body, with tears in his eyes, "I did everything I could to keep him from reaching for his gun."

Jeremiah shared Deacon Miller's prediction with Sheriff John T. Honea.

{14}

March 12, 1904
Cowtown, Texas

"I know all about Deacon Jim Miller. He's a hired assassin. Killed twelve men, some say. That's not the half of it. Unsubstantiated, but persistent, rumors claim he was only eight when he did away with a troublesome uncle and his grandparents. The first I heard of him was when he killed two men in Midland. Two of my lawman claim Miller shot Mr. Fore in self-defense. Witnesses always seem to pass away in these cases.

"He usually ambushes his victims. Miller killed a lawyer named James Jarrott two years ago. Miller shot 'im four times in the back while Jarrot watered his horses near his farm.

"Mr. Stark, I know of your reputation with a gun. A Texas Ranger told me of you. If I know your fast, you can bet Miller does too. Now, what I'm about to say, uh, I never said, if you get my drift?"

"Yes, sir, but why doesn't someone arrest him?"

"They have. Miller has a big-time lawyer and, like I said, the witnesses either lose their memory or mysteriously die.

"Now, what I was about to say is, if I were you, I would call him out before you get it in the back. Your reputation precedes you, Mr. Stark. He's no match for you, at least in a fair fight."

"Thank you, Sheriff."

"For what? We never had this conversation."

To our surprise, Miller agreed to meet Jeremiah in the street in front of Fort Worth's White Elephant. The saloon was an establishment located in the south end of town in the notorious vice district known as "Hell's Half Acre."

There were women everywhere hanging out their windows, dressed as I'd never seen, with porch lights mostly in red.

Miller strolled out the swinging doors of the White Elephant as if he'd just won a considerable poker hand. Jeremiah stood to wait for him in the middle of the street.

"Lord, protect us all. I will never speak ill of your servant Billy Sunday again," I prayed fervently.

They squared off with about 40 feet between them. Miller had no notches on his pistol.

Jeremiah held his hands loosely beside his hips. "You first."

Miller smiled, pulling his gun. Jeremiah followed suit. Miller had not cleared leather when two .45 caliber bullets hit him dead center in his chest. He did not fall. Miller aimed and ripped a shot through Jeremiah's right shoulder. He walked forward pointing his gun at Jeremiah's head.

As he approached Jeremiah to finish the deed someone fired a shotgun in the air while yelling, "Dueling is illegal, boys. You're under arrest, Miller. Get this boy a doctor." Sheriff Honea witnessed it all, from where I do not know.

"He started this," Miller said.

"Check under his coat, I know I hit him—twice." Jeremiah was bleeding and shaking. "Did you hear my bullets ricochet?" Sheriff Honea handcuffed Miller but not until he removed his long black frock coat. Underneath was a thick iron plate.

"That's not illegal, Sheriff."

"Maybe not in a Texas court of law, but I'm sure you being a man of God and all, you know it's a sin to deceive anyone in God's court."

"Since when did you become God's Sheriff?"

"The same day you became a Christian."

After throwing Miller in jail, the Sheriff walked over to the doctor's clinic. "Jeremiah, as soon as you're able, you need to leave town. His lawyer will not be long getting here, with the new railroad."

"I'm not afraid of him."

"I know you're not, but you're a wounded duck. At least go home until you're on the mend. Miller is sure to take advantage of you if you don't."

"This is not over, Sheriff. Will you be all right?"

"Yeah, I didn't make it this far by being stupid. I'll tell the judge, who's my friend, I didn't clearly understand the law in this matter. Miller will no doubt be set free, at least in this court. I doubt he will stay free for long in God's court, although I have no jurisdiction there."

Three days passed. Miller's attorney arrived in Cowtown. We packed our bags and headed to the railroad depot.

"Can't wait to get home." I bounced from foot to foot missing

Julia Ann.

"Home?" Jeremiah cracked his knuckles? "You promised to introduce us to Charles Goodnight, and I'm going to meet him with or without you!"

"Are you sure? You're frail, not out of the woods yet!"

"I'm well enough. Wasn't Goodnight the scout who tracked down the Comanche war chief Peta Nocona so Texas Ranger Sul Ross could kill him? I read all about the Battle of Pease River in a book."

"Yes, that's what Sul Ross claimed, although others swore Peta Nocona wasn't even there. Goodnight told me once it should be called the Pease River Massacre, not a battle, cause it was mostly Indian woman and children killed."

"I don't care what anyone calls it," Jeremiah retorted with a scathing tone.

"He's still the man I want to meet."

"Why?"

"He's the only man I know, or should I say, you know, who can tell me how to track down Jim Miller and hang him from a tree without getting shot again."

I agreed, but only if Jacob would return to Forest Hill and tell Julia Ann why our return trip home had been delayed.

The Stark brothers both agreed that was the best plan since I was the only one who was a friend of Charlie Goodnight.

"Now Jacob, don't burden Julia Ann with the details of the gunfight. I'll tell her later," I pleaded. He nodded his understanding.

I added, "Perhaps we should not burden Charlie Goodnight with the gunfight details either. We could make our way over to the XIT Ranch instead. They sell Longhorn bulls and even Durhams. After all, the railway now makes its way all the way to Channing, Texas, the major shipping point for the XIT. I am sure we can find a few top-grade Longhorn bulls on their three million acres, with more than 150,000 head of cattle."

None of this mattered to Jeremiah. All he could talk about was Jim Miller and Charles Goodnight. He couldn't care less about the XIT or the south end of a northbound cow.

"What kind of person is he?" Jeremiah tightened his fist.

"Is who?"

"Goodnight. I want to know what to expect?"

"He's a cowman. The kind you'd share blanket and bread with. His word is his bond, a handshake his contract. I trust Goodnight. He's a Christian gentleman with an affable nature. But like all men, he has feet of clay."

"How do you mean?"

"The flow of his tobacco juice doesn't bother me, but his profanity can be troublesome. His salty language knows no boundaries: women, preachers, animals—it doesn't matter.

"The rumors of him smoking fifty cigars a day are embellished—I've never seen him smoke more than twenty—in a row. He's not a drunkard, although he will have a toddy occasionally. He has an abiding reverence for the Good Lord, but a healthy disdain for organized religion—yet he's paid for two Baptist churches and keeps a room in his home for traveling preachers. He's an enigma."

"I don't know what an enigma is. All I want to know is how to kill Miller without him killing me."

As we pulled into the railhead and departed the train in Goodnight, Texas, we both noticed stacks of the *Fort Worth Star-Telegram* and the *Goodnight News* with bold headlines, "Gunfighter Kills Deacon Jim Miller."

"Well, Jeremiah, my friend, someone beat you to it. Miller's dead."

"Read, on down the page. They're saying that someone was me. How can that be? You can always believe what you read in newspapers, can't you?"

To that, I rolled my eyes.

S   I   X

"I wish I could find words to express the trueness,
the bravery, the hardihood, the sense of honor,
the loyalty to their trust and to each other of
the old trail hands." —*Charles Goodnight*

{15}

March 17, 1904
Armstrong County
Goodnight, Texas

Charlie met us at his front door. "Great to see you again, Daniel! I reckon your friend is Jeremiah Stark, the man who shot Jim Miller? The paper said he left Ft. Worth with you to visit me."

"It's me, sir, but he shot me, not me him."

"I can see that. Newspapers never get it right except when they write about how handsome I am." He smiled at his own humor.

"Well, come on and see my home. Molly has supper almost ready. She's been over at Goodnight College much of the day. We just chartered the Goodnight Baptist Church to help run the school. Daniel, your great-grandpa would have liked that."

"Yes, he would have. Glad to hear that, and it's good to know your concern for education."

"Truth is, it was Molly's idea. Don't get me wrong, I believe in education, although I only had six months of formal schooling. If I'd had more, maybe I would not have invested in Mexican gold and silver mining.

"Come, both of you. I want to show you my buffalo, elk, and antelope. Buffalo hunters have almost wiped the bison out! I shipped some to Yellowstone National Park. They have free-ranging there."

Jeremiah kept a steady eye on the herd. "I'm impressed that you've preserved the bison."

"I got the idea from Molly. Years ago she heard two bison calves bawling. No doubt the buffalo hunters had slaughtered their mamas. She convinced me we needed to raise them. Now, look at them. More than 250 to remind me of what greed can do. Molly saved the buffalo.

"We best head back to the house. Molly should have supper ready.

"After supper, I suspect you'll be wanting to know if all those stories about the Comanche are true?"

"How did you know that, Sir? Was that in the paper too?" Jeremiah looked like he'd just heard one of the Buffalo speak.

"No, son, if you didn't, you'd be the first visitor in forty years who failed to. For decades people have come to hear my stories and experiences. All my life I've been private, but if these stories can be of any good for future generations, I'll be like a jackass in a hail storm—stand here and take it. Don't get me wrong, I like telling the stories and showing off the buffalo, but I'd prefer not to be a tourist attraction.

"I almost forgot. A few old friends are joining us for supper.

As they gathered around Molly's table the aroma of her son-of-gun-stew and the most robust coffee this side of the Sabine filled the room. One old black man with a wind-carved face and a grey-headed Mexican even older joined them.

"Daniel Willis and Jeremiah Stark meet Bose Ikard, as good a cowboy as any Comanche. I trust him farther than any living man. This here feller is Nicholas Martinez, a Comanchero who I once used as a guide when I first came to the Palo Duro. He's since made a fortune in sheep and is here today to attempt to do the same by trading for a few of my cow ponies."

"Mr. Goodnight," the old Comanchero leaned forward. "I saw your remuda today. I bought a few horses like them before."

"Bought them while I slept, you mean!" Goodnight smiled from ear to ear.

Everyone laughed.

Bose Ikard stood with a dignity that made all of us anticipate his words as he nodded to Goodnight.

"Gentlemen, learn from this man—from his stories of triumph over tragedy—victory over adversity, for the wisdom of others blows where it wishes—like a West Texas wind."

Admiring Goodnight's long white hair, Bose Ikard lifted his glass. "You remind me of Samson. We can see the wisdom in your hair."

"Taking care to keep my hair was my top priority as a young man. It wasn't any Delilah who wanted it, only a few thousand Comanche. Now, today, my concern is how not to let flattering words cause me to lose a dime in a trade."

None of them could contain their laughter. After dining, Molly cleared the table of dishes. Everyone helped. As they walked through the Victorian-style parlor, Jeremiah stopped him to inquire about the photo of his late partner Oliver Loving.

"The bravest man I ever knew. He taught me how to be a cowman." Next to Loving's photo was another of a massive bull buffalo inscribed Old Sikes.

His rifle was in the curves of two buffalo horns above the fireplace mantle. A hewn log above the gun read: "But seek ye first the kingdom of God and his righteousness, and all these things shall be added unto you."

He directed us to the second-floor sleeping porch with spectacular views of the countryside and his bison herd. "Sit a spell, gentleman. We should retire early tonight. I have much to tell you tomorrow on our trip."

"Trip?" I asked.

"In the morning we'll take the wagon to the canyon rim, and I'll tell all about what you came here to hear. The array of colors in the Palo Duro always bring back memories—good ones—and not so good ones. The red rock cliffs carved out of steep walls remind me of all the bloodshed in vain. Molly will prepare the leftover stew and some buffalo jerky for the trip."

We arose before sunrise. On the trip to the rim of the canyon, curiosity got the best of me. "I noticed the Scripture over your fireplace mantle last night. It's good to see you're planning on Heaven."

"I've given it a lot of thought. I figure if I could take longhorns and cross-breed them into the best cattle in America in only eleven years, what could I do in eleven million?"

"You built several churches. Which one do you belong to?"

He spread his arms wide. "That one!" We stopped to look in awe at the vast Palo Duro Canyon. It stretched for more than 100 miles and was 10 miles wide in some parts and 1000 feet deep.

"There's my cathedral!"

"I have never seen a landscape with so many colors. The steep sides have layers of orange, red, brown, yellow, grey, and maroon," I said. "Look at the prickly pear, yucca, mesquite, and juniper."

"There are thousands of mesquite and juniper trees. Palo Duro is Spanish for hardwood. The canyon's named after those Junipers," Goodnight said.

"I noticed you don't cuss anymore."

"You damned right I don't."

March 18, 1904
The Cathedral
Palo Duro Canyon

Charlie fired up a cigar as they paused to survey his church.
"Gentleman, have one?"
"Yes, sir," Jeremiah said.
I also reached for one. "When did you settle here?"
"In the summer of 1876. I drove 1,600 longhorns from Pueblo, Colorado, to the edge of Palo Duro, not far from here."
"Did the Comanche try to stop you."
"Not then. Ranald Mackenzie led his Fourth United States Cavalry to the canyon two years before and defeated them.
"My involvement with the Comanche began the year I was born. My birth was one day before the siege of the Alamo ended. Two months later the Comanche kidnapped Cynthia Ann Parker. She was only nine. All this in 1836, the year I was born.
"In the autumn of 1845, I accompanied my family from Illinois to Texas riding bareback on my white-faced mare Blaze. The Republic of Texas celebrated my arrival by officially being inducted into the United States the next month.
"Much has been written about Cynthia Ann's kidnapping and recapture and my part in the latter. Oh, it all has some truth, the best lies are half-truths."
I nodded slowly. "I read about you and Cynthia Ann in DeShields's biography of her."
"I did, too. DeShields never let the truth get in the way of a good story.
"Damn newspapers. Damn dime novelists. Damn politicians."

March 18, 1904
The Cathedral
Palo Duro Canyon

"Charles, there're about twenty Indians headed straight at us and closing in fast. Are they hostile?" I asked, somewhat concerned.

"Hope not."

"Me, too, because they're now 50 yards from us and still riding hard." To my great relief, the Indian riders reined in their ponies but fanned out to encircle us. Charles smiled broadly and lifted his right hand as a peace gesture. The leader of the Indians came forward on his horse and mirrored the peace gesture.

"Daniel and Jeremiah, meet the chief of the Quahada Comanche. Correction, the chief of all Comanche. At least that's what the federal government says.

"Chief, meet Daniel Willis and Jeremiah Stark."

The biggest and toughest looking man in Texas dismounted.

"Me Quanah. Quanah Parker."

"He's the wealthiest Indian alive and the baddest man I've ever known," Goodnight said.

"I used to be bad man. Now, I citizen of United States. No fight anymore." He paused a moment, then turned his attention to Jeremiah, rubbing his chin and sizing him up.

"Jeremiah Stark? You man who killed Jim Miller?"

"No, sir. The newspapers had that wrong."

"They always wrong."

"I read your father, Peta Naconi, was killed at Peace River by Sul Ross."

"I want to fix some Texas history straight up. Some say Sul Ross and rangers kill my father, Peta Naconi. No, not so. I be eleven year old when they captured my mother, Cynthia Ann Parker, at Peace River fight. She was with party of Indians hunting buffalo. I never see her again." He paused a moment in contemplation, then continued his narrative.

"Ross no kill my father. He not there. My father sick. I see him die five years later.

"Ross friend, DeShields, wrote that to make him famous. He

becomes governor of Texas. Politicians say anything to get elected."

"I read you were living at Fort Sill, Oklahoma. You've come a long way," I noted.

"Here to hunt buffalo on Goodnight's land."

"I thought those days were long gone," Jeremiah said.

"You thought wrong. Thanks to Goodnight."

"He's too busy hunting wolves with President Theodore Roosevelt to make this trip often," Goodnight said.

"Take a couple of my beeves too."

18

March 19, 1904
The Cathedral
Palo Duro Canyon

Charles, Jeremiah and I headed back to Goodnight's home.

"When I was a boy the Comanche were lords of these plains," I said. "What happened?"

"The Comanche dominance began in Texas in the 1740s They blocked French expansion west, from your Louisiana. They drove the Apache into the mountains of northern New Mexico. They destroyed the Spanish advance from the east. The Spaniards killed more than a million Mexicans, but they were no match for the Comanche. This victory gave them horses. They became skilled horsemen, like no other people we had ever seen.

"In 1820, Spain was unable to persuade its citizens to move to Texas because of them. A year later Mexico achieved its independence. Their citizens also feared to enter Mexican Texas. The Comanche caused Mexico to allow immigration from the United States. The next year, Mexico granted a permit to Moses Austin to settle 300 families in Texas.

"He died, and his son Stephen F. Austin took charge. He brought hundreds of families into Texas on behalf of the Mexican government. They would be the ones who sacrificed their blood fighting against the Comanche to settle in Texas.

"The plan backfired 15 years later, in just 18 minutes, at San Jacinto. Sam Houston made sure of that. But, it would take another 40 years before most of Texas, including Palo Duro, could be settled because of the Comanche. They were the most powerful Indian tribe in American history.

"I started in 1857 and trailed a herd up the Brazos to the Keechi valley in Palo Pinto County. The War of Northern Aggression ended that. After the war, in 1865, Indians ran off 2,000 head of my cattle."

"Tell me more about the man in the photo at your home?" I asked.

Charles answered, "In the spring of 1858, I took on a partner,

Oliver Loving. I helped Loving send a herd through the Indian Territory to the Rocky Mountain mining camps before the war. In 1867, Loving died from wounds he received in a fight with the Comanche on the Pecos River. With the aid of Mexican traders, he reached Fort Sumner, only to die there of gangrene.

"I assured him that his wish to be buried in Texas would be carried out. He is buried in Weatherford."

*   *   *

Jeremiah rubbed his chin. "I did not want to ask this while we were with Quanah. Is it true you were the scout that led the Texas Rangers to the Comanche camp where Cynthia Ann Parker was recaptured?"

"That's about the only thing written that is true. What happened was the Texas Rangers massacred a small group of mostly women and children in December of 1860, on the Pease River. It was only newsworthy because Cynthia Ann Parker was there.

"Ranger Sul Ross embellished the story to get himself elected Governor. It worked. He did well as president of an Agricultural and Mechanical College near the post office of College Station.

"Almost thirty years later I became friends with Cynthia Ann's son Quanah Parker when he came to hunt the scarce buffalo. I made a treaty with him in which I promised two beeves every other day for Parker's followers, provided they did not disturb my herd."

Jeremiah cocked his head. "Y'all are friends even though you were the scout who led Sul Ross to their Pease River camp. How can that be? Ross said he killed his father and said you chased his sons, Quanah Parker and his brother. And Cynthia Ann Parker was recaptured and starved herself to death because of the loss of her husband and children."

"That's quite a story. The only problem is, as Quanah said, none of it is true, except the part about Cynthia Ann Parker being found. Quanah, his brother Pecos, and his father Peta Nocona were not there. Don't believe everything you read, especially when it's told by a man who wants to be a politician."

"How can you be friends with Quanah Parker after the Comanche killed your partner and the kidnapping of white Cynthia

Ann Parker?" Jeremiah asked.

"Vengeance is the Lord's. That's what I have been trying to tell you. God causes all things to work together for good." He crossed his arms as though he was done speaking, but then another thought came to mind.

"Let God handle Jim Miller. God does not need your help to right this wrong."

$$* \qquad * \qquad *$$

Jeremiah narrowed his stance and looked away. I tried to soothe things by smiling and changing the subject. "How did you manage those rough cowboys?"

"The first thing I did was strictly enforce my rules against gambling, drinking, and fighting.

"I don't know if any of this will help you get Jim Miller out of your head, Jeremiah, except to show that God has a way of taking care of an evil man like him.

"Daniel, would you be so kind as to tell me again that story about the XIT? You know the one about the real cowboys. You can leave out the part about my barbwire fences. Isn't Jeremiah in that story? It wouldn't hurt us both to hear that again."

19

XIT Ranch
The Texas Panhandle

The old-timers were spinning yarns about the weather, the scourge of the XITs, and Charlie Goodnight's barbwire fences doing away with the "real cowboys," a cattle disease called Texas Fever, and many a "she did me wrong yarn." Their laughter filled the room, and everybody was smiling until one ole cowboy who spoke with a gravelly voice, asked, "What was that young cowpoke's name? Ya know, the one that got himself thrown off a green-broke mare on the XIT. That horse was a rank one, ya know."

"I was there. His name was Jimbo. He was a praying boy," the barber said.

"Not sure that pony was green-broke though, although that's what they told young Jimbo. He came strolling out of the bunkhouse one morning when some of the cowboys started poking fun at him. He didn't have much experience, but he wanted to show them he could rope and ride."

Daddy took it all in and spoke not a word. He was spellbound.

The barber continued, "They were daring Jimbo to ride that crazy horse brought over from an XIT line camp. They couldn't handle the pony there.

"Those cowboys were mean to him. At first, Jimbo did a good job of ignoring them, but they just kept making fun of him. 'Come on, ya got religion we hear tell. You can do anything with that Jewish carpenter's help, can't ya, boy? Why don't ya wanna ride that horse? Ya scared? Maybe you're too green like that yearling cow pony. Maybe even yellow?'"

"Everybody gathered 'round to see what was gonna happen. Every eye was on Jimbo. His face was beet red. He just stood there looking at that horse and didn't move. The men laughed at him, threw up their hands and started walking away. He couldn't have been more than eighteen. The barber watched him throw his shoulders back and begin to walk toward the corral. He grabbed a bridle and opened the gate. You could hear the whispers as most of the men came back to watch.

"He bridled her and proceeded to rub the mare all over with a saddle blanket while he whispered to her. One old cowboy yelled, 'Bite her ear.' Another, 'Snub her to a post.' Another, 'She's got crazy eyes.'

"Jimbo ignored them all, except to say, 'She's not crazy, just afraid.'

"Didn't take long for him to get a saddle on her. He climbed on her real slow like and rode with a new found confidence. She seemed to trust him.

"Suddenly someone cracked a bullwhip and yelled, 'Ride 'em, cowboy.'

"She must have jumped ten feet. And, as everyone hooped and hollered, she reared up falling over backward on top of Jimbo. The horse got up but not the boy. He just lay there in the dry dusty dirt. The barber was the first one who got to him, and Jimbo sure didn't look good. He tried to talk, so he bent down close to his mouth to hear his words.

"'Please get my Book, the one that boss Jake gave me.'

"The barber thought he hadn't heard him right, but he said it real clear again.

"'Please get me my Bible.'

"He sent one of the others to fetch it from his saddlebags. He tried to make him comfortable, but there wasn't much he could do. He wondered how he'd explain all this to boss man Jake. When the Book arrived the barber showed it to him. 'Here, Jimbo, here's your Bible.'"

"'Lay it on my chest and open it to John 3:16, please. Put my finger on those words.'

"He spoke all raspy like.

"'Please, do it, please!'

"The barber found that verse and lifted his hand. Jimbo cried in pain cause his arm was broken. Daddy placed his finger on the verse.

"'Tell boss Jake that I made that decision just like he told me I should.'

"With that, he closed his eyes and was gone." The barber had tears in his eyes as he ended the story.

"Julian, that's why we nicknamed you Jake."

*   *   *

Daddy paused a minute, then said, "Boys, I made three decisions after I heard the barber's story. The first was to name the creek we now live on Barber Creek. The second was to have you boys bury me one day with my Bible opened on my chest with my finger placed on John 3:16. And the third was to give every cowboy who works with us a copy of the good Lord's Word. Your copies are in the chuck wagon. Rooster will show you where."

Jeremiah and Jacob seemed to be moved the most.

Jeremiah spoke first. "Mr. Willis, our sister Mary told us about that Carpenter. Is He for real?"

"Boys, He's as real as the skin on my bones," Daddy said.

"What does that verse say, Mr. Willis?"

"It says that whosoever puts his trust in Jesus will have everlasting life."

"What does whosoever mean? Who's that?"

Daddy replied, "I reckon, Jeremiah, that's you and me and every cowboy and cowgirl. Even the mavericks, the culls, and the undesirables. God swings a mighty big loop. But, there's many a cowboy who doesn't want His brand."

There was a peace in the camp as an unseasonably cool breeze blew in.

Then Jeremiah said, "I want His brand."

Jacob added, "Me, too."

20

March 20, 1904
Armstrong County
Goodnight, Texas

The next day Jeremiah and I packed our bags and headed to the railroad depot. We stopped to spend the night in Ft. Worth. I decided to set the *Fort Worth Star-Telegram* straight about Jeremiah's gunfight with Jim Miller. But I did not tell them that Jeremiah still vowed to kill Jim Miller.

Other newspapers began to carry the story. The newspapers quoted Jeremiah stating he did not want ever to see a cow again. In fact, he did not want to return home until he faced Jim Miller again. He would aim for his head this time.

After reading that Jeremiah was a man of faith, a man named J.M. Guffey sent him a telegraph offering him an opportunity.

The J. M. Guffey Petroleum Company had been organized four years before, in 1901. Mr. Gulley requested that Jeremiah meet him at the railroad station in West Columbia, in Brazoria County. From there they would travel to Damon Mound, located 12 miles north of West Columbia. Mr. Guffey believed the salt dome had oil beneath it.

Jeremiah answered the telegram and agreed to meet in West Columbia, but once again luck did not favor Jeremiah. He decided to make the trip in a horseless carriage introduced in Ft. Worth two years before, instead of the train. He was assured he would be there in plenty of time since the vehicle traveled at twelve miles per hour. Within two days the automobile began to make sounds like a railway locomotive. It was out of gas.

Jeremiah could not have been more dejected. Mr. Guffey had changed his plans in Houston to make a special trip to meet him. Surely God was against him. Jeremiah walked the entire way to the First Baptist Church in Fort Worth. He got on his knees and asked the Lord, "Why, Lord? Why me? What do you have against me?"

Jeremiah looked up, shook his finger at heaven. "I give up— You win. But, I'm still going to kill Jim Miller."

He walked to a nearby hotel, and as he went to sleep, he prayed he would not wake up. But wake up he did the next morning when a porter slipped the *Star-Telegram* newspaper under his door. The vast headline caught his eye from his bed: "Train Derailment! No Survivors." It was his train.

Once again he walked into the church, but this time he read Psalm 91. Before he did not believe that God had his back. But now he did, and surely God would help him kill Miller.

Mr. Guffey read the news, too, and was vexed in his soul. However, his anxiety was relieved after Jeremiah sent him a telegram to let him know he had not been on that fateful train. Mr. Guffey set the meeting again.

Once they met, Jeremiah discovered that the J. M. Guffey Petroleum Company was almost bankrupt. Jeremiah did not fret and told the Lord, "I can't wait to see what you do by noon today." Well, nothing of much of value happened by noon, except Mr. Guffey gave him 160 acres on that salt dome and some worthless stock for his trouble. In 1911, the company became part of the Gulf Oil Corporation. In 1915 Jeremiah began producing oil from his salt dome oil field. A train wreck had caused his life not to be a train wreck.

Jeremiah's desire to kill Jim Miller faded away. He realized being spared from the train wreck was not for the purpose of killing Miller, even though Miller was still executing people.

Jeremiah read Miller had assassinated a man with a scattergun. The law arrested Miller in Ada, Oklahoma. Miller shrewdly retained the best lawyer around—Moman Pruitt. Pruitt was a legend, a dynamic litigator who had never had a client executed, winning acquittals in 304 of his 342 murder cases.

The good citizens of Ada knew Miller would once again go free. Therefore, forty of them broke into the jail, overpowered two lawmen, and pulled Miller out of his cell. Down an alley they dragged him into an abandoned livery stable behind the jail. The mob wasted no time. They bound Miller with barbed wire and stood him on a box. The same type barbed wire Charles Goodnight used to become the first Texas Panhandle rancher to build fences from it. It eventually ending the open range.

The men urged Miller to confess to his many crimes.

Miller thrust his chest out. "Let the record show I've killed 51 men." He pulled off a diamond ring and asked it be given to his wife. A diamond shirt stud he left to the jailer for some kindness.

As the noose slid around his neck, Deacon Jim Miller asked for his trademark, his black broadcloth coat. "I'd like to have my coat. I don't want to die naked."

Miller shouted, "Let 'er rip!" and stepped off his box to hang. They left him overnight.

Houston's *Daily Post* interviewed Jeremiah for his reaction. "Now, I know what you're thinking. That I believe the Lord orchestrated all this. I'm not saying that. That's between the Lord and Deacon Jim.

"Then again, you might want to ask Charles Goodnight.

"Better yet, ask Billy Sunday."

21

1916
Hotel Leesville
Leesville, Louisiana

My dear wife, Julia Ann Willis, and I grew more in love on the banks of Barber Creek. We decided to visit our son, Dr. Daniel Oscar "D.O" Willis, in Leesville for a checkup. Julia Ann sensed something was not right with me.

Our son's medical clinic and office adjoined the Hotel Leesville that he built in 1907. He bought the first automobile in the parish in 1909 for $825.00. Although most of his patients did not make that much money in two years, it allowed him to make house calls faster than his horse-drawn doctor's buggy. The Model T could go 40 miles per hour.

Unfortunately, my condition worsened no matter what our son did.

FROM THE JOURNAL OF JULIA ANN WILLIS:

Here, I take up the record my late husband could not finish, for he died of Bright's disease at the home of our son. The kidney disease was named after English physician Richard Bright in 1827 after he described 25 cases. They had the same symptoms as Daniel.

Still mourning the death of his father, our son was asked to attend to a 16-year-old girl named Anna Mae Granstaff, who was brought to his office next to the Leesville Hotel. She had lost a lot of blood but could still speak to our son and the sheriff.

"He violated me in every way!" she said hoarsely.

"What do you mean in every way?" the sheriff asked.

Dr. Willis looked him in the eyes. "I'll explain later."

"At least tell me his name."

"Billy Blanchard. Billy Ray Blanchard."

"From over Tenmile Creek way?"

"Yes." She passed out and never regained consciousness.

"Now, Doc, I understand that he had his way with her. But that doesn't normally kill someone, does it?"

"Gangrene does though."

"I'll get a deputy and head to Tenmile Creek. I know of him. He's a fifty-year-old man with a family."

Billy Blanchard denied it all. His attorney from Shreveport arrived at the jail. The brash young lawyer had already made a name for himself as a defender of the friendless.

"I'm Huey P. Long. I represent the falsely accused Mr. Billy Blanchard. May I see him, sir?" A deputy led him back to the jail cells.

"Mr. Blanchard. I'm your attorney. We will speak of these fraudulent charges later. What is the best hotel in Leesville?"

"The Hotel Leesville is the only hotel in town," a deputy informed him.

As he walked to the hotel, he spied a man getting out of an automobile. "Mister, you have an automobile I see. My name is Long. Huey P. Long. I'll be your Governor someday. You will be famous if you drive me."

"No, thank you."

"Aren't you interested in being a friend of the next governor of the great state of Louisiana?"

"Not hardly."

The trial lasted only two weeks. Long made his final argument. "It's this loose woman's word against one of the most outstanding citizens of Vernon Parish. My client has a good job. Works hard. He belongs to the Baptist Church, although he has stated he's unable to attend because of his work with less fortunate girls at a home for unwed mothers. Do you think a man with three daughters and a Christian wife would ever do such a thing? Anna Mae Granstaff was white trash—God rest her soul—and forgive her."

Several in the jury nodded yes.

The jury came to its decision. The court convened at 10:00 a.m. the next day. Huey assured his client that he would be home soon.

Dr. Willis opened his office at 7:00 a.m. A patient had been waiting outside for two hours.

"Come on in, Sir. What's ailing you?"

"Justice!"

"I beg your pardon."

"Doc, how did my sister die?"

"Who are you?"

"Charles Granstaff. I got the news while working cows in East Texas. Rode as hard as my saddle horse could go. How did she die?"

"Loss of blood and gangrene."

"What caused that?"

"Sexual assault."

"Thank you for being honest. I rode once with your father and the Stark brothers on a cattle drive from East Texas to Lecompte. Like them, you do not mince words."

Charles Granstaff led his horse to the jail.

"Howdy. I'm here to congratulate my old friend Billy Blanchard."

"He will be out in a couple of hours," the jailer said.

"Cannot wait. I have business elsewhere."

"I'm sure the sheriff will not mind, you being a friend and all. Come with me.

"Mr. Blanchard, I have an old friend of yours who wants to congratulate you."

"Do I know you? What's your name, mister?"

"Justice." Charles Granstaff emptied both of his repeating pistols into Blanchard's groin area.

The Leesville newspaper interviewed Long before Blanchard's funeral. "Dr. Willis acted as judge and jury when he incited Granstaff with his erroneous conjecture. He should be convicted of manslaughter. I gave the doctor guidance once by offering him an opportunity of a lifetime. When he rejected my kindness, I should have known he was a man prone to bad choices."

"Will you assist in the prosecution of Willis?"

"I wish I had the time. I must pack in the morning. I'm off to represent a small group that's suing the giant Standard Oil."

The newspaper was on Dr. Willis's desk early the next morning. He tossed the paper aside and made his way to the hotel.

"I need the keys to Huey Long's room," Dr. Willis said to the desk clerk.

"He's not checked out yet, Sir."

"I figured as much. Give me the keys. I want to give him a special send-off."

Dr. Willis turned the keys and opened his door. "You're past my check out time."

- 77 -

"It's not but 7 a.m."

Dr. Willis grabbed Long by his collar and dragged him down the stairs.

"I'll sue you," Long screamed as he fell into horse manure in the street.

"What is your check out time?"

"6:59."

22

Dr. Willis knew the importance of available medical care to Louisiana. He was not the only descendant of Joseph Willis to understand the need for education. Poverty gripped Louisiana.

1924
Louisiana College
Pineville, Louisiana

Huey P. Long began his campaign for governor in 1924. On a sunny day he came to preach his gospel of prosperity at the Boy Scout Camp on the banks of Spring Creek near Longleaf, Louisiana.

Dr. Willis had no desire to hear him, but his brother Ran Willis did. Ran and his wife Lillie's home, the Ole Willis Place, on Barber Creek was walking distance to the Boy Scout Camp. As Ran approached with his three sons, Howard, Herman, and Julian, they could hear Long's reassuring voice.

"I'm for the poor man—all poor men, black and white, they all gotta have a chance. They gotta have a home, a job, and a decent education for their children. 'Every man a king'—that's my slogan."

Long looked straight at us. "I don't care about what the big shots say. All I care is what the boys at the forks of creeks like Barber and Spring creek think of me."

"Is he speaking to us?" Ran asked.

"I don't know, Daddy, but don't you like what he said about free textbooks for all of us?" Howard asked.

"Free! There is nothing free. We will pay for them with increased taxes. Well, I take that back. Your Uncle Doc gave Huey Long a free education four years ago at the Hotel Leesville.

"That's the same year I met a young man at Louisiana College who started his education, but with fewer advantages than we have and lot less than Huey claims.

"We became friends. He was the son of a poor sharecropper from Beech Springs in north Louisiana. He wanted to get an education like your Uncle Doc and me. He told me his family was so poor that he did not have a bed in which to sleep until he was nine.

"Upon graduation from high school, he began the task of choosing a college. One of his neighbors had a college catalog.

"He told me all about it."

"I was amazed and believed you could order a college just as you ordered something from Sears and Roebuck. I'd never seen a college, had never been on a college campus, but I read it, and it told all about Louisiana College at Pineville. I decided that's where I would try to go."

"But how could he pay for tuition, books, housing, and food? He didn't have any money or know anyone who did. He decided to try to get a job at the college. On his second day on campus, he went to the college employment office and found employment in the dining hall.

"How did you meet him, Daddy?" Howard asked.

"Through our cousin, Willie Strother.

"Willie's a history professor at Louisiana College. The young sharecropper's son attended his classes. He wished to get his degree in history.

"After acquiring the job in the cafeteria, he joined the glee club. Professor Dunwoody assigned him to the college quartet. He sang lead and received a gift, a used guitar. As winter approached, the young man became desperate for money. With his guitar, he began to sing on the street corners in Alexandria. When an officer told him to move on, he moved to another street corner."

"What was his name, Father?" Herman asked.

"Jimmie Davis. He graduated this year from Louisiana College without free textbooks.

"None of this would have happened had it not been for two encounters on the campus of Louisiana College. The last year Jimmie did not have the money to continue his education. He tried banks for a loan. They all turned him down."

"Everyone ought to be hungry and try to borrow money at least once in their life. To be broke and turned down, well, it's something," Jimmie said.

"With his dreams put on hold, Jimmie found himself in back of a mule again, plowing and picking cotton from sunup to sundown. He supplemented that by slipping back into Alexandria and singing on street corners. After one year in the cotton fields, he was able to return to Louisiana College and obtain his degree in history after

Willie Strother loaned him $120.

"But, there was another encounter on the campus of Louisiana College. It had an even greater impact on Jimmie's life. While walking across campus, a man introduced himself to Jimmie."

"The stranger was striking looking, well dressed, and friendly," Jimmie said. "At first we talked about football and baseball. The man was the son of a sharecropper, too."

He began to ask Jimmie questions and explained who he was. "I'm Robert G. Lee, and I'm holding a revival in Pineville at First Baptist tonight. Please be my guest. Jimmie, may I ask you something? If the Lord would call you today, would you be ready to go?"

"Dr. Lee, I hope He doesn't call me today because I don't think I could make it," Jimmie said.

"The Lord's been good to you, and it's something you ought to think about. I hope you'll come to church tonight."

"I realized that everything I had, everything I had ever had, and everything I would ever hope to have on this earth had come and would come through the grace of God," Jimmie said.

That night Jimmie went to church. Dr. Lee gave his most famous and beloved sermon, "Pay Day, Some Day."

"There's no doubt of it, the man had the finest command of the English language I've ever heard. Before he had finished, I was ready to go down the aisle. And when he gave the invitation, I was the first one down and made public my profession of faith and united with that church," Jimmie said.

Willie Strother was there. He was a deacon in the church.

Epilogue

December 25, 1941
The Ole Willis Place
On Barber Creek
Longleaf, Louisiana

There is nothing quite as serene as the piney woods covered in a white sheet of snow. As the sun sets and the moon rises over the snow, memories can be precious and troubling too. The death of Robert Willis on the *USS Arizona* at Pearl Harbor causes both.

"Should we have had a Christmas tree and gifts this year?" Ran asks, Lillie. He turns their Philco radio on for the news. WSM is playing "You Are My Sunshine" by Jimmie Davis, followed by a broadcast of the news.

President Roosevelt's fireside chat addresses the criticism about the White House's Christmas tree.

"There are many men and women in America—sincere and faithful men and women—who are asking themselves this Christmas:

"How can we light our trees?

"How can we give our gifts?

"How can we meet and worship with love and with uplifted spirit and heart in a world at war, a world of fighting and suffering and death?

"How can we pause, even for a day, even for Christmas Day, in our urgent labor of arming a decent humanity against the enemies which beset it?

"How can we put the world aside, as men and women put the world aside in peaceful years, to rejoice in the birth of Christ?

"And when we make ready our hearts for the labor and the suffering and the ultimate victory which lie ahead, then we observe Christmas Day—with all of its memories and all of its meanings—as we should.

"It is in that spirit, and with particular thoughtfulness of those, our sons and brothers, who serve in our armed forces on land and sea, near and far—those who serve for us and endure for us that we light our Christmas candles now across the continent from one coast to the other on this Christmas Eve."

Ran and Lillie Willis light their Christmas candle. The beckoning candle of hope illuminates their hearts!

Ran continues to leaf through his great-grandfather Joseph Willis's leather-bound journal written a century ago.

"Why did the Lord allow Robert's death? He was a good man—better than me. Did Grandpa Joseph ever write anything about that?" Julian asks.

"Not in his journal, but in a letter to my father."

Howard shifts in his chair. "Could you read that letter—please, Father? On a day like this, I need direction—advice on what path to take."

Herman runs his hands through his hair. "One minute all is good. The next all is gone. What's the Lord's purpose in that?"

Ran adjusts his spectacles. He takes a big sip of coffee and places Joseph's journal in his lap. Father must have put the letter in the journal. "Please hand me that kerosene oil lamp."

December 28, 1853

"My Dearest Grandson Dan,

I received your letter. Concerning your question, "How can a loving God allow deadly diseases like cholera, smallpox, malaria, and yellow fever in Louisiana? Yellow fever killed my best friend."

"Let me begin by apologizing in sackcloth and ashes for asking you a question first. If you had a cure for yellow fever would you have given it to your friend? Of course, you would have!

"I read in the *Alexandria Town Talk*, 1 in 15 have died in New Orleans this summer. Over 12,000 people dead from yellow fever in New Orleans alone since January, with still more deaths in rural areas like ours.

"People are dying faster than graves can be dug. 'Pretty soon people will have to dig their graves,' the paper said.

"Would you have given a cure to them? There is no need to answer for I know your heart. You would have given the treatment to every man, woman and child in Louisiana and in fact the entire earth. You would have given your life for such a great cause. How glorious it would be to provide forty additional years to a middle aged man, perhaps a hundred years to a child. What a great cause this would be. More significant than any political cause, for what can be more wonderful than the gift of life?

"Yet, there is a greater cause—an even more excellent gift than a cure for yellow fever. It does not give only an additional hundred years but eternal life. You and I have this good news. How can we not share the gift of eternal life?

"Over the last eight decades, I have received many prayer requests for physical healing, and I have never refused. My twin daughters died of honey poisoning after I prayed for days. My beloved wife died in childbirth. Do not misunderstand me; there is nothing wrong with praying for the sick. But, after their deaths, I realized I was spending more time keeping the saints out of heaven than saving the lost from hell.

"God did not answer my prayer in the way I requested, but I will be with Him and my daughters and my bride forever in heaven. The greatest tragedy is being eternally separated from Christ, not to mention my daughters and wife.

"Nothing lies beyond the reach of prayer. I believe that God heals miraculously. Sometimes God heals naturally. Sometimes He heals instantaneously. Sometimes He heals in time. God uses doctors and beyond the doctor's skills.

"But the ultimate healing is in Heaven where no disease can touch our new and perfect body. The greater miracle is not a hundred years of life free from illness, but everlasting life paid for with Christ's blood—God's lifeblood—given freely on a tree at Calvary.

"Let us tell our neighbors on our beloved Barber Creek. Let us declare this Good News in the piney woods of Rapides Parish. Let us travel our red-dirt roads to the Calcasieu and Red Rivers. And from the mighty Mississippi and Sabine Rivers to our enormous deltas and vast swamps. Let the Gospel of Jesus Christ ring forth from Driskill Mountain to the Gulf of Mexico. And let that only be the beginning!

Always, your loving Grandpa

Beckoning Candle's Characters

Randall Lee "Ran" Willis–Youngest child of Daniel Hubbard Willis and Julia Ann Graham Willis. Named after General Randall Lee Gibson. He married Lillie Gertrude Hanks. He learned to play the fiddle, by ear, after his father bought him one in East Texas on a cattle drive. He was known to be the best musician in the area. He was my grandfather, whom I was named after.

Lillie Hanks Willis–Wife of Randall Lee "Ran" Willis. They married on January 11, 1914. She was sixteen, and he was twenty-seven. They had three sons: Howard, Herman, and Julian Willis (my father).

She moved to Forest Hill, Louisiana, from Branch, Louisiana, at age eleven. She was a firm believer in Christ and was a staunch Southern Baptist.

I remember her deep reverence for the Lord and knowledge of the Word of God. As a boy, I remember walking into the Wardville Baptist Church sanctuary early on a Sunday morning in Wardville, Louisiana, with her. The pastor, Bob Galloway, was teaching a Sunday school class. He looked up from his notes and asked, "Mrs. Willis, what does Christ do with our sins?" Without hesitation, she answered, "He throws them as far as the east is from the west." I have never forgotten her words. She was my sainted grandmother and the wellspring of many of the stories in my books.

Robert Kenneth "Bobby" Willis, Jr.–Entombed in the *USS Arizona*, at the bottom of Pearl Harbor. He was the first casualty from Rapides Parish, Louisiana, in World War II.

He was my father's (Julian Willis) first cousin.

Robert was born on February 2, 1923, in Chopin, Louisiana. He graduated in 1939 from Natchitoches High School. His half-sister, Ilie Jewel Willis Close, told me that their father encouraged Bobby to join the military and "make something of himself." Bobby's mother died when he was barely eleven. Only 18, Bobby enlisted in the Navy (as Seaman First Class, S1/C), on July 31, 1940, in New Orleans. He reported aboard the *USS Arizona*, on October 8, 1940, in San Diego as Apprentice Seaman.

He served for 14 months on the *USS Arizona* before it was destroyed by the Japanese on December 7, 1941. The American Legion Post in Pineville, Louisiana was named the Robert K. Willis Jr. Post. This American Legion Post no longer exists.

Two weeks after the attack on Pearl Harbor, Bobby's father, Robert Kenneth Willis, Sr. received a message from the Rapides Parish sheriff that he was trying to reach him. He rushed to the sheriff's office. Bobby's half-sister, Ilie Willis Close, told me that when their father returned, she knew the moment he walked in the front door that Bobby was dead just from the expression on their father's face. His cousins rushed to enlist, and America's finest hours began.

Robert Kenneth Willis, Sr.–Son of Daniel Hubbard Willis, Jr. and Julia Ann Graham Willis and father of Robert Kenneth "Bobby" Willis, Jr.

Robert Kenneth Willis, Sr. married his first wife Eulah "Eula" Rosalie Hilburn, in 1903. She died on February 6, 1919, at the age of 34, in the influenza pandemic of 1918-1919. More people died in the plague than did in World War I.

Robert Kenneth Willis, Sr. married his second wife Julia Mae Johnson in 1922. Their son Robert Kenneth "Bobby" Willis, Jr. was born the next year. Julia Mae died February 17, 1934, at age 34, the same age his first wife died. Robert Kenneth "Bobby" Willis, Jr. was only eleven when his mother died.

He was my great-uncle.

Ruth Duke [Willis]–Her life's motto was, "I'd rather have Jesus." She was the best women I have ever known. She reared five children with a spirit as pure as gold and a servant's heart. She had the rare gift of encouragement and always saw the best in people. She was a Proverbs 31 woman.

She always advised me that the answer to my problems and the purpose of life was found in Christ and the Bible. Thus, even today, I often ask myself, "What would her advice be in this or that matter?" I always know that her answer would be, "Ran, what would Jesus do?"

She married her first husband, John Alex Duke, on December 23, 1933. He was 54, and she was 20. He died September 24, 1946.

John Alex Duke and my mother had four children, and thus my half-brothers and half-sisters are Johnnie Duke McDearmont, Gerald "Jerry" Duke, John "Buddy" Duke, and Marjorie Duke Eernisse.

My mother then married my father, Julian Willis, on June 26, 1948. I'm their only child.

Mother's great-grandfather was Rev. Adolphe Stagg (1834-1914). He was a pioneer Baptist preacher to the French-speaking people of Louisiana.

She was my sainted mother.

Julian "Jake" Willis–Boss Man Jake and Julian Willis in the novel. He was highly decorated in WWII in Iwo Jima and the South Pacific.

He was the son of Randall Lee Willis and Lillie Hanks Willis. He married Ruth Willis in Longleaf, Louisiana. Both are buried at Butters Cemetery near Forest Hill, Louisiana. He had two brothers, Howard Willis and Herman Willis.

Daddy had a strong work ethic. He always rose before sunrise and worked late. He wasn't much on going to church but had strong values and beliefs. He believed in Christ. He didn't care for people who used their position as an advantage for personal gain. He was a staunch Democrat (the Franklin Delano Roosevelt kind) and was extremely opinionated. He was a champion of equals rights and pay for all minorities, including women way before those beliefs were in vogue.

He was Trail Boss for many years of the Brazoria County Trail Ride and was a board member of the Brazoria County Fair and Rodeo Association in Angleton, Texas.

He was a rancher and loved horses and mules. He trained horses. We worked cows almost every week. He was patriotic. He loved to hunt and fish. He loved football, especially favoring the Dallas Cowboys.

He taught manners to me and respect for my elders and despised off-color language, especially around women. He loved to teach kids to ride horses and loved to see their excitement when they learned to ride and enjoy horses.

He had more friends than anyone I've ever known. He was the real deal; a man's man. He was a cowboy's cowboy. He was my father.

Howard and Zora Willis–My aunt and uncle. When I was growing up, Uncle Howard was our family's master storyteller and Aunt Zora was the best cook I knew. I sat for many hours mesmerized by Uncle Howard's stories. As a teenager, he worked for his uncle, Dr. Daniel Oscar Willis, at the front desk of the Hotel Leesville. At age 15, he rode freight trains with hobos during the Great Depression.

Uncle Howard shared with me the story of Huey P. Long and Dr. Willis.

He once made a house call with Dr. Willis in his Ford. As they approached the home on a long red dirt road, they could see their lights from the kerosene oil lamps through the cracks in the walls. Their home's wallpaper was made from newspapers. It was during the Great Depression in the early 1930s. The next day Uncle Howard overheard Dr. Willis's wife complain, "They will never pay us." Dr. Willis replied, "That doesn't matter. If they ever get any money they will."

Uncle Howard was full of words of wisdom. "Don't get above your raising." And, "A person ought not to be mad at a family member for long."

I once asked Aunt Zora why her tea and coffee tasted better than anyone else's. "The well water from Hurricane Creek," she replied. She was locally famous for her Old-Fashioned Buttermilk Pies. Her vegetables from her garden seemed to taste better too. But, above all, what I remember most was her kindness.

Their granddaughter (and my cousin) Kimberly Willis Holt, was inspired by them too. She is a National Book Award Winner, author of *When Zachary Beaver Came to Town*, *My Louisiana Sky*, and the *Piper Reed* series. *When Zachary Beaver Came to Town* and *My Louisiana Sky* were adapted as films of the same names.

Donnie Willis–My first-cousin. He planted the first seed in my mind to write about our 4th Great-Grandfather, Joseph Willis. Our sainted grandmother, Lillie Hanks Willis, had a treasure chest of stories about Joseph and insisted I write them down. Donnie has been pastor of Fenton Baptist Church in Fenton, Louisiana, for fifty years.

Daniel Hubbard Willis, Jr.–Great-Grandson of Reverend Joseph Willis. Cowman, Spring Hill area in Rapides Parish Constable, and Confederate veteran. He fought in many of the great battles of the Civil War, including Shiloh, Bull Run, Perryville, Murfreesboro, Missionary Ridge, and Chickamauga.

An excerpt from his obituary in the *Alexandria Town Talk*, on June 23, 1900, stated:

"He participated in all the hard battles of that army and for bravery, soldierly bearing, discipline and devotion to duty, he was unexcelled in his entire Brigade. He was made Orderly Sergeant of his Company at an early period of the war. It has always been said by his surviving comrades that when any particularly dangerous service was required, such as scouting parties to ascertain the position and movements of the enemy, he was always selected for the place, and never hesitated to go, let the danger be what it may.

"He was for a long time connected with the famous Washington Artillery, and at the battle of Chickamauga so many horses of the battery to which he was attached were killed that they had to pull the guns off the field by hand to keep them from falling in the hands of the enemy.

"He was paroled at Meridian, Miss., in May of 1865, and brought home with him a copy of General Gibson's farewell address to his soldiers and of him it can be truly said that through the remaining years of his life he followed the advice then given by his beloved commander. His love for the Southern cause, and for the men who wore the gray, was not dimmed by years, but he lived and died firmly convinced of the justice of the cause for which the South poured out so much of her best blood and treasure.

"Before death he expressed a wish that he might see his children who were at home, especially Randall L., his baby boy, whom he had named in honor of his beloved Brigadier General, Randall Lee Gibson. He also requested that his Confederate badge be pinned on his breast and buried with him.

"During an intimate acquaintance, covering a period of twenty-five years, the writer never heard a vulgar or profane word pass his lips."

He was the first of four Willis brothers to marry four Graham sisters. He married Julia Ann Graham on January 5, 1867. He affectingly called her Julieann.

When he asked her father, Robert Graham, for her hand in marriage, Robert responded, "Can you feed her, son?" Daniel replied, "I have a horse, a milk cow, a barrel of corn and a barrel of molasses." Robert exclaimed, "My goodness, you have enough to marry several of my daughters." They were married at Robert Graham's home, near Forest Hill on Barber Creek.

When Daniel died, in 1900, he left his wife Julia Ann, $35,000.00 in gold (the equivalent of $980,000.00 today), a home, land, and the woods full of cows, hogs, and horses on Barber Creek. She lived thirty-six years after his death. She never remarried and provided for her family, even during the Great Depression. Daniel made good his promise to "feed" Julia Ann...and then some.

After Daniel was made Constable of the Spring Hill area, in Rapides Parish, Julia Ann often spoke of the time he captured an outlaw from Texas who was hiding in the piney woods of Louisiana. She said it was too late to make the trip on horseback to the jail in Alexandria. Therefore Daniel handcuffed the outlaw to the foot of their bed for the overnight stay. He then told the outlaw, "You better not make a sound." She added, "Daniel slept soundly, but I didn't sleep a wink all night."

He was a successful rancher. He and his sons would buy cattle in East Texas for $4 per head and then drive them to the railroad's beef pens at Lecompte, Louisiana. They were then shipped to the northern railheads were they would fetch $40 and more per head.

Once, on a cattle drive from Texas, in 1898, the cattle stampeded in the woods. His youngest son and my grandfather, Randall Lee Willis, who was only twelve and riding drag, thought his father had been killed. But, then he saw his father's huge white hat waving high in the air, in front of the cattle.

He was my great-grandfather.

Julia Ann Graham Willis–Wife of Daniel Hubbard Willis, Jr. and daughter of Robert and Ruth Graham. She would often read her red-lettered Bible, eat an orange, including the peel. When she looked at Daniel's Civil War photo tears would come to her eyes.

When asked by her grandchildren about eating orange peels she replied, "I don't know for sure, but I think they're good for you." She was bitten by a ground rattler, at age seventy-five, and survived with home remedies. She swam in Barber Creek twice a day until age ninety. She said it prolonged her life. All her children and grandchildren loved to go swimming with her.

According to her granddaughter Ilie Close, in a letter to me, "She always had food cooked for family and friends. There were lots of blackberries, huckleberries, and fruit of all kinds for good pies. She was reared a Methodist but later joined Amiable Baptist Church and was a devoted Christian. We use to joke, she didn't think there would be anyone but Baptists in Heaven. Her hobby was making quilts, and she kept the family supplied with her handiwork."

She was my great-grandmother.

Nathaniel Willis—Born in Chettle, Dorsetshire, a county in South West England, on the English Channel coast. The county borders a county to the west that also contains my Willis roots, Devonshire. Nathaniel later moved to London, where his son John Willis was born in 1606, only fourteen years before the historic *Mayflower* voyage.

John Willis—Born in 1606 in London. John sailed for St. Christopher (a.k.a. St. Kitts) in the West Indies on April 3, 1635, on the ship *Paul* from Gravesend. Gravesend was an ancient town in northwest Kent situated on the south bank of the Thames River near London. John sailed on the *Paul* in route to the New World— America, carrying dreams that would be passed on to subsequent generations, including me.

John Willis first appears in America in Plymouth Colony, Massachusetts, in 1635, when his son John Willis, Jr. was born and again in Duxbury, in 1637, when he married Elizabeth Hodgkins Palmer, on January 2, 1637.

John Willis, a.k.a. Deacon John Willis was the first deacon in

Plymouth Church. John's brothers were also immigrants to the Plymouth Colony area. They were: Nathaniel Willis, Lawrence Willis, Jonathan Willis, and Francis Willis.

The population was about 400 in the 1630s. William Bradford was Governor of Plymouth Colony when John arrived in 1635. John Willis held offices in Duxbury in 1637 and at Bridgewater in the 1650s. In 1648, John Willis was a juror at the murder trial of Alice Bishope, who was hanged for killing her daughter, Martha Clarke.

More than a century later, John Willis's direct descendant, Joseph Willis, would marry a direct descendant of William Bradford, Rachel Bradford. I am the 4th great-grandson of Joseph Willis and Rachel Bradford Willis.

Elizabeth I—Queen of England and Ireland from 1558 until her death in 1603. Elizabeth took the reins of her country after her sister Queen Mary died. Queen Elizabeth's reign was referred to as the Golden Age or Elizabethan England. Elizabeth's reign supported the creation of works by such greats as William Shakespeare and Christopher Marlowe.

This novel begins in England during the same period, in 1575. That year Nathaniel Willis was born in Chettle, Dorsetshire, which is a county in South West England on the English Channel coast. The county borders another county to the west that contains my ancestors too: Devonshire.

Sir Walter Raleigh and Francis Drake were both born in Devonshire. In 1588, Drake served as second-in-command during the English victory over the Spanish Armada.

Raleigh was a favorite of Queen Elizabeth and helped defend England against the Spanish Armada too. She was called the Virgin Queen since she never married and had no children. Raleigh named Virginia in the New World—America—in honor of the Virgin Queen. Its state capital was named after him.

William Bradford—English Separatist leader and signatory to the *Mayflower Compact*. The Mayflower Compact was an early, successful attempt at democracy and undoubtedly played a role in future colonists seeking permanent independence from British rule and shaping the nation that eventually became the United States of

America. William Bradford is believed by many historians to have written it. Separatist are commonly referred to as Pilgrims.

The *Mayflower* arrived in Plymouth Bay on December 20, 1620. During their first winter, more than half of the 102 passengers died. As a result of hard work and assistance from local Native Americans, the Pilgrims reaped an abundant harvest after the summer of 1621. Bradford served as Plymouth Colony's Governor, intermittently, for 30 years between 1621 and 1657.

In 1623, Governor William Bradford proclaimed November 29 as a time for pilgrims, along with their Native American friends, to gather and give thanks. His proclamation contained these words: "Thanksgiving to ye Almighty God for all His blessings." It would later be known as Thanksgiving Day.

Agerton Willis—Father of Joseph. Husband of Ahyoka Willis. Wealthy Bladen County, North Carolina plantation owner.

He was my 5th great-grandfather.

Ahyoka Willis—The mother of Joseph Willis. Her real name was Mary Willis. Joseph told his children and grandchildren that his mother was a Cherokee slave.

She was my 5th great-grandmother.

Rachel Bradford Willis—First wife of Joseph Willis and daughter of William Bradford of Bladen County, North Carolina. Rachel was a direct descendant of the English Separatist leader William Bradford.

Joseph Willis married Rachel Bradford in 1784. Their first child, Agerton Willis, was born in 1785. He was named after Joseph's father Agerton Willis. Their second child, Mary Willis, was born in 1787. She was named after Joseph's half-Cherokee mother, Mary.

To honor Joseph Willis's parents, Joseph Willis and Rachel Bradford Willis waited to the birth of their third and fourth children to name an offspring after themselves. Their third child, Joseph Willis, Jr., was born in South Carolina in 1792 and their fourth child, Rachel Willis, was born in 1794.

She was my 4th great-grandmother.

Joseph Willis—Preached the first evangelical sermon west of the Mississippi River in 1798.

He was born into slavery. His mother was Cherokee and his father a wealthy English plantation owner. His family took him to court to deprive him of his inheritance, which would have made him the wealthiest plantation owner in Bladen County, North Carolina in 1776.

He fought as a patriot in the Revolutionary War under the most colorful of all the American generals, Francis Marion, The Swamp Fox.

His first wife, Rachel Bradford Willis, died in childbirth, and his second wife died only six years later, leaving him with five young children.

He crossed the mighty Mississippi River at Natchez at the peril of his own life, riding a mule! He entered hostile Spanish-controlled Louisiana Territory when the dreaded Code Noir (Black Code) was in effect. It forbade any Protestant ministers who came into the territory from preaching. His life was threatened because of the message he preached in the Louisiana Territory.

His denomination refused to ordain him until 1812 because of his race. On November 13, 1812, Joseph Willis constituted Calvary Baptist Church at Bayou Chicot, Louisiana. He went on to plant more than twenty churches in Louisiana. On October 31, 1818, Joseph Willis founded the Louisiana Baptist Association at Beulah Baptist in Cheneyville, Louisiana. Joseph Willis founded all five charter member churches. After overcoming insurmountable obstacles, he blazed a trail for others for another half-century that changed American history.

He was my 4th great-grandfather.

Dragging Canoe–Cherokee warrior and leader of the Chickamauga. He was the greatest Cherokee military leader. He once asked his father to include him in a war party against the Shawnees, but his father, Attakullakulla, refused unless he could carry a canoe. The vessel was too heavy, so the boy dragged the canoe. From that time forward, he was known as Dragging Canoe.

Daniel Oscar Willis, M.D.–Son of Daniel Hubbard Willis, Jr. and Julia Ann Graham Willis. His father died at his home in Leesville while being treated for Bright's Disease, known as Kidney Disease today. He began his medical practice in 1904 and was the first medical doctor in Vernon Parish. He owned the first automobile in the Parish. He served in United States Army Medical Corps in World War I. He owned the Hotel Leesville. After being slandered by a young lawyer in a trial, he bodily removed the lawyer from his room at the Hotel Leesville and then threw him into the street. The young lawyer's name was Huey P. Long, later governor of Louisiana and Senator. He was assassinated in 1935. Daniel Oscar Willis was my great-uncle.

John Willis–First cousin of Joseph Willis of Bladen County, North Carolina. The land that the county seat of Robeson County, Lumberton, North Carolina is located on was donated by him, from his Red Bluff Plantation.

Known as the "father of Lumberton," he went on to represent Robeson County as a state senator in 1787, 1788, 1789, 1791, and 1798. He served in the House in 1794 and 1795 and at the state convention of 1789 where North Carolina ratified the Constitution of the United States and became the twelfth state. Governor Samuel Ashe commissioned John Willis as a Brigadier General in the 4th Brigade of the Militia, Continental Army.

He gave all of this up to follow Joseph Willis to the Louisiana Territory but died in Natchez, Mississippi, on April 22, 1802.

Henry Elwa Willis–Eldest son of Daniel Hubbard Willis, Jr. and Julia Ann Graham Willis. He is buried in the Paul Cemetery in Lecompte. He named one of his eight children Kit Carson Willis after the famous dime-novel scout.

He was my great-uncle.

Jeremiah and Jacob Stark–Based upon Mary Stark Hank's brothers Rufus and Thomas Stark. Their stories in this book are purely fictional.

Mary Stark Hanks was the mother of Lillie Hanks Willis. She traveled with her parents John and Celina Marie Deroussel Stark by covered wagon to Branch, Louisiana. After the birth of six children and the premature death of her first husband, Charles Oliver, she married Arthur Allen Hanks. They had five children. He later abandoned her and their children.

Mary Stark Hanks was my maternal great-grandmother.

Billy Sunday–The most celebrated American evangelist during the first two decades of the 20th century. He was a strong supporter of Prohibition, and his preaching played a significant role in the adoption of the Eighteenth Amendment.

Jimbo–Based upon Jimmy "Jimbo" Matheson. He is a master boot and saddle maker. He makes the gun belts for the Texas Rangers. He makes my boots, chaps, and belts. And he repairs my saddles. He is my good friend.

Charlie Goodnight–He guided the Texas Rangers to the camp leading to Cynthia Ann Parker's recapture. He later became friends with her son, Quanah Parker. He developed one of the nation's finest herds through the introduction of Hereford bulls. Goodnight also invented the chuck wagon.

He was the best-known rancher in Texas history. Historian J. Frank Dobie wrote, "Goodnight approached greatness more nearly than any other cowman of history."

Quanah Parker–The last chief of the Comanche Indians, son of Peta Nocona and Cynthia Ann Parker, an Anglo-American who was kidnapped, at age nine, by the Comanche.

General Randall Lee Gibson–Confederate general in the Civil War. He was a member of the House of Representatives and U.S. Senator from Louisiana. He was president of the board of administrators of Tulane University. My grandfather, Randall Lee Willis, was named after him by his father, Daniel Hubbard Willis, Jr. who served with him in the Civil War. I was named after my grandfather.

Huey P. Long–Served as governor of Louisiana from 1928 to 1932 and as a member of the United States Senate from 1932 until his assassination in 1935.

Jimmie Davis–Singer and songwriter as well as the former governor of Louisiana. Jimmie Davis would go on to change Louisiana history and impact the lives of thousands through his music and life. In 1999, "You Are My Sunshine" was honored with a Grammy Hall of Fame Award and the Recording Industry Association of America named it one of the Songs of the Century.

Jimmie Davis would write of his beloved Louisiana College, "Every man needs God as a partner because you can't make it by yourself. I knew it was my duty to try and contribute something to life, not just take from it, and I determined to try to be a better citizen. I believe that was the most important thing I learned at Louisiana College."

Robert G. Lee–Dr. Robert G. Lee will forever be remembered as the man who warned the world that there would indeed be a "Pay Day Someday!" While he was pastor of Bellevue Baptist Church, Lee served three consecutive terms as president of the Southern Baptist Convention: 1949, 1950, and 1951. Presiding at the 1951 meeting in San Francisco, he introduced a young Billy Graham to the SBC. Evangelist Billy Graham preached on the Louisiana College campus the same year during a 1951 revival.

*   *   *

Three Winds Blowing

a nonfiction novel

Antebellum Louisiana

The son of a white man and Cherokee slave, Joseph Willis, gains his freedom and swims the mighty Mississippi on a mule.

Prologue

October 1, 1852, could be called a glorious day in Evergreen, Louisiana. A little bit of crispness still hung in the air that hinted at the colder weather yet to come. Even at noon there were only a few clouds to be seen, but enough to create a comfortable breeze, which carried the tantalizing aroma of Sunday's chicken and fresh ham for a supper on the grounds of the church near a huge brush arbor.

The rather gaunt, ninety-four-year-old preacher, Joseph Willis, made his way out of Bayou Rouge Baptist Church with the help of the menfolk in his family. It had been a morning racked with joyful emotion as Joseph had publicly blessed his grandson, Reverend Daniel Hubbard Willis, Sr., to carry on his church-plantin' and gospel-sharin' call. Each step he took seemed lighter to him now that he had passed off the torch of his ministry. He had no doubt that Daniel would become a mighty man of God. He had known that since not long after his birth in 1817, for Joseph had watched him carefully and listened to his words spoken to others. They were filled with kindness and a godly wisdom far beyond his youthful years. Joseph thought for a long time that he was a blessed man, and this morning served as confirmation in his heart.

With some careful planning and a few grunts, they were able to hoist Joseph into the hospital wagon that was headed back to

Lemuel's home in Blanche, Louisiana, where Joseph now lived. But, Joseph had decided he wished to spend a few days at his ole home place in Babb's Bridge on Spring Creek, so the wagon rolled in that direction. Daniel now owned the home, and it would be an opportunity for Joseph to visit with his family and friends from days long since past. Little did he know that his great-grandson, Daniel Jr., would use the time to draw a wealth of information from him that would forever change his life and flood Joseph's mind with memories long since passed.

There were several family members present that morning, and Joseph felt an overflowing love for them all. Being the patriarch of the huge family had given him the opportunity to celebrate the birth of his nineteen children, the legacy of love passed to his grandchildren, and even his great-grandchildren. He had shared in the joys of new babies coming into the Willis family and seen many tears shed in the cemeteries where young and old had been laid to rest.

As all found their places in the various wagons and buggies, Lemuel took the reins. Daniel tucked the traveling quilt around Joseph's legs. Daniel's wife, Anna, had sewn the quilt using the leftover scraps of material from her children's clothes. Daniel and Joseph both remembered several of the prints and plaids. With each loving stitch, she thought of another Joseph from the Bible. His father had giving him a coat of many colors. Gently, Daniel wrapped Joseph in family memories.

"Father, can I ride with you and great-grandpa?" The voice of thirteen-year-old Daniel Hubbard Willis Jr., known as Dan, could be heard from a distance as he brought a cup of strong coffee with chicory to the wagon for Joseph. Young Dan had been scoutin' out his favorites—juicy peach cobbler and dewberry pie.

Daniel glanced at Joseph, who responded with a slight nod. The wagons—some pulled by horses and some by mule teams, even some by oxen—began their steady and plodding journey down the worn path toward Babb's Bridge. The two grassless wagon ruts showed years of ongoing use. Joseph was inwardly pleased with the wear on the road. He called those ruts *love tracks* because it meant there were many people coming to and going from God's house.

Silence dominated during the first mile, and Daniel observed

Joseph with an eagle eye. He had watched his grandfather change, and it was especially noticeable today. He had lost weight, as evidenced by his more sunken cheeks. His once smooth face now sagged with many creases and wrinkles. The hair that had been so very dark now appeared totally grey. Even his once-strong hands had become gnarled with age. But, one thing had not changed, and that was Joseph's memory. With alert but dimmed eyes he still watched everybody and could take any experience and turn it into a teachable moment.

Finally, Daniel broke the silence: "Grandpa, are you comfortable?"

"Daniel, there's not a wagon known to man that's comfortable to me, but the joy of bein' with my family makes this ride easier today."

"Sir, are you too tired to talk? To tell one of my favorite stories?"

Joseph Willis's face produced a faint smile, and Daniel could read his eyes very well. It was story-tellin' time, and Daniel knew in his heart that these times were to end soon. After all, Grandpa was the oldest man he knew, so he was especially attentive to his beloved grandfather and teacher of lessons about life's rocky road. With an all-knowing little laugh, Joseph asked, "Now, Daniel, which story might that be? I've told you all of 'em by now."

"I want to hear about the sandbar fight again and how your friend Jim Bowie became famous. I want Dan to hear that story, too. Tell 'im how you were late 'cause of some green-broke molly mule. Someday, Dan wants to travel to east Texas, buy cattle, and be a cattleman. He already knows the Alamo story, but he hasn't heard *how* Jim Bowie came to be known by folks far and wide. He wants to write it all down in his diary.

Grandpa remained silent for a while as if trying to put all the pieces together in his mind. He took a deep breath and began looking intently at Dan.

"Dan, the wind of freedom first drove me from my home in North Carolina to the banks of the Mississippi, but it was a mighty, rushing wind that compelled me to swim the turbulent waters of the Mississippi River, in 1798, on my mule into the Louisiana Territory, while the dreaded Code Noir forbade me from doing so. The Territory was a land rooted in tradition and chivalry.

"It was a land that had lost its innocence. Here, I soon discovered a third wind blowing: the wind of war fueled by human bondage.

"Dan, it's an evil wind caused by this slavery issue—and I fear you and our family will be left to deal with the destruction to our property and our way of life it will most surely bring. I saw this wind blow in 1775 and its ruination when I fought with the Swamp Fox Francis Marion in 1780 in the Pee Dee River swamps of South Carolina. The cost of freedom was high then, but well worth it. Mark my words, if war comes to Louisiana, the cost will be much higher than the politicians tell ya."

Lemuel stopped the wagon to hear too. Joseph paused and studied their faces carefully. "We have all embraced the first two—*the winds of freedom and the spiritual wind.* But, my question to all three of you is this: how will you deal with the third wind, the *wind of war*?" Again, there was more silence as he stared at them. He had a way of looking past the eyes, right into the soul. "How you answer that question will determine how you deal with the war that I fear we are gonna have soon."

Silence covered the wagon like a thick blanket.

"Now, what was the question? Oh, let me tell ya the story of my friend, Jim. Here's what I remember."

An Affair of Honor: The Battle of the Sandbar

Narrative

{1}

September 6, 1827
Bennett's Store
Eldred's Bend on Bayou Boeuf

Pastor Willis felt sorry for his faithful old mule, Josh, as they both came down the dusty road leading to Bennett's store. Sweat poured off the preacher's head, and even his large hat could not sop it up fast enough. The sun was relentless, the humidity unbearable, very similar to how most of the days had been that summer and now autumn. But Bennett would have some cool water for the preacher and his mule, and maybe a new bridle could be purchased for Josh prior to an intended trip over to Mississippi.

"I know you're sufferin', Josh," said the preacher, "but this trip is important to me. We are going to Bethel Baptist Church so that I can preach a revival meeting. This'll be the first time I've been back there since I was officially ordained. Long time. This was the first church congregation I ever organized, so it has a special place in my heart."

Pastor Willis smiled as he assessed Bennett's store. It was smaller than the fancy places in Alexandria that carried needless paraphernalia, doodads, frivolous accessories, and silly contraptions. The pastor tried to keep his dear wife Hannah away from those establishments because she somehow always felt the need to purchase some "necessity" she would find there. No, Bennett's was all that was required. It was compact, functional, and diverse enough to meet the needs of farmers, cowboys, school marms, tradesmen, and itinerant preachers. Bennett even served as a makeshift postmaster for families who came to collect their mail there. Who knew that maybe Bennett may even have peeked inside those envelopes now and then, for it was for sure he knew every bit of news and gossip related to the entire region.

Arriving, the preacher noticed a one-horse buggy hitched to the rail outside. He dismounted, secured Josh, and opened the store's front door. Immediately, he was hit with a musty coolness, for the building sat under some shade trees. It was refreshing. Seconds later, his nostrils picked up the mixed aroma of cookin' herbs, leather, fresh bread, and maybe even a little sweet perfume. Bennett was able to keep his shelves stocked because he was open to swapping goods, trading materials, and bartering with local craftsmen and seamstresses. If you needed molasses and flour and cornmeal and you had handmade quilts or homemade jams and preserves to swap, Bennett would act as the middleman.

Mr. Bennett looked up and nodded to the preacher. "Welcome, friend," he said. "I'm helping Bowie here now, but I'll be with you in a moment."

Pastor Willis crossed the room and slapped the back of Jim Bowie, who whirled around and suddenly broke into a wide smile. He extended his hand. "Brother Willis, of all people I'd never expect to cross paths with today. What in the world brings you out in these parts?"

Bowie had dirty-blond hair, and as befitting a man of the frontier, he was dressed in buckskins.

"Headin' to Mississippi for revival meetings." Willis looked at a young, very attractive woman standing close to Bowie. "And who might this be?"

Beaming from ear to ear, Bowie proudly announced, "You have the honor of meeting the future Mrs. James Bowie. This is my fiancée, Miss Cecelia Wells. But she already knows you…at least by reputation."

Cecelia extended her hand and said, "Indeed, I do, Brother Willis. Jim says you're handier with a Bible than he is with a knife. And, that's saying something, sir."

The preacher chuckled at the compliment. "I hope you know the tornado you're planning to hitch yourself to, Miss."

Now she chuckled, but said, "I'll have my hands full, no doubt about that. But it won't be a boring life." Her expression turned more serious. "Jim tells me you're the Baptist man who starts churches. He says you're a friend to everyone—cattlemen, farmers, Indians, slaves, poor folks, children. I'm honored to meet your acquaintance, but I didn't know it would be this soon."

Jim lifted a hand and said, "What she means is, I told her that when we tie the knot, I was sure hopin' you'd be available to conduct the ceremony. We ain't set a specific date as yet, but if we could know your travelin' plans for the next month or so, maybe we could arrange a place and day."

By now the pastor had removed his hat in respect to the lady. "I'd be honored to conduct the rites of marriage for you, but I need to ask Miss Cecelia if she likes to cook. I say that, Miss, because this future hubby of yours loves to fish and hunt and trap."

Cecelia smiled. "I can waltz and speak some French and recite poetry," she said, "but I also can sew, plant a garden, and pluck a chicken. My mama was a librarian and a frontierswoman. I got the best of both of her skills."

Teasingly, Pastor Willis turned to Jim and said, "You're marrying up, amigo. I guess even an ole blind hog finds an acorn now and then."

Jim laughed in agreement. "I'm blessed, no doubt about it. So, good, you'll do the vow exchanges. That pleases me more than you can imagine."

Mr. Bennett came over from where he had gone to unpack some crates. "Is there anything else you may need, Miss Wells?"

Cecelia told Jim and the preacher to go outside and tend to the animals while she sashayed a time or two more through the store. She touched her ringlets to make sure none had moved too far from her tidy bow. She held her bonnet with its dangling ribbons by her side. It matched the blue of her dress and her eyes.

Once outside, the preacher found a bucket, went to a nearby well, drew some water and came and placed it by Josh, who eagerly put his nose and mouth inside. The preacher pulled it back after a minute and said, "Not too much all at once." He scratched Josh's ears.

"So, you're finally getting' married and settlin' down, eh?"

Bowie looked somewhat perplexed. "To me, the two don't mean the same thing, Preacher. Yes, I'm getting' married, but I'll still be lookin' for the next new adventure. In fact, I've got my eyes focused on Texas. It's big with opportunities. But first, there are some matters closer at hand that have to be resolved."

The preacher's eyes narrowed. "I've heard bits and pieces of news about trouble brewing around here. What's the straight talk about that?"

Bowie frowned. "A scoundrel—a so-called doctor named Thomas Maddox—and his patrons have been sayin' a lot of disrespectful remarks about our womenfolk, and there's been some shootin's and stabbin's along the way, too. Some of it is political, but there sure is lots of tension. A friend of mine, Samuel Wells, is not going to put up with much more from those rascals. Their feud is gettin' ugly. The two of 'em will have to fight it out in order for this to end, and that'll be a *real* barn-burner, too!"

"Whoa, Jim, are you talking about an affair of honor? Please tell me you won't get involved in something like that."

Jim lifted his buckskin shirt and showed a long, red wound across his ribs. "Too late for warnin' me, Pastor. I've tangled with Wright—you know that snake—once too often. I went to his bank for a loan to start a business, and he turned me down flat. Later, we had words and he wounded me with his pistol. I can't let that pass. I need satisfaction. The whole feud is heatin' up. It's too big now for me, alone, to put a stop to. Anyway, ya know I don't have to carry a gun 'cause I just don't trust 'em. I just got this 'toad-stabbin' knife that I carry. Only important men with titles in front of their names, whether real or made-up, can fight it out like that. I'm just a guy who likes adventure." He ran his hand up and down the sheath in his belt as he spoke.

That look told the preacher a whole lot more about his ability to protect himself than he let on. That was one thing anyone could say for Jim Bowie: he was hardheaded for sure, but he never talked about himself. That was the first thing about him that had impressed Pastor Willis.

"But you know what the Bible says about fightin' like that. Not only is it 'gainst man's law, but it's 'gainst God's law, too. I got a bad feelin' that nothin' good will come out of this, Jim."

"Pastor, just as your heart tells you I should not get involved in this, my gut tells me I *must!*"

The silence caused discomfort for both men. Jim changed the subject and walked inside to collect his supplies and lady.

With Cecelia on his one arm and a parcel in the other, they walked to the buggy. "It was good seein' you again." He paused and looked at the preacher. "I'll be careful. Ya won't read my name in any obituary column. Don't ya worry 'bout me." Cecelia was seated, and he climbed aboard. "I'm serious about the weddin', Pastor. I will be in touch with ya."

"That would be most enjoyable, my friend. And, Jim, I'm serious about this fightin', too. I don't see how it could possibly bring ya any honor. Think about it." The minister could not help but see the questions and concern written on Miss Wells's face. "There is also someone else to think about now, too." He nodded toward Jim's fiancée.

Same Day
Outside Ezra Bennett's Store

Just as they were ready to leave, a young man rode up on his lathered horse. He greeted everyone and seemed friendly enough, in an arrogant sort of way. He was talking even before he climbed out of his saddle. "Howdy. I'm Edwin Epps. You folks from 'round here?"

Jim climbed back down out of the buggy and did the introductions. "I'm Jim Bowie, and this here is my fiancée, Cecelia Wells. That guy over there is Preacher Joseph Willis. Nice to meet ya."

Epps bowed to Miss Wells and shook everyone's hands. He studied Jim's face for a few seconds and asked, "Are you the Bowie friend of Jean Lafitte? You the one who sold slaves down in N'Orleans with 'im? Someday I'm gonna have me a big cotton plantation, so I'll be findin' ya so as you can get me some niggers to work on my land. You live around here?"

Pastor Willis could tell Jim was uncomfortable just by the way he looked at the ground and eyed the other man askance. Jim answered vaguely, "I travel a lot, but I don't live too far from here."

Epps looked directly at Willis and said, "Preacher, I heard of you, too! You're the one who gets churches started. You're friends with many of the plantation owners—*and their slaves*. Right?"

Rev. Willis nodded and wondered where he was going with this conversation. It did not take Epps long to explain.

"Yup, I'm gonna have me some slaves who dance to the whip and never give me problems. They won't be like those ignorant darkies down in the André and Meuillion Plantations. You hear'd what they did to 'em slaves, right?"

Jim and the preacher stood there, trying not to flinch hearing the sordid details. Miss Wells was now looking off in the distance. But Epps, kept right on talking.

"Back in 1811, there was a bunch of 'em niggers, over 200 or so, who thought they could have a revolt and be free. What foolishness! They marched toward N'Orleans and were caught and rightly punished for bein' stupid. About forty-five were killed in the fightin', but I really like what they did to the ones they caught alive. They cut off their heads and put 'em on spikes, and stood 'em up along the Mississippi River levee for many miles. Served as a reminder for those other uppity niggers to mind their manners and obey their masters. Ain't heard of no more trouble since then." Epps scratched his head, "Oh, yeah, their leader...what was his name? Deslondes, or somethin' like that. Got his hands chopped off, and then they shot him in both legs and roasted him like a pig in some straw. What a great way for a nigger agitator to end his life! Don't y'all agree?"

Pastor Willis found it very difficult to speak to this young man after hearing his hateful words. He looked the younger man directly in the eyes and said, "Mr. Epps, I'm not sure if you are serious about all this or not, but I can tell you in the eyes of the Lord you would never have such a right. To do so would be murder."

"Oh, yes, I would, Preacher, 'cause they ain't got no souls, anyway. Surely, you know that!" His face was bright red with anger and hatred. "If you live 'round here, too, you have to know Peter Tanner, your fellow Baptist. He's a brother-in-law of William Prince Ford, a big plantation owner. I heard Tanner tell some plantation owners that the niggers had no souls."

"That's not what Scripture teaches," Pastor Willis retorted. "Tanner is not speaking the truth. We all are made in God's image."

Epps stopped for a moment, paused in thought, and then said with a smirk, "Oh, that's right, Preacher, I forgot. You're mix't with Indian. You were once a slave, weren't ya? Well, least ya got *half* a soul."

Pastor Willis could feel his human nature getting aroused to anger. His blood was getting hot. It wasn't just that Epps had tried to insult him because of his heritage, it was more for the man's disrespect to sound teachings of doctrine. In a flash, however, the love of Christ ruled the preacher's countenance, and he became more concerned about saving this man's soul than knocking him down a peg or two for his prideful behavior.

With a peaceful but commanding voice, the pastor said, "The Bible says, 'Let every man be a liar and God be the truth,' and Mr.

Epps, *this is wrong.*"

Epps flinched. His eyes narrowed. In his brash youthfulness and position of wealth, he was not used to being contradicted nor corrected. "You callin' me a liar, Preacher?" Epps curled his fingers into fists. "Oh, if you wasn't a preacher, I'd...."

Jim, whose arms had been folded on his chest, let them drop to his sides. His hand was but maybe an inch away from his sheathed knife. "Well, Epps, I ain't no preacher, and I can tell you that I feel the same way as my friend."

Epps looked at that nine-inch knife in Jim's belt and it was obvious he had heard of Bowie's reputation. He seemed to lose some of his arrogance. He offered a twisted smile and said, "This talk may be better suited for when a refined lady is not present, gentlemen. No need for us to get carried away."

He tipped his hat toward Jim's fiancée. "It was a pleasure to meet you, Miss Wells. And good day to y'all." Epps went into Bennett's store and quickly returned. Everyone was still silent as he mounted and left.

No one knew what to say. His words had left a foul stench in the air. Pastor Willis whispered to Jim, "Young men like that concern me deeply. He is on a mission in life, and it is not healthy, loving, or productive. I see and hear heartless cruelty in young Epps."

"It's been bred into him," said Jim. "He's grown up hearing masters speak bitterly to their slaves, and he's watched slaves get whipped, hanged, separated from their families, and he's been told there's nothing wrong with it. Hard to change a man's thinkin' at this stage of his life."

"Only too true," agreed the preacher, "but I'll pray for Epps and his entire family. I'll pray that he sees the light and has a change of heart."

"You do that, friend," said Jim. "Take care until we cross paths again."

Pastor Willis tugged at Jim's arm. "Once again, please be wise about this debt of honor situation you talked about earlier. Do the right thing, Jim. Think carefully 'bout this fighin' and realize it cannot come to any good end. Rational thinkin' is not cowardice."

Jim nodded but gave no response. He popped the reins and the horse started to pull the buggy away. Both Jim and Cecelia leaned back and waved at the pastor as their buggy turned and disappeared around the bend.

The minister gave old Josh another drink of the water, and told him, "I'm gonna go inside and buy you a new bridle. You'll have time to get used to it before our trip to Bethel Baptist.

September 19, 1827
Vidalia, Louisiana

Pastor Willis spent a lot of time in prayer as he rode old Josh. It was a six day trip from Bayou Chicot to Vidalia, Louisiana. He planned to cross the Mississippi River there on a barge and then head on to Bethel Baptist Church in Woodville, Mississippi. His mind was pulled in two directions emotionally, however. On the one hand, he was really looking forward to seeing his old friends at the church and also meeting new ones. On the other hand, as he traversed his miles, he met passing travelers who carried news about a pending series of duels at the Vandalia Sandbar. Prominent in this duel would be his friend Jim Bowie.

As word came, it seemed that the sandbar was far enough afield in the Mississippi River that no one could claim actual jurisdiction for it. Thus, even though dueling was outlawed, there would be no one to enforce it there on the midstream sandbar. Just as Bowie had said to Joseph Willis, the build-up to the duel had been a long time in coming. The wealthy Cuny and Wells families were close relatives. They were firmly established in the region, and they took issue with the newer families who came in and took over farming land, felled standing timber, initiated independent businesses, and started rearing large broods of children.

The Cuny clan was accused of fixing the election of the local sheriff so that grievances would go in their favor. The Wells clan denied loans to the influx of newcomers. One very outspoken adversary of the establishment was Dr. Thomas H. Maddox, who openly challenged Samuel L. Wells III to a duel. Twice the duels were delayed: first, because the parties could not agree on the terms of engagement and wound up screaming and name calling; and the next time because the seconds were informed that by participating, they, too, would go to jail for breaking the laws against dueling. So it was that Vadalia, Louisiana was chosen as the venue wherein this duel could finally be staged and the issue of honor resolved. However, in one of these previous encounters, Major Norris Wright, a supporter of the Wells clan, shot Jim Bowie. Though wounded, Bowie charged Wright and would have killed him had not several bystanders intervened and held him back. Bowie's ire was raised from that day forward.

Pastor Willis reached the Mississippi River on a Wednesday morning intent on catching a barge. His mind was now made up to move as quickly as possible to reach the sandbar and stop Jim Bowie from risking his life. Possibly, he could witness the love of Christ to the others involved and, thus, belay the entire faceoff by the duelists. It was worth a try. However, upon getting to the water's edge, he was stunned to see not a single barge anywhere. There was one plump old man sitting on a crate with a fishing pole, surrounded by some hungry, brown pelicans.

"Where's all the barges?" asked the preacher. "I need to cross to Natchez today. It's a matter of life and death, not to mention that I also need to conduct special church meetin's later this week."

The barge tender laid down his pole, got up slowly, and walked over to the minister. He was a rough one and spoke with gruffness in his voice. "Well, you can wait 'til they come back tonight and leave in the mornin', or you can swim it, mister. Ain't no barges to be had *today*. Nope, no barges! Some crazy men from Alexandria took all the barges this mornin'. Yup, they's *crossin' the river*."

"*All* of the barges? Why all of them?"

"You been livin' under a rock, mister? It's the boys what's gonna have the shootout on the sandbar. The two duelists came, then there was their seconds, then a couple of sawbones carrying their doctor bags, a few former military men still calling themselves 'major' and 'colonel,' and a bunch of others who were kinfolk and undertakers and newspaper writers. Yes, sir, filled up every barge and paid to have them wait to take them back. Crazy as bats, the lot of 'em, but they paid up front, so I got no complaints."

Pastor Willis looked chagrined. "They're actin' like this is some kind of county fair or circus show. Men's lives—their souls—are at stake. This has got to be stopped. I need to get to them. Now!"

"Unless you and that mule can fly, you ain't goin' nowhere today, friend."

"When those men crossed, did one have sandy hair and a large knife strapped to his side?"

The fat man grinned. "You talkin' about Jim Bowie?

Heavens, yes, he was with 'em. His boots was shined and he looked like he'd had a fresh shave. It was like he was expectin' to be one of the leaders of that parade."

Pastor Willis lowered his head and whispered a silent prayer. "That settles it," he said. "I've got to get across this river this very mornin'. My mule and I will swim it."

The fat man raised both hands. "I don't know if ya'all are from these parts, but let me explain to you why you won't be crossin' this river, crazy though you may be. First, this time of year the current is so strong it will wash you down river right away. Second, even if that mule is sure-footed, the bottom of the banks on both sides are thick with reeds, wild grass, and tangled roots. That mule will get snarled, be pulled under, and drown. Third, that water is infested with snappin' turtles, poison snakes, and mosquitoes."

He paused a moment to let all that sink in, then added, "Now, there is an old legend that says that many a year back some fool hearty young preacher who thought he could walk on water actually did ride a mule across and live, but that was before my time and I never believed it, even though I heard it from some trustworthy folks. No, mister, if you go in that water today, someone'll be fishin' your carcass out of the river a few miles downstream. If you're a prayin' man, you'd better make your peace with your Maker."

Joseph Willis nodded and said, "We're about to see if history can repeat itself, brother. I was that crazy young preacher who swam it years ago, and I'm set on tryin' it again today. And, yep, I've made my peace with my Maker. I hope the same can be said for you."

The fat man looked at the preacher as if he'd just heard a dog talk. With more respect he said, "Well, sir, if you do intend to ford this blasted river, may I suggest you do it with a mule younger, stronger, and less swaybacked than this critter you rode up on?"

The preacher turned and sized up Josh. Reality struck him hard when he saw him. Josh had served him well, but he really was too old now, and though he'd die trying, the pastor knew he couldn't swim it again. Joseph wasn't sure he could, either, but he stood a better chance on a younger mule.

"Where can I buy a mule colt? A molly will work, too.

Quickly, tell me! Please."

"Go down that street a stretch, and you'll find a horse trader. You can git a good mule there, but be careful. If you got *any* horse sense, use it well. Ya know what I mean?"

"Sure do," Joseph muttered as he walked away. "All too well…some of 'em are like some preachers I hear tell of."

Pastor Willis found the place without any trouble and went up to the trader. "Mornin'. Do you have any mules for sale? I gotta get 'cross that river today!"

The man looked at the stranger with curiosity. He seemed to study the preacher as he walked to the stall. After fumbling with the gate, he led out the only mule in the stable.

"This here's a good molly mule. She's a good'un', and she'll give ya some good years. She's as fit as a fiddle."

"Not to give you a sob story," said Pastor Willis, "but I've got to travel all the way to Bethel Baptist Church to deliver a series of sermons in a few days, but before that I've got to try to stop a donnybrook from breakin' out down river. I need a broke mule, not just a green-broke mule, 'cause I have no time for trainin'. Usually, I don't ask for favoritism for me being a man of the cloth, but this time I've got a close friend whose life is on the line. Can you help me out?"

He just kind of smiled, nodding the whole time Joseph was talkin', and finally said, "Yup, here's the one for you. I will sell her to you for a good price, 'cause of you bein' a preach'r man."

"Let me look her over," said the preacher. He took the mule and tethered it to a nearby tree. He pried her jaws apart and examined the lines of her teeth and judged her to be about three years old. He walked around and touched her and even tried to spook her. She didn't respond except to look back with her big, brown eyes as if to say, "You got the St. Vitus Dance or something?" He climbed on her back. She flinched only enough to indicate it would take her a few miles to get used to a new set of hips and legs.

"How much?" called out the preacher.

"Fifty in gold or silver," came the answer.

"The streets of heaven may be made of gold, but I'm not there yet. If I was payin' fifty, I'd want a stallion that had just won a race. I'll give you twenty, plus I'll let you have the old mule I rode in on. His name is Josh, and he'll still be good for ridin' and reasonable wagon pullin' for a few more years."

Josh looked Joseph in the eyes. "Never mind, I'll pay ya to keep 'im 'til I get back next week but I can only afford twenty bucks. He don't eat much," Joseph added, changing his mind.

The trader laughed out loud. "You caught me on a lucky day. It's a deal."

It didn't take Joseph but a minute to settle on a name for the new mule. To him, she just looked like a *Sally*. She looked older than her years because of her flea-bitten, gray-hair coat, so he altered it to Ole Sally."

The ride back to the waterfront was easy. The river between Vidalia and Natchez was narrower, but it was still a far piece to swim. Ole Sally was cooperative as she and the pastor eyed the water near the barge dock. Joseph took a deep seat, gave a faraway look, and focused his mind on that opposite shore. Suddenly, he remembered his late wife Rachel once telling him, "Joseph, no river is too wide if you want what's on the other side."
Well, the preacher wanted Jim Bowie to live, but obviously Rachel had not seen the Mississippi. Nevertheless, in order to reach the sandbar yet this day, he'd have to risk everything. After securing everything on Sally's saddle tightly, he nudged her forward.

"Here we go, girl," he said.

From the distance, the fat man said, "If by any fool chance you do make it to the other side today, you will convince me there is a God. I'll be on the front row of that Bethel church next Sunday when you're preachin' there."

"I'll be watchin' for you."

{4}

September 19, 1827
Vidalia, Louisiana, at the sandbar

The Maddoz partisans and the Wells partisans faced off before each other.

"We are here to conduct an honorable gentlemen's duel today," said Col. Robert A Crain. "I will serve as second to Dr. Thomas A. Maddox, and Major George McWorter will serve as second to Mr. Samuel L. Wells. Attendants for Dr. Maddox will be Major Norris Wright, and Misters Alfred and Carey Blanchard. Attendants for Mr. Wells will be Mr. James Bowie, Mr. Jefferson Wells, and General Samuel Cuny. Two physicians, Dr. Richard Cuny, who has traveled with us from our home, and Dr. James A. Denny, a local physician, will provide medical attention as may be required. Any other observers will need to keep back from the engagement."

Crain surveyed the gathered small crowd of witnesses. Two plantation owners were present, several slaves, a man in buckskins who served as a local guide, and two more men who claimed to have gained medical experience in northern schools.

"Gentlemen, do you have any questions or do either of you wish to make a statement?"

"I'm content," said Maddox. His hair was pulled back and his mustache was curled.

"I, too, am ready," said Wells. He wore a tweed suit, despite the unbearable heat.

Pistols were handed to each man, one per each hand. The observers and seconds stepped back. The duelists, with backs to each other, paced off 14 steps.

"Turn and fire," came the command.

Much too swiftly, Maddox whirled, aimed wildly, and discharged one pistol. His bullet hit the ground some six feet in front of Wells. Startled by such a quick response, Wells acted instinctively and lifted his arm and squeezed off a round. His bullet went high and wide of Maddox.

Immediately, both men started to sweat profusely, realizing that each had dared to try to kill another man, and that another man had tried to kill him.

Acting more deliberately, Maddox switched his loaded pistol to his right hand and lifted it to aim more carefully this time. However, he was surprised to find that his hand was shaking uncontrollably. He was scared of getting killed, but he also was appalled at the idea of shooting Wells dead over what now seemed to him to be inconsequential matters of property and banking and name calling. But it was too late to back down now. He held the weapon at full arm's length, closed his eyes, and pulled the trigger. The shot went far to the left of Wells.

For his part, Wells was relieved to realize that Maddox had fired both times and had not come even close to injuring him. But now, how was he to behave? Should he wait until his nerves settled, and then calmly take aim and shoot Maddox square in the chest and kill the man? It would be ruled an honorable shot, but could he, himself, abide with such callous behavior? True, he had often wished ill fate against Maddox, but to kill him in cold blood? No, no…harsh businessman though he may be, he was not a wanton murderer. He lifted the pistol, pointed it above the head of Maddox, fired, and missed. The duel was over.

"I do not wish to continue, if you feel you are satisfied, sir," Wells yelled to Maddox.

Catching his breath, Maddox responded, "I am most satisfied, sir, and I even wish to offer you my hand in resolution." He dropped both pistols in the sand, lifted his hand, and started to walk directly toward Wells.

Wells, equally gratified that the entire matter was finished at no embarrassment nor injury to either of them, strode forward, also extending his hand. The two adversaries met midfield and shook hands.

And that should have ended the matter.

But fate or pent-up ill will or misunderstood actions combined to set a string of events in motion that would very quickly turn the placid white drifts of the sandbar into a blood-stained arena of carnage, agony, and death.

{5}

At the Mississippi River
still September 19, 1927

Ole Sally waded into the warm, muddy water. At first it was sandy, but then the bottom became thick with sludge, mud, and plant life almost as thick as a swamp. She walked and stumbled until she could no longer touch the bottom, but then it seemed she enjoyed a sense of freedom as she was able to kick all four feet. Being free of that thick, weighty mud was a welcomed relief. She swam for a short distance, keeping her nose above water and staying focused on the distant shore. But as she gained the half-way point in the crossing, the current became fast and strong and relentless. Ole Sally's eyes widened, and she began to lunge frantically in the river.

"Easy, girl, you were doing fine," coaxed Joseph. "You can fight this. You're strong. What got you spooked?" He rubbed her neck, all the while scanning the horizon to try to discover what had suddenly panicked the animal. Then, following Sally's line of sight, the preacher spotted a pair of deadly water moccasins.

"Dear Lord, save us!" he called out. For some reason his mind flashed back to the story of Aaron turning his staff into a snake before Pharaoh, and how Pharaoh's magicians turned their staffs into snakes using satanic powers. But the snake from Aaron's staff devoured the two demonic snakes before turning back into a staff.

"Deliver me from these snakes, just like that, Precious Lord," Joseph cried aloud.

Sally wanted freedom from her saddle and her rider. Horses and mules hate snakes, whether on land or water, and Sally was no exception. Eying the snakes moving in on her, she dove under the waves and thrashed to put distance between herself and the two predators. Joseph felt as though he was on a bucking horse. Fearing to lose his grip, he held the reins and was pulled below the water. An eternity later Sally rose to the surface, and both she and the preacher were spitting water, gagging, and coughing.

Joseph debated whether to stay with Sally or try to go it on his own. The decision was made for him, however, when he discovered that his pigging string, which secured his rope to the saddle horn, suddenly broke and the rope flew off in every direction, tangling the preacher. Down he went again when Sally took another plunge. Struggle as he may, he could not release himself from his binding. He prayed Sally would need air and rise, and, praise the Lord, she did.

Together, Sally and Joseph came atop the water, and to Joseph's great relief, there was no sign of the two water moccasins any longer. One hurdle cleared, but more to go. Struggling like a man wrapped as a mummy, the preacher managed to extricate a knife that had been gifted to him a few weeks earlier by his friend Bowie. He used one hand to stay atop Sally and the other to saw away the rope loops. The blade was razor sharp, and very quickly Joseph could move his arms again. That proved fortunate, because it was at that moment that Ole Sally saw the shore and determined to reach it at any cost. She lunged forward and kicked her back legs high. Preacher Willis, in the midst of dislodging the ropes, went flying through the air in a back flip. He got a fast slap in the face from Sally's tail, which he had the good sense to grab hold of.

"Pull...swim...move!" gasped Joseph, admonishing Sally to reach the land. She needed no directions or encouragements. With steady strides, she put the full range of her muscles to work in swimming to the shore. When she reached the shallows, onlookers came to the edge to help guide the mule and to pull the wretched crazy man out of the river.

An aged fellow in a weather beaten rowboat rowed near the shore. "I wanted to help y'all," he said, "but this little dingy of mine couldn't go head to head with a charging mule. I'm glad you survived. I would have bet money you both were gonna be goners. What was so dad-blamed important that was worth riskin' gettin' drown over?"

Pastor Willis, now on his knees on the shore trying to suck in clean, fresh air, muttered, "I've got to get to the sandbar down the road. There's supposed to be a duel today, and I need to try to stop it. I'm a preacher, but I'd do it anyway. One of my best friends is involved."

The man in the rowboat pushed back his faded cap, pulled in his oars, and said, "I'm 'fraid I got some bad news for you, Preacher Man. It's been hours since those barges hit this shore.

Those folks all left on horseback or rented carriages. Hired a local guide to direct them. Fella name of Bradshaw. Even if this Molly mule of yours wasn't exhausted from that swim cross the Missisip, you wouldn't stand a chance of getting' there before the shootin' starts."

The preacher emptied water from his boots, squeezed his socks and pant legs, wrung out his coat, and unknotted his kerchief from his neck and used it to start wiping mud, and reeds from Ole Sally's eyes, nostrils, and ears. Without turning to direct his response specifically to the man in the rowboat, he said, "Got to try anyway." He coughed twice, spit rank-tasting muddy water from his throat and repeated, "Got to try anyway."

September 19, 1827
Vadalia, Louisiana, at the sandbar, mid-afternoon

Relieved that the duel was over and both men being content that honor had been observed, the small group of duelists and seconds and physicians walked as a group of six across the sandbar. They moseyed toward the group of Maddox supporters, assuming there was no need to fear additional hostilities. However, Col. Crain still toted the two loaded pistols he had been allowed to carry while serving as second to Dr. Maddox.

Not feeling comfortable with three of their members getting so close to the large group of Maddox partisans, three members of the Wells contingency rapidly moved to intersect and join their relatives and friends. They were carrying loaded pistols. Misinterpreting this as potential aggression against the Maddox clan, members of their family started to run over as back-up support against the supposed Wells aggressors.

Gen. Sam Cuny saw that Col. Crain was still armed with two pistols. These two men had tangled weeks earlier. Cuny yelled, "Col. Crain, this is a good time to settle our previous difficulty." Caught off-guard by the challenge, Crain jerked his hand up and discharged one of the pistols in Cuny's direction. It was a wild shot and came nowhere near Cuny, but, to everyone's horror, the bullet struck Jim Bowie in the hip and dropped him on the ground. Cuny took careful aim, but was a long way from Crain. He fired and nicked Crain in the left arm. Crain, now outraged, took several deliberate steps forward, extended his second pistol, and carefully aimed at Gen. Cuny's heart. He squeezed the trigger and the bullet found its mark. Cuny grasped his chest, gave a loud moaning sound, dropped to his knees, spat out a stream of blood and fell forward, dead.

Jim Bowie gritted his teeth, struggled to get back upright, drew his huge knife and came stumbling straight for Crain, intent on slitting the man's throat. But Bowie had lost blood and his attempt at running worked to make him dizzy. When he actually reached Crain, he was staggering. Crain wasted no time in taking advantage of the situation. He turned his empty pistol in his hand

and slammed the handle down on Bowie's head, hitting him so violently, the pistol broke into its various parts. Bowie was stunned senseless and collapsed to the sand.

By this time Major Norris Wright came rushing upon the scene, pulling his pistol and firing at the prostrate Bowie. His shot missed. "I shot you once, Bowie, and now I'll finish my task." He pulled a very thin blade from the inside of his gentleman's walking stick. He drove the blade straight into Bowie's chest. It hit Bowie's sternum and the blade snapped. Bowie, now regaining his strength, also remembered their former standoff. He grabbed Wright's dress shirt, pulled him down, and rammed the full length of his famous knife into the man's heart, killing him instantly.

Bowie pushed the dead man's body off of him, which turned out to be a tactical mistake. It left Bowie open, vulnerable, and weak. Two members of the Maddox clan ran toward Bowie. One shot Bowie, causing a flesh wound, and the other stabbed Bowie in the shoulder and then ran off. Somehow, Bowie brushed aside his pain and managed to stand once more. He screamed obscenities at his adversaries. Alfred and Carey Blanchard simultaneously rushed at Bowie, both firing their pistols. One of the bullets hit Bowie in the left arm, but as Alfred charged by, Bowie grabbed him by the hair, yanked him back, took his huge knife and sliced out the entire muscle formations of Alfred's right forearm. Seeing his brother in great distress, Carey came running back, firing another pistol at Bowie, but missing. He lifted Alfred and started to carry him to safety, but unknown to him, he and his brother were being pursued by Jefferson Wells and Major McWorter. Wells got off a shot at the fleeing brothers and was able to put a bullet into the left arm of Alfred. McWorter fired but missed both brothers.

Suddenly, the shooting and screaming and cussing ceased. The sandbar was traced with blood, and soft moaning could be heard in several directions, but there was no energy left to continue the violence. The entire melee had lasted less than two minutes, but when the dust settled, Samuel Cuny and Norris Wright were dead, Alfred Blanchard was crippled for life, and Jim Bowie was maimed and scarred in ways in which he would know discomfort and pain for the rest of his life. A few bystanders had also been injured by the random discharge of weapons, including innocent Dr. James A. Denny, who sustained a wound to one leg and one finger being grazed by a bullet.

As with many a battle, once the chaos has ended and the combatants have had a few moments to assess what they have wrought on others, a true sense of remorse and guilt and shame settles upon them.

Col. Crain approached Jim Bowie. "You need medical attention, sir. Allow me to assist you in finding the doctors." He lifted Bowie, had him put his arm around his shoulders, then cinched his arm around Bowie's waist and half-carried him across the sandbar.

Bowie responded, "Col. Crain, I do not think, under the circumstances, you ought to have shot me." The other man vouchsafed no reply.

Five men with medical training set to work on Bowie, extracting pieces of lead, cleaning and sewing up stab wounds, and putting plaster castings on various cuts and abrasions. When at last he was allowed to sit up again, Bowie was amazed to find the sandbar deserted. "Where is everyone?" he asked.

"Skedaddled," said one of the doctors. "They took boats back across the river somewhere downstream and rushed out of here as quickly as possible. With two killings and many wounded others, there's bound to be some constables or sheriffs come looking for someone to put in the slammer. There isn't any *neutral* territory when that much bloodshed transpires."

"Then I best find me a way out of here, too," said Bowie. "Anyone who takes one look at me will think I've been wrestling gators or been in the brawl of a lifetime."

7

At the Mississippi barge crossing
September 19, 1827

Pastor Willis asked directions to the sandbar, and he and Ole Sally did their best to head in that direction. The hot sun actually was welcomed by both of them. The preacher's clothes dried out, and Ole Sally's legs got warm. They had a lot working against them, however. The effort to cross the Mississippi River had pulled them downstream, pushing them farther away from their destination of the sandbar. They needed to cover ground to get back north to Natchez. The odds of them making it there by noon were slim.

Speaking aloud to Ole Sally, Joseph said, "Maybe we should have just gone up the river's edge despite all those rocks and trees. Then again, it would have been rough terrain. No time to second guess now."

Man and beast were tired, but they did their best to maintain a steady pace. As often as possible, the preacher guided Sally to the edge of the road if trees were casting any shade at all.

More than once, they came across long links of slaves, chained at the ankles or at the neck or around the wrists. Many of the men were barebacked, showing hideous scars from the whip, some old wounds and some fresh. *What possibly could they have done to deserve that*, Pastor Willis wondered. His heart ached for them, and he quietly prayed for each slave's well-being.

One particular scene seared the preacher's heart. He watched one slave woman on the road that day doing her best to run behind a carriage she was tied to. She needed water and rest, but if she dared to stumble, she would have been dragged. It brought vivid memories of the minister's own mother, who had been a Cherokee slave.

Somehow, the preacher's pocket watch had not been ruined in the crossing of the river earlier that day. When he and Sally finally reached Natchez it was after 1:00. Indeed, the townsfolk were alive with the gossip and rumors and secondhand stories of the battle that had taken place earlier on the sandbar. No one was definite about the details, except to say that it had been far more than a duel. Some were saying that the families had scurried away with their dead and wounded. The preacher's heart sank, and he had a sick feeling in his stomach. Was his dear friend Jim Bowie wounded...dead...missing?

He and Sally made their way to the water's edge. Three young men were standing there. The preacher called to them. "Am I on the right road to where the duel was?"

The men turned. "It's over, sir. Two dead and four wounded seriously."

"Who? Do you know who, exactly, died or was hurt?

Joseph dismounted and led Ole Sally to the top of a grassy knoll. From there he could see the deserted sandbar and some barges going back across the river.

"We was in the woods over here," said one of the young men. "We could see things quite well, but we was out of range of the weapons. When the folks started hightailing it for the boats, we come down here and pieced some of the details together. You a member of one of these families?"

"No," said Joseph, "but I'm a close friend of one of the men who was an attendant for the Wells family. What details did ya get?"

"It's still a bit cloudy regardin' specifics, we gotta admit," said another lad, "but we know that some feller named Wright was killed and so was some other man who had 'general' in front of his name. And, you probably heard of Jim Bowie, ain't ya? Well, he got shot and stabbed, but somehow they patched him up and he let out of here 'bout half an hour ago."

The preacher eased down on the grass, feeling immense relief that Jim had not been killed, but at the same time feeling overwhelming regret that he had not arrived in time possibly to have averted the entire conflict. He lowered his head and prayed, "Lord, it's in your hands now. I ask you to mend those who were hurt and to comfort those who have lost loved ones. I did my best to get here, but it just wasn't meant to be. If there's a lesson to be learned from this tragedy, please make it known to me so that I can use it in my preachin' duties. Amen."

8

October 1, 1852 On Bayou Boeuf
Southeast of Cheneyville, Louisiana

After having regaled his progeny with the saga of Bowie at the sandbar, old Joseph had napped soundly for several miles and seemed to be stirring some under the elder Daniel's watchful eyes. "Grandpa, you doin' well?"

Lemuel stopped the wagon, and both Daniel and his son Dan helped Joseph to sit up. Lemuel had arranged for the hospital wagon and felt this would provide more comfort for his father. There was a raised pallet nailed to the floor of the wagon so it wouldn't move about. It had raised edges to keep him in place, almost like a cradle. The linseed-oiled cloth covering could be pulled over the frame to protect them all from any inclement weather.

Joseph took in all of the scenery. His face showed great peace as the broad-winged hawks flew overhead and blue jays screamed warnings of intruders to one another. Neither of the Daniels wanted to interrupt his reflection. After a few moments Joseph looked around, carefully inspecting their location. He had traveled that road for decades. Not much had changed except the number of people now traveling on it.

He spoke to Daniel with tender authority. "Up about half a mile is a perfect place to stay the night on Bayou Boeuf."

The elder Daniel was not going to rush his grandfather on this trip. He did not care if the three-day trip back turned into a week; he just wanted the old preacher to be comfortable. The other family wagons had moved past for the sake of the teething babies and nursing mothers, and that just left the four of them to make their way at their own pace.

Within a short distance, Lemuel could see the exact place his father had described. The partially cleared area appeared to have had some overnight use in the recent past. There were big stones already set in a circle for their evening campfire. Some previously cut cedar stumps were set back a ways from the fire.

That night, they ate some fried chicken and biscuits with mayhaw jelly, along with some huckleberry pie that Lemuel's wife, Emeline, had slipped into the basket. Their conversation was rich with family chatter, and Joseph answered questions from the men. Young Dan sat and listened with great interest.

It was past sunset when there was a lull in the conversation, and Dan asked his great-grandfather, "Great-Grandpa, ya ever been scared?"

Everyone stopped and looked at Joseph, who was still eating his favorite pie, dewberry. "Son, that's a mighty interestin' question. What makes ya ask?"

"Great-Grandpa, ya swam the Mississippi on a mule twice and fought with the Swamp Fox. Didn't ya ever feel afraid?" Dan had a curious look on his young face.

"There are lot of times I've been afraid, including those times you mentioned, but I always knew the good Lord was with me." Joseph sensed that Dan was a little uncomfortable, so he decided to lighten the conversation. He thought for a few moments and spoke. "Son, did your father ever tell ya 'bout the time he was afraid when he got chased by a screamin' woman?"

Young Dan's mood changed quickly. He looked at Joseph and then at Daniel. "Father, did that really happen? Is Great-Grandpa pullin' my leg?"

Daniel's face got red, and he put his head down. Lemuel gave a hearty laugh.

Joseph's head turned slightly toward Daniel, even though he was still looking into the fire. "I thought by now you'd have already told 'im 'bout that screamin' woman you heard in the woods."

Joseph had obviously caught Daniel off guard. "Um, no, sir, I hadn't told 'im that story, and didn't see any need for 'im to hear it from me. Ya know, Grandpa, you really don't have to share it. I'm sure there are plenty of others he'd like better...."

Dan interrupted his father's protest. "Great-Grandfather, please tell me the story." Dan grinned. "It must be a good 'un if my father doesn't want me to hear it. Right?"

9

March 15, 1830
Cocodrie Lake near Bayou Chicot, Louisiana

"Dan, years ago, your father and your grandfather Agerton had come for a visit, and we decided to take a fishin' trip. Your father was about your age, and we were campin' on the south side of Cocodrie Lake. Anyway, he slipped away and disappeared from the campfire one night and was gone for quite a spell. We were gettin' worried 'bout 'im, 'cause he didn't have a good sense of direction and, you know, his eyesight has never been that good. There was a big moon that night, but it was dippin' in and out behind the clouds."

"Was he *really* lost in the woods?" Dan asked as he stirred the fire with a green stick.

"Well, let's just say we couldn't find 'im. He didn't respond to our call, and he'd gone farther than he should have."

Young Dan had stirred up the embers enough to get a good look at both of their faces. Joseph seemed to be enjoying every minute of this story, but the elder Daniel not so much.

"My mind started playin' all kinds of tricks on me, and I knew there were some mean, large critters out there just waitin' for a tasty meal like Daniel. Also knew they might just come after our horses, too."

The elder Daniel interrupted his grandfather. "Are you sure you don't have another story you'd like to tell instead?"

Joseph shook his head firmly, "No, I kinda like this one." He turned back to young Dan. "Well, the time passed, and Daniel still didn't return. We were beginnin' to worry, when all of a sudden there was a screamin'—the sound of which we'd never heard before. It sounded like a woman screamin' who was bein' hurt...and then another hollerin' commenced. We recognized the second sound as your father. He was yellin' at the top of his lungs and thrashin' through the blackjack and post oak. There was silence again, and then this blood-curdlin' scream filled the woods.

"Daniel musta caught sight of the campfire, and he ran as fast as he could to the clearnin'. Totally out of breath and half-silly with fear, he told us, 'There's some insane woman out in the woods! She's chasing me. Don't let her get me! Please save me! Get the gun and shoot her, 'cause she really is crazy! She's gonna hurt us all!'"

Joseph stopped for a moment and winked at Dan, then turned to speak to the elder Daniel. "Do you want to tell 'im who the screamin' woman was, or do you want me to?"

"Grandfather." Daniel hung his head. "You're havin' way too much fun with this to stop now. You go ahead and finish the story." While appearin' a little embarrassed, he still could not resist the opportunity to let Joseph spin his yarn.

"Well, we grabbed our weapons as we prepared to catch her. Her chillin' scream cut the silence again and made everyone uneasy, especially the horses. Your father was hidin' under the wagon by this time and could not be coaxed from his safe place."

The young Dan stopped his great-grandfather and asked, "Why didn't she just come out of the woods? Why? Was she insane? What made her scream so bad?"

"Those are right good questions, Dan. You see, the 'screamin' woman' who chased your father in the woods was not a woman at all. It was a hungry panther who could smell a meal on four legs. She wasn't after your father. She wanted the horses. We could hear her claws hit the bark of a pine tree. She must have been climbin' high to watch and wait for a chance at our horses. She was a big one and probably had hungry kittens not far off."

Dan asked with all sincerity, "Were ya really gonna shoot and kill her?"

"Only if she had come too close to our family or the horses. She was hungry, and her instincts were strong, but her need for survival was greater. She did what came natural to her. We fired three shots into the air, and it scared her back into the woods."

Everyone sat quietly, just staring into the fire. Young Dan seemed uncomfortable as he looked up into the nearby pine trees.

"So, we teased your father for quite some time, didn't we, Lemuel?" Joseph chuckled. "Throughout the years, I must 'ave thought of that night more 'an a dozen times." Joseph shifted his focus to the elder Daniel and asked, "Did ya learn any lessons from that frightful night?" Joseph's curiosity urged him on. "Tell us."

Daniel laughed and rolled his eyes. "Only that your story-tellin' is mighty excitin', Grandfather."

Young Dan was on the edge of his stump, hugging his knees.

Daniel looked at his son and said, "Son, here's what I gained from my 'night of terror' in the woods. Me and the horses came close to bein' supper for a panther 'cause I wandered off from the safety of the group. When we stray away too far from our family, there's no tellin' what might happen. It's the same when we stray too far from the Lord. We aren't well-protected when we go our own way."

Daniel paused, and a great big grin seemed to cover his whole face. "And, as for that panther, it really did sound like a crazy woman screamin'. T'was the most chillin', scary sound I ever heard in my life."

Joseph couldn't stifle his amusement and again broke into a big laugh. They all laughed that night around the campfire, until they heard the scream of a panther in the distance. They looked at each other, and one by one said, "Goodnight!"

Except young Dan, who added, "I hope so."

Oh, how the old preacher Joseph loved his Louisiana—the piney woods, the sights and sounds…lovely Louisiana. Paradise for a young boy like Dan and the not-so-young boys, too! He rose and retreated to his comfy bed in the wagon and within minutes was asleep and dreaming of older times and younger folks.

{10}

October 2, 1852 Early Morning
Southeast of Cheneyville, Louisiana, on Bayou Boeuf

Old Pastor Willis awakened early, and his stirring caused a chain reaction in the camp. Wood ducks could be heard in the bayou, and the little ducklings welcomed the day from a hollow cypress tree trunk. He was intrigued with a lone, green-head mallard that seemed to be looking for his mate. The morning promised good traveling weather, as the blue sky held not a cloud.

"Smells like the coffee is already brewing," said Joseph, coming near the rekindled fire pit. The delicious aroma of fresh coffee was one of his favorite enticements.

"Yes, sir, and we got some biscuits and leftover ham from our Sunday supper on the grounds. Help yourself."

After a quick meal, the fire was doused, the packing was completed, and they made ready to move on down the red dirt path. Before they left, however, Joseph led them in prayer asking for safety. He then recited the part of Psalm 91 that says, "He shall give His angels charge over you." He prayed further for all of his children by name and their families.

As they settled in for the morning's ride, Daniel drove the team of horses, and Lemuel sat on the bench in the back beside Dan. Joseph rode semi-reclined, soaking in the beauty all around him.

Joseph noticed that something was bothering young Dan and finally asked, "What's on your mind this morning? Ya got a question for me?"

"Yes, sir, I do. But, I don't want to make you upset or sad."

"Go ahead and ask. There ain't much these days that can pull me down to a frown."

With some hesitation, Dan began. "Great-Grandfather, I noticed that you asked the Lord to bless all seventeen of your children this mornin'. I've heard many times from Father 'bout the other two, but he never gave any details."

The look on Joseph's face changed. He did not respond quickly as he shifted his position on the pallet. Lemuel's expression was even more distraught.

Joseph sighed, then said, "Life gives us some huge challenges. The story you're askin' about was the biggest emotional and spiritual challenge I ever faced. But, you're old enough now to have the details shared with you."

June 17, 1830
Near Oakdale, Louisiana
On a visit to Joseph's son William's home

The twin Willis girls, Ruth and Naomi, were absolutely beautiful! Their dark hair framed their little faces in such a way that they could have posed for artists wanting to do paintings or sculptures of angels.

The girls were always together, playing with dolls or making up stories or trapesing off to do a little exploring. They used to come home with some of the most unusual treasures—a bird's nest, shiny pebbles, huge pine cones, an ancient arrowhead, some colorful bird feathers. They were little ragamuffins, in that dressing them in linens and lace and frills only resulted in torn and tattered outfits.

On a bright and cloudless day the girls became fidgety staying indoors. Hannah asked William if it would be safe to let the girls go to the barn and frolic awhile in the hayloft and to feed the animals.

"I reckon they'll be fine doin' that," said William, "but be sure to tell them not to leave the barn without tellin' us first. The black bears are out of hibernation now that summer's here. They usually keep to their own territory, but I don't want to take any chances."

Hannah turned to the girls and said, "It's cooler in the big barn, so stay inside of it. If you get hungry, come on back and I'll fix you something to eat. Take your dolls with you. You can make a little homestead with the hay in the loft. Have fun, but don't go farther than the barn."

Both girls nodded their understanding and said, "Yes, Mama." They raced off toward the barn, swinging their dolls in their hands. Hannah enjoyed hearing the girls giggling and laughing. It had been a tremendous strain bringing two babies into the world on the same day, but now all she thought about was how the Lord had doubled her love and joy by giving her a set of twins.

The sun continued to rise. The day was a scorcher. For a time, Hannah could hear the girls calling to each other in the barn and playing games. But then there seemed to be a lull. To Hannah, it was unnatural for two girls to go twenty or thirty minutes without causing some kind of ruckus. She went to the door and looked toward the barn. There was no movement.

"Naomi...Ruth," she called. "Come on back for some dinner."

There was no reply. Were they teasing her, perhaps playing hide and seek and not wanting to be discovered? Worse yet, had one of them climbed to the hayloft and fallen?

"Come back to the house right now, girls," Hannah yelled forcefully. "This isn't game time. Mama wants you back here now!"

Again she heard nothing—no replies, no laughter, no pleas for more playtime.

With genuine concern, Hannah called, "Lemuel, go check on the girls. I can't get them to answer me. They were in the barn."

Lemuel took off at a quick gait, but within minutes he emerged from the barn and called, "They ain't here. I checked the stalls, the loft, and the seed bins. One of the dolls is here, but no sign of the children."

Hannah's mind immediately went to William's warning about black bears. She threw her apron aside and knocked over the bowl of beans she'd been snapping. She started running full speed toward the barn. Within seconds, she was there, as was everyone else.

At the back of the barn was a small exit. The little door was ajar. William and Hannah moved quickly toward it. There, in the dirt, was the other doll, and all around it were claw marks and bear tracks. Hannah's face went pale, and she gripped the side of the barn to keep from fainting.

"Bear tracks," said Joseph, arriving just then. "But, we heard nothing. No screams, no sounds of a struggle. Quickly, spread out and start a search. If a bear had dragged one away, we would have heard the screams. We need to get out there fast. This bear may be tracking the girls by smell."

Hannah cried, "Oh, my God! Let us find my babies before that bear does."

Oddly enough, all the tracks seemed to be together. William, Joseph, and Lemuel followed them to the edge of the woods.

There, they discovered a huge, hollow log with a swarm of honey bees buzzing around it. And that's where the tracks split up. The bear's tracks went one way, and the girls' tracks went another.

"Stay with the girls," Joseph instructed. The men advanced along the trail, but suddenly the tracks veered off and were lost in thick brush. Joseph's heart raced! Where were his girls? Where was that bear? Had the bear somehow lured them into following it deeper into the woods?

"What'll we do now, Father?" asked Lemuel.

Joseph surveyed the area and directed each man along a separate route. "Split up and keep callin' their names." Off they went, doing their best to push through the gnarled blackjack. Calls of "Naomi! Ruth!" echoed from left, right, and out front, but no responses were heard from either little girl. Suddenly, a female voice joined in, and Joseph realized that Hannah and come into the woods to become part of the search party.

Time seemed to crawl, but then from far into the brush and undergrowth Lemuel yelled, "Over here! I found them! I need help. Hurry!"

Hannah could be heard to say, "Oh, thank God!"

Everyone converged on where Lemuel waved his arms and continued to call out. At first, there was an immediate sense of relief and praise for the fact that both girls were located and neither had been mauled by a bear. However, this euphoria soon morphed into a state of confusion and bewilderment as the girls evidenced behavior totally unlike the movements or speech of children their age.

"Their faces are all bright red," said Lemuel. "I pulled them up, and they just staggered around and fell back on the ground. They were moaning when I got here."

Hannah picked Naomi into her arms, smoothed back her hair. Suddenly, Naomi lurched forward and began to vomit violently. She gagged, couldn't catch her breath for a full minute, then sagged back into Hannah's arms.

Meanwhile, Joseph had lifted Ruth into his embrace. "We've got to get them back to the house—cold compresses, beds, soft pillows." As he spoke, Ruth averted her head and vomited a sickly mass of her morning breakfast along with some sort of sap and grease. "They act like they've been poisoned. I can't think of anything in the barn that they would have eaten. Hurry! William, carry Naomi."

Naomi moaned and then said, "I can't see, Papa. I'm blind. I can't feel my legs. I'm really sick." Again, she went into a fit of vomiting.

Knowing that the nearest practicing physician was 45 miles away, Joseph called to William, "Have one of your boys go fetch that horse doctor. Tell him we've got two really sick girls, and we need any help he can provide us. Send 'em. Go!"

When they reached the cabin, Hannah laid blankets on the floor in the dogtrot and Joseph stretched the girls there, hoping they would catch a bit of breeze coming in.

Joseph prayed, "Lord Jesus, show us what to do. Please, let our babies be well again."

Lemuel and William's wife, Rhoda, watched over all the other children while Hannah and Joseph sat with the twins and continued to put cool rags on their foreheads. They could tell it didn't seem to do much good. The girls had their lids open, but they were glassy-eyed and burning with fever.

The girls were blind and disoriented. Continuously, they called for help from their parents. Their frail little voices asked, "Mama, where are you? Papa, help me!"

They were slipping away, and all the preacher and his wife could do was cry out, "Lord, help 'em. Deliver these poor children."

Hannah took a washcloth of cool water and did her best to clean Ruth's face. Turning to Joseph she asked, "What is this? There's some kind of sap or sticky syrup stuck to their hands and chins and on their play shirts."

Joseph leaned closer and sniffed. "Smells like honey, only with a bit of bitterness to it. Can't place it. Did they have honey with their biscuits this morning?"

"No," said Hannah. "They both took some of my blackberry jam. I don't know what this sticky oozing is."

"Where's that horse doctor? Why can't he get here? I pray he's not off delivering some foal at one of the farms."

Hannah shed more tears. "They ain't movin' anymore, Joseph. They ain't callin' our names or coughin'. I can't tell if they're breathin', but I'm not lettin' go."

"Me neither," said Joseph. "Not till that horse doctor gets here and takes a look. But I done enough funerals to know when the spirit has departed, Sweetheart. Our little darlin's are with Jesus now. Their struggle is over, and ours has just begun."

Hannah was bereft. She insisted that Joseph put both girls in her arms. She clung to her daughters, willing her own life to flow into the children. How could this be? That very morning her six year old girls had been running, giggling, and living life to its fullest. And now, a mere several hours later, they both were gone. It just couldn't be possible.

But, sadly...it was.

*   *   *

The veterinarian arrived about five o'clock. He went into the dogtrot to find Hannah still holding both girls on her lap. What happened next was most difficult. The doctor, William, and Joseph had to pry the girls from her grip and carry them into a bedroom so the doctor could try to find out what happened.

As gently as possible, Joseph pulled Hannah up and led her out of the room. Rhoda tried to comfort Hannah while the doctor did his work, but Hannah was drowning in a sea of sorrow. The doctor's arrival had given her just a slight glimmer of hope. But, when he came out, he just shook his head and said, "Pastor, they're gone. Been dead at least two hours. I'm sorry I was so far away, but I don't think I could have done anything anyway. Let me look at the clothes they were wearing."

Joseph located one of the dresses that was covered with the vomit and sticky substance the girls had emitted. Slowly, the vet examined the material, smelled the discharge, and nodded solemnly.

"Yep, just as I suspected," he said. "I'm no people doctor, but I've encountered this before. What I see and smell here, and what you described as the symptoms the girls showed, convinces me that they were swallowing poison honey."

Joseph was baffled. "Poison? Why, we eat honey nearly every day. We got hives in the back of our spread here. My boy and I go there with smoke, drive the bees away for a while, harvest some of the honey, and my wife uses it for baking and for sweetin' on top of biscuits or pancakes. Ain't never once caused any of us any harm."

"What you're talking about is called cultured honey," explained the vet. "But out in the wild, bees sometimes find an open field of flowers that have poison nectar. They retrieve it and never get harmed. But the honey they create from it has that poison transferred to it. It's lethal to animals and to people."

"You think our girls ate some of that?"

The doctor pulled up a chair and motioned for Joseph to sit opposite him.

"I do," he said. "They probably went for a stroll, saw a honeycomb with very few bees around it, and maybe decided they'd bring it back as a gift for you and their mother. Of course, they couldn't resist giving it a taste test first. And, probably it appealed to them, although a slight bit tart. It would only take three or four swallows to have the poison quickly enter their bloodstream."

"We warned them not to leave the barn," Joseph said almost inaudibly.

"Funny thing is," continued the vet, "bears and fox and other animals somehow can tell from the smell that it's poison. They don't eat it. I've been around dying and dead animals for 25 years, and I've never seen even one that died of poison honey. This will make the sixth time, however, that I've seen human beings die from it."

"What can be done?"

"Actually, nothing," replied the doctor. "Even if you had a top notch physician here to tend the girls, he wouldn't have a potion or medication or concoction that could cure someone who has ingested poison honey. And that's why we need to take steps to keep this from happening again. I'll get with your boys here, and we'll go back to the woods and burn out those hives and destroy that honey. I know they are in mourning, but we've got to keep this from poisoning someone else. You understand, don't you, Pastor?"

Almost trancelike, Joseph said, "Yes...of course...they'll help...don't want anyone else to...."

The doctor rose and patted Joseph on the shoulder. "You try to comfort your dear wife. I'll see to the destruction of the poison hives. After that, I'll ride back home, but if you need me again, send word."

{12}

Heartbreaking Aftermath, Funeral Arrangements

Hannah was inconsolable. Upon finally comprehending that both twins were dead, she went into a state of shock. She sat alone and didn't move, didn't speak, didn't respond when spoken to. She stared blankly out the window, as though expecting to see a vision of her little girls come traipsing across the yard, arms burdened with wildflowers, faces dirty, and shoes untied.

After a full day and night of immobility, Hannah allowed herself to be given a drink of water, but she refused food. She took to her bed and wept pitifully. Her sobs were heard throughout the house, as was her fists thrashing against the pillows. She could be heard asking, "Why not me? Why not Joseph? What reason could You have for taking our babies?" The crying continued unabated, day and night. For moments at a time, utter exhaustion would send Hannah into a fitful slumber, only to find her jerking back awake and once again resuming her vigil of mourning, crying, and bewailing her lost daughters.

Joseph was beside himself. His anguish weighed on him like a fallen tree. He was too numb to pray, too grief stricken to do his daily farm chores. When he told the other womenfolk what had transpired, it was as if someone else was speaking, not himself declaring that Ruth and Naomi were really departed.

Finally, the day after the girls died, Lemuel approached his mournful parent.

"Father," said Lemuel, "my heart is broken, and I know your pain in grievous. But you're still head of this family, and you're also the only parson that folks round here have for funerals. We're gonna have to pull ourselves together and plan a proper burial for the twins. When you've thought it through, you tell me what to do. I'll try to be strong and do right by my sisters."

Lemuel's words made an impact on Joseph. The boy was right. The twins needed—yea, deserved—a proper burial and graveside service. There would be a lifetime for grieving, but only a day or two before the bodies would start to decompose in such wretched heat. Undertakers and morticians didn't set up practice in the hinterlands. No, the farmers and homesteaders and Indians buried their dead respectfully, but quickly.

"Yes, son, thank you," said Joseph. "I'm not thinkin' straight just now. You're a good boy. I need to talk to your mama about this. You fetch William to the back porch in a bit. I'll have some directions for ya'll by then."

Lemuel nodded and moved away. Joseph stood a moment, collecting his thoughts. Indeed, he was head of the family, and he was a pastor. He could not collapse when those around him needed his leadership most. He straightened his back, lifted his chin. "Lord, give me supernatural strength to face the duties before me. Lift me, Holy Spirit, when my soul grows weak."

With a determined step, he walked to his cabin and entered. Gently, but quite directly, he entered the bedroom where Hannah yet laid, absorbed in her grief.

"Dear wife," he said softly, "the Scriptures tell us there is a time to grieve and a time to laugh. But we've had it backward. Those little girls gave us six years of laughter and joy and happiness. And now, with their passing, we will have to experience levels of grief we never knew existed."

He paused long enough to sit on the side of the bed. He reached out and placed a hand on Hannah's shoulder.

"If someone were to ask me if I'd rather not have had those little girls for six years, knowin' in advance that they'd be taken away from me, I can tell you sure 'nuff, I'd say I'd want those six years. They was good years for us, Hannah. And we'll see those young'uns again up yonder one day. And that's when we'll share happy memories, and we'll see their pretty faces, and we'll hear their laughter."

Hannah, not turning to face Joseph, mumbled, "Oh...to have that day now."

"It's a blessed hope," said Joseph. "And I know you feel hollow, feel empty, feel sick with sorrow. But Lemuel reminded me that our duty to our girls ain't over yet. We need to show everyone that our love for those babies is as strong now as it ever was. We need to stop ignoring them and give them a respectful burial. I need your help in that, darlin'. You're their mama. You're the one who best knows what's proper in putting them to rest."

Slowly, as though waking from a trance, Hannah lifted herself onto one elbow. Then, she turned and stared at her husband.

"Oh, dear me," she said, with genuine consternation. "Dear, dear me. My girls. Yes, yes, they need me now. They need both of us, Joseph. Oh, how could I have neglected them? Help me up. I must go to them. I *will* go to them."

"We'll go together," said Joseph. As Hannah rose from the bed, she was visibly weak and shaken from extensive crying, lack of sleep and having not eaten. Joseph pulled her against his chest and held her reassuringly for a full minute.

"The girls are still laid out in their bedroom," he said softly. "They've been covered with a sheet. I want you to comb your hair, put on a fresh dress, and then I'll have the other womenfolk meet you there. You can wash our girls, dress them in their Sunday best, put ribbons in their hair…"

"Yes, yes, we will," said Hannah. "We'll take care of our girls. Yes, surely, we will. Oh, dear me, my girls."

Joseph left Hannah, knowing she would be all right now that she had a maternal sense of mission. He went and found Lemuel and William.

"I have a big task for you boys. I want you to go out into the woods and along the river's edge. Search until you find a hollow cypress stump. Pry it out, bring it back, and get some of the neighbors to help you carve a coffin that will fit both girls. They came into the world together, so it's only fittin' they should depart together."

"What do you want on the lid, sir?" asked William.

Joseph squinted in thought, then replied, "Put both of their names and then carve MATTHEW 19:14 beside it."

The duties of preparing for the burial somehow brought unity to the family and the neighboring community. Hannah took nourishment and regained a measure of strength. She and the ladies showed great reverence and respect to the little bodies they attended to. In deference to Joseph's Cherokee heritage, Hannah anointed the girls with oil and lavender, as Joseph's mother would have done had she been present. This gave a measure of special comfort to the preacher.

The funeral was not drawn out. Two songs were sung, verses of Scripture were read, and Lemuel and Joseph each said a prayer. Then the casket was placed in the back of a wagon and was driven by Lemuel and William to a place down the trail where a grave had been opened beneath large shade trees. "We'll have a more proper funeral after we've had time to notify the local folks," Joseph had explained. He rode on Ole Sally, following the wagon and later helping to lower the casket into the grave.

Thus, to his credit, Pastor Willis had risen to the challenge of burying his daughters with dignity, reverence, honor, and grace. He had shown strength, leadership, and authority.

But, he was just a man. Being a minister did not make him immune to loss, to agony, to guilt, to worry, to regret, to unimaginable grief.

No, he would not break down in front of his family or his congregation. But, once alone with his Lord, he would unveil his misery, and he would seek some kind of understanding as to why, why, *why* such a tragedy could befall him and his sweet wife.

Alone, along the trail down the Calcasieu

Joseph told his family to carry on the farm chores and family duties. He wanted to spend some special time in prayer. This was not unusual, particularly if he was planning a series of revival meetings or if he was seeking special guidance from the Lord.

He cinched Ole Sally and began riding down the trail. He may have gone one mile or five, for his mind was not on the road but on how his life had been changed so radically in the space of just a few days. He had been forced to endure the deaths of his two daughters, but he also had come to recognize maturity and wisdom in his son Lemuel, who had given him counsel and direction when needed. He had shared searing grief with Hannah, but he had also witnessed his wife show renewed strength when she had been needed in preparing the girls for their internment.

All this made him marvel at how life had odd balances. Ecclesiastes proclaimed that life was a series of such balances—times to plant and times to reap; times to rejoice and times to be sorrowful; times to build up and times to tear down. He had this very week experienced such odd balances. Could it be that in rending his heart the Lord had also made him more sensitive to the needs of others? Could it have been that by discovering his wife's amazing inner strength that the Lord was showing shown him they *both* were destined for a greater calling?

These matters he pondered and scrutinized and analyzed until he found himself at a clearing surrounded by shade trees. He dismounted and tethered Ole Sally where she would be cool. Joseph extracted his worn Bible from his saddlebag and sat on a large rock.

"Lord, I confess that I cannot comprehend the deaths of my sweet Ruth and Naomi. I would never challenge your goodness and care, but in my limited capacity, I struggle to know why such a calamity should have befallen these innocent girls. Gladly would I have given my own life in place of them. You know my sincerity about that. But…such was not your choosing. All I ask, Holy One, is that you help me understand your will in all this. If I can but know your purpose, it will provide direction and encouragement for me."

This prayer was not followed by a clap of thunder, nor a whirling dust cloud, nor any audible voice from heaven. But, for some odd reason, the preacher's weather beaten Bible fell open to the story of Jonah. *Jonah?*

Pastor Willis wondered what possible answers were evident in the book of Jonah. How did any of that story relate to him? It was a story of a man who went in one direction when called by God to go in another direction. It was a story of a man on a ship wherein all the cargo was thrown overboard to make the vessel more seaworthy. It was a story of a man who found new zeal in proclaiming the message of Jehovah to heathen nations greatly in need of salvation and redemption.

Joseph dropped to his knees. Then he put his face into the dust. He spread out his hands.

"Oh, Lord, am I this Jonah? Have I stayed too long in one place, when from the start You have called me to travel far afield to plant new churches and to spread your word to tribes and peoples who do not know You? Have you forced me to lose my cargo that I may not be hindered in seeking to fulfill my calling?"

Tears came forth, both for the cost of what this renewed calling would require, but also for the joy of gaining the direction and response from God he so sincerely sought. For the next half hour, Joseph remained facedown before his Lord, asking for a vision, for guidance, for forgiveness, for an open door.

When at last Joseph arose, he knew exactly what he had to do. He fetched Ole Sally, mounted her, and said, "Let's go home, girl. We've got a special meeting to arrange." Off they galloped back to the homestead.

{14}

June 27, 1830
On the banks of the Calcasieu River

Pastor Willis was dressed in his Sunday preaching clothes. He stood tall on the back of a wagon so that his voice would carry. Before him was assembled an outdoor congregation of family, neighbors, church members, some tradesmen, cowboys, and slaves, and even three Indians. It was a tradition to uphold the local folks in time of grief, whether you were close friends or not. Word had gone out that Brother Willis was going to do a tribute service to his departed twin daughters, so folks showed up to show respect and offer comfort. Folks came from Alex, Bayou Chicot, and Bayou Boeuf.

"I want to thank you all for comin' to this spot on the Calcasieu today. The girls would've enjoyed playin' under this flowerin' red buckeye tree. Oh, how they loved flowers. The girls have been in Beulah land for ten days now.

"I'm sure many of you are askin' why we buried 'em here and not at the church cemetery. Probably many more of you are wonderin' why their service was not held back in Bayou Chicot at our beloved Calvary Baptist Church.

"I have to confess that in the days after that tragic loss, I felt weak and confused. I just had to get away by myself, so I rode my mule to this very spot. I got off and fell to my knees. I asked the Lord, 'Why? I'm seventy-two! Why not take *me*? They had so much life left to live. Haven't I been obedient to Your callin'? Why, *why,* Lord, *why*?'

"The silence was deafenin'. Again, I talked to Him, sayin', 'I don't understand, but when I get to heaven, it will be the first question I ask You.'

"It was then that the Lord spoke to my heart. 'Joseph, when you get to heaven, you won't need to ask that question....Will you abandon Me now?'

"'No, Lord, where would I go? Only You hold the keys to eternal life.' I remained quiet for a moment and then spoke to the Lord with the faith of a grain of mustard seed. 'Lord, even if You take away the rest of my children, You slay all of 'em today, and take my salvation from me and then cast my soul into hell, I will still praise Your holy name. Lord, I will *never* forsake You. Never, never…never again!'

"My Bible fell open to the story of Jonah, and through that story I felt, once again, the Lord spoke to my heart, sayin', 'Joseph, you are to cross this river into the so-called No-Man's-Land. That's where I'm sending you next.'

"We chose this place to bury the girls 'cause this is where the Lord has called me to cross another river on this journey called life. Unlike Jonah, I won't flee this port, but will traverse this water.

"Hannah and me—to honor my mother—cut a piece from the hems of the girls' dresses and replaced 'em with my mother's Cherokee colors from a dress of hers. We have purposed in our hearts to take these pieces of cloth from their dresses 'cross the Calcasieu and bury 'em under that big oak tree you see o'er yonder on the other side."

At the back of the crowd were three Cherokee. They had come across the river from No-Man's-Land. Joseph remembered them from when he planted Antioch Church more than three years ago on the upper reaches of the Calcasieu. He could tell by their faces that they approved of what he did that day.

Again addressing the assembly, Joseph said, "My Hannah and I wept bitter tears, and I have even grieved in my sleep. I cried so hard that it woke me up. Scripture says that it's all right to grieve, but we're not to grieve as others who have no hope. We have a Blessed Hope. His name is Jesus.

"The Lord called me to cross the Mississippi River, and now He has called me to cross the Calcasieu River. But, there's yet another river we will cross someday soon, called Jordon. We will see our little Naomi and Ruth and the face of our Blessed Hope as we arrive on the other side."

The preacher paused, then asked to be handed a bucket. He grabbed it and held it high for all to see.

"My mother was Cherokee, and it was her people's custom during a time of mourning and grief to have the men smear ashes on their heads to show pain over the loss of loved ones. This bucket contains ashes. I crossed the Calcasieu River yesterday and brought back these ashes from a fire I made under the oak durin' my time with the Lord."

At that, he reached into the bucket, withdrew moist ashes, and made the sign of the cross on his forehead. William and Lemuel did likewise. Then a line formed as dozens of people wanted to come forward and have ashes put upon their foreheads, too. Not a word was spoken as they took turns making the sign of the cross on their foreheads.

Joseph realized that the death of his dear daughters had caused a revival this day among the people of their community and places far beyond. They had not died in vain.

"Praise you, Lord. Praise you, Lord," was all he could say over and over.

15

Late Afternoon, October 1, 1852
Hurricane Creek as it flows into Cocodrie Lake

For several miles, no one spoke a word in the wagon, for all were lost in thought.

Lemuel watched his father carefully throughout the afternoon as he slept. The bouncy wagon ride would have kept most awake; but, then again, most people were not ninety-four. He knew it had to be the hand of the Lord that had kept Joseph alive this long. Lemuel thought, *I'm already forty. Young Dan has already started writin'. I also need to start writin' Father's stories down for my grandchildren. Perhaps someday their grandchildren will write 'em down, too.*

When Joseph finally stirred, his eyes seemed keen and alert as he again started looking for landmarks that indicated their exact location. He immediately recognized where they were as memories flooded his mind. He spoke to Daniel, who was at the reins. "Up here not far is a little veer-off into the woods. Doesn't look like much, but this was one of my favorite fishin' holes. You'll see why when we get there."

Joseph turned and spoke to his great-grandson, "Now, Dan, I know ya asked me yesterday 'bout Mr. Epps and Solomon Northup. What I didn't tell ya was that Epps wasn't Solomon's first owner. He was first owned by a close friend of mine. That's how I became friends and pastor to Solomon."

"What was his name, Great-Grandpa?"

"William Prince Ford."

"You mean *your* friend owned Solomon Northup?

"Yes, but it was before Epps bought 'im. Fact is, William Prince Ford and I used to come to this very spot to fish and talk. He asked me almost as many questions as you do. I knew his father back in South Carolina and have known William since he was a small boy.

"When I organized the church near Forest Hill in '41 that you and your father belong to today, Spring Hill Baptist, William Prince Ford was the first church clerk. He would bring Solomon and his other slaves to church with 'im. One of his slaves, Judy, even helped us organize Spring Hill. They made William a deacon the next year, and I ordained 'em in '44 to preach Jesus. The next year, though, in '45, they kicked 'em out of Spring Hill for teachin' the beliefs of Alexander Campbell. Some call 'em Campbellites today.

"Before that happened and he moved away, we'd ride down the banks of Hurricane Creek to this very spot to catch a mess of fish. But, he's still a faithful friend of mine to this very day. Some have a problem with that. I told 'em I can fish with anyone from any church I want, 'cept those that handle 'em snakes. They're welcome to fish with 'em, though."

The bumpy ground jostled them as the elder Daniel followed his grandfather's instructions. Sure enough, Joseph had remembered correctly. He seemed a little disappointed as he looked for his landmarks, because it was obvious that others had also discovered his fishing hole. He spotted a small child's footprints in the sand. He smiled and said, "Oh, well, that's all right."

The woods cleared, and right down next to Hurricane Creek as it flowed into Cocodrie Lake was a perfect place to fish for supper and camp for the night.

"You and Dan can go down and catch some crappie for our supper, and I can sit here and watch from the wagon. That sound good to ya? I'm really hungry!"

Within just a few steps, the warm water tickled the shore.

"Great-Grandfather, this is gonna be fun! I'm gonna catch me some brim, and we can eat 'em for supper."

Dan's face beamed with excitement as he and his father cut a couple of cane poles from the banks of the lake. The elder Daniel had brought an axe, a sharp knife, and a loaded gun. The elder Daniel really knew very little about guns, but they all agreed it was wise to bring some form of protection, more than a filletin' knife.

Lemuel unhitched and unharnessed the horses, which he had named Pete and Repete. He took them down to the banks of the creek to water them. He tied both to a rope, separated them, and strung it between two trees. He had brought some oats along for them and would tend to them while the others fished. As Lemuel waited for the fun to begin, he took the axe and cut some wood for the evening fire. He then set about collecting pine cones and pine straw for kindling. Lemuel knew the scent of a pine smoke fire couldn't be matched, in Joseph's mind.

They had the back of the wagon facing the creek so Joseph could enjoy watching them fish. Dan had found some crickets in the tall grass and poked around under an old log for a few worms. It didn't take too long before he had a good strike. It took him a good while to get his fish to the bank because he had to be careful not to snap his cane pole. He finally pulled out a nice-sized bluegill that fought like a big-mouth bass, to Dan's way of thinking.

Joseph encouraged him the entire time he struggled with what was Jonah's whale to him! "Dan, wear 'im down! Keep playin' with 'im! That's our supper—you can do it!"

Young Dan could hear Joseph laughing with Lemuel in the background. His father had moved out of sight and had no idea about this. When Dan finally got the fish up on dry land, he sat on a rock to calm down.

"Great-Grandfather, my knees feel kind of wobbly! That was fun, but I was 'fraid I'd see moccasins, or even worse, that my fish would get away. Any gators in there?"

"Dan, don't ya know what Cocodrie means?"

"No sir...what, Great-Grandfather?"

"It means *alligator*."

Dan's jaw dropped. Joseph put his head back and gave a hearty laugh. Dan could not tell if he was laughing at him or if there was something else funny that he had missed, so he politely smiled but remained quiet.

It wasn't but a little while later that Daniel came around the bend in the creek and held up his string of various-sized perch for everyone to see.

Dan announced, "I caught a fish, Father!"

But, before Dan could display his catch, Daniel put his fatherly hand on Dan's shoulder. "Ya only caught *one* fish, son? Don't feel bad. Jonah only caught one fish! At least yours isn't big enough to swallow ya."

They all laughed.

Joseph came to young Dan's rescue. "Don't get ahead of yourself, Daniel. Your son did right well. Show 'em, Dan."

Dan held up his one *bigger* fish.

His father's eyes got huge, and he seemed to stumble over his own words. "How'd you catch that? Were you over by some big ole cypress stump? What bait did you use?" He scratched his head and kept looking at that one fish still dangling from the line. "Who helped you?" He glanced at Lemuel for an answer.

Dan looked at Joseph and smiled. "Great-Grandfather guided me with what *he* called 'the Alpha and Omega' of fishin'."

Joseph's smile could not be mistaken as he nodded in agreement. Again, they all laughed.

The elder Daniel looked at the three of them and shrugged. "I've heard that fishin' advice before—a few hundred times. But, that's just like your great-grandfather. He has such an encouragin' way with folks. Always had and always will."

Joseph spoke to Dan. "Son, ya did good. I can remember the first time that your father went fishin'. He didn't catch a single fish for supper that night."

The fish were cleaned and cooked over an open fire, and Dan had never tasted anything quite so good in his entire life.

The fire crackled as the bullfrogs sang their chorus from the edges of the lake. The men could hear an old hoot owl back in the woods. Dan, still being full of energy, caught some fireflies and saved them in a tin can while the men sat ruminating about good family memories.

At Joseph's insistence, they helped him down out of the wagon, and he joined them at the campfire. One of the small benches from the wagon served as his seat, and he appeared to be comfortable for the time being between the Daniels. Lemuel sat on the other side of the fire.

Joseph said to Dan, "Sure am glad we got this strong breeze tonight to keep the mosquitoes down. I can remember times when the air hung heavy with 'em. In fact, they grew so big that you could saddle 'em and ride 'em. Remember those times, boys?"

Dan smiled, waving his hand in the air, "*Awww*, Great-Grandpa."

Lemuel and Daniel could both recall spending many a night swatting at those pests. Lemuel added, "I don't know which caused us more trouble, the buzzin' around or the bites they gave us."

Dan piled some logs on the fire, and it blazed bright. He sat close to his great-grandpa this time.

Dan whispered, "Great-Grandpa, I sure do love you."

Joseph whispered back, "I love you, too, Dan."

Dan sat quietly for a moment and then said, "I've got a couple more questions."

"Go ahead, ask away."

"How'd ya meet Miss Elvy, and did ya ever see your friend Mr. Bowie again?"

Lemuel and Daniel snickered a little.

Joseph's response was somewhere between a laugh, a sigh, and surprise at Dan's question about Miss Elvy. "Dan, I'm not sure you're old enough for this story."

"Please, Great-Grandpa, I'm all fetched up! I'm thirteen and a half as of yesterday. I want to hear about Aimuewell and Samuel's mother and how you met her."

"Dan, I need to think about this tonight. Tomorrow, we'll have lots of time to talk at your father's home on Spring Creek. You know, it used to be my ole home place. I built it in 1827 before I moved the family there for good."

Dan was the last one to go to sleep and the first one to wake up the next morning. They prepared to move out after their breakfast of hard-boiled eggs and homemade bread with dewberry and mayhaw jelly.

Joseph could tell that Dan was just itching for the story to begin. Daniel and Lemuel were also curious about how he would handle all this.

"Dan, before I tell about Miss Elvy, first things first. I need to help you understand a little more about those years between 1826 and 1833. Now, all this time, I had been travelin' and plantin' churches like Antioch in '26, Amiable in '28, and Occupy Baptist Church in 1833. Hannah, my third wife, got the fever in '31, a year after our girls died. She succumbed to it, and I took her to the banks of the Calcasieu River to be buried near the twins. I made several more trips into No-Man's-Land when I heard of a settlement down the river that wanted a church. So, I hopped a steamer to see if I could help 'em. When I think back on *that* riverboat trip, I can't help but smile. You asked for it, Dan...."

16

April 5, 1833 Alexandria, Louisiana
Riverboat *Rodoph* on the Red River

Joseph was bent on finding this new location for a possible church planting. He approached the captain of the Riverboat *Rodoph*.

"Cap'n, are you a God-fearing man?"

"I don't get to church often," replied the captain, "what with all the traveling I'm required to do. But I have a Bible in my cabin, and I turn to it now and then."

"Good enough," said Joseph. "I'd like to give you a firsthand opportunity to take part in spreadin' the Gospel. This here mule of mine and I need to get to a bend upriver. It ain't one of your regular stops, and I know you ain't steering the ark. But I'd be obliged if you'd make an exception and let this mule and me ride to that spot. I aim to try to establish a church there."

The captain gave it a moment of thought, and then replied, "I'll do it and only charge you the fare for yourself, not the mule. But on the condition that when you hit your knees in prayer tonight, you'll put in a good word for me with our Maker."

"I accept," said Joseph, a wide grin forming. "I'll do it for a week." He led Ole Sally forward across a gangplank and toward the back of the boat.

The captain came to greet him with a handshake. "I appreciate your prayers, preacher," he said, "and I can tell you there's another onboard who could use some religious guidance. It's a card shark name of George Smith. He's cleaned out several of my passengers since coming on board. I can't boot him off. He's done no wrong. But I don't like the man." He looked up, then whispered, "Speak of the devil."

George Smith, wearing a tailored waistcoat, a shiny vest with an expensive pocket watch and gold chain dangling outside, pleated pants, and hand tooled boots, approached the two men. He extended his hand.

"I couldn't help but overhear your conversation before you boarded," said Smith, shaking Joseph's hand. "So, you're a man of the cloth, eh? My name is Smith…George Smith, previously of

Memphis and now ensconced primarily in New Orleans. I take a leisure cruise such as this every month or so to exercise games of skill."

"You gamble," stated Joseph flatly.

"I detest such labels," said Smith. "No, sir, I prefer to say I engage in skill rather than fool luck or mere chance. If I put money down at the Fleetfield Race Track at Natchez, you can be assured that I've examined the steeds and learned about their riders. And if I sit for a round of vingt-et-un, you can feel confident that I've thought carefully about the cards and the odds of how they will fall to each player. I'm not a card sharp, just a sporting man using his wits and experience to make a living. I'm sure you would find favor with that, am I right?"

"Not hardly," said Joseph, "but I do wish you a nice day. I need to get some water for my mule. One jackass is all I can attend to at a time, sir."

The spring weather was pleasant enough that day—not too hot yet, and there was a nice breeze blowing on the river, and the fog had long since lifted. Joseph's thoughts were on visiting Bethel Baptist Church again at Woodville, Mississippi, at the request of Mississippi Governor Abram Scott. Joseph had helped establish that church in 1798, and the Governor was now a trustee. He felt concern about the cholera epidemic, the same sickness that had claimed the life of Hannah, for it was continuing to spread throughout the area and was even thought to be carried by the riverboats. He had asked Joseph to lead a prayer meeting in which he and the congregation would invoke the protective power of Jesus, the Great Physician, in avoiding the plague. At first, Joseph had some concerns about traveling by riverboat, if that is actually how the fever was being spread, but then he recalled that he had stayed at Hannah's bedside right until she died, and he had not become sick with fever. Maybe he had a natural immunity, or perhaps the Lord was already putting a protective hand upon him.

The day wore on and Joseph decided to stretch his legs by taking a tour of the steamboat. He was on the far end of the deck when he saw a long-time friend, Johnson Sweat, and a young female.

Joseph quickly approached his friend and said, "It's good to see you again. I think the last time we spoke was at your father's school in Bayou Chicot. My children always thought he was a good teacher, and they learned readin', writin' and cipherin' better than I ever did."

Johnson Sweat laughed in agreement. "He had a gift for teaching, and he spoke favorably about your children." He paused and looked back and forth between the young lady and Joseph. "Pastor, I'd like you to meet my daughter, Elvy. Today is her thirty-first birthday, and I promised to take her down the Red River to the Mighty Mississippi on this riverboat—down to Red Stick, you know. I just love Baton Rouge."

Joseph removed his hat and bowed slightly to the lady. "Pleased to make your acquaintance, miss. And happy birthday."

"Thank you, pastor." She smiled, showing even teeth and dimples in each cheek. Slowly, she twirled her lacey parasol.

Having spent most of his days amidst pioneers, farmers, sharecroppers, Indians, slaves, and cowboys, Joseph was unaccustomed to the style of dress Elvy was wearing. It had lace, ruffles, bows, and ribbons, but it was cut low enough to allow some of her shoulders to be bare and exposed. This was rather awkward for Joseph, but he tried to avoid appearing the part of a hayseed or country bumpkin. He avoided staring at her and tried to take her appearance in stride.

"Do you have one church," asked Elvy, "or are you an itinerant pastor?"

"A bit of both," said Joseph. "I support myself mainly by working a farm, but each week I preach at a specific church near my homestead. However, the Lord has called me to share the Gospel in revival meetin's and as a church planter, so I do get around quite a bit."

"And your wife Hannah?" asked Johnson. "How is she and your family these days?"

Joseph cleared his throat. "Been a long time since you and I crossed paths, Johnson, my friend, so you wouldn't know that my twin girls died, and this past year Hannah got the fever and she's buried next to them."

Mr. Sweat blanched. "Seriously? No, no, Brother Willis, word had not reached me of this. You have my sincerest condolences. I'm truly sorry for your losses. But...your other children...?"

"Fine, fine," Joseph assured him. "And blessings to me, to be sure. No, the fever didn't fall on them. My little girls didn't die of fever. But I don't want to revisit that matter just now. The Lord has given me a new vision to expand my ministry by plantin' more churches. I'm on my way right now to scout out a location."

"I admire your resilience, sir," said Elvy. "And your sense of commitment. But while we have you cornered here on this boat, would you allow me to ask some questions of you related to Scripture?"

"If I can offer clarity on a matter, consider me your servant, miss."

She glanced at her father with an amusing sparkle in her eyes and then back at Joseph. "My father says *if* and *when* I get married, I have to be submissive and do what the Bible teaches. What are your thoughts on that, Pastor Willis?"

"Miss Elvy, the way I see it is this: do you remember the story in Genesis of the creation?"

"Yes, Pastor, I do, but not in detail."

"The story goes that Adam told God, 'I want a wife that will cook, clean, help me take care of these animals, and do whatever I tell her to do. How much will that kind of submissiveness cost me?'

"'An arm and a leg.'

"Adam scratched his head and asked, 'What kind of submissiveness will a rib get me?'

"'Not much!'"

She giggled, but her father laughed right out loud.

After a moment of reverie, Joseph said, "Let me be serious for a moment, Miss Elvy. It does say in Ephesians that a wife should submit to her husband, but it also says in the Bible that they both should submit to each other. In fact, Miss Elvy, it says that a man should be willin' to give his life for his wife, just as Jesus did for His bride. As I figure, it's not a fifty-fifty arrangement as many say today. It's a ninety-ten deal. Each gives ninety percent and expects ten percent in return. If they both do that, then as I see it, they got a good chance of makin' it work. If you meet such a man, then you'll have one worth your interest."

"Oh, my, I never thought of that, Pastor. Is that what you did? You've been married. Did you and your wife feel that way?"

"Actually, I've outlived two wives. When I was married to Rachel, my first wife, we made a decision to get down on our knees every night and pray for each other. You know, Miss Elvy, it's hard to stay angry with someone you're prayin' for."

Joseph studied her face and waited for a response. He suddenly realized she was mixed with Indian, too. She had dark eyes and high cheekbones. A different kind of beauty, inside and out. Joseph found her very attractive, but she was half his age. Nevertheless, he found himself unable to make small talk with her, feeling like a school boy with his first twinge of love. Talking about the Bible was one thing, but trying to extend the conversation in other directions found him floundering.

"Brother Willis, you were right when you said we have not crossed paths in a long while," said Johnson Sweat. "Can we remedy that by having dinner tonight here on the boat, say around seven. I'm sure Elvy would like more company than just me for her birthday meal."

"Yes, yes, do join us, please," said Elvy. "I'm eager to hear of your work in these parts."

"Well, if you're sure I wouldn't be intrudin' on your celebration. Thank you. I'll see you then."

Joseph could not help keeping his eyes of Elvy and she turned and gracefully strolled along the railing, her parasol over one shoulder and her arm interlocked with her proud father.

Joseph wanted to look respectable for the dinner. He retrieved his saddlebag and used his razor to trim his beard. He always carried a brush to use on Ole Sally, but today he found it useful in brushing his own dust ridden clothes. By seven, he was as spruced up as he could get, improvising with what he had available to work with. He grabbed a discarded rag and wiped his boots then headed for the dining room. He hoped that Johnson Sweat would do most of the talking; for a fact, Joseph could tell Miss Elvy had some refinement, and if she started to talk about literature or history or world travels, she would soon discover he had areas of mental poverty he had yet to overcome.

To his amazement and immediate dismay, he looked up to see Miss Elvy arrive alone. She walked right up to him and said, "Poor, poor Father. He should not have taken that extended walk earlier today in that hot sun. His gout has flared up, and he's quite lame this evening. He won't be able to join us. I hope you're not too disappointed. Father says that I talk enough for two people, so maybe we won't miss him. Shall we be seated?"

Caught off-guard, Joseph mumbled, "Yes, miss...I suppose...well, that...that would be all right...given the situation."

They were directed to a table and Joseph pulled the chair out for Elvy. Fortunately, he had brought some traveling money with him, but it had not been his plan to dine in such an elegant fashion. His saddlebag contained cornbread, a flask of buttermilk, some hardboiled eggs, raw carrots and onions and potatoes, and one piece of fried chicken. That would have been enough to sustain him until he reached church folks who would provide meals for him.

He looked at the menu and was perplexed. He wasn't sure what was proper to order in a formal establishment.

Perhaps Miss Elvy sensed his unease, or maybe she was a mite presumptuous, but either way, Joseph was relieved when she said, "Since it is my birthday, I believe I'm entitled to choose our meals tonight." She turned to the waiter and said, "We would like pistolettes stuffed with crawfish etoufee. And bring bowls of shrimp and okra jumbo." Turning to Joseph, she asked coyly, "Will that suit you, Pastor?"

"I could not have said it any better," he replied, quite well meaning it.

As they waited for their food to arrive, Elvy was very much at ease in drawing Joseph into a conversation. She asked about where he was born, who his parents were, how he had felt a calling to enter the ministry, and what prompted him to venture into lands others might feel were forbidden and dangerous. Strangely enough, Joseph no longer felt ill at ease around her. He shared a couple of more of his jokes with her, asked about her own background, and even explained to her the circumstances of how he had come to know her father and her grandfather.

When the plates and bowls of food arrived, the aroma made Joseph's mouth water. His Hannah had been French, and she could work miracles with celery, onions, peppers and shrimp. Her file gumbo had always put a smile on Joseph's face. Certainly this riverboat fixings could not compare to Hannah's cooking, but it was close enough to bring back fond memories of times around the table as a family.

"Today, you said that you lost your wife to the fever," Elvy said, respectfully. "I know that cholera has ravaged many families these past few years. My father and I were so sorry to hear about your loss. How have you been coping with that?"

Joseph did not feel she was prying. Instead, he sensed a kindness in her desire to let him share his grief with a kindred spirit. Briefly, he recounted the incident of the poison honey and how the burial of his twins had led to a major revival on the riverfront. He also told of receiving a new calling from God to cross the Calcasieu into No-Man's-Land and share the Gospel.

However, fearing he was directing the conversation too much on himself, he asked innocently, "And in what ways have you filled your life, Miss Elvy?"

And that's all it took. She retold stories she had read in novels. She talked about reading in newspapers and gazettes about how women in France were gaining formal educations and taking on leadership roles and obtaining more respect and responsibilities. She recounted adventures she had read about in history and geography books. She told of science lessons her grandfather, the teacher, had demonstrated to her. She explained how she used the mathematical lessons from her grandfather to design her own unique patterns for quilts and bedspreads.

Joseph was at first startled by Elvy's confidence and brashness, but soon he discovered that he found her to be distinctive, refreshing, truly stimulating. She was entertaining, captivating, lively, vibrant, and very pretty. He found himself wishing the evening could go on and on.

Finally, at the conclusion of one of her narratives, Elvy said, "My meal is getting cold. I ramble once I get started. You are a good listener, Pastor Willis. But, please, allow me to enjoy some of my birthday feast. Tell me now of your enjoyments."

Joseph pushed his empty plate forward, folded his napkin and laid it beside his plate. He lifted his cup to his mouth and enjoyed a last swallow of strong coffee.

"My pleasures are somewhat basic," he began. "I like meetin' new people and seein' how I can help 'em. I enjoy my study time with my Bible, and I like all the aspects of being a minister. I give sermons, but I also baptize folks, perform weddin's, preach funerals, anoint the sick, encourage the lonely, and try to defend the weak."

Miss Elvy nodded, but did not interrupt.

"I love my children, grandchildren, and now even great-grandchildren," Joseph continued. "I'll take a couple of them at a time to a favorite fishin' hole, and we'll spend the day hauling in catfish and bluegill and crappie, and then sometimes clean them right there on the riverbank, build us a fire, and have a private fish fry. That's pure joy to me. And, if I need private time, I get up on my faithful old mule Sally and take a ride through the tall yellow pines and commune with nature and with God."

He paused and looked around the room, then confessed, "And, ya know, I'm startin' to take a shine to these riverboats. Might want to board one again someday."

The waiter approached, coughed to gain attention, and asked, "Will there be anything else, folks?"

Joseph looked around, and to his surprise, the room was practically empty. Obviously, the waiter wanted to do his final clean-up chores and turn in for the night.

"No," said Joseph. "We'll just pay and be on our way, thank you."

"Oh, the meal has been taken care of already, sir," said the waiter. "Compliments of Mr. Sweat, in honor of his daughter's birthday."

"Yes, my daddy will pamper me on special occasions," said Elvy. "Shall we take a breath of air before you walk me to my cabin, Pastor Willis?"

They stood at the railing and just listened to the bullfrogs on the banks of the roaring river. The moon was really bright that night, and passengers could see the cotton and sugarcane fields glistening in its light. An occasional fire dotted the banks, and it was bright enough to see people fishing for river catfish. The steamer almost had a heartbeat of its own. The steady sound, along with the fresh air, moonlight, and a few lights from the fires was very peaceful. But all of a sudden, down below, the crack of a whip could be heard, followed by a cry of pain. Elvy winced at the sound.

"Pastor, I'd like to get your opinion on that someday."

"Miss?"

"Slavery."

"We'll save that for another day."

Her question told Joseph a great deal about her. He felt a need to move her away.

"Miss Elvy, I think we have both heard enough. It's gettin' late."

She put her hand on his arm, and he walked her to the door. He said, "Happy birthday. This was a most enjoyable evenin'. Tell your father I hope he recovers soon, and that I will mention him in my prayers. I hope to see both of you tomorrow before they let me off when we reach the Mississippi."

"I'm sure you will, Pastor Joseph Willis. Lord willing and the river doesn't rise."

She smiled and disappeared into the room.

Joseph was also smiling as he made his way back to the main deck. That night, he sat on a bench for a good long time and wondered, *What just happened?* For a passing moment, he pondered the idea that Mr. Sweat might have been playing matchmaker. No, probably not. Either way, she was a very charming young woman, and totally in contrast to his two wives. Surely, it was a memorable night.

*   *   *

Joseph awoke early, found the food he'd carried in his saddlebag, enjoyed a makeshift breakfast, gave some oats to Ole Sally and a drink of water, and then made his way to the deck area. The day was sunny, clear, and already getting humid.

"Morning, Brother Willis," called Johnson Sweat, walking briskly toward the preacher.

Joseph turned and smiled. "You look as though you've had quite a recovery."

Johnson shrugged and said, "Oh, you know how these summer sniffles can be. Gone overnight."

Joseph wrinkled his forehead. "Sniffles? I thought Miss Elvy said you suffered from gout."

"Uh…and that, too, seems to have passed during the night. Fine day, isn't it?"

"You've raised a lovely daughter, and I compliment you. She's a lively conversationalist. Wide range of interests. I was very impressed."

Johnson Sweat crossed his arms and slowly shook his head. "Kind of you to say so, friend. But I fear her opinions and candor and prattle have chased away any man who might have been a suitor. At this rate she'll become an old maid and live with me until I pass on."

"I'm sure she feels blessed to have had a grandfather who was a teacher. And you, too, in providin' books for her. She's nobody's fool."

"I hear you're going to leave us soon, so let me extend a sincere invitation to you to visit our humble home the next time you are in the Tenmile Creek area. It's been a little lonely since my wife died. I think Elvy would like that, too. What do you say, Pastor?"

Joseph was now sure that his earlier suspicion about Mr. Sweat trying to line up his daughter with this preacher was a fact. And, if he'd been 20 years younger, he would have jumped at the chance. But he was drawn in two emotional directions. On the one hand, like his biblical namesake, he wanted to run away from this feminine temptation. On the other hand, he could not help but be curious as to whether such a sophisticated, educated, refined lady as Miss Elvy would seriously consider him as someone worthy of courting her.

"There you are, gentlemen," spoke the soft voice of Elvy Sweat. Slowly, she ambled across the deck. If possible, Joseph felt she looked even prettier than the prior evening. With a different dress on, but still one that revealed her graceful shoulders, and a hint of rouge on her cheeks, she looked like no "old maid" Joseph had even seen.

Johnson Sweat smiled and said, "I was just extending a personal welcome to Brother Willis, asking him to stop by our home the next time he finds himself in the Tenmile area." Turning to Joseph, he asked, "Is there any truth to the rumor that you are even considering the idea of starting a church at Tenmile?"

"No rumor to it," asserted Joseph. "It's a fact. We've already bought the land for the church right down on bank of the creek. We plan to call it Occupy Baptist Church. Mind you, there's still a lot of work facin' us. We need to clear the land, lay the foundation, cut the timber, erect the building. I'll be spendin' a considerable amount of time in Tenmile. I would hope you both would attend the church, perhaps consider becoming members."

Johnson Sweat was ebullient. "You can count on that. And since you'll be in the area for a spell, please consider staying with us. Our home is not grandiose, but it is comfortable."

Miss Elvy looked boldly at Joseph and said, "And I could prove useful. I could swing an axe in helping to clear the land, and I could bake you a very tasty huckleberry or dewberry pie."

Joseph tipped his hat and said, "How can I say no to that?"

But he smiled to himself as he said it, for he knew those delicate hands had never wielded an axe, a plow, or even a hoe. And, yes, she probably could handle a needle, what with her enjoyment of those arithmetic figures she said she created for her quilts and bedspreads, but he also doubted she could make a pie...or biscuits or cornbread or green beans with pork fat. But, then again, she seemed to learn things fast. So...who knew? Maybe she'd catch on fast if she had the proper motivation.

The captain ordered a layby so that the preacher and his mule could disembark.

Joseph looked at Johnson and Elvy Sweat and said, "This is where I get off. I'll be returnin' to this exact spot in two days to catch this same riverboat home. Hope to see y'all soon."

"No doubt you will, friend," said Johnson. "We had planned to be upriver for three days, but things have now been cut short. I have a business matter to attend to, and I'm eager to get home to soak my feet in a solution that seems to help ease the pain of my gout. So, we'll probably see you onboard again in a couple of days. Best regards, preacher, in your work until then."

*   *   *

Joseph fulfilled his promise to Governor Scott to conduct the church meetings to pray for healing and protection in regard to the cholera epidemic. He was fed well and given a comfortable place to sleep each night, and when he packed to go, the womenfolk of the church made sure he had a good supply of vittles.

The preacher mounted Ole Sally and rode back down to the spot on the river where the captain had promised to pick him up on the return trip. With a couple of hours on his hands, Joseph cut a cane pole for some idle fishing. He sat pondering his situation with the Sweats. Intuitively, he knew that it would help his ministry and his own wellbeing if he could find a wife to share his life with. But could he live in harmony with a woman—a lady—who had book learning and more modern views of life?

The riverboat gave a blast to announce it was ready for Joseph and his mount to come on board. Ole Sally went right up the gang plank with the confidence of a Louisiana politician. It was as though she enjoyed that riverboat ride, or maybe it was the attention the other passengers gave her, especially the sugarcane the kids offered to her.

After Joseph got onboard, he looked around the deck for the Sweats. At first he didn't see them, but then they came down the narrow passageway. They greeted each other warmly and chatted for several minutes about the church meetings.

But then, Joseph stopped, squinted, and stared hard into the near distance. At first, he could not believe his eyes. But, yes, there, right before him was none other than Jim Bowie, walking along the deck, toting a leather bag, wearing his standard buckskins, and his knife flashing in the bright sunlight. But it wasn't the same Jim Bowie whom Pastor Willis had crossed paths with some time back. This man was slumped shouldered, sad-eyed, and grizzled, in the sense that he needed a haircut, a shave, and a bath.

Pastor Willis excused himself from the Sweats and moved quickly to intersect Jim Bowie.

Bowie looked up, at first disoriented, and then relieved.

"Brother Willis," said Bowie. "If ever there was a time I could use your company...."

The men embraced and then took a seat on a nearby bench. Pastor Willis could smell strong liquor on Jim's breath.

"You looked tuckered, Jim. What's happened since I last saw you...outside of the fact that you were shot and stabbed during that faceoff on the sandbar? I got there too late to be of help, but I heard most of the details."

Jim shook his head. "Ah, partner, that weren't nuthin' to

speak of. It's since then that I've become a most miserable man. Had a wonderful wife named Ursula. You never met her, but she was as sweet as could be. She gave me two darlin' youngun's, too. But the cholera hit our family, and all three of 'em died in the space of two weeks. Weren't a dad blame thing anyone could do to help them." He paused briefly, then added, "And word came downriver that you lost Hannah and your twins. That doubled my grief, preacher. Truly it did."

"My heart was broken for them," said Joseph, "and now it's broken for you. I'm so sorry."

Jim raked his fingers through his long hair, let out a large puff of air, and actually groaned.

"I wish I could just make some sense of it," said Jim. "They never did no one no harm. But me...I'm a scallywag from way back. If anyone deserved to be...."

Joseph put his hand on Jim's shoulder. "I understand those thoughts. I had the same questions. Why not an old roustabout like me instead of those little six year old girls?"

"Get any answers?"

"Some, yes," said Joseph, "and I'll share that with you later. I've got some good fixin's in my saddlebag that the church ladies sent with me. We'll share 'em and talk. First, however, I'd like you to meet a couple of friends of mine, then I'll catch up with you later."

Jim rose and followed Joseph down the deck.

"Mr. Sweat, Miss Elvy, this is my friend Jim Bowie."

Elvy moved a step closer and examined Jim. After a moment, she said, "I've heard of your exploits, sir, and I stand amazed that you are actually here, alive. The newspapers told of the duel and outbreak at the sandbar. It was reported that you were shot and stabbed. The report also said that, despite being wounded, you killed one of your adversaries. That's truly amazing!"

Bowie shrugged. "I wouldn't put too much store in what newspapers tell ya, miss. I only use 'em to wrap fish in."

"Ah, modest, too," said Elvy. "I can see why you and Pastor Willis get along. It's obvious you have catching up to do. My father and I will hope to talk more with you tomorrow."

"My pleasure, Miss," said Bowie. He bowed slightly and then started to move off. Joseph said he would see them after he had had a chance to commune with his friend.

Joseph led Bowie to where Ole Sally had been tethered. He had him sit in a cane back chair. He rummaged in the saddlebag for a moment, then set a slice of wheat bread, a small jar of molasses, and some cold chicken before Jim. He also located a piece of apple pie and set that out, too. He ordered Jim to eat, which he did, slowly.

"You asked if I had any answers, Jim. You eat while I talk. I ain't sure I'm goin' to bring you much comfort, but at least it may put some different perspective on things."

For the next twenty minutes, Joseph told about the crisis with the poison honey, the burial of his daughters, the attendance at the internment by settlers, farmers, cowboys, tradesmen, slaves, and three Cherokees. He told of his new calling, and then of the loss of Hannah. And he told of his vision of erecting the new church at Tenmile."

"I 'spose you're sayin' that life must go on," said Jim. "And I reckon that's the bare truth of it all. I confess to ya, I've tried to find comfort at the bottom of a bottle, but there ain't nothin' it offers 'cept bloodshot eyes and a head-splittin' hangover. But after hearin' your tale, maybe I can pull myself together and see about fulfillin' that dream I had years ago of headin' to Texas."

Pastor Willis nodded. "Jim, I really admire you. I've never once heard you use vulgarity or profanity, and you never talk about yourself. I know the pain you feel, 'cause I've had it myself. But, you're right in figurin' the bottle is not goin' to solve any of your problems."

Jim licked some molasses from his fingers and said, "Even bloodshot eyes can see that Miss Elvy is partial to you, Parson. And I sense that her papa ain't against the idea of her hitchin' up to you. But, oh, my, if you come struttin' into that new church with a young filly like that on your arm, the old widows and spinsters are gonna have tongues a waggin', trust me on that."

"Well, to begin with, there's been no talk of marriage," asserted Joseph. "But, if there was, I'm sure it would only serve to provide plenty of topics for my sermons—gossipin', backstabbin', spreadin' rumors, and lyin'."

"Ah, the tongue," said Bowie. "I believe it was James who said it controlled the body."

"My, my, Jim," said Joseph. "You actually have cracked a Bible. Wonder of wonders."

"Thanks for the grub. I'm gonna make myself more presentable. I've got a cabin. I'll shave, wash up, take a rest, and then meet you and the Sweats for dinner in the dining commons, say around six. I've heard they do a good job of serving up catfish."

"I'll relay that invitation to the Sweats and see you tonight. By the way, where are you goin', Jim?"

"N'Orleans for about a week on some business. But one day I truly am gonna make it back to Texas again."

*   *   *

That evening Bowie arrived sober, rested, and clean. He recommended the pan-fried catfish with cornmeal batter and all four were soon served. Both Johnson and his daughter pressed Bowie to tell of his travels, his development of his famous knife, and his future plans. Thus, it was with genuine relief that their table was interrupted by a visit from the ship's cabin.

"Don't let me disrupt your fellowship," said the captain, "but I have some rather good news to pass along. Some days ago Pastor Willis cleverly convinced me to let him and his mule take a ride with us to a location where he was going to preach a series of sermons. He said I'd be doing the Lord's work if I helped him. Well, I passed that notion along to the owners of our line of riverboats, and, believe it or not, that is now a new policy. From now on, preachers on their way to plant new churches or lead revivals or minister to distant folks will travel free and be let off wherever it best suits them."

"That's mighty generous of you folks," said Joseph. "I'm much obliged."

"Indeed, we are delighted," said the captain. "In fact, we're very soon going to pick up another pastor right around the bend. You might even know the man."

Joseph smiled and said, "Who would that be?"

"Reverend Murrell," said the captain. "Reverend John Murrell."

Bowie nearly gagged on the bite of cornbread he had just

bitten into, and Joseph's eyes bulged in astonishment. A cold chill went up the preacher's spine.

17

April 9, 1833
Riverboat *Rodoph*
On the Red River

Joseph woke up late. He decided to go to the dining area and see if he could buy a cup of coffee to go with the remaining food he had stored in his saddle bag. To his good fortune, one of the waiters saw him walk in and said, "We are just closing, but if you'd like to help yourself to a couple of leftover beignets and few hard boiled eggs, it'll be on the house. No charge. You can take it out on the deck with some coffee. We'll open again at noon, sir."

The hot French roast coffee helped Joseph wake up. He didn't see any of his friends, who had probably dined earlier. So, he just sat quietly and enjoyed the ride.

After twenty minutes, Joseph returned to the door of the dining room to set his coffee mug inside. As he turned, he found himself face to face with Rev. John Murrell, who had spotted Joseph and had made a beeline to him. Joseph's blood ran cold.

"You miserable scoundrel," said Murrell. "I knew I'd find you again one day!" He pushed Joseph back against an outside wall and pinned his shoulders there. His face was beet red and his eyes were glazed. His breath was sour.

"It's been a long time, Willis, but I've never forgotten what you and your friend Bowie did to me back in 1810." He was so angry he was spittin' his words. "I vowed I'd get my revenge one day, and this is going to be that day."

"We only told the truth," said Joseph.

"You both were lyin' through your teeth," asserted Murrell. "You embarrassed me in front of all my friends. You accused me of stealin' horses from a meetin' where I had just shared the gospel. I was just plunderin' hell and populating heaven, and you erroneously blamed me for stealin' from the flock! Your friend Bowie got the jump on me, put a knife to my throat and made me apologize. I still have the scar where his impatience cost me a little bit of my blood. Do you remember that?"

Joseph swallowed hard but did not flinch.

"Yes, I certainly do recall how you preached a sermon and

ended it by tellin' 'em to sing a couple of hymns. I was there that night. Did you know I went just to hear you? I had to minister to those folks after they went out to find you had plundered their horses and mules. What you did was wrong. You tried to steal from 'em."

Murrell moved in closer. "No, what *you* did was wrong. You humiliated me in front of my friends...and strangers. But, your friend with the Arkansas toothpick is not here to protect you now."

"You'd be surprised how the Good Lord plans things," Joseph said. "For a fact, Jim Bowie *is* on this riverboat right now. He and I had dinner together last night."

Murrell gave a menacing grin. "My, my...now, I've heard some whoppers before, but that one tops them all. For a preacher, you're a pretty good liar. I know for a fact that Bowie was heading to New Orleans to do some slave trading. I heard it upriver. He's probably already there by now. I'll get to him at a later time."

From his waistband Murrell pulled a silver plated ivory handled pistol.

"Jesus fed thousands, and today so will you," said Murrell. "When you hit the bottom of the riverbed the crayfish and catfish and gators will make quick work of you. You're old and tough, but they'll all be grateful for a free lunch. Move out on the deck. Now!"

Joseph turned, as ordered, and took a step forward, silently praying as he went, "Lord, I could use some divine intervention 'bout now."

Just as Murrell cocked the pistol there came a *swoosh* and a loud *thump*. A huge knife tore across Murrell's hand and stuck in the wall three inches from Joseph's head. Murrell screamed in pain, dropped the pistol, causing it to discharge, sending a bullet into the boat's side railing. Almost instantly, Jim Bowie was atop Murrell, giving him a right cross to the jaw. Jim retrieved Murrell's pistol and put it in his pocket.

"You look like ya seen a ghost, Murrell," said Jim.

Murrell pulled a handkerchief from his pocket and wrapped it around his bloody hand. "Look what you've done to me."

"That's just a little blood to help draw the gators," said Jim. "You was right about someone goin' swimmin' today, but it ain't gonna be Brother Willis." Bowie pulled his knife from the wall and brandished it toward Murrell. "Step to the edge."

Munnell's eyes widened. "No, you can't do this. I'm not a strong swimmer. The banks a long way off."

"All right," said Bowie, "I'll just slit your throat and end your worries."

Joseph laid a hand on Bowie's arm. "Don't kill him, Jim. I know he wouldn't have shown the same mercy to me, but I don't want his blood on our hands."

Bowie grimaced, but withdrew the knife. Murrell let out a long breath. However, just as he was about to turn to walk away, Bowie grabbed him by the collar and the seat of his pants, lifted him high, and threw him over the guard rail. Murrell dropped like a stone into the river, then came up spitting and gasping and cussing.

"Throw me a rope," begged Murrell. "My clothes…my money…."

Bowie waved goodbye as the riverboat continued to move forward. He called back, "Brother Willis will donate your belongin's to the folks you stole from. Hey, look out. I think that may be a water moccasin movin' up on ya. Swim! Your life depends on it."

Bowie and Pastor Willis shared a laugh as they watched Murrell scramble to make it to the shore, splashing and waving and screaming all the way, bobbing like a cork. It was better than a traveling carnival show. Fortunately, he was near a bend where the shore was closer than usual. He'd survive, but he'd be out of sorts for a long time.

Joseph turned to his friend and asked, "Jim, how'd you know you were gonna hit Murrell with the knife and not me?"

Bowie smiled. "I just assumed the Lord would look after ya, brother."

By now a small crowd had assembled on the deck, all looking at the famous Jim Bowie, but no one actually wanting to go near him just yet. The dining room door opened and the waiter who had served Joseph earlier stepped out.

"Saw the whole thing, I did," he said. "That villain got what he deserved. We don't open until noon, but if you two gentlemen would like to come in and cool off, I do believe I could find some sarsaparilla to bring to you."

Jim and Joseph nodded and stepped inside. The waiter

locked the door behind them.

"This here's Murrell's fancy pistol," said Jim, pulling the weapon from his pocket. "I heard tell about this one. They call it a Denix...Italian made. Pretty, ain't it? What would you guess...fifteen inches long? And look at the ornate carving on it. Where would a backwoods drifter like Murrell get something like this?" Jim paused a moment and then said, "Stole it, that's for sure."

"Why don't you keep it, Jim? I'll give Murrell's money and extra clothes to the needy, as you said, but I believe you earned that little toy today. You saved my bacon. I'm obliged."

Jim turned the gun over and back, examining it. "Believe I will, friend. If I ever see Murrell again, I'll use it on him."

The two men finished their cool beverages. They left to find Murrell's stateroom and to retrieve his belongings. Joseph shook his head as he examined the booty. "Look here, Jim. Three pocket watches, four pairs of fancy cufflinks, ridin' boots and walkin' boots, five shirts, four leather belts, two hats, a hickory cane with a silver grip, tobacco, a pair of spectacles, and six pieces of gold. Oh...and for window dressin' one almost-new Bible."

Jim pulled a carpet bag from the floor and opened it. "Put it all inside here and you can tote it to the storage area where you've got your mule tied. You can take it off with you when you leave. Some of this stuff you'll have to sell or barter. It'll all go to good use in the long run. Give one of those gold pieces to the captain for the trouble he went to on behalf of Murrell."

After storing the carpet bag and giving Ole Sally oats and water, the men were surprised to discover it was almost noon.

"I kept the pistol," said Jim, "and I believe a tithe is appropriate for you, preacher. So, take one of those gold coins and buy lunch for me, you, and the Sweats. I'm sure they'll be in the dining room by now."

And, indeed, Johnson Sweat and Miss Elvy were seated at a table for four when Jim and Joseph arrived, making it obvious they were hoping to be joined by them. Miss Elvy looked radiate in a green dress with brocaded lace around the waist.

"Everyone's saying there was a ruckus a couple of hours ago," said Mr. Sweat. "You boys know anything about that?"

Jim gave an innocent look and said, "I believe someone tried to take a ride without paying the fare, and he wound up in the river. Probably just routine business for a riverboat. What looks good on the menu today? Our friend, Brother Willis, insists on paying."

*   *   *

Lunch included sweet potatoes, ham, rice, collard greens, black-eyed peas and tea. Miss Elvy talked about her grandfather, the teacher, and of the schools he ran and how his students went on to become successful in business, politics, law enforcement, and the military. Jim Bowie talked of his desire to spend more time in Texas, of the yearning the locals had to be shed of Mexican rule, and how the land was perfect for raising and breeding cattle. Jim spoke respectfully of Steven F. Austin, a man who felt Texas was destined for independence.

"It sounds as though battles will have to take place if Texas truly desires independence from Mexico," said Mr. Sweat. "Are you in favor of that, Pastor?"

Joseph gave a moment of thought to the question and then responded, "I am not fit to pass judgment on Jim or anyone else who hears a call for freedom. I, myself, fought alongside Francis Marion, the famed Swamp Fox, when I felt we Americans had a right to seek our freedom from British rule. I believe that noble causes will attract noble men."

"Pecan pie, anyone?" suggested Miss Elvy in an effort to turn the conversation to something less dramatic. "I plan to indulge and then retire to my room for a nap during this heat. But I look forward to seeing you both again here for dinner."

Her smile lingered on Pastor Willis.

18

December 23, 1833
Riverboat *Rodoph* on the Red River

Once the Sweats had departed for their quarters, Joseph coaxed Bowie to sit out in a veranda area where they could put their feet up and relax and have a long private talk.

"Jim, you've been like kinfolk to me," Joseph began, "so I'd like us to bare our souls before we have to part ways again. Ain't too many men we can be so honest with, so I, for one, don't want to pass this opportunity to unburden some of my recent misfortunes. And I want to hear you out, too. I'll start by saying that I could hardly believe my ears when word came to me that your lovely fiancée, Cecelia Wells, took ill and died not two weeks before I was to perform your weddin' ceremony. I remember her well, Jim. She was beautiful in appearance and in spirit, and I know you loved her dearly."

Bowie looked into the distance, as though going back in time.

"I've been wounded more than once," he said, "but that was nothin' to the pain I felt in losing that dear gal. I can close my eyes at night and still see her smile." He paused, then said, "But it just wasn't meant to be. And to tell you the truth, I feared I'd never find anyone who could touch my heart the way Cecelia did. But it was you who once told me that even a blind hog can find an acorn now and then. And I did. But it was in Texas."

"I know you are an adventure-seeking hombre, Jim, but what led you to go so far away?"

Bowie shrugged. "Reckon I had the fool notion that if I put enough distance between me and Cecelia's grave, it would lessen the heartache. Nonsense, that. But it carried me all the way to a place as close to Paradise as I'd ever discovered. The Mexicans call it *Coahuila y Tejas.*

It has huge rivers full of fish and turtles and birds of every color and design. The prairie grass is thick, and the antelope are enormous and have gigantic racks. Mustangs run free across the land, and there's an odd blend of cactus, hardwood trees, and wildflowers. The local people grow corn and tomatoes and beans, and they keep chickens, milk cows, pigs, and goats. The wind comes in during the evenin's and makes it cool for restin'. Folks have been livin' there for five or six generations, some in adobe houses, some in soddies, some even in large tents. I felt right at home as soon as I arrived. And it was there I found love, tragedy...and my new call of duty."

"Whoa," said Joseph. "Sounds like three stories, not just one."

"Quite so," Jim confirmed. "The love story is centered on a senorita named Maria Ursula Vermamendi. Her hair was long and soft and as black as coal. Her brown eyes were deep, and she had a soft laugh that I found alluring and sweet. The only reason I can figure she agreed to take up with me was because she was pretty much related to about everyone else in that village in one way or another.

Anyway, we found a padre and I understood enough of the Spanish to know what I was agreein' to, and we said our vows. Part of the agreement, however, was that I had to take an oath of allegiance to the Mexican government. With the way things was runnin' locally, I had no problem doin' that. But that began to change as time wore on."

"You started a family?" asked the preacher.

"We did," said Jim. "Two children came along, and thank goodness they looked more like their mama than they did me. Pretty, pretty children. I rode 'em on my back, taught 'em to speak English, picked flowers with 'em. I bought us some land, built a place, and settled in. I did some tradin', a bit of farmin', ran a string line of fish, broke some horses. We managed."

"Sounds like you had some happy years there."

"True enough," said Jim. "But even before the cholera took my wife and two children, things started to go bad. The government in Mexico made the people of Texas surrender their weapons. They levied burdensome taxes. They conscripted young boys to serve in the army. They confiscated food, animals, and personal belongings. What once had been a land of singin' and dancin' and joy became a place of dread, worry, and anger. The people of our village weren't askin' for much. They just wanted justice, freedom, and a safe place to bring up their youngun's."

"Who did all the changin' of things, Jim?"

Bowie spat, then said, "The new *presidente* of Mexico, a weasel named Antonio Lopez de Santa Anna. His henchman is a crazy general named Jose de las Piedras. It was ol' Jose who said everyone had to turn in their guns and knives. You can imagine how well that went over with a brawler like me. I was away on business when that edict was invoked, but I hurried back home. We tried to make our complaints known by serving grievance papers and signin' petitions. Fat lot of good that did. General Piedras sent out a hundred of his cavalry and led a full charge against us."

"But isn't Texas a lot different from Mexico?" asked Joseph. "I mean, sure, ya got your Spaniards who've been there for decades. But ya also got Indians and white settlers and open range cowboys and runaway slaves. Think anyone could get them to organize into one body and resist those corrupt sidewinders from Mexico?"

"Yep, I do believe there is such a man," said Bowie. "Ever heard of Sam Houston?"

*   *   *

Pastor Willis shifted his legs and grinned. "I'm gonna catch you off-guard when I say this, Jim, but I actually do know somethin' about Sam Houston. But my source may surprise you."

"Do tell."

"Well, sir, we do get newspapers in Louisiana and in Mississippi, so I'm not completely cut off from the outside world," said Joseph. "So, sure, I've read about Sam Houston bein' a lawyer who became a congressman and then governor of Tennessee. Personal friend of Andy Jackson, as the story goes, because of Houston's bravery during the War of 1812."

"That's the very man," said Bowie.

Joseph said, "But why I know so much about Houston is because my mother's people carried tales of this white man who lived as one of them. They told of how when he was a young man, he spent time in Cherokee villages, learning to speak the language, to ride ponies bareback, to throw a tomahawk. They taught him how to track deer, set traps for rabbits, tan hides. He later went into politics, but he fell out of favor after his marriage went bad, so he moved back among his friends in the land of the Cherokee. As I recall, I believe it was in 1829."

"There's more to his story," said Jim, "but what your Cherokee kinfolk passed on to you is true. Anyway, last year Houston came to Texas.

Sam Houston witnessed firsthand what I told you about the harsh treatment the folks livin' in Texas been dealin' with. Bein' a lawyer and a former politician, he tried a few angles in approachin' the Mexican government, but all for naught. They laughed him off. But I believe they may have underestimated this feller. He's fought in a war. He's learned to live off the land. And he's got book learnin', too. That's a dangerous combination of elements. Reminds me of a story my old mother used to tell."

"What's that?" asked Joseph.

Bowie smiled. "Well, she said that she hated the taste of lard, hated the taste of raw flour, and hated the taste of buttermilk. However, when she mixed 'em up all together, they made some of the best biscuits anyone ever chewed on. I believe those Mexicans may find out that there are a lot of raw ingredients in Mr. Sam Houston, but they combine to make one fine leader."

"So, you're sayin' Houston is focusin' on liberatin' the people in Texas?"

Bowie shrugged. "I'm sayin' that if anyone could unite the suppressed people to throw off their chains, it would be someone like Sam Houston. And, since I'm not giv'n up my land without a fight, if he organizes an army, I'll be one of his first recruits."

"You know some Spanish, Jim, but do you know what my mother's people call Houston? In Cherokee he is known as *Colonneh*. It means raven. He had black hair, but the name implies his love of being free like a bird. He actually married a Cherokee squaw when he lived with a tribe led by Ahuludegi."

"How did you learn all this?" asked Bowie.

"Got it firsthand," said the preacher. "You remember I told ya about my call to cross the river and bring the Gospel to No-Man's-Land, where some Cherokee are settled? Well, when Andy Jackson sent the army to force the Indians off their land and make them move far west—a place the Choctaw call *okla humma*—some of the Cherokee jumped off the steamboats and ran away and settled in what is now No-Man's-Land. They knew the stories of Sam Houston and his anger over how Jackson treated the Indians, about Houston's background with the Cherokee. They don't trust many white men, but they think of Sam Houston as an adopted brother."

"I've actually met the man," said Bowie. "Briefly, mind you."

"Under what circumstances?"

Jim responded, "We got to know each other during thirteen days back in April of this year when we were both representatives at San Felipe de Austin at a convention. We drafted a list of our grievances to be delivered to the Mexican government."

"Yeah, you mentioned they tried paperwork first."

"I gave a letter of introduction to Stephen F. Austin from one of his father's original three hundred colonists. Now, Austin is another man you'd admire. We immediately took a likin' to each other because of our dreams for the future of *Tejas*.

Austin asked me to see if I could help resolve this issue without bloodshed. In August of last year, several of us marched into Nacogdoches to present our demands to Piedras. Before we reached the officials' offices, we were attacked by about one hundred men with the Mexican cavalry. You remember I told you earlier about that. Well, we returned fire and it became obvious that both sides were intent on a fierce battle. And I don't just mean that particular skirmish. It sparked a wildfire for independence."

"I truly hope it won't end in a great deal of bloodshed," said Joseph.

Bowie lifted his chin as though a new thought had struck him.

"Preacher, why don't you pick up and go with me? I'm serious. They need churches in Texas as much as anywhere else. I've got to get back to my home in San Antonio de Béxar, and I know that things are fixin' to change. My late father-in-law's home was near Mission San José. My Maria Ursula loved it there, and she would say, 'It's a shame that we don't have more missions like Mission San José and like the way *Mission San Antonio de Valero, the Alamo* used to be, before Mexican soldiers made it into a fort.' The fields are ripe for harvest in *Tejas*, Preacher."

"Well, it's temptin' if for no other reason than how much I'd enjoy spendin' more time with you, good friend," said Joseph.

"But I've been in Louisiana for three decades, and my work is still not done here."

Bowie weighed that, then said, "I can appreciate a man with a mission. I'm feelin' the same way about Texas independence. I have to warn ya though, that crazy Santa Anna is a madman. He has talked about crossin' the Gulf of Mexico and invadin' Cuba for its sugarcane fields. I just hope he won't cross the Sabine and make his way to your beloved Calcasieu River."

"I gotta feelin' you and Mr. Austin and Mr. Houston will put a stop to it long before that ever happin's," said Joseph. They shook hands, both understanding that this would probably be the last time they would ever see each other.

19

October 3, 1852
Near Babb's Bridge, Louisiana
On Spring Creek

Pastor Joseph Willis appeared still lost in his memory as the team of horses followed the banks of Cocodrie Lake, heading due west.

"So, you never met up with Jim Bowie after that trip on the riverboat?" asked young Dan.

"No, son, I never did," said his great grandfather. "But I said many a grateful prayer to the Lord for lettin' me spend a couple of days just then with one of the best friends I ever had. Not to mention that fact that Jim prevented ol' Murrell from puttin' a bullet in my back and dumpin' me in the river."

Everyone chuckled. "Yeah, there was that small matter," someone said.

"How'd it all end for him?" asked Young Dan.

"Well, I got part of it from the newspapers and part of it from folks who came through Louisiana after leavin' Texas," said old Joseph. "Jim agreed to lead his volunteers to defend the Alamo against Santa Anna. He was supposed to get everyone out and destroy the fort but he didn't have the oxen or horses needed to move the heavy artillery, and there was very little ammunition.

That's the story that's been handed down, but I've often wondered if the real reason that he volunteered in the first place and didn't want to leave once he got there was because it was his home. His beloved wife grew up near Mission San José. He married her there, his children were born there, and he converted to the Catholic faith there. Knowin' Jim as I did—he wasn't leaving. Can you blame 'em? From what I've heard, Jim was sicker than a dog most of those thirteen days that they stood against the forces of evil. Small wonder, all the times he was shot and stabbed and punched and wrestled. Time takes a toll even on a strong man's body.

"Boys, my heart hurt when I heard the news in 1836, but I also know that he died defendin' freedom. Jim Bowie and those other brave men were willin' to lay down their lives. That is exactly what happened at the Alamo. The Good Book says, 'There is no greater love than a man lay down his life for a friend.' That's what they did at the little mission fort. Son, as I see this woman that Jim called Liberty, I can understand their passion for this lone star called Texas today which shines so bright. It's men and women like Jim Bowie that make it shine so bright, even today."

The elder Daniel asked his grandfather, "Did you ever *really* consider followin' Mr. Bowie to Texas?"

"Yes, I sure did, and I almost made it there."

*   *   *

Young Dan watched his great-grandfather carefully and finally spoke. "You've told me so much about your life, but do you mind if I ask more questions?"

"I thought you might. Go ahead."

"Grandpa, I have a few questions of my own." Daniel was nodding.

Lemuel chimed in, "Me, too, Father!"

Joseph just grinned and said, "We have a few more miles to go, so maybe I can help ya make sense of things before we get to your home, Daniel. Dan, what did you want to ask?"

"You told us you *almost* went to Texas. Why didn't you?"

"I had decided I wanted to see Texas, plant a church or two, and maybe even find Jim. I felt excited about the idea of headin' farther west. I saddled Ole Sally, loaded my packhorse, and headed west to the Sabine River. The closer I got to Burr's Ferry, the less sure I was about my decision. I got right up to the river's edge and was gettin' ready to pay my toll when I got this real uneasy feelin'. As clear as I'm talkin' to you boys, I heard the Lord tellin' me, 'This is not what I've called you to do.'

"At that moment, I knew I had made a terrible mistake. I had made my own plans without askin' the Lord. Ole Sally, my packhorse, and I turned back, and I'm certainly glad we did.

"Ya know, there's a legend that says that John Murrell, the devil preacher, buried his loot in some caves not far from there. Who knows, maybe there are a few gold pocket watches there that he stole from my friends, but that was not my concern that day."

Joseph smiled.

"Great-Grandpa, did he ever get caught?"

"Yes, Dan, if I rightly remember, he went to prison for ten years, and I heard that he died soon after leavin' prison. Now, Daniel, did you have a question for me?"

"Grandpa, when ya headed back, did ya see Miss Elvy again?"

"I surely did! It was on my way back, after I stopped at a café in Natchitoches. I was havin' some supper and struck up a conversation with a man named Jean Baptiste Louis Metoyer. He was buyin' lumber to build a new plantation house, and when he noticed I was dark-skinned he told me how his grandmother, Marie Thérèse Coincoin, had once been a slave. Her generous master of nineteen years gave her and her children their freedom. He even left his plantation to her. Jean Baptiste told me stories 'bout growin' up and havin' slaves waitin' on 'im. He invited me to come visit 'im at his thrivin' Melrose Plantation. I did so on one of my trips to Natchitoches, and he showed me some great hospitality. What a grand place it is along the Cane River. We became good friends.

"When I went back to pastor Occupy Baptist Church, I visited Miss Elvy. She attended Occupy, and we got to know each other much better. Boys, she never wanted me to go to Texas, so she was very glad when I told her my plans had changed. We spent many hours sittin' and talkin' on the courtin' couch in Mr. Sweat's parlor. It was in early May of '34 when I asked Mr. Sweat for her hand in marriage. Now, I know the age difference was a problem for her, because she used to tell me how her brothers teased her. If they weren't calling her an *old maid*, they were laughin' at her for being too young for me. When we finally got engaged, the teasing stopped. Miss Elvy was a headstrong young woman and still is.

"I was grateful to have so many family members and friends there at our wedding in late June of '34. She was a beautiful bride in her white dress, especially with those dark eyes and long black hair all the way down to her waist. I can remember her talkin' 'bout havin' an instant family and how happy she was to be surrounded, loved, and accepted by all of you. We settled into marriage quickly, and I continued workin' with Occupy Church."

Lemuel asked, "What was it like in No-Man's-Land back

then?"

"Oh, my, son! You'll have to imagine a place where there was no law and no one to enforce a law if there had been any. In those days, it was a vast land strechin' all the way to the Sabine and claimed by no nation. In No-Man's-Land at that time, there were outlaws, pirates, counterfeiters, runaway slaves, and fugitives from other states. There were tribes such as the Choctaw and others who lived peaceably. There were also the Cherokee Jim spoke of, those who had escaped off the steamboats headed up the Mississippi to take 'em away from their native lands to reservations. I made a point of becomin' friends with many of these tribes, especially my mother's and my people, the Cherokee.

"I tried to minister to as many of the outlaws, runaway slaves, fugitives, and others as best I could. Fed and clothed 'em when they were in need and shared the gospel when they'd listen. I baptized many an Indian and fugitive from who knows where in those days. Many memories flood my mind, like once when I was on a trip up on the Ouachita River. I met a Choctaw man who was very sick, along with his wife, Ohoyo. I prayed for 'em and was able to hunt for some game for 'em. They both went on the mend. What a blessin' that was to me.

"They were the last, the least, and the lost in that hostile land—exactly the kind of folks the good Lord had called me to. I loved it. They were sorta like the Samaritans who were despised in the Bible.

"Some were dangerous men. However, there were many others who were not that and had grown up there. They called it *home*. Not everyone who lived there was a fugitive. Some were doin' their very best to survive, like Miss Elvy and 'er family.

"She grew up there. Bein' mixed with Choctaw, she was accepted and got along well with those who had escaped from the Trail of Tears. My Cherokee roots helped me aplenty as I preached in that lawless land.

"Years before, there was another place that was just as dangerous as No-Man's-Land that I dared to venture into the Louisiana Territory. It was in March of 1800, down in Vermilionville, and the law of the land was the Spanish Black Code. It forbade any preachin' other than Catholicism. They came after me in the middle of the night. A friend of mine, Jacques

Cormier, caught wind of the mob's plans and warned me. They were goin' to sell me to the silver mines in Mexico, or even worse, *kill me*. I fled so fast that I didn't have time to put on my boots. That's when they started callin' me the 'Barefoot Preacher' and the Apostle to the Opelousas."

Everyone listening to Joseph's account laughed as he continued.

*　　*　　*

"The good Lord has saved me from many dangers. Once, when I was travelin' through No-Man's-Land, I stopped at an inn for the night. Inside, there was a man burnin' up with fever. I asked 'im, 'What's your name?' He said, 'Malachi. Malachi Perkins...from Tenmile Creek.' I asked him if he knew Jesus as his Lord and Savior and Redeemer and he affirmed boldly that he did. I told him that I felt that was a good thing because, to be honest, he might not make it through the night in his fevered condition.

"I did what I could to comfort Malachi, giving him a bit to eat, providing water, and putting cool cloths on his forehead. After we prayed, he drifted into a sleep, so I went off to get some rest in my own room. A few hours later there was a faint knock at my door. I got up, opened the door, and saw Malachi leanin' against the door frame. He was sweatin' something terrible, but he had forced himself out of bed.

"He looked pleadingly at me and said, "Y'all gotta skedaddle, preacher. I overheard two men talkin' about robbing and killing you. They think you have money. Let me tell you of a trail you can use as an escape route. I'm in your debt for caring for me.'

"I dressed quickly, and this time I put on my boots and went out the window. I saddled Ole Sally in the barn next to the inn and off we went in the early hours of the mornin'. She could run like a deer back then. Thank God for a full moon, for I found the path he was talkin' about and got away without any trouble. It kind of reminded me of the story of how the angel came to Joseph and told 'im to take Mary and baby Jesus and flee into Egypt. This was not the first time, nor would it be the last, that the Lord sent a messenger to warn me of danger.

*   *   *

Young Dan asked another question. "Great-Grandpa, why did Uncle Lemuel send a hospital wagon to bring you to live with his family? I've asked 'im, and he would never say. Why aren't you still livin' with Miss Elvy?"

The elder Daniel spoke up. "Dan, you don't ask your great-grandpa personal questions like that."

The silence felt uncomfortable. "It's a reasonable question, Daniel. I don't mind if he knows. Dan, I understand why you're askin'." Joseph nodded, then noticed Daniel and Lemuel's eyes were open—wide. They could not believe that Dan had asked the question or much less that Joseph was going to answer it.

"You see, when I married Miss Elvy, she was only thirty-one, and I was seventy-something. She was a wife like the woman described in Proverbs 31, and as you know, she blessed me with two more sons, Samuel in '36 and Aimuewell in '37. We had many happy years together. But, as I grew older and needed more help, she just couldn't take care of me. I think it got to be too much for her. She sometimes sounded so tired and frustrated that it made me feel sad for her.

"Out of her exhaustion, she began to speak unkind words. I know those were not her true feelin's, but she was just so weary. When Lemuel and his family came to visit a few months back, I told 'im that I was makin' her unhappy. I did not want to be a burden to her. I can't blame Miss Elvy. I still love her, and I know she still loves me too. Now, it's my turn to ask a question." Everyone looked rather surprised as Joseph changed the subject. "Dan, there is something I've been meanin' to ask you since we left Evergreen."

"Yes, sir."

"What are ya gonna do with Jesus?"

"Sir, I don't understand."

"Jesus hung between two thieves on a cross. One of 'em rejected Him that day, but the other one asked Him, 'Will You remember me when You enter Your kingdom?' Now, Dan, both of those men were guilty. One said yes to Jesus, and the other said no. One put his trust in Jesus, and the other chose not to. The question is, which thief on the cross are you?"

"Great-Grandpa, I want to be like the one who said yes."

"Dan, there's a Scripture that I love, and it explains things so simply that even I can understand. It says, 'If thou shalt confess with thy mouth the Lord Jesus, and shalt believe in thine heart that God hath raised him from the dead, thou shalt be saved. For with the heart man believeth unto righteousness; and with the mouth confession is made unto salvation.' Dan, you can settle this question right now in heaven and on earth."

"Sir?"

"By sayin' yes to Jesus, just as that one thief did on the cross. It's just as this old Cherokee slave that you call Great-Grandpa once did, too."

"Yes, sir, I want to do that. But, how?"

"I'll tell ya how I did it as a young boy 'bout your age."

"How was that?"

"I just said a prayer to the Lord. There are no exact words. And prayin' is just talkin' to the Lord."

"Will you help me do that, Great-Grandpa?"

"I sure will. I'll pray, and if these words are how you feel in your heart, you can repeat 'em. "Heavenly Father..." Dan began to pray, too. "I come to You in prayer, askin' for the forgiveness of my sins. I confess with my mouth and believe with my heart that Jesus is Your Son, And that He died on the cross at Calvary that I might be forgiven. Father, I believe that Jesus rose from the dead, and I ask You right now to come into my life and be my personal Lord and Savior. I repent of my sins and will worship You all the days of my life. Because Your word is truth, I confess with my mouth that I am born again and cleansed by the blood of Jesus! In Jesus' Name I pray. Amen!"

"I do believe that in my heart, Great-Grandpa."

"Praise the Lord, Dan! Ya know, after *I* made my decision, I got myself baptized."

"Why?"

"Because the Lord said to."

"Great-Grandpa, I want to do that, too!"

"We're 'bout a mile from your home on Spring Creek, and

that'll be a good place to get baptized. The other wagons should already be there from Evergreen."

The elder Daniel looked puzzled. "Grandpa, are *you* gonna baptize 'im?"

"No, Daniel, I think you should. The strength has mostly gone from this temporary home."

"Dan, I'm sure your mama and sisters and brothers will want to witness this glorious occasion."

Joseph smiled and spoke quietly under his breath, "Lord, who is likened unto You?" This was a day that all would remember in the Willis family.

Dan leaned in close to his great-grandfather and gave him a big hug. He whispered in his ear, "I sure do love you, Great-Grandpa...and my Jesus, too."

Lemuel reined the team of horses around the bend. "We'll be at Daniel's home shortly."

Joseph was grateful, because his bones were sore from being jostled for three days. When they pulled up, everyone came out to greet them. It was a joyous reunion, especially when they took young Dan down to Spring Creek to be baptized. Lemuel and Daniel carried Joseph down the path to the creek. Dan and his father stepped into the cold creek, and when young Dan came up out of the water shivering, he had the biggest smile his family had ever seen!

Dan walked right up to his great-grandfather. "Great-Grandpa, what do I do now?"

"I'll give you two words of advice my mother gave me many times. She would say, 'Son, the only Bible that most people ever read is our lives.' And Dan, every time I went to her for advice, her answer was always the same: 'Joseph, what would Jesus do?' Write those two down in your tablet, son, and write them on the tablet of your heart, too. Pray and trust Him at all times, and study God's Word, and count your blessin's daily. And, Dan, remember that it's what you sow that multiplies, not what you keep in barn."

As they carried Joseph back to the house, he could smell a savory stew. The fragrance of fresh bread filled the air, and Joseph's stomach growled. When he was settled, they brought him a bowl of piping-hot venison stew. He gave thanks and ate slowly, enjoying every single bite. He also gave thanks for finally having a soft chair to sit in.

Dan brought his plate of food over closer to his great-grandfather so he could sit and talk. Joseph could see that something was troubling him. "You look like something's on your mind. Let's hear it."

Everyone stopped eating to hear Dan's question. "Will ya tell me about Mr. Ford's slave, Solomon Northup?"

"I'll do that, but I first need to get some rest and read the Word. We can talk about it in the mornin'."

Joseph had a peaceful rest that night. He awoke the next morning at the break of dawn with the sound of an old rooster crowing and the smell of Louisiana dark roast coffee and biscuits baking in a cast-iron skillet.

Daniel's wife, Anna, had cooked a hearty breakfast of fried eggs, ham, and biscuits with gravy, and there were mayhaw and dewberry jellies, too. After Joseph got cleaned up, they carried him out and placed him gently in a chair at the head of the table. Young Dan took a seat right next to him.

Joseph had hardly given thanks and swallowed his first bite when Dan asked, "Are you ready to tell us about Mr. Ford and Solomon Northup?"

"Yes, Dan, I am, but first let me tell you what led up to me meetin' Solomon Northup. I hope you're ready to hear all this."

20

August 8, 1841
Spring Hill Baptist Church on Hurricane Creek
Near Forest Hill, Louisiana

What a memorable day Sunday, August 8, 1841, turned out to be! It was the day Pastor Joseph Willis founded Spring Hill Baptist Church, which would be the last church he would ever organized. All sixteen organizing members were present, including William Prince Ford, and Judy, a slave woman of color owned by William. William brought all his slaves that day, including two newly bought ones whom Pastor Willis did not recognize. There was standing room only, and it was a scorcher! Many of the plantation owners and their slaves were there, too. The preacher's heart was filled with joy.

P.W. Robert, William Prince Ford, and Robert Tanner each stood and spoke encouraging words about the new church. They had asked Pastor Willis to come and deliver the message that morning, and he'd gladly accepted. He spoke to them about making good choices. He told them what his mother always taught him to ask when making a decision: 'What would Jesus do?' Joseph warned them that all churches, and especially new churches, face adversities. To this he received a chorus of "amens" and "that's right, brother," with heads nodding and handheld fans waving. The pastor then led the assembly in singing "Rock of Ages" and "Amazing Grace."

With the official dedication ended and the morning's sermon delivered, William Prince Ford came forward and asked the crowd to stay yet another minute.

He declared, "I'd like to say a few words. This is a great day for our community. My wife, Martha, and I were plannin' on having a small celebration at our plantation this afternoon, but after talkin' to Pastor Willis, we want to make it very special and invite everyone in our community. At Pastor Willis's request, we are goin' to make it a celebration of thanksgivin'."

The congregants smiled with great expectations.

"So, next Saturday, we're havin' some of the best eatin' this parish has ever seen, with music and games for the children too—

young and not so young. Did I mention the hayrides and a horse race or two? Also, Daniel Willis wants to organize a new game from up North called baseball. He explained it to me. It will never catch on, but y'all can sign up with 'im."

Mr. Ford allowed for folks to share a laugh, then he continued, "Ladies, please bring your favorite covered dishes! I'm thinkin' we'll have plenty of corn on the cob, potatoes, fresh produce from your gardens, and, of course, some mouth-waterin' desserts. We're gonna have fresh-smoked hams from my new smokehouse. And, we're also gonna serve up a couple of dozen smoked turkeys, a side of beef cooked over an open fire, and with any luck we'll have some fresh venison." William looked at a couple of the best local hunters and grinned. "And that's what Martha came up with in the last ten minutes."

Everyone laughed again and applauded, and the planning for the celebration of thanksgiving was underway.

To his recollection, Pastor Willis couldn't recall anything like that ever happening before around those parts. It reminded him of a celebration his late wife Rachel would often speak of that was handed down from her ancestor, William Bradford. The folks in the new church started getting excited just thinking about a day of thanksgiving, fellowship, fun, and Southern recipes. The week passed quickly, and everywhere the preacher went, people were talking about the pending gathering.

21

August 14, 1841
William Prince Ford Wallfield Plantation
On Hurricane Creek near Forest Hill
Louisiana Feast of Thanksgiving Celebration

Saturday proved to be a perfect day for a community celebration. A gentle, cool breeze off Hurricane Creek and some lofty clouds kept the normally stifling heat suppressed. The turnout was massive—more people than Pastor Willis could get a count of. All across the Fords' Wallfield plantation everybody was enjoying fellowship. Several small groups of men gathered to talk about politics, about who had the fastest horse, and, of course, about crops and hunting and the weather. The womenfolk were busy cooking in the log kitchen, getting the food in order, taking care of the babies, and watching the toddlers. Their conversations were as lively as the youngsters.

The older children were down in the field competing in sack races and swinging off a rope into the creek's swimming hole. The younger girls played hopscotch and pick-up sticks, and there were dolls everywhere. It had all the makings of an unforgettable day.

At first, Pastor Willis and Elvy made the rounds together, greeting old friends and meeting new ones. There were people from Cheneyville, Bayou Chicot, Bayou Boeuf, Alex, No-Man's-Land, and as far away as N'Orleans. Some of the plantation owners' wives wore the newest fashions, including William Prince Ford's wife, Martha Tanner Ford. She looked like she had been shopping in N'Orleans's finest stores. And Madam Mary McCoy, the beloved angel of mercy from Norwood Plantation, walked around in finery rumored to be from Paris and greeted all the guests, including the slaves. Madam McCoy was known for the Christmas parties she provided for the slaves down Bayou Boeuf way. After a time, Elvy, in her crisp, blue gingham dress, chose to stay with the women and children, so Brother Willis excused himself to go talk with several of the men. The savory smell of the meats being smoked gave everyone a sharpened appetite. There was an abundance of food and it all looked good!

"You said there'd be dancin'," complained a little girl who

had come in a starched dress and ribbons in her hair.

"So I did," responded Mr. Ford. He signaled for one of his slaves to grab a fiddle, and soon the happy "Skip to My Lou" was being played and the children were prancing in circles. When that tune ended, the slave strolled among the guests accepting and performing requests. He could do Virginia reels, barn dance jigs, French love tunes, well known hymns, and traditional lullabies.

Pastor Willis cornered William Prince Ford and asked, "Where did a slave learn to perform like that on a violin? I remember seein' him in church last Sunday with you. He listened to everything I had to say. He's a quite remarkable fellow."

"Ah! My fiddler! Yes, he is pretty good, isn't he?" Ford said. "His name is Platt, and he belongs to me. I bought 'im down in N'Orleans a few weeks back. He works at my lumber mill up on Indian Creek. Seems to be a good worker so far, and...well, he's lots smarter than most."

At that moment the slave Platt began to play an old hymn called "Sweet Canaan," and from behind him a woman's angelic voice began singing the lyrics from deep in her heart. Everyone stopped talking, stopped playing, stopped moving and gave full attention to the fiddler and the vocalist. There was a soulful, almost mournful pouring forth of the words, as the vocalist told of a better land, a better place, and a sacred time when everyone would know peace. True, the song was written about heaven, but Pastor Willis could sense that the Negress who was singing it was picturing in her mind a time and place without slavery.

When after several verses and choruses the twosome finished, there was a moment of stillness, a special calmness that settled over the crowd. Then, Mr. Ford started to clap his hands, and others awoke from the reverie and joined in, so the fiddler and the singer made a quick bow and then scurried off to do their assigned chores for the day.

Mr. Ford rang a bell, summoning everyone to the tables of food. "Y'all gather round now and find a place. Brother Willis will say a few words and then asked the Lord's blessin' on the food."

Joseph allowed a moment for folks to find seats, and in that interval he said to Mr. Ford, "Would you mind if I asked your fiddler to play some more tunes for me? I love the old Negro spirituals, especially."

"Oh, he can play just about anything," said Mr. Ford. "Sure, find him after the meal and make your requests."

Pastor Willis raised his arms to signify the need for order. Silence fell across the assemblage.

"Friends, before I say the prayer, I want to tell you 'bout another feast of thanksgivin'. I remember hearin' my late wife Rachel talk about the harvest feast back in the days of the Pilgrim leader, William Bradford. He was her ancestor. He traveled to this New World in 1620 on the *Mayflower* to seek religious freedom. They were not prepared for what they found, and had it not been for the kindness and generosity of the Indians livin' up there near Plymouth Colony, we might not be here today having *this* feast of thanksgivin'.

"Those Indians remind me of my Indian friends in No-Man's-Land and the Carolinas. William Bradford wrote a proclamation as governor of the colony three years later that contained these words: 'Thanksgiving to ye Almighty God for all His blessings.' We need to do the same today, and I think it would be nice to have this celebration every year. Let's make it a tradition!"

There were some echoes of "amen" and "I'm for it," from the crowd. Pastor Willis then said grace and sat down next to William. He noticed a light-skinned slave who was serving lemonade. As with the fiddle player, he recognized her from the church dedication service the week before. She would not look up, nor did she speak to anyone—except Platt. Her face had no life. She did her work, but it was as if someone had ripped out her joy.

After some small talk with William, the preacher said, "I'd also like to speak to your female slave. I saw her at church last week."

With a questioning glance, William wrinkled up his sun-tanned forehead and asked, "Oh, you mean Dradey?"

"Yes, William. Platt intrigues me, but your Dradey…well, she makes my heart hurt, and I want to know why her pain grieves the Spirit within me."

Conversation during the rest of the meal was most lighthearted. Elvy had rejoined Joseph and sat close beside him, freely joining in on most topics that the other women dared not venture into. Samuel and Aimuewell sat right across the table and ate like field hands before they asked to be excused to go swim in Hurricane Creek. There were three older boys who volunteered to watch the children swim, so the adults had little concern. The food was delicious, and there were many choices, from the cornbread and biscuits to the mouth-watering ham with all the fixings. And, of course, there was the pastor's favorite dish, dewberry pie.

The table talk was about newly acquired livestock; the new school, Spring Creek Academy; the death of President William Henry Harrison from pneumonia earlier that year; the new President, "His Accidency" John Tyler; and about what the members at Spring Hill Baptist were going to do about the Campbellites. A couple of times, the conversation drifted, mostly because of two men, toward how the slaves needed to be kept in line and disciplined. William Prince Ford quickly changed the discussion each time, wanting to keep the celebration mood of the day and prevent arguments.

What with eating and chatting a full hour passed at the tables.

"Husband, let's mingle a bit with some of the folks we hardly ever see," coaxed Elvy, rising from the table and pulling at Joseph's arm. They made their way to talk with William's brother-in-law, Peter Tanner. However, when they drew near him, Pastor Willis was dismayed to discover that Peter was engaged in conversation with none other than Edwin Epps, the man who had strongly espoused brutality as a way of managing slaves.

Epps studied Joseph's face a moment, then said, "Why, we've met before. Back some time, yes, but I remember. It was at Bennett's store on Bayou Boeuf. You were there with the famed Jim Bowie and his lady...Miss Cicely or Cecelia or Cynthia...something like that. How is she, by the way?"

"It was Cecelia Wells," said Pastor Willis, "and I regret to tell you that she fell victim to the fever and died two weeks before their weddin' was to take place."

"Do tell," said Epps. "I read about your friend Bowie's death because of some misguided loyalty at the Alamo."

Elvy clinched Joseph's right hand tightly. "This is my wife, Mrs. Elvy Willis. We're just makin' the rounds, seein' old friends. Please excuse us."

Epps raised a hand. "Hold one moment," he said. "You ride a mule, as I recall, so your insight may be of value to us in a discussion I've been having. I've purchased two new blacksnake whips to use on my slaves, and I do believe the Bible condoned the use of stripes as a form of discipline, both on animals and on people. Can you verify that for us, preacher man?"

Joseph felt heat rising on his neck. He had not liked Epps the first time he had met him, and his opinion had not changed today.

"Our Lord was whipped so badly, the Scriptures say he was unrecognizable as a man," said Joseph. "I don't interpret that as condonin' such treatment. Now, if you'll excuse us, our sons are down at the swimmin' hole. We need to check on them. Good day, gentlemen."

On the way to the water, Elvy steered Joseph to where Ruth and Robert Graham were standing. The preacher knew from discussions with the local folk that the Grahams had recently moved from Jackson Parish to Forest Hill on Barber Creek, about a mile away. That creek had long been a safe haven for Joseph, a place of refuge from the cares of life. He hoped they wouldn't mind seeing him down there from time to time.

"You're settled in, are you?" asked Elvy.

"For the most part, yes," said Ruth. "Please come for a visit when time permits. Robert has put in a crop already, and I've started a modest garden. Do you sew? We could sit and work on a project and talk about our children. You could fill me in on the local history."

"I'd like that," said Elvy. "But let me ask you, so that my husband won't have to be so brash about it, are you folks Baptists?"

Robert smiled and shook his head. "No, ma'am, we're Methodists."

"Well, ya won't find a Methodist church anywhere nearby," proclaimed Joseph, "so join us Baptists on Sunday. We won't report you to the Wesleys."

Robert and Ruth laughed and agreed they would, indeed, make it a point to visit Spring Hill Baptist Church. Joseph and Elvy took an immediate liking to them.

"I've got to fetch my two sons and get them into some dry clothes," said Elvy. "I will come for a visit soon, Miss Ruth."

Joseph promised to catch up with her in half an hour. He turned and spotted William Prince Ford talking to his slave Pratt. He moved quickly to join them, and William smiled as he saw Joseph approach.

"Brother Willis, this is Pratt," said William. "A mighty good worker, and, as you already know, a man with a fine ear for music."

Joseph extended his hand, and said, "A pleasure to meet you, Platt."

Platt humbly accepted the handshake, having to shift his bow to the hand holding his fiddle. He was about thirty years old, with a weathered face, long dexterous fingers, and bright eyes that seem to be alert to the world around him.

William saw other guests who were getting ready to depart, so he excused himself to bid farewell to them. Joseph turned and looked Platt directly in the face. He said, "I'm a good judge of character, Platt. But you puzzle me a bit. I can tell that you have a love for music and a great talent at performin' it. And, from watchin' you at my service last week, I can tell you listen well and like to learn."

"You a fine preacher, suh."

"But I also sense that you've got another part to your story," Joseph continued. "I see some sorrow in your walk, some sadness in your smile. Can you share, in confidence, some of your background with me?"

Platt lowered his head and said softly, "I felt the sting of the whip too many times in 'dis here life, I has. Said some things what got me in serious trouble. It done cause me to tells lies 'bout who I really is, suh."

"Master Ford beats you?"

Platt looked stunned. "Oh, no, suh, fo' sure not him. He a fine Christian man. Never laid a hand on me or any of the other slaves 'round here."

"What's your given name?" asked Joseph. "Your birth name?"

Platt shook his head. "Ain't never s'pose to say it."

"If anyone asks, I'll say, rightfully so, that I insisted you tell me."

"Well, then, suh, I was 'riginally called Solomon, like in de

Bible. Solomon Northrup."

"That's what I'm goin' to call you from now on. If anyone has a problem with that, they can take it up with me personally."

Joseph watched Solomon's hand clutch his fiddle more tightly, and the look in his eyes changed. There was an intensity that could not be ignored, and it seemed he wanted to say something.

He finally spoke with a hushed but strong voice. "Pastor, I done heard you speak last Sunday at church 'bout the advice yuh mama done give you when you had a decision to make. I gots but one question for you."

"What's that, Solomon?"

He laid down his shiny fiddle and bow, untucked his shirt, pulled it up, and turned to show the parson his back. "What would your Jesus do 'bout this here?"

William must have seen this exchange by the surprised look on his face. He quickly came over and spoke to Solomon. "What are you doin'? Pull your shirt down, and show respect to Pastor Willis."

"William, he has done nothin' wrong."

"Platt, please go and continue playin' for our guests." William's voice was commanding.

"Yes, suh, I gonna do exactly that." He tucked his white cotton shirt into his trousers and got himself ready to play his tunes. Before he moved on, his eyes fixed on the eyes of Brother Willis, and the unspoken words between them hung heavy.

It was obvious Solomon carried deep, ugly stripes from the slave pens. For the preacher, it brought to mind the stripes borne by the Savior.

Joseph watched Solomon stand up straight and tall, playing his fiddle, and he heard all kinds of music, from hymns to square dance tunes. He had a confidence that could only come from a good upbringing. He was like no slave Joseph had ever met.

Pastor Willis didn't know what to say when Solomon asked, "What would Jesus do?"

William said, "Pastor, you're missin' the pie-eatin' contest. Are you sure nothin's wrong?"

"No, William, all is favorable. By the way, would you mind if I come to Spring Hill to deliver the message next Sunday mornin'?"

William's face brightened. "Of course not. We'd be honored. I know I can speak for the others."

"Good! I'm gonna walk down to Hurricane Creek for a spell. I need to talk with my mama!"

William looked puzzled.

22

August 18, 1841
William Prince Ford Wallfield Plantation
On Hurricane Creek Near Forest Hill, Louisiana

Unannounced, Joseph rode out to the Williams plantation only a few days after the thanksgiving celebration. He arrived on Ole Sally at midmorning.

"Why, Brother Willis, what a pleasant surprise," said William, coming out on the front porch. "I didn't spec to see y'all until Sunday. My wife made some shortening bread this morning. Come share some with me and some coffee."

A house staff slave brought the plates, food, and coffee to the porch and served the men. William told the server to have one of the men take Ole Sally to the barn for some water and oats.

"Is this merely a social call, or do you have pastoral duties out this way?"

Joseph swallowed the last of his coffee. "Remember last Saturday when I said I wanted to meet your slave, Dradey? I am here to minister to her. Her heart is very heavy. Can you find her for me?"

"I think she's down in a cabin. She's feelin' poorly today." William looked curious and confused.

"Do you mind showin' me which cabin?"

"Better yet, I'll walk you there."

William went inside and retrieved a straw hat. He led the preacher through a small orchard of pear, peach, and orange trees and down a narrow path to a group of shotgun slave cabins. When they reached the second cabin, William called out, "Dradey? Dradey, come on out here."

The door opened slowly, and she walked out, wiping her hands on her dress. "Yah, suh?"

"Pastor Willis is here to talk with you. You heard 'im preach last week at church." William stood there and made no effort to leave.

When Dradey made no response, Joseph knew immediately that she was intimidated in the presence of her master.

"William, I mean no disrespect, but it's best I minister to her *alone.*"

"Ah, I see. Well, then, I believe I'll make my way back to the porch for another piece of that shortening bread. Join me when you're ready."

Wanting to put Dradey at ease, Pastor Willis pointed to a rocking chair and said, "Would you mind sittin' a spell and visitin' with me?"

Cautiously, she eased down but still seemed weary. Her face evidenced she had been crying recently. Joseph sat on the top step of the weather-rotted porch, and Dradey immediately clutched her knees and put her head down, staring at the sparse grass in the little yard.

"Mr. Ford told me your name is Dradey. Is that your given name? Your Christian name?"

"No, suh. My true name be Eliza."

"I'm goin' to call you Eliza, if you don't mind. Eliza! That's a special name to me. I have a granddaughter and a great-granddaughter named Eliza."

She stared at Joseph with uncertainty.

"Eliza, I'm not sure what happened to you, but I know someone who can heal your broken heart."

She said nothing, only commenced to rocking back and forth slowly, and not in a comfortable way.

"Eliza, you can talk to me. I want to pray for you and help you if I can."

"Pastor, if'n that *someone* you speak of really had loved me, He wouldn't have allowed dem babies of mine to be torn from my arms. I be mad at God!"

Joseph nodded slowly. "I've lost my babies, too, Eliza, and I know that kind of pain. There is no salve or balm or ointment or cure for it. But there is One who understands and listens and offers spiritual peace. What you say to me stays between us, I promise. Share your story with me."

"I been a slave all m'life," she began hesitantly. "Master Berry, he be my owner back in Maryland, and he be kind to me. He da father of my two chillin' and he were a good man to me and my Randall and my Emily. He done give us good clothes, 'nuff food, and even brings my babies some candy and toys when he come back from a trip."

She paused, and her expression changed to something akin to both anger and fear.

"But he got a white daughter name Jane, and she all time be jealous of how Master Berry be spoilin' my chillin'. She try ever'thing to convince him to sell us, but he say no. One day Master Berry leave on a trip, and Miss Jane, she say the next day that she gonna get rid of us by givin' us our freedom papers. I was so happy, I done believed it, even knowin' I shouldn't trust dat woman."

Eliza's eyes narrowed as she recalled what happened next.

"Miss Jane have a friend name of Jacob Brooks. He and some other man come round with'n a big ol' wagon and say fo' us to get in with our clothes. We goin' to town to gets our freedom papers. So, we done pack up and climb up in dat wagon. Well, off we go, but in what seem to me to be da wrong direction. I ain't gonna complain, long's we gets our freedom papers."

"I can tell already that it didn't turn out that way, right?" said Pastor Willis.

"No, suh," asserted Eliza. "We was a couple miles down de road when Jacob Brooks pull the wagon to the side. He and da other man came to da back, grab our clothes and throw 'em in da nearby stream. He say we ain't gonna need no fine clothes where we be goin'.

"I tole him we wants to go back to Master Berry's place, but the stranger man say he gonna knock me senseless if'n I don't sit down and shut up. I grabbed my Randall and Emily and pull 'em close to me. I cried out, 'Oh, Lord, help us!' and dat stranger man, he spit some tobacco and he say, 'Nigger, you gonna need all the prayers you can say where you goin'.'

"My babies was scared. They askin' me why dem men threw away their clothes and toys, so I jest speak some lovin' words to 'em and sing some songs. We done rode in dat wagon all day, and when night come, my chillin' fall asleep. By mornin' we arrive at a big, big city and the wagon pull up at a old buildin'. Our two drivers started yellin' about makin' us move. They pounded on a door, and when it open, they push us through it. Dey was an old, dirty, scary man with long hair and only a few teeth. He grabbed my Randall and pulled 'im away from me. My boy cried for me, but 'fore I could do anythin', they push Randall through another door and then shove me and Emily into a big ol' cold empty room with a dirt floor."

"Did you have any idea where you were?" asked Pastor Willis.

"Wouldn't know," said Emily. "Never been to no big city before. Dey done kept us in that nasty place three days, only once a day bringin' us some water and pieces of stale bread. I give mos' mine to Emily. She always be lookin' at me with that innocent little face and askin' what gonna happen to us. And me, I jes' keep prayin' to the Lord, askin' Him to protect my babies."

She paused a moment and tears coursed down her cheeks. After a moment she cleared her throat.

"Well, come a day when dey open da door and take us outside in the sunshine and tell us we need to be cleanin' up. While I be washin' Emily's arms, I done hear my Randall screamin' fo' me. He run up to me and hug me. And I can tell, he ain't been eatin' right. He cryin' and shakin'. But dem slavers, dey crack de whip and tell us we gots to get clean, so I cleans Emily and Randall and me, too.

"That night dey put the three of us and some other slaves in a big wagon, and dey cover us with a tarp. After a long ride, we come to da river and I sees da biggest steamboat of my life. Dey tell us to walk up that gangplank, so we does. Then they take us down into the belly of dat boat where there's mo' slaves. Mos' dem slaves was men, and when dey see my chillin', dey look so sad it makes me sick to my stomach, causin' I'm thinkin' dey know somethin' I don't know, and it gotta be bad.

"We down in the belly o' dat boat for days, and it smell like oil and grease and puke and sweat. At nights, I curl Randall on one side o' me and Emily on da other, and the churnin' of that boat lull them to sleep. While we was back at that cleanin' time in the slavers' yard, I done met Solomon Northup. He a kind man. He, ever' day, be sharin' his small supply of food with my chillin'."

"How long were you on that boat?" asked the preacher.

"Near five days, as I recollect," said Eliza. "When it stop, they take us off and put us in a slave pen worse'n dat one from dat other city. But after a day, they bring us out and say, 'Clean up. Here's water and soap. Wash your hair, too. Rub dis oil on your skin and make it shine. Put on these clean clothes.' Dey had whips, so we done what dey tell us to do. I prayed dey would let me stay with my babies. I cuddled 'em and kept tellin' 'em how much I loved 'em."

"How old were your children?"

"Randall be ten and Emily be seven. Dat day some impo'tent man named Master Burch come around and look at us. He be dressed in a fine blue suit and fancy lace shirt and a tall hat. He look at us and say, 'Now you goin' to da market.' My babies started to smile and giggle. Dey don't know what no slave market is, dey just know that when Master Berry go to da market, he come home with candy and toys."

Eliza wiped a tear from her eyes and ran her fingers through her hair. Her shoulders slumped, and for a time Pastor Willis wondered if she would be able to finish her story. However, in time, she lifted her face and showed a defiance that indicated she was determined that someone should hear her entire tale of woe.

"So, Master Burch, he warn us that when we gets to the selling place, we gots to step lively and show respect to da white folks who gonna be there. He say that if'n we cause any trouble, he gonna have us skinned.

"Dey done took us to a big room and had us stand 'round like horses. Dey move us women to one side and da men to the other side. Fancy-dressed men be walkin' around, some pinchin' me, some lookin' at my teeth, some grabbin' my arms. They wives just be walkin' behind 'em, like it be some stroll in a park.

"I hear one man say to his wife that he bought David and Caroline, who done come down the river with us, but the man say he need a house boy, too, for his place in Natchez. He seen my Randall and asked Master Burch's slave trader, Freeman, how much for dat boy. My heart start breakin' and I run to dat man from Natchez and fall at his knees and beg him to keep us as a family. I promise him I gonna do the wash and ironin' and cookin' and garden work and mendin' and cleanin'. I tole him dat boy gonna work harder for 'im if'n his mama is with 'im teachin' 'im how to do things right."

"What happened then?" asked Brother Willis.

"Freeman rush over and lift a whip over my head, but I kep' on a beggin' fo' dat man to keep us together as a family. Da man's wife say dey don't need no more maids or field workers, but dat I could have two minutes to say good-bye to my boy. So, I cover Randall's face with my kisses and I keep tellin' him to be a good boy and do what he be told to do, and he say, yeah, he gonna do that. Then Freeman have two men come and take my boy away. Dat's da last I ever see of him."

At that point Eliza could not contain her grief. She sobbed uncontrollably, pounded her fists against the side of the rocker, and even stomped her feet. This continued for several minutes. Then, suddenly, her body stopped shaking and her breathing slowed. She lifted her face and fixed her eyes on Pastor Willis.

Through gritted teeth, she said, "Las' Sunday, you be askin' us to behave by askin' ourselves what would Jesus do. Well, I gots a question for you. Where be your Jesus the day dey took my Randall from me? Why didn't Jesus do somethin'?

Pastor Willis sat quietly for several minutes, then he uttered, "I, too, am searchin' for the answer to that question, sister. I'm prayin' that the Lord will give me some wisdom in that regard. I've lost two wives and two daughters, and I still trust my Savior. But, like you, I surely do wish I had a better understandin' of His ways."

23

August 18, 1841
William Prince Ford's Wallfield Plantation On Hurricane Creek
Near Forest Hill, Louisiana

Joseph allowed Eliza to rock a few moments, saying nothing, only contemplating the events of her life. In due time, he said, "I know there is more to this story, and I believe you need to share it with someone who understands. Please tell me what happened after Randal was taken away from you that day."

Eliza wiped tears from her cheeks. With head still bowed, she said, "No one bought Emily and me dat day, so we was sent back to the slave pen. During the night we all got real sick, and they took us to the hospital. The doctor say Emily and me had smallpox. I prayed that Randall didn't catch it, too. Solomon Northup was the most sick. It took us a few weeks to gain our strength back, but when we did, we was sent back to dat slave pen. Burch told us how mad he had been when we had not made a good enough showin' on that first day for the plantation owners. "You niggers are costin' me money! Now, do it right this time, or else." After he threatened to beat us, we were told to act better, but I had no strength to obey. My heart ached for Randall, and I missed 'im so much. Emily clung to my hand as we made our way into the market house again."

Eliza lifted her face and wrinkled her forehead, testing her memory.

"Dis time a different group of people come see us, and the talk was louder. Freeman tapped me on the shoulders, tellin' the buyers, 'Come, see her arms! She can pick lots of cotton for ya. And work your sugarcane fields, too.' In a minute, dis man come in da room and start lookin' around. He didn't touch any of us, and he spoke calm. He say, can I cook and can I pick cotton, and I say dat I's can work hard. I say dat I a good mama, and I beg him to take me and my li'l girl. We promise never to run off."

"What did he say?" asked Joseph.

"Nuthin' right then," said Eliza. "He jest move into the next room. But Freeman come 'a roarin' at me askin' what did I be sayin' to Mister Ford, and I says dat all I say was dat I'd be a good slave. Freeman be thinkin' I made him leave. I didn't."

"Did William Prince Ford come back again?" asked Joseph.

"Well, furst dey was another man who come in and be starin' at my little Emily. He turn her around couple times, pinch her cheeks, and rub her hair. Den he turns to Freeman and say he gonna buy dis girl, but Freeman shake his head and say, no, he gots special plans for this one. He gonna use her in his own house fo' couple of years, den he knows how he can makes some big money usin' her. Oh, Lord, when I hear dat, my soul cried out. I almos' faint right there."

Eliza's tears returned at the thought of that terrible day.

"Then good Massa Ford, he come in and say he gonna buy me and my little girl and Solomon and few other slaves, and I'm on my knees beggin' Freeman to let Emily go with us. But, no, he cold-hearted. I'm sayin' dat my boy done been takin' from me and I needs to care fo' dis little girl. And Massa Ford, he offer extra money, but Freeman say that one day Emily gonna be a regular source of income for him. He won't sell her. Finally, Massa Ford pay da money and dey point me and Solomon and the others to a wagon, but I grabs my Emily. Two big men pins my arms, so I bends down and kisses my li'l girl and tells her how much I loves her. She cryin' and screaming, but Freeman jest hold her tight, and he smile an evil smile as he look down on my little angel."

Eliza halted her story, assuming Joseph could figure out the rest for himself.

"And that's how you wound up here?" asked Joseph.

"Oh, my heart breaks day and night for my chillin'. I talks to my Randall and my Emily, but dey don't answer me. Solomon be tellin' me dat I shouldn't do that, but ain't nuthin' gonna make me stop missin' and stop lovin' my babies. Ever since dat wagon done brought me here, I done prayed that I would get the small pox again and die."

"Oh, I truly hope that prayer will not be answered, Eliza. We must always hold out hope."

"My hope gone, Preacher. Last week you be sayin' we ought to ask what Jesus would be doin'. Well, I'm askin' where was dis Jesus when dey took my chillin' from me? And where is He now, when my ol' heart be breakin' ever' day?"

"He's here, Eliza, and just as heartbroken as you are," the

pastor said softly. "And my heart is broken, too, after hearing your story. The Bible tells us the Lord moves in mysterious ways. I can testify that His ways, indeed, are often mysterious to me. I wish I had a clear cut answer for you. I can only tell you this: after my twin girls died, I was depressed beyond belief, but the Lord called me to deliver a sermon of revival at their burial. And, to my astonishment, when I finished preachin' that day, an endless line of repentant sinners came forward to dedicate their lives to Christ. Now, I ain't saying it was for *that* that my little girls were taken from me…just that it might have been part of it. All I *can* say is that I have to believe that the Good Lord has a plan, and, hard though it may be, I need to trust His guidance and mercy and grace. Without that, none of life's hardships and challenges make any sense at all."

Joseph rose slowly. "I will pray for you and for your children. And I will check back on you from time to time, if you'll permit that. If you need someone to talk to, send word for me."

Eliza offered no response, just lowered her head and tried to control her sobbing. Pastor Willis turned and walked back across the yard and through the orchards, coming back to where William was seated on his porch reading a newspaper and sipping coffee. The preacher took a seat but did not speak. Neither did William. He poured a cup of coffee for his friend. They sat in total silence for a long time.

24

August 18, 1841
William Prince Ford's Wallfield Plantation
Hurricane Creek Near Forest Hill, Louisiana

After a considerable time of recuperating emotionally, Pastor Willis said to William, "I've often wondered if anyone could ever understand the pain my wife and I endured when we lost our six year old girls. Well, today, I can say for a fact, I met a woman who has a true understanding of that kind of agony."

William nodded slowly and said, "I know you mean Dradey. I brought her here to be a housekeeper for Martha, but she is so sorrowful, she cannot do her duties. I've talked to Solomon about it, telling him we may need to replace her. He's tried to help her think differently, to do her work, but it's like she's just a shell of a person. Were you able to help her in any way today?"

"I'm not sure," admitted Joseph. "I gave her a sympathetic ear, and I shared with her about the loss of my little girls. I promised to pray for her and to come back for another visit. But she's terribly heartsick. I saw it like that in my wife. Sometimes we can move on, but we can never forget. And for women—the ones who carried the children nine months and went through the birthing process—it has to be more personal than even we men can comprehend."

"I did all I could to try to keep the little girl with us."

"I mean no accusation," said Joseph, softly, "but can you tell me your version of what happened that day, William?"

William leaned forward, rested his chin on his palm, squinted his eyes, and said, "It was a routine business trip. I needed some hearty workers to expand the work bein' done at my sawmill. And Martha asked me to see if there might be a woman who could do some housework and cookin' when not out in the cotton fields. So, I went to Mr. Freeman's auction house and, believe it or not, Platt was there playin' music. You heard of the expression 'fit as a fiddle.' Well, here was a man who could actually fill that bill. He was strong and healthy, and he really was fit to fiddle. So, I knew I wanted him. I also chose two other men."

"But what about Eliza—about Dradey?"

"Well, I had seen her when I passed through to look at the men, and she seemed right for what Martha would need, so I came back to make a bid for her. Problem was, she was beggin' to have her little girl go with her. I had limited funds. By the time I added up what I'd have to pay for the three men, plus the cost of Dradey, my capital was runnin' low."

"And Freeman wouldn't negotiate?"

"No, not unless someone was willing to pay five thousand dollars just for the child," said William. "Another man wanted to buy her, but Freeman said he was keeping her. I didn't have that kind of money left. I pleaded with him to show mercy, but I could tell he was thinkin' long range."

Joseph frowned. "Meaning what?"

"You may be a preacher, but you're a man of the world," said William. "That little girl had a white papa, so she had deep green eyes, light tan skin, smooth hair, well-defined features. Freeman knew he could own her as a slave, but could hire her out to men as a mostly-white girl. I believe they start that as young as twelve or fourteen. It's a shame, a disgrace, but it's within the law because they actually are *property* of their owners. Freeman probably figured to use her that way for several years, then sell her off completely. I brought Dradey here and gave her a clean place to live, plenty to eat, and new clothes, but she walked around like she was drunk or half-asleep."

"She's numb," said Joseph. "Her feelings exist only for her children. Everything else is an illusion. I looked at her clothes. They're hangin' on her. She's not eatin'. No appetite for life means no appetite for food. She told me she wants to die. I believe her."

"I've never whipped her," said William, "and I've been lenient when she says she's feelin' too poorly to go into the fields. But I'm no sawbones. I don't know how to fix what ails her...and apparently, you don't either. I could make a suggestion, though."

"Speak."

"You might want to have a talk with Platt, the fiddler. He traveled with her and her children, and he was there the day the two youngun's were taken from her. I know he's tried to talk to her. He's due back for the noontime meal about now."

Pastor Willis sat upright. "That's a good suggestion. It certainly can't hurt to get another view of this. Is that him coming now with that group of men?"

William turned. "It is. He's the one on the right. You already know him."

"I'll go meet him."

Platt smiled as he saw Pastor Willis approaching him. "Good day, Brother Willis. Back again so soon?"

Joseph touched Solomon's arm and guided him to one side. Very briefly, he recounted his visit with Eliza. He asked Solomon for insights on her life.

"Well, sir, seems like you already got a good summary of what happened to her," Solomon responded. "She had a good life with her white master in the North, but that man's daughter was afraid of the affection her daddy was giving those two other off-spring of his. She tricked Dradey into thinkin' she was sending her to get her freedom papers, and instead she had her taken down river and sold."

Pastor Willis was doubly intrigued: first, by the story Solomon was sharing, but second by the fact that Solomon did not talk now with a slurred Negro dialect as he had when around his white masters during the thanksgiving picnic. His much better diction, combined with his training in music, led the preacher to speculate that somewhere along the line, Solomon had gained a white man's education…at least on some basic level.

Solomon confirmed that William had tried to buy Emily so that she could stay with Eliza, but Freeman refused to give in.

"Master Ford's been patient with Dradey, but I think she's goin' crazy," said Solomon. "She talks to her children. She sets places for them at her table. She even unraveled one of her blankets and started sewing a scarf for little Emily. I tried to tell her she can't do that, but she's like a child playin' in a pretend world."

"It's her way of trying to cope with the situation," said the preacher. "Thank you for telling me about her life before she came here. That's helpful. You go on now and get your meal. I'll be back on Sunday, bringin' the message. Try to get Eliza to come to church with you. With the Lord's help, maybe I'll have something to say that will encourage her…and you, my friend."

{25}

August 21, 1841 On Barber Creek
Near Babb's Bridge, Louisiana

On Saturday morning Pastor Willis was awake at the first crow of his five month old Dominicker rooster. After washing and dressing, he came to the stable and saddled Ole Sally. He told her, "This is the day which the Lord hath made. We will rejoice and be glad in it." To Ole Sally one day was no different than another, so long as she got her oats and water and a decent night's rest. "We're goin' to Spring Creek Academy so that I can give a little talk, Sally."

"William Prince Ford was the president of the school's board of trustees. William had told Joseph that the principal, Joseph Eastburn, had requested he come and speak to the children. Joseph agreed, on the condition he could tell stories from the Bible. William had told Joseph that when the legislature chartered the school in 1837, it insisted no one could be refused admission because of their religious tenets. Joseph did not want to break the law, but William assured him it would not be a problem."

There was more than one reason the academy was reached only after a considerable ride. It has purposely been set far from the Red River because of the belief that riverboat passengers spread small pox, cholera, and yellow fever as they moved from port to port. Additionally, by setting the academy on Spring Creek, it was close enough to the Texas Road so that students could get there from their plantations on Bayou Boeuf and as far away as Orleans Parish.

Several planters settled here after leaving their bottomland. The summer heat was less oppressive, there were fewer mosquitoes, and for some reason malaria was far less rampant. William Prince Ford married well. His wife Martha provided 200 acres of prime farmland on Bayou Boeuf, across from her brother, Peter Tanner, as a dowry. But William allowed Peter to manage that land on a cash rent basis, and he and Martha created their plantation near Hurricane Creek instead. They never regretted it.

"We're gonna take a slight detour, Ole Sally," Pastor Willis informed his molly mule. "You will love the taste of those cold

Barber Creek waters, and I'll enjoy being back where I've always come to clear my mind and sit a spell with the Lord."

Joseph used to tell friends that the waters of Barber Creek were so clear, he could have dropped his Bible on the creek bed and still been able to look in and read the Scriptures. After dismounting Sally, Joseph sat and listened to the bird calls, the wind humming through the tree branches, the gurgling of the moving water, and the scuffling of small animals. All week he had carried heavy burdens, memories of the whiplash marks on Solomon's back and of the tragic story of Eliza losing her two children. He opened to the Old Testament and read the words God spoke to Isaiah: "And thine ears shall hear a word behind thee, saying, this is the way, walk ye in it."

The old preacher dropped to his knees. "I need such a word, Dear Jesus. My new friends Solomon and Eliza have broken spirits. They seek answers. What, Merciful Father, should I tell them? I know your heart is broken over their anguish, so break my heart in a way that my words will be genuine to them and comforting."

Joseph knew that his feelings about slavery were already settled. His mother's time as a slave had given him a heritage of sympathy for those who suffered under that yoke. No, it wasn't the issue of slavery that he had to deal with regarding Solomon and Eliza. He would share with them that they were joint heirs with Jesus. They were free in Christ. They wanted answers to different questions…questions about how real the love of God was, how secure they would be in the arms of Christ, and how truly they could trust the Lord to sustain them.

Joseph knew the Lord was preparing him for a revelation. He would wait for it, expect it, prepare for it.

The journey to the academy was not long, especially since Ole Sally had had such a delicious drink of cold water. Pastor Willis enjoyed telling the children the story of David and Goliath. He explained that giants aren't always men. Sometimes they can be sickness, like small pox or yellow fever, and sometimes they can be drought or wildfire or hail storms or the loss of a loved one. These giants have to be faced in a fearless manner, too.

At the end of his talk, one little boy named Josh stood up and said, "I reckon David was willing to fight all afternoon, Pastor."

"What makes you think that, son?" asked Joseph.

"Well, when you read that story, it said he picked up five stones. I'm thinkin' that if the first one didn't do the job, he'd have tried four more times."

Pastor Willis smiled and said, "You've got a good point there, and from now on I'm gonna add that fact to my sermon. Give some thought to becomin' a preacher when you grow up, young man. Some say Goliath had four brothers. In any case David was prepared for more than one giant that day. We need to do the same."

Mr. Eastburn shook hands with Joseph and thanked him for speaking to the children. "I know you are speaking at Spring Hill Baptist in the morning, so may I invite you to spend the night at our home. My wife and I would enjoy your company."

"I'm obliged," said Joseph, "but William Prince Ford already has invited me to spend the night at his home. But I'll take you up on your offer the next time I get back to these parts."

"Ah, very well," said the principal, "but do come next door and let my wife pack you something to eat as you travel."

Joseph rode several miles, then stopped to eat a buckwheat cake and some fresh vegetables Mrs. Eastburn had sent with him. He felt the need for solitude so that he could plumb the depths of the Scriptures and listen for the voice of God.

"We're gonna sleep here in the wild tonight, ol' girl," Joseph told Sally. "You can graze and sleep and enjoy the cool breeze." He located a comfortable spot on the banks of Hurricane Creek, not far from the Baptist church where he was due the next morning. He and Sally got settled down under some longleaf pines and used the pine straw to shape a natural bed. Soon, he finished off most of the food he'd carried and he looked to the stars coming out. He had been in Louisiana for almost half a century. It was home. It felt good to lie down against the land and recall memories of earlier days.

Joseph became one with the land. A large whitetail buck wandered nearby and went on downstream for a drink of water, reminding the preacher of David's psalm in which he compared how the deer panted for water the way his soul panted for fellowship with the Lord. Joseph could understand that longing. In the distance were sounds of a lone coyote, a screaming panther, a growling bear, and more nearby were the sounds of scurrying gray squirrels. Sally was tethered with a long rope, so she wandered down to the river and got a drink. She seemed in her natural element with the chirping crickets, jumping fish, and croaking bullfrogs. She hardly noticed as a mama raccoon and her three babies came to the creek's edge and put their paws in the cool water.

Once the sun set, it turned somewhat colder, so Joseph assembled some pine cones, dry brush, and small branches and built a fire. As he did so, he prayed, "You are the Lord of Creation. You alone are!" He recalled vividly coming to Louisiana Territory in 1798. There were no inns and few people. He had slept many a night under the stars near a campfire in those days.

The moon made its way slowly across the sky, and Joseph quoted, "The heavens declare the glory of God, and the firmament sheweth his handiwork."

He fetched a blanket from his saddlebag and went into a contented sleep.

*   *   *

The next morning he didn't need his rooster to wake him. Two loud green-head mallards started quacking, and a blue heron started squawking, as if to brag about all the crawfish he'd caught that morning.

Joseph made his way to the creek to wash, feeling fully rested. The sun was just climbing in the eastern sky, giving faint hints of red and orange mixed with low clouds, meaning a storm was brewing but hopefully not too soon. And speaking of brewing, he brought water back and made himself some coffee over his rekindled fire. Two biscuits were left from the vittles given him by Mrs. Eastburn. He dusted off his clothes, cleaned up his campsite and mounted Ole Sally for the ride. Upon arriving, he was pleased to see that folks were coming early, indicating a good turnout for his sermon.

He studied the arrivals. Plantation owners and their wives and children came, and some allowed their slaves to come, too. There were farmers, tradesmen, trappers, and a few folks of the professions, including a horse doctor and a lawyer and a school marm.

"Lord, give me the words needed for Your people today," he prayed silently.

26

August 22, 1841
Spring Hill Baptist Church on Hurricane Creek
Near Forest Hill, Louisiana

William Prince Ford rode up and tied his saddle horse to one of the hitching rails next to Ole Sally. He smiled and said, "Mornin', Pastor. We missed you last night. Looks like another great day at Spring Hill. You look rested this mornin'."

"Yes, William, sorry we did not make it to your place yesterday, but thank you for the invitation. I decided to sleep under the stars. It was refreshin'!"

The men started to walk toward the church, but then Pastor Willis stopped abruptly. "William, I've done more thinkin' about our talk. I need to ask you why you went ahead and bought Dradey when you knew she couldn't be with her children?"

William shrugged. "Well, sir, Freeman didn't want Dradey, just the girl. And the boy was already gone by then. I felt I could at least provide a decent place for Dradey to live and work. Would you have done it any differently?"

"I like to think I would," said Pastor Willis. "I would like to believe that I would have mounted Ole Sally and followed those children wherever they were taken, and I would have gotten that money to buy them and bring them back to their mama. You acted on what you thought was a charitable way of behavin', but it still led to the breakup of a mother and her children."

William was about half a step behind the parson as they walked up to the front door, and it was obvious William wanted to make a reply in his defense, but a crowd of well wishers assembled at the door.

"Nice to see you, Mr. Ford," said a neighbor.

Peter Tanner came up and shook Brother Willis's hand. "Can't wait to hear your sermon, Pastor."

Another added, "Isn't this a nice day!"

Joseph smiled at the folks, but William didn't respond to their interruptions, and his red face carried an expression that was hard to interpret. He caught up to Brother Willis, who was working his way down the aisle greeting folks.

William tugged at Joseph's coat and whispered, "Pastor, you're beginnin' to sound like one of those abolitionists from the Northern churches. You're not 'gainst slavery, are you?"

Joseph turned and replied over his shoulder, "You might be onto somethin' there, William." He moved forward, getting ready to sing the day's hymns. Silently, he prayed, *If ever I needed to be in the Spirit, it's right now.*

The preacher scanned the sanctuary for Solomon and Eliza and was happy to see they were there. Solomon was seated with the men slaves, and Eliza was seated with the women slaves at the back of the church, for there was no balcony.

After the singing concluded, Joseph rose and asked, "Which of you children can recite the Golden Rule?"

A young boy sitting next to Peter Tanner stood and said, "Treat others the way you want to be treated."

"That's very good. It actually says, 'Therefore all things whatsoever ye would that men should do to you, do ye even so to them: for this is the law and the prophets.' I just spoke yesterday at your school. "

All the children clapped. "Can you tell me what that verse means?"

Another young boy raised his hand and stood. "Pastor, it means that however I treat others is goin' to come back on me, like if I'm mean to someone during recess, they're gonna be mean back to me." Everyone nodded in agreement.

"Well said, young man. That's one way to look at it." The boy sat down. "Now, let me ask you adults, how many of *you* believe in the Golden Rule?" All hands went up, and everyone was looking around.

"Good. My next question is, 'Who's your brother?'"

Peter Tanner stood and said, "Bible says that everyone is our brother. Jesus taught that in the story about the good Samaritan."

"You have answered correctly, for Jesus' own half-brother, James, wrote in the Word of God that we are to treat everyone the same. My father told me many times that the test of a man's character is how he treats those who can do nothin' for 'im. Those who know me often hear me tell stories about my mama, who was a Cherokee slave. When I was facin' a big decision, she would always give me the same advice: 'Joseph, ask yourself the question, "What would Jesus do?' I had to ask the Lord that question yesterday on Barber Creek."

Joseph paused for emphasis, then explained, " I fell to my knees and I asked Him, 'What would You have me do?' I then said, 'Lord, You don't have to answer that, because You gave me that answer already when I was a Cherokee slave many years ago, in my own family on my own property.' I grew up on the Cape Fear River in Bladen County, North Carolina. My father would often tell me, 'Joseph, see 'em boats? A risin' tide should lift all boats.' That's how he described the Golden Rule." Again he paused to give the congregation time to weigh that.

"The Lord then spoke to my heart yesterday, saying, 'My question to you, Joseph, is what are *you* going to do?' I'm now goin' to call a few men up to the front. Peter and William, would you mind comin' forward." Peter came forward quickly, but William was slow to cooperate.

"Gentlemen, would you mind showin' us your backs? Nothing immodest, please, but just lift your shirts a little.' The two men stood there stunned and did *not* do it. Pastor Willis then pulled out a whip from his travel bag. "Who would like to volunteer to lay one hundred stripes on the backs of these men?" The people gasped, and Joseph saw a few women put their hands over their mouths.

"Do I have a slave who wants to whip these men for disobeying my request?"

No one moved. Not one person came forward to take the whip from the preacher's hand. He stood there, looking at the faces of the men and women he had known for a long time. "Gentlemen, you may sit down now." Slowly, they did so.

"I came here in 1798, and I have watched this sin called *slavery* grow, and I have done nothin' to stop it. I have not spoken out against the horrible treatment of my brothers and sisters. I have allowed God's Word to be used against 'em. I have heard the tragic stories of families being torn apart and of lost children, and I have sinned by my silence. I was once a slave, but never again, and neither should any other man be!"

With that, Peter Tanner stormed down the aisle and pulled his wife out of the pew. In his anger, he proclaimed, "This preacher is senile and has lost his mind. I am not staying for any more of this nonsense." Several more got up and walked out after him. But, to Joseph's surprise, most did not. He continued to stand there, holding the whip.

The thunder that s u d d e n l y boomed outside was not as loud as inside. The storm clouds had opened, and the rain pelted the church building and the church body. Needing to say no more, Pastor Willis bowed his head and closed the service in a word of prayer. When he opened his eyes and looked at Solomon, he could detect a nod of affirmation, and when he looked upon Eliza, her eyes were dry, and she had one raised and seemed to be praising the Lord.

The news of that day's sermon spread throughout Rapides Parish like a wildfire. Brother Willis was one of the most talked about men in Central Louisiana, but he didn't care. He was at peace.

27

September 14, 1841
Joseph Willis's Home on Spring Creek
Babb's Bridge, Louisiana

In the weeks that passed since his sermon against slavery, Pastor Willis had experienced a variety of reactions. At his own home church, Amiable Baptist, four regular families no longer showed up, slave owners all. However, three new families got up early to travel long distances just to be in the service; each had some mixed blood in their family trees and had experienced the scorn of rejection and mockery. Surprising most of all was that two families from over at Spring Hill Baptist shared a wagon and rode all the way to Pastor Willis's church on Sundays.

One day about an hour after breakfast, Joseph was seated with his Bible studying a series of passages that were starting to form a relationship in his thinking. Before he could complete his studies, however, there came a knock at his front door.

Joseph found himself facing William Prince Ford and friends of his who represented regional churches established by the Methodists, other Baptists, the Presbyterians, and the Disciples of Christ.

Without batting an eye, Joseph waved the men inside, saying, "I've been saving some fresh-baked root chicory for a special occasion, so have a seat, gents, while my dear wife, Miss Elvy, sets it to boiling. Seems the longer I'm here, the more I grow to like that bitter taste."

William removed his hat and joined his friends in finding chairs to bring to the table. He looked at Joseph and said, "You don't act surprised to see a flock of clergymen at your home this mornin'."

"Well, I'm assuming they all didn't come so that I could convert them to bein' Baptists," said Joseph, "so I'm gonna speculate it has somethin' to do with my outspoken stance against slavery."

The men around the table gave a laugh, and one said, "Right on both counts."

William accepted coffee from Elvy, who served all of her

guests and then left the men to whatever their business-at-hand might be.

"I, personally, have worried for a long time about the legitimacy of slavery," said William, "and when you laid it out that Sunday morning, it sealed it for me. At first, my reaction was like that of my brother-in-law Peter, but I'm glad I stayed to show support for you. These men are like minded with me and with you."

The ministers nodded, said, "Amen to that," and "True, very true."

Pastor Willis leaned his elbows on the table and moved his gaze from man to man, then said, "If that is how we all feel, and that is what we all believe, and if despite our doctrinal differences that is what we feel our Bible tells us, why have we been so timid for so long in makin' this known?"

"I've made excuses for myself by saying my sermons have focused on *other* valuable lessons from the Holy Word," said one minister, "but I confess that it was cowardice on my part. I didn't want to be hated by my parishioners."

"As for me," said another preacher, "it was a fear of not being able to feed my family. The plantation owners contribute most to the collection plate each week. Without that steady stream of cash, I'd have no salary and the church could not be maintained. I shamefully turned a blind eye to how that money was being earned."

"I'm in a similar circumstance," explained another pastor. "Our national denomination has taken a strong stance against slavery where our churches are located in the northern states. However, here in the south and west, the members still endorse slavery. And, to keep me and others like me in line, they pay us in cotton gin receipts that we can only spend in stores owned and controlled by them. If I want a pair of shoes or a pound of coffee, I have to use cotton gin receipts. That actually *traps* me in my community."

Joseph nodded solemnly. He said, "I cannot fault you fellers 'cause I'm been as neglectful as y'all. I've made my stand, but I can tell you that this slavery question is going to impact the whole country...and sooner than later. There's already a movement afoot for us Baptists down here to break off from our brothers in the north. Our Home Mission Society was formed in 1832 and it is not sanctioning missionaries if they've been slave owners. So, folks down here are decidin' to form a separate mission board and to put its blessin' on whoever they feel fit to ordain and send forth. It's like people in Louisiana and Pennsylvania ain't even in the same country any more. Lots of division."

William eased sideways in his chair and cleared his throat. He said, "I believe you preachers have got a lot of decisions to make, and I don't envy you tryin' to find a balance between your conscience and your basic survival. But I need to take a moment and explain somethin' to Brother Willis here. On the mornin' of his sermon, he brought me up short for buying a slave woman when it meant separating her from her two children. He told me that I should have chased after that boy and girl and paid whatever the cost was so that they could stay with their mama."

"I'm sorry, William, but I still feel that way," asserted Joseph.

"And that's because everyone thinks I am rich," said William. "But I signed a bank note for my brother and used my wife's land as collateral, as well as the land my home rests on. Things have gone bad. My brother's wife died of small pox, some of his slaves came down with malaria and yellow fever, and there wasn't enough rain to sustain his crops. He was foreclosed on, and so was I. I'm fightin' to stay afloat."

Joseph seemed shocked. "But, you organized the big thanksgiving celebration and you had food and music. From all appearances you seemed to be thriving."

"And that's how fast things can change," said William, his face showing deep lines of worry and concern. "Since then—and I know you will be terribly upset to hear this news—I've had to pay my debts by selling eight of my slaves. One of 'em was Dradey, the one you call Eliza. Dradey was too depressed all the time, so she was no help to my wife Martha. I will probably have to sell Platt, my fiddler, too."

"I can hardly believe this," said Joseph. "You actually sold your slaves?"

William slumped. "I could sit here and tell you that my conscience bothered me so much, I did not want to be a slave owner any longer. And, to a point, that would be true. But, when facing reality, it came down to the necessity of raisin' money or being evicted from my home and land."

One of the ministers spoke up. "William came to us and told us about this slave woman and her children. If possible, we'd like to ease his burden of guilt by trying to reunite that little family. Maybe we can take up a collection or perhaps get word to the plantation owner who fathered those two children."

Joseph realized that this group of men was turning to him for leadership. He had been the first to take a stand as a preacher against slavery, so they admired him. Joseph knew that a few of these men had attended seminaries in the North and had obtained diplomas. He had none of that formal training. Nevertheless, they weren't looking right now for someone who could translate Hebrew or Greek. No, they were looking for someone who could set them on a path of redemption, new vision, and healing.

"We've got to settle one big issue first," said Joseph, "and then we can concentrate on important, but secondary, matters. Please wait here while I fetch somethin' from my study desk."

When Joseph returned, he was carrying papers.

"Friends, when I was a young preacher, and even before I was ordained, I was influenced by the Great Awakenin' preacher George Whitefield. He could do no wrong in my eyes. I read the letters that he sent to Benjamin Franklin after Franklin printed 'em, and I was greatly influenced by his thinkin'."

Joseph unfolded several parched, yellow, aged papers. "Let me just relay what Reverend Whitefield wrote in 1740 to his friend, Mr. Franklin, about the plantation owners' treatment of their slaves. 'God has a quarrel with you for your abuse of and cruelty to the poor Negroes.' Now, here's what Ben Franklin said of Whitefield: 'He excoriated the slave masters for mercilessly beating their laborers, and for failing to provide basic food and clothing for them. He also suggested that white Southerners were keeping the gospel of Christianity from the slaves for fear that salvation would make them restless for freedom.'"

Joseph explained, "Ya see, Whitefield thought they should be evangelized. That's why they took their slaves to church, and that's why the plantation owners do today. Whitefield believed that Negroes were the spiritual equals of whites, and that masters should not abuse their slaves. Gentlemen, I have always believed that, too.

"With all that said by Whitefield, he still believed it was all right to own slaves. In fact, he later owned a plantation with slaves. That's how many in the churches got the notion it was all right. I say to you all today, as Paul the Apostle said, 'Let God be true, but every man a liar.'"

The Presbyterian said, "Pastor, I've read those articles, too. I thought it was all right, so I bought slaves. I treated 'em right, was kind, and took 'em to church. Like Whitefield, I thought it was acceptable in God's eyes."

The Baptist said, "Whitefield wasn't alone. Thomas Jefferson, the writer of our own Declaration of Independence, owned slaves. And, he's not alone either. Eight out of our ten Presidents have owned slaves."

Joseph asked them again, "Gentlemen, how did we get to this point? Louisiana has become rich off the backs of slave labor, and it's wrong that I have not spoken out against it. I have sinned by omission. Not sure my words would have made a difference, but I know my silence has! Brothers, these are basically the same words I spoke a few weeks ago at Spring Hill that have caused all this upheaval. I might add I knew slavery was wrong in my heart of hearts. How could I have become so numb to it when I had been a Cherokee slave as a boy? We must never follow the crowd and lose the fact that we are called to be salt and light. Salt can heal, but it can sting, too. Our words must sting the conscience of Louisiana and heal the victims of slavery. Light always drives darkness away. Let us purpose to be the light in this darkness. If we don't, and Louisiana does not repent of this injustice, we can rest assured that God's favor will be lifted, and His rod of judgment may well fall upon our land."

Pastor Willis looked deep into the eyes of the men who sat around the table and said, "I believe we have gotten caught up in the religion of influence. I've watched worldliness and ambition break the spirit of our brothers and sisters whose skin is a different color. As a boy, I saw firsthand the arrogance of prejudice against my own family back in North Carolina because of my dark skin. Today, I see the same ungodly arrogance in some of our Louisiana neighbors and even a few of our own church members. I've seen it help destroy our nation's two great spiritual awakenings.

"Because we did not come together and voice our beliefs as the Body of Christ, the plantation owners have grown very rich, bought more slaves, and found bigger and better ways to get their cotton and sugar up North.

"It would appear that not only are our brothers and sisters slaves, but by tradition we are slaves as well. I do not say this to bring shame upon us. I speak the truth and do not know how to right this wrong. But, there is a wind startin' to blow—the wind of war. Mark my words, our children and our children's children will have to pay for our sins of silence."

No one spoke. Several of the men had tears in their eyes, and others sat stoically trying to put his words into perspective.

The youngest pastor, from the Disciples of Christ, said, "Pastor, I agree with you totally, but I have a family to feed. I cannot speak my mind freely and still put food on my table. I love my wife, and I have eight children to think about. Our founder, Alexander Campbell, has written against the terrible treatment of slaves in his *Millennial Harbinger*, but there has been much opposition to its circulation in Louisiana, and he lives in Virginia, not here."

The Methodist added, "We all agree. It's a shame that there are so many denominations today. Even though there are some things that divide us, there're also many things that unite us."

Joseph stood and spoke. "Ya know, Jesus healed the blind in different ways. He put spittle once on a blind man's eyes, and he could see. Another time he healed a blind man by usin' mud to anoint his eyes. And, Jesus even once just touched a blind man's eyes to give 'im his sight. In the religious age we live in today, out of that would have come three denominations: the spitites, the mudtites, and the touchites." Everyone laughed. "But seriously, gentlemen, we are surrounded by religion and spiritual blindness. The question remains, 'What would Jesus do?'"

They all agreed.

"I believe slavery is a sin, and for the rest of my days, I'm goin' to speak out against it to any and all who will listen."

William's face showed grave concern. "Pastor, have you thought about what men like Epps and Burns might do to you?"

"William, fear and faith do not mix well. They're like oil and water. The most often-mentioned words in the Bible are 'Fear not'— over 360 times, I've been told. Even if harm did come to me, that would only hasten my graduation day to glory. If God is for you, who can be against you?

Pastor Willis looked around at their faces and saw mixed expressions. He offered them more coffee and some spice cake Miss Elvy had baked early that morning. Wanting to establish a bond with these men, Joseph steered the conversation in ways to show personal interest in them. He had them talk about their families, their church work, their recent sermons, and what they did when not engaged in church activities. One man enjoyed helping with the garden. Another was a student of history. Another was trying to learn to speak French. Yet another did woodworking. Joseph did not turn the discussion back to slavery, but when the men rose to leave, he knew that they were of one mind on that subject. How they would deal with it was yet to be seen, but this day's meeting had been fruitful.

*   *   *

Joseph wanted to lead by example. He went to Amiable Baptist Church and preached another sermon that was anti-slavery. As before, some folks walked out, others stayed to listen and pray. A few days later word came to him that some of the area plantation owners feared his sermons were going to cause another slave revolt. They sent messengers telling him to stop talking about slavery as being against the teachings of the Bible.

When Elvy asked Joseph if he feared for his life, he smiled and told her he had been reading the story of Jeohshaphat. He was facing three mighty armies with a force of his own that was small in number and limited in military resources. In faith, he turned the battle over to the Lord, who delivered him and his soldiers.

Joseph said to his wife, "The Lord doesn't lose battles. Never. I'll let Him handle it."

"And what are you going to do in the meantime?" asked Elvy.

"Reckon I'll go down to Spring Creek, cut me a cane pole, and come back here later on with a mess of brim that we can have for supper."

28

October 24, 1841
Joseph Willis's Home on Spring Creek
Babb's Bridge, Louisiana

William rode up to Joseph's home early Sunday evening saying, "Pastor, may I have a moment with you? I know I'm interruptin' your day of rest, but this is real important."

"Come on in, William. Want some coffee, or perhaps a glass of buttermilk? Wish you had been here this mornin', 'cause Miss Elvy made her famous grits for breakfast. I sometimes feel I'm diggin' my grave with my fork with her fine cookin'."

"Coffee only, Pastor, 'cause I been up a long time." He looked to see if Miss Elvy was in hearing range and leaned in close to speak. "Pastor, seems there's trouble headed your way. Peter Tanner rode all the way from Bayou Boeuf to my home yesterday. He personally wanted me to know what happened Friday when he went to Bennett's General Store. He had walked over to buy some cotton sacks when Epps and Burns came ridin' up. They didn't see Peter walkin' over the bridge on Bayou Boeuf from his home, but he heard enough of their conversation to know they got some evil plans for you."

Joseph evidenced surprise. "That right? I thought Peter was mad at me."

"Well, he is, sorta…'bout the slavery issue, but he doesn't want any harm to come to you. He thinks of you as a 'pioneer,' and you have done a lot for everyone 'round here. That's why he came to tell Martha and me about what they're plannin'. Burns and Epps have concocted a plan to ambush ya. They're bringin' along a couple of riffraff they hired out of N'Orleans."

"William, when is all this comin' down?"

"When you leave for Amiable Baptist next Sunday, they are gonna ambush you on your way to church. They want to shut you up—for good."

Joseph got really quiet. "But, William…Miss Elvy, Samuel, and Aimuewell will be with me."

"They don't care, Pastor. They're bushwackin' cowards. They are gonna ambush ya 'bout a quarter mile from here, and they don't worry about who else gets hurt."

Joseph took a deep breath as he motioned for Miss Elvy to join them at the table.

"Miss Elvy, it seems there is goin' to be some unwanted visitors 'round here. You need to hear this."

Elvy wiped her hands on her apron and sat down.

"William, there have been two other times that the Lord has sent messengers to warn me of danger. Once was down in Vermilionville, when a friend, Jacques Cormier, warned me to flee because the religious folk there didn't like what I was preachin' and were gonna kill me to shut me up. Another was at an inn in No-Man's-Land when Malachi Perkins warned me to flee in the middle of the night 'cause two men were gonna ambush me for what little money I had. Today, you are the third messenger to warn me of danger. You risked your life and reputation to come here today, and I want to thank you."

Then Joseph fell silent, letting all this sink in. "I know it's time to leave and take Elvy and the boys across the Calcasieu to Tenmile Creek. William, we're gonna take the important things…but I'm leavin' one thing behind."

"What's that, Pastor?"

Joseph got up, walked to the mantle, and took down a large tin box and brought it over to the table, slowly opening it. "I started writin' down my journey in life many years ago, back in Bladen County, North Carolina, in this here journal. I want you to have it for future generations."

"But, Pastor, you have children who…."

Joseph looked at him like a father correcting his son. "William, I have already spoken to my sons and daughters, and they're all in agreement that you should hold this diary. It's a journal of the history of the events in my life. You are an educated man, church clerk. You love history, and you love the Lord. You are like a son to me." Joseph held the record in his hand as his fingers rubbed the familiar worn-leather cover.

William did not move quickly. "Pastor, I don't know what to say. I have learned much from you—you're my mentor. To think… your *entire life* is in this journal?"

Joseph winked and said, "Well, hopefully, not yet. There's still work to be done, but I'm eighty-three, and I have no promise of tomorrow, at least not here. Take good care of it."

"I will, sir, I will!" Tears welled up in William's eyes, and he had to look away. "Now, Pastor, about next Sunday...."

"I know!" Joseph sighed a breath of relief as he turned to Miss Elvy. "We need to start packin' soon."

William stood and walked to the door. Once outside, Joseph spoke. "William, I want to thank you again for comin' here today and warnin' me."

William reached to give me the right hand of Christian fellowship, but Joseph pulled him in to give him a big bear hug. "And please, tell Peter I'm grateful for his help, too! I know this could put him in harm's way."

"Pastor, I will. Take good care of yourself and your family."

Joseph watched him ride off down the red-dirt road and 'round the bend.

*   *   *

Five days later, the Willises loaded up the wagon and took the ferry across the Calcasieu River. They went straight to Johnson Sweat's home on Tenmile Creek. When Joseph explained what had happened, Johnson said, "I just finished buildin' this new home, but my old house, the one where you came a-courtin' Elvy, is empty. Why don't ya'll stay there?"

That next Saturday night, Epps, Burns, and the two scoundrels they'd hired from N'Orleans built their camp on Barber Creek, not far from Joseph's home. They were up and ready on Sunday mornin', but hours went by, and the Willises' wagon never rolled down the red-dirt road to church. After several uneventful hours, they decided to sneak up to Joseph's house and look around. It looked abandoned, but wagon tracks led toward the Calcasieu.

*   *   *

What happened next would always been attributed to the hand of the Lord by Pastor Willis. Two young boys from Spring Creek Academy were playing hooky and swimming in Barber Creek when they thought they saw some Indians. They heard all kinds of commotion just up around the bend of the creek. Cautiously, they crawled up on a sandbar and laid on their bellies to see what the commotion was about. What they saw was Epps and Burns and two other men changing out of Choctaw disguises and putting their regular clothes back on. The men were angry and arguing. They were yelling and making bets about who had warned the preacher about their plan. Thankfully, no one mentioned William or Peter.

The boys watched quietly, and one whispered, "That's Mr. Epps! My daddy told me 'bout him. He was at the feast of thanksgiving at Mr. Ford's plantation."

Now, these boys were in a bit of a pickle, because they knew they'd be in trouble for playing hooky if they told anyone what they had heard and seen. They also knew these men were up to no good. They did the right thing, though, and went and told their daddies.

The man who ran the ferry later gave Joseph more details about the story. He said that after the men got back in their regular clothes, they rode back to follow the wagon tracks and discovered that they led to his ferry at the Calcasieu. The younger man from N'Orleans sat in his saddle and shook his head, sayin', "I ain't crossin' this here river. You're not paying me enough to go into No-Man's-Land."

Epps and Burns just glared at 'em. Burns barked at the other man, 'You feel that way, too?"

"Yup! There are pirates, savages, and all kinds of outlaws over there."

"And you're not like any of 'em, right?" Burns had no time for their cowardly comments. "Epps, let's give 'em part of the money and be done with 'em."

"Wait, we want what you promised to pay us—*all of it*," said the thinner man.

"But, you didn't do anythin'."

"It's not *our* fault that the preacher didn't show up."

Epps responded, "You better be glad to be gettin' away with your lives!" With that, Epps pulled his gun out and took aim. The two quickly found out that Burns and Epps were as bad as any bandits in No-Man's-Land.

It took Epps and Burns a couple of days to ride back to

Bayou Boeuf, but by then the news had already spread all the way to the Red River. The story the two boys shared was carried from farm to farm, cabin to cabin, church to church. Epps and Burns denied taking part in any plan to do me harm, but everybody was talking about what happened and how they'd been seen. They told everyone who was in earshot, "We ain't killers! We're Southern gentlemen and planters. We're good Christians, just like the preacher." They were smart enough to steer clear of the Spring Creek area, though.

All was real quiet in Tenmile Creek for about two weeks, until William came riding up again, this time to where the Willis family had relocated.

"William, it's good to see you again so soon!"

"You, too, Pastor!" He slid off his saddle horse quickly like a man on a mission and tied his mare to a cedar tree. "Remember what we talked about a couple of weeks ago, at your ole home place at Babb's Bridge? Do you mind if we talk again?"

Joseph chuckled and said, "I heard they came dressed as Choctaws. Heard, too, they were spotted changin' clothes on Barber Creek by some young'uns from the academy. They should've known it would take more than a fake Indian to sneak up on a Cherokee."

William then noticed a stranger standing beside the pastor. "I don't mean to interrupt you and your guest. We can talk later."

The short, bearded man of about forty years spoke to William before Joseph could introduce them: "I hear tell that you're the third messenger."

William looked confused. "Pardon me?"

The stranger continued, "I'm the second messenger, Malachi Perkins."

He put his whittlin' knife down, stepped toward William, and shook his hand. "Brother Ford, everybody knows 'bout what those scoundrels tried to do, and their dastardly conduct has spread from the Red to the Sabine Rivers. But now that the cat is out of the bag, they don't dare come around these here parts."

William spoke directly to Joseph. "That's true, but nobody knows what I'm fixin' to tell ya now. Pastor, these men are comin' for you again! Don't know how, but they're comin'!"

Malachi asked William, "How do you know this?"

"I don't know Epps or Burns very well, but Ezra Bennett sure does. They go to his store often to buy supplies and get their mail, and he told me last week that this isn't over. He said, 'I'm not sayin' they *did* or *didn't* do it, but I do know men like Epps and Burns will never let it end until it is finished.'"

William looked at me with concern and continued, "They told Mr. Bennett that you're puttin' a hurtin' on their money, and you're leavin' 'em no choice but to stop you. They think your words are gonna cause a slave revolt. They think if men like them don't make an example of you to the other preachers, then others might start preachin' 'gainst slavery, too. They won't have it. I believe Mr. Bennett's right. *They're coming!*"

"What do you mean, *'They're* comin'?'" Malachi asked. "We all know what *they* look like. Let 'em come. We'll be havin' a little meetin' here in a couple of days 'bout 'em. Care to stay and join us?"

"Thanks for your offer." William thought for a moment and nodded. "I told Martha I wasn't sure how long my trip might take, so I might just do that." William then looked at Joseph and asked, "So, what are you gonna do, Pastor?"

"Ya mean right now, William?"

"Well, yes, sir."

"William, the Bible says, 'Be still and know that I am God.' Maybe I'll get some fishin' in…but I'll be still while I fish. You can catch more fish that way—and plantations owners, too. Wanna go with me?"

William considered that and replied, "I will feel better if I'm at your side these next few days. So, yes, let's set some hooks."

29

November 1, 1841
Johnson Sweat's Home
Tenmile Creek, Louisiana

Malachi sent out runners to announce a meeting. The day was a busy one! Several local men brought smoked turkeys and venison. Squash had come into season, and it was baked to perfection. The house was filled with the smell of freshly baked cornbread.

It was late afternoon when Malachi welcomed one old Choctaw. As he invited him in. The Indian greeted Pastor Willis by name, who didn't immediately recognize him.

The Choctaw spoke English well. "Pastor, we heard that those *hatak haksi,* or as you say, bad men, dressed up like us."

Joseph looked at him with confusion. "Friend, where do I know you from?"

"You did good for me, up on the Ouachita. When sick, you hunted *issi* for food. You saved life of wife, Ohoyo, when our didanawisgi did no good. I come to pay back."

Before Joseph could respond, there was another knock, and Malachi opened the door. An old Cherokee entered with a younger one and nodded to Joseph, saying, "Osiyo."

Joseph replied, "Ostu iga." They looked at each other, studying the lines and wrinkles that seemed to map out two lives filled with adventures and the cares of life.

The old Cherokee said, "Pastor, we have come to help. The words you spoke changed my life and my Ageya's life. I was at the funeral when you buried your little girls, Ruth and Naomi. I stood far away with my brothers. This is my grandson, Degotoga. I wanted 'im to meet you."

"Siyo, Degotoga. What does your name mean?"

"Sir, it means *standing together.*" The young man moved closer to his grandfather.

Joseph was filled with humility. "I thought so. That's what we need today."

Elvy came forward. "Please, everyone, I've made cornbread, bacon, coffee and other food. Join us."

Joseph had never provided a favor or service to anyone with the intention of one day calling it back. Nevertheless, here were people showing up to provide aid to him in his hour of need because years ago he had been a servant to them. He thought of how King David provided a life of comfort for the crippled son of Jonathan because David never forgot the loyal friendship of Jonathan.

Elvy poured Joseph a fresh cup of coffee, and as he sat enjoying it three more strangers entered the home. Malachi spoke to each of 'em as they made their way over to the table.

"Pastor, we're printers, and we're here to lend a hand!"

Another man in the room wrinkled up his forehead and quickly asked, "Printers of what?"

No one responded for a moment, then the man resumed his introduction. "I know he knows what we print. Brother Willis, you probably don't remember this, but before I got into *this* trade, I came to you when we needed food for our children. You went out to your corn crib and got some vegetables, a barrel of molasses, browned flour, and you gave us milk from your Jersey cow. I've never forgotten! This here is my son, Joseph. I named 'im after you."

One after another folks arrived and shared their connection to old Joseph. Seated next to Joseph was William, and he listened carefully as people reminded the preacher of how he had crossed paths with them. Of special interest was a man who walked with a cane and had long, greyish hair tied back with a piece of rope. He walked slowly toward Joseph with measured steps. He looked the preacher straight in the eyes.

"Reckon we're about the same age, and not sure what I can do to assist, but I'm here 'cause of a friend of yours and mine I knew down in N'Orleans back when I sailed with Jean Lafitte. He talked good things 'bout you and said he'd come runnin' if ya ever needed 'im. Preacher, Jim Bowie respected ya. He can't come runnin' with that big knife now, since the Alamo, but I can be here for 'im."

Malachi said, "I'm sure we can use you. Always admired Lafitte after he helped General Jackson defeat those Brits in the Battle of N'Orleans."

"I was there!" The old pirate smiled a toothless grin. "And

you're right, General Jackson did help us give 'em there Redcoats a good whippin'. I know these bayouques like the back of my hand and every alligator by name. My boots are made from one alligator that tried to have me for supper." He limped over to the bench, sat, and helped himself to some pipin'-hot filé gumbo.

They kept coming in. Each time the door opened, Joseph wondered which chapter from his life he would experience next.

Then, some rough-looking cowhands lumbered in. They had guns on their hips, and they looked like they could whip a black bear with a switch. Malachi spoke quietly to them and then brought them over to talk.

The roughest-looking one, with black, curly hair and a scar on his left cheek, asked, "Preacher, do you remember me?"

"My eyes are not what they used to be, my memory neither. I've got sometimer's disease: sometimes I can remember, and sometimes I can't."

"When my little girl was real sick, you came and prayed for her on your knees by her sick bed, and she got well."

The other added, "My son died of the yellow fever, and times were hard. We had no money to bury my boy, and we were hungry. You took care of everything and then invited us into your home and fed us. It didn't matter to you that I was an outcast. You treated me and my family with kindness. You never condemned us."

Words caught in Joseph's throat. He wasn't feeling proud, but he felt he was being given a sign from the Lord of what it would be like one day in heaven when he would stand before the judgment seat of Christ. His work in Louisiana had not been for naught. Today was tangible evidence of that.

*   *   *

In total, some fifteen men assembled that day. They kicked around ideas on how to handle the pending invasion by the forces of Burns and Epps. After the humiliating ordeal of the fake Indian ambush, no one believed those two men would physically be part of any new threat. But they would plan and fund it.

One of the cowhands spoke up: "This ain't no Bayou Boeuf,

Cheneyville, or Bayou Chicot. This here's No-Man's-Land. Neither of those scoundrels would be crazy enough to show his face here."

Another said, "My gut feelin' is they'll hire some outsiders to do the dirty work. Ain't hard to find drifters wantin' to make some easy money."

Speculation and debate continued until Joseph stood and raised his hands for silence. "I welcome you all, friends. With those who were already here and those of you who have arrived this mornin', I believe we're about thirty strong. Before we make any plans of action, I want to share a favorite story of mine. I call it 'The Fourth Man in the Fire.' If you've heard me preach it before, consider it a reminder."

At hearing Joseph's confident voice, many in the group started to feel more at ease. But others—men who had been involved in skirmishes, battles, and brawls—maintained an attitude of vigilance.

30

November 15, 1841
Johnson Sweat's Home
Tenmile Creek, Louisiana

Joseph had thanked everyone who had come to meet with him in response to Malachi's runners. He said that if he felt threatened, he would sound the alarm and ask for their support. Two weeks then passed with no one making an attempt to harm Joseph or his family. But just as it seemed the threat had passed, a new warning came by way of a stranger on horseback.

Malachi and Joseph were seated on the front porch when a man wearing a gunslinger's holster came riding up on a lathered chestnut mare. Both rider and horse seemed hot, tired, and dirty.

The man dismounted, and with breathless words announced, "I need to find the preacher Joseph Willis. I have to speak with 'im."

"Not wearin' that sidearm, you ain't," said Malachi. "Who are you, stranger?"

"I understand," said the man. He unbuckled his belt and holster and wrapped it around his gun, then put it away in his saddlebag. "It's vital that I speak to Joseph Willis."

"I'm Pastor Willis. Come up here and sit with us. You look tuckered."

"I am, indeed, tuckered, but I'm relieved to know that I got to you first."

"First?" said Malachi. "What do you mean by that?"

"Fact is, I've been ridin' hard from Nacogdoches to warn you there are three outlaws on their way to harm you."

"And you would know this because…?" asked Malachi.

"I met 'em two years ago in San Augustine County, Texas, during the Regulator-Moderator War. I was hired by one of the Moderators, Edward Merchant. The three of 'em were workin' for the Regulators, Charles Jackson and Charles Moorman. The feud is still ragin'. Vigilantism is the only form of justice, so our kind of work is in high demand. I left Louisiana to make a better livin' in East Texas."

Joseph nodded his understanding. "Son, I know well about

that feud. The roots of it began here in No-Man's-Land, with fraud and land swindlin'. I met Charles Jackson once in Natchez when he was a Mississippi riverboat captain. He's a fugitive from Louisiana justice now. I hear tell he shot a man named Joseph Goodbread last year and then organized the Regulators to prevent cattle rustling."

The rider responded, "That's the pot callin' the kettle black. The news out of Texas is that the hostilities escalated four months ago, at Jackson's trial."

"Anyway, son, what does all that have to do with me?"

With narrowing eyes he informed us, "A man by the name of Epps hired these three outlaw assassins. They're 'bout two days' ride behind me. You need to be ready for 'em. They're good with their guns. They're a bad lot...been known to shoot men in the back."

"This fellow here is my friend Malachi, but you haven't told me your name."

"Cormier, sir," he replied. "Theo Cormier."

Joseph paused and then asked, "Might you be any kin to a man named Jacques Cormier from Vermilionville?"

Theo looked amazed. "Why, you're talkin' about my grandpappy." He waited a beat then said, "I'll be danged. I may know of you, sir. In your younger days, did folks call you the Barefoot Preacher?"

Joseph smiled, "They truly did, and it was because your grandpa was a messenger who helped me escape from some religious folks who intended to do me harm because they did not like what I was preaching. I hustled away so fast, I didn't even have time to lace my shoes or put on my socks."

"You had a lot of nicknames," said Theo. "My grandfather and others called you the Apostle to the Opelousas. He truly admired you. And I feel honored that I can be of service to you now."

Joseph put a hand on Theo's shoulder. "You sit here a minute while I go inside and get you something cool to drink. Then I want you to start from the beginning and tell Malachi and me how you came to know about these hired guns who are comin' to put me in my grave."

Epps rode into Nacogdoches after a long and dusty ride. But it was obvious from his countenance that he was a man on a mission. When he put up his horse, he asked an old timer at the livery stable, "If a fella was lookin' for someone good with a gun, where might he go to find 'im?"

"The Dirty Dog Saloon is your best bet."

"And who might he ask for?"

"That's easy. Theo Cormier. He's the fastest with a gun, and he packs a big knife, too. He's proved his skills time and time again, but if you don't rile him, he's a pretty affable fellow."

Epps left his horse and went into the saloon, where he asked the bartender, "Where can I find Theo Cormier?"

The bartender tilted his chin and pointed. "He's sittin' over there playin' poker. Can't miss 'im. He's the one with the Bowie knife on his belt and the low-slung pistol."

Epps approached him. "Excuse me, Mr. Cormier, might we speak in private?"

Cormier did not look up from the cards he was holding.

"Let me finish playin' this hand. Lady Luck been smilin' a bit on me today and I do believe Mr. Derkins over here has called me." Cormier laid down four sixes and a king. The other three men at the table folded their cards in disgust. Cormier smiled as he gathered up a huge stack of money, gladly folded it, and abandoned his chair.

Cormier asked Epps, "How can I help you, stranger?"

"Can we talk in private?"

They moved over to a table on the far side. Epps introduced himself. "My name is Edwin Epps, and I've got a job for a man with your skills."

"What kind of job?"

"I have a problem, and I need someone to take care of this here...umm...problem for me. Heard you were pretty good at what you do."

"Well, you just saw me clean out those fellers at the table," said Cormier, "so if it's a card shark you need, then I may be your man. But I'm guessing you're probably talkin' about higher stakes.

Does this *problem* of yours carry a gun?"

"Nope, he don't carry a gun at all." Epps moved to the edge of his wooden chair. "Look, I'm willin' to pay ya good money to take care of this for me."

"What's your problem's name?"

"Willis. His name is Joseph Willis, and he's gone to ground in No-Man's-Land."

Theo scowled and got a strange feeling in the pit of his stomach. "You mean the Louisiana parson, Joseph Willis? The preacher friend of Jim Bowie?"

Now it was Epps's turn to look confused. "Yes, they were friends. But Bowie's dead."

He spoke sternly to Epps and shook his head. "Ya got the wrong card player, mister. I don't know this man personally, but I heard of him. Can't see how he's done anyone any harm. No, I ain't gonna take care of no parson problem."

Epps tried to back off a bit. "Oh, Mr. Cormier, I didn't mean to kill 'im. I just wanted you to scare 'im."

"Sure, and you're gonna pay a lot of money just to scare somebody! I doubt you rode all the way to Texas just to hire someone to scare that old man."

Epps began sweating l i k e a L o u i s i a n a politician in church as he tried to clean up his newest mess. He saw no evidence of a sheriff or peacemaker in this town, but he didn't want to be found out about his plans. It had been bad enough when he and Burns and the two men he hired had bungled the ambush. He didn't need a repeat of that.

"Hey, you ain't gonna tell the pastor about this, are ya?"

"Epps, I ain't got no dog in this here fight. I don't even know 'im. Never met 'im."

He went back to his poker game but kept one eye on Epps.

Epps walked up to the bar. The bartender had seen him with Theo and asked, "You and Cormier friends?"

"Old friends. I had some work for 'im, but unfortunately he's busy. You know someone else who might be in the same line of work as Cormier?"

"Well, I know some Mexican *hombres* that might. Not as good as Theo, but they'd probably help ya. "

Epps looked around to find them. The bartender just laughed

and said, "Don't serve their kind here. They're down at Los Cuchos. Be careful down there! Lots of crazy fights over nothin'." The bartender laughed again. "Go on down there, and you'll find the brothers, Fernando and Julio, drinkin' mescal no doubt."

Epps laid a coin on the counter and nodded his thanks to the barkeeper. He walked down the street and located the cantina. He found the Fernandez brothers and laid out his proposition. They listened carefully and seemed to be interested until he said the intended target was a minister. Cold-blooded as they may have been, Julio and Fernando wanted no part in killing someone they considered to be a priest. "*Es muy malo*," said Julio. "Very bad. We dun't kill no padre."

Feeling frustrated, Epps went back to the livery stable to talk to the old man and get another suggestion. "You said Cormier was the best, but who is second best? I've been down to that Mexican watering hole, and that didn't work either."

The old man played with his grey mustache and smirked. "Who sent you to that cantina?"

"Bartender."

"Ya could've been killed there for blinkin' an eye. You're a lucky man. I know another feller who has two bad friends. They're in the same line of work as Cormier, but without his scruples, and they're here in town today. They're good with a gun. They're just plain ole no-good cowpunchers that made a name in the Regulator-Moderator War. Go back to the Dirty Dog, and look for a bald headed, beady-eyed man named Scar Bartholomew, with two friends who are so ugly they'd scare a funeral up an alley. He wears a bull-hide hat most of the time. I hear tell he stole that bull."

Epps went back to the saloon and found the men standing at the bar. From the scar on his cheek, it was obvious who Bartholomew was. Epps approached him and said, "It's been a long day, and it hasn't been a good one. Can I buy you and your friends a drink?"

They all nodded and one by one said to the bartender, "Make it a double of your best whiskey!" Epps motioned them to a table at the back and they all took seats. Bolstered by the effects of a brandy he had ordered and swallowed in two gulps, Epps told the three men of his needs.

Bartholomew reflected a moment, then said, "I heard tell of this Willis fellow. He's got a reputation. Lots of people hold him in high regard. Getting' rid of someone like that is gonna take some special effort. We can do it, but it's gonna cost ya."

"How much?" asked Epps.

"I'll need two thousand for my fee and all the plannin' and travel expenses, plus a thousand each for my two partners here. Half up front and the rest when you get word that the job is done. Sound fair?"

"I can pay that upfront amount today, and I'll meet you in Alex for the balance of payment when the deed is done."

The next day, as Epps's newly hired assassins were preparing to head to Tenmile Creek, Theo Cormier walked into the stable.

"You boys takin' a trip?"

"Yup, we got us a nice job over in Tenmile Creek, Louisiana. Supposed to take care of some problem. The feud is a little slow this week, and *this* pays much better."

Theo nodded. "Heard the problem's a preacher."

They looked surprised, and Scar asked, "How'd ya hear that?"

"Epps asked me first, but I turned 'im down. Been havin' a good run with the cards and don't want to quit while I'm hot. You boys watch yourselves in No-Man's-Land. It ain't no *Tejas*!"

They finished packing and asked Theo, "You're from over that way. What's the best trail to take? We're thinkin' 'bout takin' the El Camino Real, then south along the Arroyo Hondo, and then over to Tenmile. What do you think?"

Theo smiled. "It'll do."

"See ya in a couple of weeks, Cormier. No hard feelin's that we're not on the same side in the feud. Tell your boss we'll change sides if he'll pay us more.'

*   *   *

Normally, Theo Cormier wasn't a man of strict conscience. If he was hired to protect someone, he'd do the job. He didn't care about the man's politics or family history or business. It was just a job, as far as he was concerned. But something about this planned murder of the old parson didn't sit well with him.

He went back to his room and pulled out some old letters from Jim Bowie. He sat there and read one of them three or four times. In it, Bowie told the story of how he and his friend Brother Willis had tossed a rogue preacher into the Red River after the scoundrel tried to kill Willis with a fancy pistol. That settled it for Theo. He decided right then and there he should warn Brother Willis. Any friend of Jim's was his friend, too.

He went to the stable, got his saddle horse, and asked the man at the livery stable for the quickest way to Tenmile. Wasn't long before Theo lit out on the Texas Road to Burrs Ferry on his way to Tenmile Creek.

He was told if he could find an old Choctaw trail to the north of Tenmile, it would make his trip even shorter. He started down an Indian trail but felt uncertain of his choice. He finally saw several Choctaws riding up ahead. They saw him, stopped, and circled him. Theo was concerned but spoke: "Do you speak any English or French? I'm 'fraid I might be gettin' lost. Can you help me? I'm in a hurry…I need to get to Tenmile Creek. "Lookin' for a preacher named Joseph Willis?"

They watched his movements very carefully. "Why you go see Willis?"

"I have important information for 'im. He's in danger!"

The Choctaws took notice of the weapons Cormier was wearing. Maybe he was coming as a friend, but maybe he was coming to do harm to their friend. They decided to accompany this stranger.

"We'll take you to 'im. He is a friend. We will trust the Great Spirit of the preacher to make journey safe."

"Thank that spirit!" Theo spoke under his breath, but there were only a few who heard him and smiled. Theo and the Choctaw got to Tenmile two days ahead of the three outlaws. After Theo shared his story, Malachi asked the Choctaw, who had turned out to be a huntin' party, to warn everyone that Joseph was in harm's way.

31

November 15, 1841
Johnson Sweat's Home
Tenmile Creek, Louisiana

Theo was exhausted after his long, hard trip and slept well that night. With the news that Malachi sent out the day before, people began showing up by sunrise from as far away as the Red River. In the morning Joseph took a cup of hot coffee Elvy had made and went out on the porch. He was amazed to see the field filling up with folks of all ages.

In one sense it was exciting to see all those people, but it was also a mite unsettling, too, for they arrived from every corner and were armed with guns, knives, and even pitchforks.

Malachi walked out amongst the group and greeted them. It was early afternoon when he came back to talk to Joseph about his plan. He had sent a few scouts to send back a warning of the outlaws' arrival. Malachi's plan was for everyone to come together just before dawn the next morning and for them to wait for the outlaws at the ferry crossing on the Calcasieu.

"Don't you worry, Pastor," he said. "We're gonna take care of all of this for ya."

"I'm goin' with ya'll, Malachi," Joseph insisted.

Malachi stared at his friend for a moment. "Pastor, can I talk ya out of that?"

"Not hardly! Remember that old paintin' in the inn where you gave me the warnin'? The one with Daniel in the lions' den."

"Yes, Pastor, I do remember."

"What was Daniel lookin' at?"

"As I remember, Pastor, he was lookin' at the light."

"That's right, Malachi. He wasn't lookin' at the lions. Neither am I."

*   *   *

The next morning came quickly and quietly. Joseph was somewhat caught off-guard to see that a couple of women had joined the group since the previous night. He raised his eyebrows at their rather loud comradery. They were hanging on a gentleman's arms. Joseph remembered the man from meeting him on the Riverboat *Rodoph* on the Red River.

Joseph gestured for the man to come over. He quickly came forward with his lady friends. Malachi asked him, "Didn't see you last evening. How long ya been here?"

"Just arrived from Alexandria. You were always kind to me, Pastor Willis, every time I saw you. No other preacher was, what with knowin' I'm a scamp who plays the cards and likes the ladies."

Joseph was a bit perplexed. He asked, "Is that all I did?"

"That was a lot to me at the time. Besides, I can't stand Epps. He cheated me once in a gentleman's game of chance on the Riverboat *Rodoph*."

Malachi asked the gentleman, "Have you known your lady friends long?"

"Not really. I met 'em at a poker game. We had a bet on a single cut of the cards. High card wins. If I won, they had to come. As you can see, I won." With a wink, he added, "Forgot to tell ya, I had the honor of cuttin' the deck."

Malachi spoke to all of them. "Well, thanks for comin'." But he added under his breath as the three walked back into the crowd, "Preacher, is he one of your converts?"

Joseph mumbled just loud enough for Malachi to hear, "God only knows."

Miss Elvy caught Joseph's attention. He went over to her. She took his hand. He could feel her trembling.

"Pastor Joseph Willis, I know there's a lot going on right now, but I want you to know just how much I love you. I know I've fallen pitifully short on the obey thing, but there is no one whom I respect and trust more."

"Miss Elvy, I love you, too." He could see that look of concern on her face. "Are you worried about this here meetin'? Ya know, everything's gonna be all right. Their weapons will not prosper, nor can they."

"Yes, I believe that, but I could never forgive myself if I didn't say those words…especially if something goes wrong."

She put her head on her husband's chest, and for a moment

he just stood there and held her. He could see lots of stirring out there and could feel the stirring in Elvy's and his hearts. *Why does it take somethin' like this to get us to tell the one we love just how much we care?*

Anxiety and tension hung heavy in the air as a group of about two hundred men and a couple of women started moving toward the Calcasieu in buggies and wagons, on horses and mules, and even some on foot. Malachi again, and now Theo, tried to persuade Joseph not to go.

Theo said, "Pastor, I don't think it's a good idea for you to go with us. It's just too dangerous. This kind of work is not for a preacher, not to mention your...."

"Theo, I'm goin'! See Ole Sally standin' there like an oak? We once swam the mighty Mississippi together. We haven't lost but 'bout half a step since then." Ole Sally turned her head and gave me one of her looks. "Well...maybe a full step." She backed her ears and looked at him again. "All right, ole girl, maybe two. But Theo, to me she's still a high-stepper—a real thoroughbred! And I'm just now gettin' into my prime."

Theo grinned and said, "Pastor, now I see why my grandpappy admired you so much."

When the sun finally came up, it was amazing to see all those determined faces. They were lined up deep and wide. It was about mid-morning when the group reached the halfway point to the ferry crossing. One of the scouts came riding down the trail from the Calcasieu. "They'll be at the ferry in 'bout two hours, so you need to hurry. There's three of 'em armed to the teeth."

Like Moses leading the children of Israel, Joseph pressed his entourage forward. They reached the ferry a mere fifteen minutes before the outlaws. The talking had stopped, and there was hardly a sound to be heard as the crowd approached the ferry.

Hoping that an envoy might serve to diffuse the conflict, Joseph signaled for Theo to approach the three men. He rode out and came to a stop before them.

"Nice to see you 'gain, boys. What was it you said in Nacogdoches as to what and why you were comin' here?"

Scar hesitated for a moment, then said, "We're here to...to buy some cattle. You remember, don't ya? Theo, I had no idea you were headed to this neck of the woods, too. What are *you* doin' here? Who are all these people?"

"Oh, these are just a few of preacher Joseph Willis's friends. We're here to hang some misguided cattlemen from Texas who are comin' to do him harm. I hear tell they're wanted in Texas, so the law's on our side. Might even be a reward. But, that doesn't matter here in No-Man's-Land. Here they just hang those kind and ask questions later."

The three men surveyed the mob, taking note of dozens of pistols, rifles, knives, pitchforks, hanging ropes, bullwhips, and even bows and arrows. The trio acted as if they'd just heard Ole Sally talk.

Theo continued, "I reckon your cattle business is 'bout done here in Louisiana, ain't it?"

All three shook their heads. Scar confirmed, "Yes, sir. Our business here is over."

"Thought so! By the way, are ya comin' back to these parts to buy any more cattle in the future?"

"No. I think we're gonna buy 'em over in Waterloo, Texas, on the Shawnee Trail. You know the town, but I hear they changed the name to Austin two years ago. Prices are low there for longhorns, and we hear tell they fetch good money in some parts."

"How do you know so much about the cattle business? I heard tell that you acquired some longhorns recently, for next to nothin'…more like free." Theo just stared at Scar and his friends. "Anyway, good to know ya don't got plans to come back this way again."

"None I can think of."

"Good choice. If ya ever have another hankerin' to come back *here* to buy cattle, I'll be seein' ya 'gain in Nacogdoches, and we'll be havin' a little talk *outside* the Dirty Dog about the high cost of Louisiana cows. Scar, ya got that?"

"I got it, Theo. When I was a little boy, you could slap the kid sittin' next to me in school, and I picked it up."

They turned their horses around and started to leave. Scar stopped and turned back. "That Joseph Willis must be quite a man, to have this many friends. I would like to meet 'im someday…but not on any cattle-buyin' trip."

Before anyone could stop the preacher, he gave Ole Sally a cue with his legs to moved forward. "I'm Joseph Willis!"

"Well, I'll be!" Scar took his hat off and sat there a few moments, looking at the country preacher sitting tall in the saddle while Ole Sally backed her ears as far as she could.

Brother Willis wasted no time. "Are you ready to meet the Lord?"

"No, sir. Why do you ask?"

"'Cause you came mighty close to meetin' Him today. I'll pray you'll have a safe trip back to Texas, young man, and that you get out of the cattle-buyin' business. Give my regards to Mr. Epps."

Scar put his hat back on, laughed, and rode off with the other two. With the conflict averted, Joseph thanked everyone for their support and bade them a good day and sent them home.

Later that afternoon Theo, Malachi, and Elvy were on the porch, visiting and sipping tea. The preacher suggested quietly to Theo, "How 'bout if we take a little walk down by Tenmile Creek? I'd like to talk to you about your grandfather."

"Sure, Preacher."

They made their way down to the creek, and Joseph asked, "Theo, do you know Jesus?"

"Pastor, my grandpappy said Jesus had bought my ticket to heaven. If I've been pardoned like he said, why should I do anything?"

"Theo, a dozen years ago in 1829, there was a man named George Wilson who was found guilty and given the death sentence for murder. But, Wilson had some friends who petitioned President Andrew Jackson for a pardon. Jackson granted the pardon, and it was brought to prison and given to Wilson. To everyone's surprise, Wilson said, 'I am going to hang.'

"There had never been a refusal to a pardon, so the courts didn't know what to do. The case went all the way to the Supreme Court, and Chief Justice John Marshall gave the ruling. I keep a copy of it in my wallet. Let me read to you what Marshall wrote: 'A pardon is a piece of paper, the value of which depends upon the acceptance by the person implicated. If he does not accept the pardon, then he must be executed.' God loves you, Theo, and, yes, He has provided a pardon for you and me, paid for with Christ's own life-blood, but you have the right to refuse the pardon. Jesus was crucified between two thieves. One thief said yes to Jesus, but the other said no to Him. One accepted the pardon, and the other refused it. The question to you and me today is the same as it was 1,800 years ago: which thief on the cross are you? The one who said yes to Christ's pardon or the one that said no to His pardon? I have chosen to say yes. Theo, you have the same choice."

"Pastor, you have given me much to think about on my way back to Texas."

"Son, I'm not going to talk to you as a preacher now, but as a friend of your grandfather's. I knew him real well. He was a good, honest man. I don't know how you got into this line of work, but I know he would want me to tell you to find some other way to make a livin'. This is not going to end well for you, and you have a good family name to pass on."

"I hear ya, Pastor, and I'll give it some thought. But, most preachers I've known just wanted my money, and I just can't stand those Christians who say one thing and do another. I once went to hear John Murrell, that man you and Jim Bowie threw overboard into the Red River. He said he loved Jesus and then stole my horse. That's why I came to warn you, after readin' Jim's letter about what you and Jim did to 'im. The French call people like Murrell an *ipocrite*. The English call 'em hypocrites. What do you call 'em, Preacher Willis?"

"Lost! Theo, there will come a day when you will meet Jesus. He will not ask you if you put your trust in Murrell, me, a church, religion, denomination, or any other person. He will ask you why you refused to put your trust in Him after He gave His life-blood for you. Ask yourself, how has He wronged you? How has He deceived you?"

Theo remained silent. Joseph reached into his side pocket, pulled out a Bible, and handed it to him. "I want you to read this. It will help you find your way."

Theo took the Bible, smiled, and said, "Just for you, I'm gonna put this in the inside pocket of my new coat...right over my heart. I'll keep it here, in honor of you and my grandpappy."

32

May 19, 1843
Edwin Epps's Plantation
Near Holmesville, Louisiana

Edwin Epps and his co-conspirator Jim Burns failed in both of their attempts to waylay and kill Pastor Joseph Willis. Not only had both endeavors resulted in personal humiliation, they also had cost the men thousands of dollars in wasted expenses. Each blamed the other for the outcome, with Burns faulting Epps for drinking secret sips of brandy from his saddlebags during the thanksgiving celebration at William Prince Ford's plantation and thus causing him to speak brashly, overconfidently, and stupidly. Epps, counterpointed this by blaming Burns for behaving so obviously dastardly to his slaves, everyone in the community immediately knew who to suspect if there was a plot to close the mouth of anyone—including a preacher—who spoke out against slavery. The two men screamed at each other, made threats, yelled, cursed, and shook fists, but in the end, they both knew they were defeated. Neither ever again tried to plan an assault on Brother Willis, and Burns and Epps made it a point never to see each other or talk to each other the rest of their lives.

But that did not mean they stop harboring hatred toward Joseph Willis or anyone who called him "friend." And each found ways to make life miserable for such individuals.

*   *   *

Edwin Epps came to own Solomon, the fiddle playing slave, in May of 1843. Epps as a very large, portly man with high cheekbones and a huge nose. He had cold blue eyes, thinnin' hair, and he stood a full six feet tall. Solomon considered his new master to be repulsive, coarse, without manners, and clearly a poorly educated man who used vulgarity whether sober or drunk. With the possible exception of his former partner Jim Burns, Epps was the cruelest man Pastor Willis or William Prince Ford or the slave Solomon ever knew. And, sadly, he was Solomon's owner and master for nine years.

Joseph Willis had only seen Solomon once since William had been forced to sell him to cover overwhelming debts. It was on a trip back to Evergreen to preach at Bayou Rouge Baptist Church. After the service, Ole Sally and Joseph traveled through Holmesville on their way to Bayou Chicot to preach a funeral. Little did Joseph know that journey would take him right by Epps's plantation on Bayou Boeuf. After stopping to water Ole Sally in the bayou, there stood Solomon. Joseph saw a couple of other slaves step out of the trees with heavy iron collars around their necks.

As Solomon approached the preacher, Joseph could see lash scars from Epps's whip. "What are all those bruises on your neck...and those cuts on your arms?"

"I'd rather not say, if you don't mind, sir."

"Solomon, I insist. Please, tell me how this happened."

"Well, sir...Master Epps got drunk 'bout a week ago. It was rainin' real hard. The thunder was crackin' every few seconds. We had all been sleepin' for several hours when he barged in and started screamin' at us, 'Get up, you no-good, lazy niggers! You got some work to do.' He was so drunk that he slurred his words, but we still understood 'im. In his hand was his favorite whip, and he made it crack—almost as loud as the thunder. 'Get outside and line up. We're goin' for a ride.'

"I stepped up and asked if he wanted the team of horses made ready, but he just laughed at me and said, 'Get all the harnesses and bridles, and bring 'em to me.' Runnin' to the barn for fear of bein' whipped, I made quick time to meet all of Master Epps's demands.

"He began sortin' out all the tack and told us to get over to his carriage. He roped us together...got real mad when the horses' harnesses were too big for us. He then cracked his whip and told us we were gonna pull his carriage.

"There was so much mud that we could hardly get any footin'. Each time we slid or fell, we felt the lash of his whip. He screamed for us to go faster and got mad when we couldn't do it! He kept drinkin' and cussin' and crackin' that whip on us. This went on for a couple of hours, until Master Epps passed out in his covered carriage. We all went back to our cabins and tried to get dry. We heard 'im holler a few more times, and everybody froze, but he never came back into the cabins again that night...except for Patsey."

"This is a mighty hard life for you, Solomon," said Joseph. "I've taken a stand against slavery, but I'm just a voice in the wilderness."

"Master Epps don't know that I can read, so sometimes he leaves his newspapers where I can see them," said Solomon. "Lots of talk about folks in the North wantin' to force southerners to free all the slaves. Whenever anyone asks Master Epps about it, he always says, 'Over my dead body.' And, tell you the truth, Pastor, I believe that's where this is all headed. I think it may lead to a war."

Joseph grimaced and said, "I've read the same articles and editorials, and it breaks my heart to have to agree with you. I fought in a war. Even when you're the winner, you're the loser. Lost lives, destroyed homes, disrupted families, civilian and military casualties, sickness and disease, ruined crops and burned forests. And afterward, the bitterness lasts for decades. Victory comes at a very high price."

"Deed, so, sir," said Solomon, "but some things be worth fightin' for."

Joseph nodded his understanding. "I'm sympathetic to your need for freedom, dear brother. I just wish it didn't have to come at such a high cost to all humanity."

The preacher paused a moment, then asked, "Tell me, do you still have opportunities to saw that fiddle of yours?"

Solomon smiled. "So happens, I got to play it this past Christmas. All of us slaves was invited by Madame Mary McCoy of Norwood Plantation. We all call her 'the beauty and glory of Bayou Boeuf.' She treated us with kindness and generosity."

Joseph scratched his head, then said, "Oh, yes. I met her at that thanksgivin' celebration at the Ford plantation. Very charming and gracious lady."

"Yes, sir, that would be her," Solomon confirmed. "She knows the slaves by name and was at the door to greet us personally. She presented each of us with a jar of jam or jelly from her larder made from the fruits of her personal orchards. We knew she was gonna do that, so some of us came with little gifts for her.

I whittled some manger animals for her to put on her mantle, and some others brought doilies they crocheted. She was an angel of mercy to us."

"Edwin Epps allowed you to go?"

"Oh, not out of kindness," said Solomon. "He figured if someone wanted to feed his slaves for a day, it would save him money. And feed us she did, Pastor. We sat at a table with china dishes and linen tablecloths. She brought out tortes and cakes and pies and coffee and cream and butter and sugar and molasses and sourdough bread. What we couldn't eat, she told us to wrap in our handkerchiefs and carry back home with us."

"And you played your fiddle?"

"I played the fiddle and Miss Mary, herself, played the piano. There was dancin' and singin' and laughin' for hours, till finally we all settled down and sang *Silent Night* together before leavin'. I know there's gonna be a special place in heaven for that fine woman."

"I'm glad you've had some moments of joy in your life, Solomon," said Joseph, "but I wonder if you could tell me whatever happen to Eliza, the dear soul who was called Dradey?"

Solomon's countenance sagged and he cast his eyes downward.

"She's dead, Brother Willis. You know how sad she was when she was owned by Master Ford. Well, he sold her to someone who didn't have the patience Master and Miz Ford had. The new master whipped Eliza, but she didn't care. She actually wanted to be beaten to death. Finally, the slave driver put her in a dirty little cabin and cut off her food. Told the other slaves not to go near her. And, one day, she was found dead in there."

Joseph looked puzzled. "But wasn't there some talk about trying to relocate her two children?"

"Yes, sir, but talk is all it came to. Master Ford had no money. He hoped to help her find her little ones, even tried to get a message to the white man who was father to them, but no answer came back. Finally, as you probably already know, Master Ford sold all of his slaves, all of his crops and animals, and even most of the furniture in his fine home. Didn't even have a horse to ride. Now, he and his wife just sit in that big ol' house. If it weren't for help from Master Peter, the brother of Mistress Ford, they'd starve."

"A mansion is the goal of many in this life," said Joseph softly, "William has one in the life to come to look forward to."

33

May 19, 1852
Rev. Daniel Hubbard Willis, Sr.'s Home
Babb's Bridge, Louisiana

His reminiscences drawn to a conclusion for the moment, 92-year-old Pastor Joseph Willis brought his mind back to the current time. He surveyed those around him who had been listening intently and respectively—son, grandson, great-grandson.

Young Dan asked, "You had your ups and downs, sir, but were there any times of real happiness?"

Joseph turned directly toward him. "Dan, 1845 began with good news and celebration when your best friend, Julia Ann Graham, was born in February." He gave the boy a wink and said, "Ya know, son, she just might make you a good wife someday. She comes from good stock—Robert and Ruth Graham from over on Barber Creek."

Dan's face blushed a bright red. "Aww, Great-Grandpa, she's only seven years old. I tried to teach her how to fish. She was 'fraid to even put a worm on her hook, and she wouldn't help me clean 'em. All she would say was, 'Eww!'"

"I understand, Dan. Those are mighty important things for a young man of your age." With a twinkle in his eye, Joseph said, "She probably can't cook, milk a cow, or saddle a mule yet either. My eyesight has dimmed, and I thought she was your age, but son, it's never too soon to pray for the needs, protection, and salvation of your future bride, even though you might not even know her name yet. Who knows, the Lord may put a desire in her heart to like fishin' someday. Then again, He may not, but nevertheless she needs your prayers."

Joseph dusted off his spectacles and continued: "I learned from my mother to pray for my children and children's children, as well as future generations of our family, and yes, my future bride, even though I did not know who she would be at the time."

"Great-Grandpa, what *else* happened in 1845 that made it such a year to remember for our family?"

"It was a year of new beginnin's. Life is a series of new beginnin's, Dan. After Julia Ann's birth, President Polk was sworn into office in March. We were blessed again with yet another addition to our family when your cousin Polk was born in June. Your great-uncle Lemuel named him James K. Polk Willis. I sure was glad when President Polk turned out to be a great president, or Lemuel would have had to change his name." Joseph laughed.

"President Polk accomplished all he had promised to do, includin' annexin' Texas, which he did in '45, before the cholera killed him like it did my Hannah and Jim's wife, Ursula.

"But, just when I thought it couldn't get any better, your father was the first in our family to follow me into the ministry. What a day that was! Do you remember that Sunday, Daniel?"

"Great-Grandpa, how could I forget? It was close to my sixth birthday, and Father and I celebrated together. There was only standin' room in the church, and all us kids had to sit on the hard floor. It was a very *long* mornin'. What I remember most was supper on the grounds after church. My father told me to stop eatin' so much, but I didn't listen 'cause everything tasted so good."

Joseph chuckled. "Dan, what I remember most was the look on your father's face durin' the service. He almost glowed, and his heart seemed 'bout to burst with love and gratitude. Don't know which of us was more thankful that day—me for havin' a family that loved the Lord, or your father finally surrenderin' to God's call.

"It was a year of change. 'Bout the same time as your father strapped on the sword of the Spirit, we Baptists broke apart over the slavery issue. In May of '45, we in the South split from our Northern brothers to form the Southern Baptist Convention. I could see it comin'. Louisiana Baptists have been splittin' over a lot less ever since. Some say it's cause we're autonomous. That may be true, but I tend to think some people's pride makes 'em think they got to have it their way, from the music to the hitchin' posts for the horses. There's a lot of chiefs and not enough of us Indians."

Joseph sat very still. He got a faraway look on his face, and it was one that Dan could not easily read. Finally, Dan asked, "Are you all right?"

"Dan, I remember once in '45 when the Lord spoke to my heart while we were headin' home from church. Lemuel, Aimuewell, your father, and I were near Forest Hill. The Lord put it on my heart to stop the wagon and walk out to a farmer who was workin' a turnin' plough pulled by a team of oxen in the middle of a small field. He was all by himself—at least, that's what he thought. I poured him a cup from the water barrel on the side of our wagon and took it out to 'im.

"The farmer told me, 'You must be the angel I prayed for with that there water! I sure am thirsty.'

"I told 'im, 'I'm no angel, mister, but I have news of livin' water, too.'"

"'What kinda water is that, sir?'

"'The kind that if you will drink of it, you'll never thirst 'gain.' Then I shared the story of the Samaritan woman at the well as I took his hand.

"He said, 'I'm an outcast like her, mister. People call me a Redbone, and they sneer at me 'cause of my dark skin.' I could feel his warm tears as they fell on our hands. We knelt in the red dirt together, surrounded by blown pine straw, and settled his future for eternity.

"That red dirt reminded me of the scarlet thread that runs from Genesis to Revelation. Apart from Jesus' blood, there is no redemption, hope, or salvation. Those Louisiana golden pine needles reminded me of yet another thread. It, too, runs from the beginning to the end in God's Word. It is the golden thread of the Second Coming of our Lord Jesus Christ. It tells us that our Blessed Hope Jesus is comin' again. Soon, I hope.

"But, it wasn't all unity in that year. In March of '45, William Prince Ford was excommunicated from Spring Hill Baptist. He was frequentin' too much with the Campbellites to suit the leaders there. Some said William was ordaining Campbellite preachers, too. When the good folks at Spring Hill got wind of it, they gave 'im the boot. Brothers Wright and Rand talked to 'im.

"William told me Brother Rand said, 'You were ordained to follow the tenants of the Baptist faith.' Mr. Wright told William that he'd gotten off course. The conversation went downhill from there. I'm sure he knew it was gonna happen, but it caused a big stir from Forest Hill all the way over to Beulah Baptist in Cheneyville.

"William asked me if I wanted my journal back. I told 'im, 'Not hardly!' There were some who would not even speak to 'im or give 'em the time of day.

"If that wasn't enough, Dan, I had to put Ole Sally out to pasture that year. She had been a good and faithful servant to this old hayseed preacher. We both knew she was way past the time that most mules would have just lain down and quit. But, like me, quittin' was not in her, so I had to make the decision for her. It was time to find her replacement, although I knew that was near impossible.

"I searched and searched, but couldn't find a one that looked like it might measure up to Ole Sally. Finally, I got the idea that I'd just let her choose. We went over to No-Man's-Land and found some printers of sort who I knew also traded in mules. I put her in a pen with about a dozen others and just let her have her way. She did not take a likin' to any of 'em. When other molly mules came near her, she backed her ears and made some horrible brayin' sounds. She moved to the far end of the pen and after about half an hour, I went over and spoke in her ear: 'Ole girl, I still have more travelin' to do before I go, and I can't walk it anymore, so I need your cooperation here. You know the Lord hates pride, Ole Sally, so help me out.' She looked at me as if she understood every word I'd said.

"She moved back toward the front and again backed her ears and brayed when the other mules came near. There was, however, this one John mule that trotted up to her. She looked at 'im and didn't back her ears. I took that as a sign from heaven and quickly made the deal before she changed her mind. I named him Bo. Don't ask me why. I suppose 'cause it was easy for me to remember.

"He was more patient than Ole Sally but not as sure-footed. I never got the opportunity to see if he could swim the mighty Mississippi, thank God. He was more obstinate than Ole Sally, and that's sayin' something, but perhaps even a step or two faster. They both were smarter than a couple of plantation owners I knew of, though."

"Great-Grandpa, do you think that when I get to heaven, I might be able to ride Ole Sally?"

"If a lion can lie down with a lamb, then I 'spect you can climb on Ole Sally's back—that is, if she'll let ya. She might just tell ya—if she can talk like that donkey did to Balaam—that she's already laid down her burdens. But, Dan, let's not get ahead of ourselves. She's still got a few years left here. She's out to pasture, not dead. Now, son, speakin' of animals, how 'bout you go milk the cows and gather up the eggs from the hen house, too."

Dan was hesitant as he sat on the edge of his chair. "Great-Grandpa, please tell me just one more excitin' story that happened in 1845."

"You go and do your chores, and when you come back, I'll tell ya one you'll never forget."

{34}

May 19, 1852
Rev. Daniel Hubbard Willis, Sr.'s Home
Babb's Bridge, Louisiana

Joseph had time to reflect on a very special time in his life, and when Dan returned, he was ready.

"Miss Elvy and I took a little trip to N'Orleans. I had been asked to speak at Half Moon Bluff Baptist Church, which is in Louisiana but on the eastern side of the Mississippi. I asked Miss Elvy to go with me, and she agreed, but only if we caught a riverboat at Baton Rouge after I preached at Half Moon and took a side trip to N'Orleans. She had our return trip all mapped out in her mind. I knew I didn't want to make this journey alone, so we left the boys with Lemuel's clan. She talked eagerly for several weeks ahead 'bout how we'd catch the Riverboat *Natchez* at Baton Rouge for our voyage.

"I hadn't been to Red Stick in a long time, and I'd never been to N'Orleans, but Miss Elvy had seen the sights before. I remember how her eyes danced with the excitement of a child on Christmas mornin' when she saw all the lights and steamers. Miss Elvy and I were both intrigued with watchin' the riverboats with their paddle wheels churnin' the muddy waters of the mighty Mississippi. There were lots of new riverboats from up north. An inventor named Fulton was mostly responsible for this boom when he took an interest in steam engines and started usin' 'em in boats. And, Jim Bowie and I never had cookin' like they now served. That night the bill of fare gave us a meal I won't soon forget. We both ate sauce piquante."

"Great-Grandpa, what else did you eat?"

"My mouth is startin' to water just thinkin' 'bout it. I had andouille and red beans and rice. For dessert, she had pecan pralines, and I devoured the warm bread puddin' with cream on it. We sat and talked for a long time as we sipped our steamin' hot coffee. It was a delightful evenin', and we decided to stroll out on the deck. I still can remember the aroma of the jasmine and honeysuckle. We stood for a long time just lookin' over the riverbanks of the Big Muddy River. At dusk, a log floated by. Miss

Elvy tugged on my shirt and pointed. 'What's that down there...on that log?'

"'I'd say that's an alligator snappin' turtle—the kind of turtle that can snap your finger off quicker than a duck jumps on a June bug.'

"'Looks kinda scary!' She kept her eyes focused on the black, spikey shell.

"We slowly came around a bend as we neared the Hamptons' House, the Crown Jewel of plantations in Louisiana with more than 300,000 acres. Today, it's the largest producer of sugarcane in our entire country. But, it was the Houmas Indians who first owned the land. They should name it the Houmas House after 'em. Miss Elvy asked me if I'd like one of those. I told her I already have a mansion waitin' for me, but not built with human hands—slave or free. I reckon my corncrib in heaven is bigger than that mansion.

"The many oil lamps and candles from the windows glistened on the river like hundreds of stars. It was light enough for Miss Elvy to see a tall building standin' apart on the grounds, and she asked me about it. I hesitantly told her, 'My dear, that is called a garçonnière. It is a house where bachelors entertain guests. I hear tell that is where some of the less honorable ones take female slaves at times. I told Miss Elvy, 'My eyes don't see as well as they used to, so tell me 'bout all those other buildin's.'

"I heard hesitation in her voice as she said, 'Looks like slave quarters.' I took her hand, and we walked to the back of the *Natchez*. She stopped and got the biggest smile. 'Pastor Joseph Willis, didn't you promise to buy me one of these big plantations...or was that one of my other suitors?' I said, 'Had to be one of the others, 'cause I'm sure I only could afford a mule and milk cow at the time. Come to think of it, I've not added much to my estate throughout the years.'

"Miss Elvy smiled sweetly. 'Not much, you say? Not much except a place called home and nineteen children.' We both laughed and talked 'bout what we'd been through in our eleven years together. We talked of how our love for each other had grown. Dan, love can fade at times, but what kept us together through the hills and valleys is trust and respect. It is what mattered most when our love seemed to flicker like the light of a candle.

"So, next mornin' Miss Elvy and I got up as the mist was risin' off the water. We shared a pipin' hot cup of coffee and watched the sun come up over the eastern banks of the river in N'Orleans. As we greeted the daybreak, we heard a most unusual sound. Miss Elvy's eyes got real big. 'Joseph, what is makin' that hideous noise?'

"'I do believe those are trumpeter swans,' I told her as I looked over toward the edge of the river. We were comin' into the city, and there were some shallower little marshes along the banks. I motioned for Miss Elvy to come and see.

"'They are the most beautiful birds I've ever seen,' she told me. 'By the way, how do you know about trumpeter swans, anyway?'

"'When I was visitin' Jim Bowie once on the Mississippi, I saw plenty of 'em. Besides, I read an article by that artist James Audubon sayin' how they used to sell 'em in the markets here in N'Orleans. Sure are beautiful, aren't they? They say they mate for life.'

"As we got farther into N'Orleans, there were many steamers comin' and goin'. The noise, sights, and smells were not to this here country preacher's likin', but Miss Elvy enjoyed every bit of it. I now knew how Jonah felt in Nineveh, but I had a nicer whale to get me there.

"We found an inn and registered. I asked her what she wanted to do for the day, and she told me she was interested in seein' some fashion. Now, Dan, I sure can't say that was top on my list, but I wanted to make her happy, so I told her that would be all right if we could also see Jackson Square.

"Miss Elvy commented, 'I didn't know you were an admirer of President Andrew Jackson.'

"'Never said I was…I just want to see the statue of 'im.' Miss Elvy smiled and said, 'Well, I declare, why?'

"I told her it would be better if I just showed her. We took a carriage over to Jackson Square. I told her a most fascinatin' story about Micaela Almonester de Pontalba."

"Great-Grandpa, who was she? That is a very long name, so she must've been somebody important."

"She was a baroness and *the* richest woman in N'Orleans. I

told Miss Elvy how she got married when she was fifteen and went to Paris, but she was not in love with her husband. Her new father-in-law didn't like her and shot her four times in the chest, then ended his own life. She survived and went back to N'Orleans. Seems she made a visit to Washington, and President Jackson caught wind that she was in town and sent a buggy for her. She was a mighty independent woman. I told Miss Elvy she kind of reminded me of her.

"Miss Elvy quickly turned her eyes to mine. 'Whatever do you mean, Joseph?'

"'Oh, nothin',''' I assured her.

"Dan, the baroness spent lots of money fixin' up Jackson Square. I heard tell that she used to go to the work sites wearin' men's trousers. The story goes that the President didn't like that and told her he wouldn't tip his hat to her if she continued to be seen in public wearin' pants. The baroness was a bit strong-willed and decided she'd have a statue built of President Jackson. You see, he's facin' her quarters as he tips his hat. I'd like to think of 'im today as tippin' his hat to my Cherokee people that he dishonored.

"Anyway, that day Elvy and I retained that carriage, taking in all the sights, until the driver slowed down, turned with a most unusual look on his face, and made the comment, 'We are now comin' near the home of the voodoo queen, Marie Laveau. Heard she's havin' a two-for-one special today on love potions and pincushion dolls. Are you in the market today?'

"'Not hardly. Please drive on!' I proclaimed, but Miss Elvy giggled like a little girl.

"We stopped a little later for café au lait and some fresh beignets. I spent time with Miss Elvy in Vieux Carré, where she roamed through store after store and tried on many a dress. Then we walked back to the Victorian Inn in Vieux Carré.

"Toward the end of '45, there were more joyous events. One would change our lives forever. There was also news from Theo!"

{35}

June 1, 1844
Pinta Trail Crossing on the Guadalupe River
The Hill Country of Texas

The sounds of change brought glorious news that blew like trumpets from heaven. The first trumpet sounded with a story Theo Cormier shared with Joseph in a letter.

A group of fifteen Texas Rangers rode out from their headquarters in San Antonio to look for a Comanche war party that was raiding and terrorizing the settlers. The Rangers traveled on the Pinta Trail as far as the Pedernales River without a trace of any Comanches. After nine days, the Rangers decided to turn back and make camp at a crossing on the Guadalupe River. One Ranger saw a large band of Comanches after climbing a bee tree. "Must be a thousand of 'em!" he yelled. It was there that those fifteen rangers found what they'd been looking for…and then some.

Theo had ventured to San Antonio, looking for employment. A couple of German immigrants hired him as protection while they explored the Pedernales River for a place to start a settlement. They told Theo they wanted to name the town after Prince Frederick of Prussia. One wanted to call it Fritztown, and another suggested Fredericksburg. When they returned on the Pinta Trail, they heard the sound of guns being fired as never before. Theo figured there must have been a hundred or so firing by the number of shots. He quickly discovered the number to be only fifteen.

Theo told the immigrants to wait for him down the trail. "I got to know what kind of guns they're usin'," he said. He managed to identify himself to the leader of the men and soon discovered they were Texas Rangers. Remembering our friend Jim Bowie, who had been a Ranger, Theo began to fire. The Ranger told him, 'Your gun will be of little effect again' 'em. Use one of my five-shooters!'

Those Indians started yelling bad things in Spanish at the Rangers. They called them cowards and all sorts of things. The leader of the Rangers recognized the leader of the Comanches, Yellow Wolf, and said something to the effect of, "Yellow Dog, son of a dog-mother, the Comanche liver is white!" That's when the fighting really began picking up. Theo thought, *Who* is *this man?*

Theo began to shoot and soon discovered he was no match to that Ranger. Within five minutes, Theo was hit with an arrow. It knocked him to the ground, and he lay there stunned. He lifted his head and could see the shaft of his demise sticking straight up in the air. He asked himself, "Why ain't I dead?"

With a trembling hand, he reached inside his coat. There was no blood. As Theo sought to find his wound, he touched the hard Bible that was in the pocket of his coat. He thought, *I'll be! It would seem this little Book has saved my life!*

*   *   *

"Great-Grandpa, was that the Bible *you* gave him?"

"Sure was! And when he opened it, the tip of that arrow's head stopped right on the verse talkin' 'bout how the thief on the cross asked the Lord, "Would You remember me when You enter Your kingdom?" That was the moment in Theo's life when everything changed forever."

Joseph added, "Theo said he made two decisions that day, one for Jesus, and the other to make sure he had one of those Colt Paterson rapid-firin' revolvers. He said one Comanche who took part in the fight later complained that the Rangers 'had a shot for every finger on their hand.'"

"Great-Grandpa, who was the Ranger who gave Theo that gun?"

"I'm gettin' to that, Dan. Hold your horses. Theo told the Ranger, 'I've never seen anybody shoot like that. Who are you, sir?'

"'Hays, Captain John Coffee Hays, but my friends just call me Jack.'

"Theo also said that Hays's uncle was President Andrew Jackson, the same president who had my people driven from their land in North Carolina. Hays, who was also friends with Sam Houston, admired Jim Bowie and was a very brave man that day, so Theo decided to make an effort to be his friend. Hays moved to California in '49 durin' the Gold Rush, where he became the first sheriff of a place called San Francisco.

Theo ended his letter with, "One Riot, One Ranger. One Sinner, One Saviour. Theo."

November 22, 1845
Joseph Willis's Home
Babb's Bridge, Louisiana
Willis Feast of Thanksgiving

November of 1845 was once again time for the annual feast of thanksgiving. A cool autumn breeze seemed to carry the excitement that was in the air across the scented pine planks at Babb's Bridge to all the Willis neighbors and friends. There was a hint of crispness in the piney woods that reminded folks that winter was just around the corner, but that Saturday was perfect in more ways than just the weather. That day would change our lives forever.

There was nary a cloud in the sky, and the sun took care of the heavy dew on the pine straw as tables and chairs were being set up. The smell of turkeys smoking was just a hint of what was to come as far as the food was concerned. The place was alive with great anticipation as family and friends began to arrive. Womenfolk were busy cooking all kinds of Louisiana recipes. They'd been preparing for days. There were sweet potatoes, okra, fresh-baked buttermilk biscuits, cornbread, butter beans, turnip greens with bacon, venison, hams with brown sugar glaze, apple pie, and Joseph's favorite, dewberry pie that Miss Elvy made. Naturally, there was plenty of coffee with chicory, too.

Mary McCoy from over Bayou Boeuf way brought a recipe with all the ingredients for a servant of hers to prepare. He served the many trays of French beignets covered with powdered sugar and some with fruit on top. They were kept hot in one of the brick ovens. Joseph mused, *If I die today from eatin' too much, the French would have been able to do to me what they could not do in Vermilionville forty years before.* The preacher felt they had much to be grateful and thankful for that day, and for the entire year, for that matter.

*   *   *

The family started arriving around mid-morning. Little Samuel and Aimuewell were of great help. Being eight and nine, they were responsible boys, and their mother kept them busy. There were probably four hundred people there throughout the day.

The Willis family mingled with friends, and everyone felt at home. Even Brother Robert Sawyer was there. He had been asked to leave the church a few months back for partaking of ardent spirits and had promised never to touch another drop. He seemed to be having way too much fun for such an early hour. He was talking and making gestures to Malachi when Joseph approached.

Malachi turned and quietly said, "Pastor, if I didn't know better, I'd say he was higher than a Louisiana pine."

Joseph looked at Brother Sawyer and asked, "Have you been into something stronger than the lemonade?"

"Oh, no, Pastor. I tasted a little of the cookin' sherry that your sweet ladies were usin' up at the kitchen to make sure it had not gone bad. You know I don't partake of the devil's poison anymore, since Spring Hill Church put me on the straight and narrow path. I told 'em I'd sign a pledge with my own blood drawn from my veins if they'd let me back in."

The preacher just shook his head and said, "Brother, these here Baptist women don't use cookin' sherry. Most of 'em don't, that is. Some say otherwise."

Sawyer had a sheepish grin.

Malachi smiled and asked, "Is *he* another one of your converts, Pastor?"

"Yes, sir. At least that's what I hear he's been tellin' everyone from the Calcasieu to as far away as the Red River."

"Well, look here," said Malachi, pointing.

Brother Willis turned and was most surprised and happy to see Theo come riding up in a one-horse buggy made for two. He had a young woman with him, and when he saw the preacher, he jumped out of the wagon, leaving his lady friend just sitting there. The burly bear hug he gave Joseph almost took his breath away, but it was a wonderful reunion.

"I got your letter," Joseph told him. "But first, see to your guest. She's most welcome today, too."

Theo laughed and apologized to her as he helped her down. "Pastor, I'd like you to meet my fiancée, Adelaide Chevalier. She's from Baton Rouge by way of N'Orleans—and quite the cook."

"Theo, I can see you been eatin' a lot of her exquisite cookin'! It is a pleasure to meet you, Miss Chevalier. I pray that the two of you will be very blessed together."

Adelaide gave a small curtsy to the parson, and extended her hand for him to shake.

Theo said, "Pastor, I wanted to thank you in person for your words down on Tenmile Creek. Although it took a Comanche's arrow a half-inch from my heart to change my life."

Theo then told his entire story to the crowd that had gathered around, and when he had finished, everyone extended the right hand of fellowship to him. Theo also shared the story of their engagement after getting alone with Brother Willis, Elvy, and Malachi.

*   *   *

"So, I went to Mr. Chevalier's home to ask for Adelaide's hand in marriage. We stood outside on the front steps to talk. He asked me, 'Can ya feed her, Theo?'

"I felt as poor as Job's turkey. 'Mr. Chevalier, sir, I got a barrel of molasses, a barrel of corn, a milk cow, and a mule that can jump any object he can see over.'

"He replied, 'My, you *are* richer than I was at your age, son.'

"'Sir, I love your daughter and would do anythin' for her."

"He said, 'Oh, well, we will see. Are you a Christian, Theo?'

"'Yes, sir, I am.'

"'Do ya believe the story of Jacob in the Bible is true?'

"'Yes, sir, I do, Mr. Chevalier.'

"'You know Jacob had to work seven years for his wife. You willin' to work for me for seven years for my daughter?'

"I didn't know what to say. All I could do was nod my head a little. Suddenly, there was a lot of laughin' goin' on inside the house. Mr. Chevalier thought it was quite funny, too, and said, 'Son, you can have my blessin' *and* my daughter. She's been readin' 'bout those liberated women in Paris, so ya don't have to worry 'bout feedin' her, 'cause she can do that for herself now. At least, that's what she tells everyone who will listen.'

"Mr. Chevalier told me, 'Adelaide is behind that wall listenin' to see just how much you love her.' When Miss Adelaide came out, she was gigglin'. Mr. Chevalier explained that when his father-in-law asked 'im the same question, he tried to bargain 'im down to one year. I told Adelaide, 'I would have done the full seven years.'

"She said, 'Sure you would have, Theo. *Sure.*' Then she smiled at me with a twinkle in her eye."

While Theo told his story, other folks were active. The children were involved in games of hide and go seek, tag, and blind man's bluff. A few of the more hearty ones even braved the frigid waters of Spring Creek for a final swim before the onset of winter. Young Dan was the leader in that adventure. He would swim year round if his parents would let him.

It was early afternoon when everyone finally sat at the tables and some on the ground to enjoy the meal together. Joseph looked around for William Prince Ford but did not see him anywhere. He had hoped to have him offering the blessing. Instead, Dan said grace, and then everyone dug in. Plates were passed, food was enjoyed, and everyone was talking and laughing and enjoying each other's company.

A special event of that day was a presentation of a lineback dun gelding from Joseph to Dan. The gelding stood taller than Bo. Dan was so proud, he became tongue-tied. Joseph rubbed his head, gave him a manly hug, and said, "Let's see what kind of cowboy you can turn into. I've heard tell you're already better than most of 'em Texas boys."

There was one huge surprise left to be revealed later that day. As the evening approached, Pastor Willis stood and announced that he wanted to point out the many members of his family who were there that day. He named off Agerton, Daniel, Dan, Mary, Joseph Junior, Rachel, Jemima, Sally, Sarah, William, Lemuel, John, Martha, Samuel, and Aimuewell.

Then he added, "And my surrogate son too, William Prince Ford. It would seem he could not make it today. He's been through a lot lately."

At that very moment, however, Dan, still seated on his new mount, proclaimed, "Great-Grandpa, I see Mr. Ford comin' this way in an open carriage."

Malachi was standing right next to the table and hopped up on it. "Pastor, it is William, and it looks like he's got some folks with 'im."

"Malachi, my eyes are dim. Who's he got with 'im? Is it Martha and Peter? I so hope so!"

William had to leave his carriage far away in the field because of all the other wagons, horses, and mules.

Malachi said, "Pastor, he seems to have three others with 'im. Looks like a nice-lookin' family: a woman in a lace bonnet with two well-dressed children."

Joseph said, "I suppose they are Martha's people from Bayou Boeuf."

The closer they got, Joseph could see that the woman was holding the hands of two children. William was walking in front of them and smiling. Pastor Willis suddenly recognized the woman. "Eliza? Is it really you?"

"Yes, Pastor, and I want you to meet my children, Randall and Emily."

Joseph looked up toward heaven and said, "Who is likened unto You, Lord?" He then bent down to Randall's eye level, shook his hand, and hugged Emily. "I'm pleased to meet you, Mr. Randall, Miss Emily."

They both smiled and said, "Thank you, sir."

"But…but, Eliza, I heard that you had died. How is it that…?"

Eliza smiled. "Well, suh, I was left fo' dead, and I accepted that. I would never run away. I had no feelin' to live without these chillin' of mine. So, when dey done come to bury me, Master Ford show up and say he want to claim da body. Well, dat be fine with my new master, 'cause it save him money. They dump my body in a wagon, and after we done get five mile away, Master Ford shake me awake and give me water and food and then tell me to rest. He saved me, dat good man."

Brother Willis looked at William with astonishment and admiration. "Whatever motivated you to attempt such a thing, William?"

"You did, Pastor," he replied. "You shamed me when you said that if our roles had been reversed, you would have followed the two children until you could rescue them and bring them back.

So, after Martha and I nursed Eliza back to health, we sold Martha's jewelry, and I took a personal loan from her brother Peter, and Eliza and I spent more than a month tracing down her two children. To be bluntly honest with you, I had to use force to make Freeman sell me Emily, but he could see I was determined not to leave without that child."

Malachi told William, "The version of the story we got from Solomon was that an angel of the Lord came to get Eliza. He meant you. He wanted to guard your secret. My admiration of you knows no limit, sir."

Joseph embraced William. "I just had told this gathering that you were a surrogate son of mine. Well, to quote the Good Book, 'This is my son in whom I am well pleased.'"

Epilogue

December 25, 1852
Excerpted from Daniel Hubbard Willis, Jr.'s Diary
Babb's Bridge, Louisiana

Great-Grandpa Joseph Willis relived much of his life in Louisiana on the wagon trip in October of 1852 from Evergreen to Babb's Bridge. He poured out his heart to us, and I discovered a joy in writing and keeping an account of all his stories.

Just when it seemed that no day in our family would ever top the 1845 Willis Feast of Thanksgiving…it did. It all began the first time ever I saw a white Christmas, December 25, 1852, in Babb's Bridge, and the entire family was there. Each family member brought a decoration for our tree. The cedar was so big that we had to cut it down three times just to get it inside the door. There were strings of popcorn, wooden figures, sugared fruit, paper dolls cut out by the girls, gingerbread, and somebody even brought a bird's nest.

We had ornaments that had meanings, too, like a pine tree, which symbolized eternity, pinecones that meant warmth, and a teapot that signified hospitality, which has always been taught by our family. There were candy canes with the Good Shepherd's crook, with white stripes for the purity of Jesus and his virgin birth and the bold red stripes for Christ's shed blood. At the top of the tree was the star of Bethlehem made from a quilt. And, the Christmas stockings stuffed with nuts, candy, and fruit hung on every available nail.

I'll never forget the looks on my cousins', brothers', and sisters' faces. Dolls, books, tablets, pencils, wooden soldiers, and even a rocking horse were unwrapped that happy morn. I got a new writing tablet that I started using to write this.

Christmas Day started with a few flurries, and everyone ran out to see the snow. Mother taught us to make something I'd never eaten before—ice cream. She showed us how to add milk, cream, butter, and eggs with the snow in a pewter pot. She had read where President Thomas Jefferson had even made ice cream with split vanilla beans. Imagine that! Our traditional hot spiced cider warmed us from the cold. The smell of roasting chestnuts in Mama's cast-iron skillet in the fireplace brought back precious memories of Christmas past.

As the flakes began to fall steadily, more guests arrived, including Mr. Cormier and Miss Adelaide. She was with child, due in many months. Mr. Cormier told Great-Grandpa, "If the baby is a boy, we are gonna name him Joseph." Great-Grandpa's face shone with an all-knowing peace. You could hear the excitement in their voices as Mr. and Mrs. Cormier brushed the snow off.

Mr. Malachi Perkins, Miss Eliza, Randall, and Emily came in together. Mr. Perkins went right up to Great-Grandpa and gave him a hug, saying, "Pastor, we consider ourselves engaged, but as you know by Louisiana law, we can't get married. We've fallen in love, and if it was legal, we'd be hitched already." He hesitated, then went on, "We so want to do what's right in the eyes of the Lord. I remember ya tellin' me how your mama and daddy had a clandestine weddin'. I don't want to bother ya on this special day, but would ya mind thinkin' 'bout it in a few days and lettin' us know if ya'd perform our weddin' ceremony?"

Great-Grandpa took all of two seconds, grinned, and said, "Ain't gotta think about it, Malachi. I'd be honored...if ya don't mind if I do the ceremony sittin' down. I'm a half-step slower than I used to be." Everybody laughed.

"Ya know, Pastor, ya could get in trouble for doin' it!"

"Yes, I know, but I'm ninety-four, and my race here is almost run. What are they gonna do, shoot me? They already tried that, when I was only knee-high to a grasshopper."

The entire room seemed to be filled with a sweet joy. We all cheered and clapped. Randall and Emily looked the happiest. Great-Grandpa motioned for me to come over and whispered in a voice real low, "Quite a few folks are named after me now. If you ever have a son, Dan, you should name him Randall, after Eliza's son. You can even nickname 'im Randy, if you so like. That way, our descendants will remember that miracle and share it with their children."

We watched the storm bringing heavier snow, which seemed to be driven by a blue norther as our neighbors Mr. and Mrs. Robert Graham arrived. And, yes, Julia Ann was with them. Great-Grandfather asked to be carried to the barn to talk to his aged four-legged friend, Ole Sally. He told her he had a gift for her—a mule blanket that all the Willis women had made. They had made a matching blanket for him, too.

I listened to him sweet-talk her in her ear. He thanked her for being a good friend and told her that he could never have done it without 'er. As Ole Sally leaned over the stall gate, Great-Grandpa kissed 'er on the nose. She backed her ears, and he laughed, saying, "Aww, you know you like it."

We carried him back to the house, and then I asked him to share his annual Christmas story once again. Everyone gathered around the fireplace. He looked like he was doing what he loved best.

The wind was blowing the snow so hard we didn't hear Mr. Ford arrive with Mr. and Mrs. Peter Tanner, the brother and sister-in-law of his late wife. Mr. Ford rushed through the door with a great big smile, saying, "Looks like Solomon Northup will be freed on January 3rd. He's gonna be a free man!" Again, everyone clapped and cheered.

Great-Grandpa's heart was full of joy. Mine, too! He beamed as he said, "I don't see how a Christmas could get any better than this."

He'd started to tell the Christmas story when there was a knock at the door. I jumped up to answer the door. There stood a snow-covered, half-frozen woman in a green hooded cape. Her hair was all wet and matted. All of a sudden, I recognized her—and so did everyone else. There were a few gasps and then lots of hugs. Great-Grandpa couldn't see very well, as his eyes were dimmed by age. He asked, "Who's that? Who's here?"

She put her finger up to her lips to keep everyone silent. No one said a word as she went over to Great-Grandpa, hugged him, and said, "Merry Christmas, Pastor Joseph Willis. I love you with all my heart."

His eyes glistened as he pulled her to him and said, "I love you even more, Miss Elvy Willis. Welcome home! I've saved a place beside me for ya. You're just in time to hear my favorite Christmas story again.

"He was born in a little-known village. He was brought up in another community that people said nothing good would ever come out of. He worked with his hands in a carpenter shop until he was thirty, and then for three years, he traveled as a country preacher. He never wrote a book. He never held an office. He never commanded an army. He never owned a home. He never went to college. He never traveled more than a couple of hundred miles from the place where he was born.

"He was rejected by the religious folk of that day. While he was still a young man, the tide of popular opinion turned against him. One friend denied him. Another betrayed him. Many even hated him. He was turned over to his enemies. He went through the mockery of a trial and was then nailed to the cross rightfully prepared for a notorious prisoner named Barabbas' and lifted between two thieves. His executors gambled for his only possession—his cloak.

"Most of his friends had abandoned him by then. When he died, he was laid in a borrowed grave. Then, on the next Sunday mornin', he rose from the dead. As we look back across eighteen hundred years and examine the evidence and sum up his influence, we must conclude that all the armies that ever marched, all the ships that ever sailed, all the governments that ever sat, all the kings that ever reigned, and all the presidents who ever led combined have not had the influence on mankind that this one Country Preacher has had!"

Not a sound was heard 'til Great-Grandpa said, "Merry Christmas, everyone!

I got a stirring in my heart and started singing, "Joy to the world, the Lord is come!"

Great-Grandpa and Miss Elvy joined in: "Let earth receive her King; let every heart prepare Him room...." Finally, everyone was singing. "And Heaven and nature sing, and Heaven and nature sing, and Heaven, and Heaven, and nature sing. Joy to the earth, the Savior reigns!"

*   *   *

Three Winds Blowing's Characters

William Prince Ford and Solomon Northup—Neighbor, mentor, and friend of Joseph Willis. Ford had bought the slave Solomon Northup on June 23, 1841, in New Orleans. He immediately brought him to his Wallfield Plantation. Just forty-six days later, Joseph Willis and William Prince Ford founded Spring Hill Baptist Church, on August 8, 1841. Ford's slaves attended the church too, which was the custom in pre-Civil War Louisiana.

The plantation was located on Hurricane Creek, a 1/4 mile east of present-day Forest Hill, Louisiana. It was located on the crest of a hill, on the Texas Road that ran alongside a ridge. Northup called this area, in his book *Twelve Years a Slave*, "The Great Piney Woods." Ford was also the headmaster of Spring Creek Academy located near his plantation and Spring Hill Baptist Church. It was near there, in 1841, that Joseph Willis would live and entrust his diary to his protégé William Prince Ford, according to historian W.E. Paxton.

Ford was not a Baptist preacher when he purchased Solomon Northup and the slave Eliza, a.k.a. Dradey, in 1841, as many books, articles, blogs, and the movie *12 Years a Slave* have portrayed.

The first part of the Spring Hill Baptist Church minutes are written in Ford's own handwriting since he was the first church secretary and also the first church clerk. The minutes reveal that on July 7, 1842, Ford was elected deacon. On December 11, 1842, Ford became the church treasurer, too. It was during the winter of 1842 that Ford sold a 60% share of Northup to John M. Tibeats. Ford's remaining 40% was later conveyed to Edwin Epps, on April 9, 1843. It was not until February 10, 1844, that Ford was ordained as a Baptist preacher. A year later, on April 12, 1845, Ford was excommunicated for "communing with the Campbellite Church at Cheneyville." But, Ford's later writings reveal that he remained close friends with his neighbor and mentor Joseph Willis.

As a child Randy Willis lived near Longleaf Louisiana. As a

teenager, he would work cows with his family there on the open range, owned by lumber companies. Seven generations of his family have lived there, beginning with his 4th great-grandfather—Joseph Willis. He would often ride his horse through his family's neighboring property, which was once William Prince Ford's Wallfield Plantation, not realizing the significance of his ancestor's connection to Solomon Northup and William Prince Ford.

Jim Bowie—Neighbor of Joseph. Famous for his knife used at the Sandbar Fight (1827), as well as fighting to defend the Alamo (1836).

Jim Bowie was a neighbor of Joseph Willis when they both lived near Bayou Chicot. Jim's brother, Rezin Bowie, was a neighbor to Joseph's eldest son Agerton Willis and eldest grandson, Daniel Hubbard Willis, Sr., for four years (1824-1827) in the village of Bayou Boeuf. The name changed to Holmesville in 1834, and is located near present-day Eola. It was at Holmesville, on Bayou Boeuf, that Edwin Epps enslaved Solomon Northup for almost ten years of his twelve year indenture. It was here that Joseph's eldest son and Randy Willis's 3rd great-grandfather Agerton Willis met and married Sophie Story.

Edwin Epps—Last owner of Solomon Northrup for ten of twelve years of his captivity. He was a cruel and brutal plantation owner.

Jim Burns—Plantation owner and neighbor of Epps. He boasted of his cruelty to slaves. Solomon called him a barbarian.

Eliza aka Dradey and her children Randall and Emily—Friend of Solomon Northup. While in a slave pen, Solomon makes the acquaintance of several other slaves, including Eliza. After surviving a bout of smallpox, Northup and Eliza are purchased by William Prince Ford and taken to his Wallfield Plantation on Hurricane Creek near present-day Forest Hill, Louisiana. Her children Randall and Emily were sold to other owners.

Peter Tanner—Plantation owner, brother-in-law of William Prince Ford.

Ezra Bennett—Owner of Bennett's Store on Bayou Boeuf. The store was a place where men bought cloth, socialized, got their mail, told stories and shared gossip reinforced by traditional antebellum roles. Because the land across from the store was owned by Randal Eldred, the curve in Bayou Boeuf became known as Eldred's Bend. It was later named Bennett's Store. Ezra Bennett married the daughter of Randal Eldred and niece of William Prince Ford's first wife, Martha Tanner Ford. Eldred was a member of Spring Hill Baptist Church that Joseph founded, in 1841, along with William Prince Ford. Eldred moved to Bayou Boeuf from Woodville, Mississippi, the location of yet another church founded by Joseph Willis.

Captain Jack C. Hays—Legendary Texas Ranger. Hays built a reputation fighting marauding Indians and Mexican bandits. An Indian who switched sides and rode with Hays and his men called the young Ranger Captain "bravo too much." Rachel Jackson, wife of Andrew Jackson, was his great aunt. In 1836, at the age of 19, Hays migrated to the Republic of Texas. Sam Houston appointed him as a member of a company of Texas Rangers because he knew the Hays family from Tennessee. Jack met with Sam Houston and delivered a letter of recommendation from his uncle Andrew Jackson. After moving to California during the gold rush he was elected sheriff of San Francisco County in 1850 and later became one of the founders of the city of Oakland. Hays County, Texas, is named in his honor. Randy Willis lives in Hays County, Texas.

Madam Mary McCoy—The "beauty and glory of Bayou Boeuf" according to Solomon Northup. He also said she was beloved by all her slaves and he remembered the Christmas parties she provided for them.

Baroness Micela Almonester de Pontalba—Wealthy New Orleans born aristocrat. She was responsible for the design and construction of the famous Pontalba Buildings in Jackson Square.

On a trip to Washington DC President Andrew Jackson sent his own carriage and secretary of state Martin Van Buren to bring her to the White House as his guest. The celebrated Battle of New Orleans in which Jackson had defeated the invading British, in 1814, had been fought on the grounds of the Chalmette Plantation belonging to her uncle and aunt.

As their friendship grew Jackson scolded her many times for wearing pants, for being on the work site and for ordering the workmen about. He told her that she was not acting as a proper lady and that he would refuse to tip his hat to her (gesture of respect from men to women of those days) until she started behaving like a lady again.

She financed the bronze equestrian statue of Jackson that stands in the very center of the Jackson Square today—and had it built directly facing her apartment in the building—with Andrew Jackson tipping his hat directly at her balcony.

Her interlaced initials "AP" can be seen on the wrought iron balconies of the buildings around the Square today, too.

Marie Catherine Laveau—Louisiana Creole practitioner of Voodoo renowned in New Orleans.

Sam Houston—aka The Raven—Governor of Texas and U.S Senator from Texas. He ran away from home to live with the Cherokees on Hiwasee Island in the Tennessee River. Joseph's mother was a Cherokee. One of the same rivers Joseph migrates to Louisiana on. Adopted by Cherokee Chief Oo-Loo-Te-Ka and is given the Indian name, "The Raven."

Listed ahead of Andrew Jackson on purpose because of Jackson's treatment of Native Americans.

Andrew Jackson—President of the United States. More than 30-years after Joseph crossed the mighty Mississippi River into the Louisiana Territory his maternal cousins would be driven out of North Carolina on the "Trail of Tears." In 1830 Congress passed the Indian Removal Act, which directed the executive branch to negotiate for Indian lands. This act caused the Cherokee Nation to bring suit in the U.S. Supreme Court. In Cherokee Nation v. Georgia (1831) Chief Justice John Marshall, writing for the majority, held that the Cherokee Nation was a "domestic dependent nation," and therefore Georgia state law applied to them. President Jackson refused to enforce the court's decision stating "John Marshall has made his decision, now let him enforce it." The Cherokee nation was forced to give up its lands east of the Mississippi River and to migrate to an area in present-day Oklahoma. The Cherokee people called this journey the "Trail of Tears," because of its devastating effects. The migrants faced hunger, disease, and exhaustion on the forced march. Some 4,000 out of 15,000 of the Cherokees died.

John Murrell—The Reverend Devil. His father was a Methodist minister and his mother a prostitute. He despised his father and learned his thievery from his mother. He became one of the most notorious outlaws who roamed No Man's Land a.k.a. The Neutral Zone.

Jean Lafitte—Well-known pirate of the Mississippi and Gulf of Mexico dealing primarily in illegal slave trade. Became a hero after joining General Andrew Jackson and the Americans at the Battle of New Orleans.

Maria Ursala de Veramendi—Wife of Jim Bowie. She and their children succumbed to cholera in 1833.

Brother Robert Sawyer (based on Robert Snoddy)—Joseph's convert. After twice before promising not to "partake of ardent spirits" any more, Robert Snoddy had the fellowship of the church withdrawn from him on May 31, 1851. A month later Snoddy sent this letter to the church explaining his actions:

"Dear Brethren, Having been overtaken in an error I set down to confess it. I did use liquor too freely, but did not say anything or do anything out of the way. In as much as I do expect to be at the conference I send you my thoughts. I did promise you that I would refrain from using the poison, but I having broken my promise I have therefore rendered myself unworthy of your fellowship and cannot murmur if you exclude me. I suppose it is no use to tell you that I have been sincerely punished for my crime in as much as I have confessed the same to you before but I make this last request of you for forgiveness or is your forgiveness exhausted towards me. It is necessary that I say to you that I sorely repented for my guilt, but my brethren if you have in your wisdom supposed that my life brings to much reproach on that most respectful of all causes, exclude me, exclude me, Oh exclude me. But I do love the cause so well that I will try to be at the door of the temple of the Lord. Brethren whilst you are dealing with me do it mercifully prayerfully and candidly. I was presented by a beloved brother with a temperance pledge to which I replied I would think about it but if I could of obtained enough of my hearts blood to fill my pen to write my name I would have done it. It is my determination to join it yet – and never taste another drop of the deathly cup whilst I live at the peril of my life. Nothing more but I request your prayers dear brethren – Robert Snoddy"

Robert Snoddy was restored to membership. Four months later he was once again reported drinking and once again excluded.

Antonio López de Santa Anna—President of Mexico defeated by the Texian Army led by General Sam Houston at the Battle of San Jacinto. Three weeks later, he signed the peace treaty that dictated that the Mexican army leave the region, paving the way for the Republic of Texas to become an independent country.

Malachi Perkin—Based upon the real man whom Joseph tended to at an inn. He warned Joseph to flee for his life the next morning.

Theo Cormier—He was a friend of Randy Willis who preached his grandmother's funeral. He was a Louisiana Baptist missionary and host of the radio program the French Baptist Hour in South Louisiana. He was a student of the history of Joseph Willis. His character is 100% fictional.

George Smith aka George Adams—Based upon the famous Mississippi riverboat gambler, George Devol. He was born in 1829 and worked the river for more than forty years and made a fortune playing cards.

Joseph Willis—He was born (1758-1854) a Cherokee slave in Bladen County, North Carolina. Preached the first evangelical sermon west of the Mississippi River in 1798. He was born into slavery. His mother was Cherokee and his father a wealthy English plantation owner. His family took him to court to deprive him of his inheritance, which would have made him the wealthiest plantation owner in Bladen County, North Carolina in 1776. He fought as a patriot in the Revolutionary War under the most colorful of all the American generals, Francis Marion, The Swamp Fox. His first wife, Rachel Bradford Willis, died in childbirth, and his second wife died only six years later, leaving him with five young children. He crossed the mighty Mississippi River at Natchez at the peril of his own life, riding a mule! He entered hostile Spanish-controlled Louisiana Territory when the dreaded Code Noir (Black Code) was in effect. It forbade any Protestant ministers who came into the territory from preaching. His life was threatened there because of the message he preached. His denomination refused to ordain him until 1812 because of his race. On November 13, 1812, Joseph Willis constituted Calvary Baptist Church at Bayou Chicot, Louisiana. He went on to plant more than twenty churches in Louisiana. On October 31, 1818, Joseph Willis founded the Louisiana Baptist Association at Beulah Baptist in Cheneyville, Louisiana. Joseph Willis founded all five charter member churches. After overcoming insurmountable obstacles, he blazed a trail for others for another half-century that changed American history. Joseph Willis was Randy Willis's 4th great-grandfather.

Daniel Hubbard "Dan" Willis, Jr.—Thirteen-year-old great-grandson of Joseph. The eldest son of Daniel Hubbard Willis, Sr. and Anna Slaughter Willis. He was reared on Barber Creek near Longleaf, Louisiana. He married Julia Ann Graham on January 5, 1867. Daniel Hubbard Willis, Jr. was the first of four Willis brothers to marry four of Robert and Ruth Graham's daughters. He fought under General Randall Lee Gibson in the Civil War in many of the great battles including Shiloh, Bull Run, Perryville, Murfreesboro, Missionary Ridge and Chickamauga. He named his youngest son, Randall Lee Willis, after General Gibson. Randy Willis was named after his grandfather. Daniel Hubbard Willis, Jr. was Randy Willis's great-grandfather.

Reverend Daniel Hubbard Willis, Sr.—(1817-1887) He was the first of Joseph's descendants to follow him into the ministry. The eldest son of Agerton Willis and the eldest grandson of Joseph Willis. He was born in the village of Bayou Boeuf and was a neighbor of Jim Bowie's brother Rezin for four years. The name changed to Holmesville in 1834. It was here that Rezin lived between 1824-1827. It was also here later that the brutal plantation owner Edwin Epps enslaved Solomon Northup for almost ten years of his twelve years as a slave before being freed. Daniel married Anna Slaughter in 1838. They settled on Spring Creek at Babb's Bridge. Both are buried at the Amiable Baptist Church Cemetery near Babb's Bridge (present-day Longleaf, Louisiana.) He was Randy Willis's great-great-grandfather.

Ahyoka Willis—The mother of Joseph Willis. Her real name was Mary Willis. Joseph told his children and grandchildren that his mother was a Cherokee slave. She was Randy Willis's 5th great-grandmother.

Ruth and Naomi Willis—Joseph's twin children. Joseph had nineteen children. For the sake of this book they are the twin daughters of Joseph and Hannah Willis that died of honey poisoning at age six, but early historians wrote they were two sons who died "poisoned on honey and were buried a half mile from the present town of Oakdale, Louisiana."

Elvy Sweat Willis—Fourth wife of Pastor Joseph Willis. She was much younger than him.

Hannah Willis—Third wife of Joseph. Hannah was not her real name, although she was married to Joseph the longest of his four wives. She married Joseph after Sarah's death. Her real name was probably Sarah Johnson. The author changed her name to Hannah in order for her not to be confused with Joseph's second wife Sarah. Three of Joseph and Hannah aka Sarah Johnson's sons, Joseph Jr., William, and Lemuel all had daughters named Sarah.

Rachel Bradford Willis—First wife of Joseph Willis and daughter of William Bradford of Bladen County, North Carolina. Rachel was a descendant of another William Bradford, too. He was an English Separatist leader and signatory to the *Mayflower Compact*. He served as the Plymouth Colony Governor five times. The combination of hard work and assistance from local Native Americans meant that the Pilgrims reaped an abundant harvest after the summer of 1621. The celebration that we now regard as the First Thanksgiving was the Pilgrims' 3-day feast celebrated in November of 1621.

Bradford helped organize the celebration. She was Randy Willis's 4th great-grandmother.

Agerton Willis—Eldest son of Joseph and father of Reverend Daniel Hubbard Willis Sr. Named after his grandfather. He was a neighbor to Jim Bowie's brother, Rezin Bowie, for four years (1824-1827) in the village of Bayou Boeuf. The name changed to Holmesville in 1834 and is located today near present-day Eola. It was also at Holmesville, on Bayou Boeuf, that the brutal plantation owner Edwin Epps enslaved Solomon Northup for almost ten years of his twelve years as a slave. Agerton married Sophie Story, an Irish orphan brought from Tennessee by a Mr. Park, who lived near Holmesville. He was Randy Willis's 3rd great-grandfather.

Agerton Willis—Father of Joseph. Husband of Ahyoka Willis. Wealthy Bladen County, North Carolina plantation owner. He was Randy Willis's 5th great-grandfather.

William Willis—Son of Joseph and eldest son of Sarah Johnson Willis (known as Hannah in the novel).

Lemuel Willis—Son of Joseph and Hannah Willis in the novel. Hannah's real name was probably Sarah Johnson. Three of

Joseph and Sarah's sons, Joseph, William, and Lemuel all had daughters named Sarah. He married Emeline Perkins in 1833. They were living in Blanche, Louisiana in 1852. Blanche was three miles from present-day Glenmora towards Oakdale.

Samuel Willis—Son of Joseph and Elvy Sweat Willis.

Aimuewell Willis—Youngest of 19 children of Joseph. His mother was Elvy Sweat Willis.

Johnson Sweat—Father of Elvy Sweat Willis.

Ephriam Sweat—Father of Johnson Sweat and grandfather of Levy Sweat. He taught Joseph's children at Bayou Chicot.

Julia Ann Graham Willis—Wife of Daniel "Dan" Hubbard Willis, Jr. Daughter of Robert and Ruth Graham. She was Randy Willis's great-grandmother.

Robert and Ruth Graham—Father-in-law of Daniel Hubbard Willis, Jr. Four of Robert Graham's daughters married four of Rev. Daniel Hubbard Willis's sons, inluding Daniel, Jr. whom married Julia Ann Graham. They were Randy Willis's maternal great-great-grandparents.

Joseph Willis's children—Joseph married four times, with three of his wives dying before he did. He had nineteen children. According to the 1850 Rapides parish census Joseph's fourth wife Elvy Sweat was born in 1820. This is unlikely. Joseph had 19 children by four wives. They were in order of birth: (1) Agerton Willis (1785), (2) Mary Willis (1787), (3) Joseph Willis, Jr., (1792), (4) Rachel Willis (1794), (5) Jemima Willis (1796), (6) Sarah Willis (1798), (7) Sally Willis (1802), (Although she could be the same as Sarah Willis in 1798), (8) William Willis (1804), (9) Lemuel Willis (1812), (10) John Willis (1814), (11) Martha Willis (1825), (12-15) (four females listed in the 1830 census between the ages of 5-20), (16) Samuel Willis (1836), (17) Aimuewell Willis (1837- 1937), and two sons (18-19) that died "poisoned on honey and were buried a half mile from Oakdale.

The Animals

Josh—Joseph's first mule that swam the Mississippi with him early in his ministry. His real name is unknown. Randy Willis named him after one of his three sons just for fun.

Ole Sally—She refused at first to be listed with the animals.—Molly mule that Joseph bought in Vidalia to swim the Mississippi River and carry him on mission trips. Her real name is unknown.

Trixie and Dixie—Two mules named in honor of two of Randy Willis's father's mules.

Beau "Bo" (the mule) and Dollar (the horse)—Named after two different horses, Dollor and Dollar, that John Wayne rode in his final westerns. The horses are often confused. It is Dollor aka Beau (the name the author chose to avoid the same confusion) that carries Wayne when he makes his famous charge, reins in his teeth, in his Oscar-winning portrayal of Rooster Cogburn in *True Grit*. And it's Dollar that Wayne rides in the sequel, *Rooster Cogburn*.

Louisiana Wind

a novel of Louisiana

INTRODUCTION

"The best men I've known have been cowmen. There's a
code they live by—it's their way of life. It starts with an abiding
reverence for the Good Lord. They're taught to honor and respect
their parents and to share both blanket and bread. Their words are
their bond, a handshake their contract. They're good stewards of
His creation, the land. They believe the words in His Book.

Learn from these men—from their stories of triumph over
tragedy—victory over adversity, for the wisdom of others blows
where it wishes—like a *Louisiana Wind*." —Daniel Hubbard
Willis, Jr., 1900

This is the story of such men....

PROLOGUE

March 20, 1900
Barber Creek
Babb's Bridge, Louisiana

I'd give anything to be mounted on a fast saddle horse again. I'd give him his head and point him due West—West to East Texas, that is. There, I'd buy another herd of longhorns, maybe even a Hereford bull or two.

My son, Daniel Oscar, says I might have Bright's Disease and may never be able to ride and rope again. I don't believe it, not for a Yankee minute. He's studying to be a medical doctor. I told him I'm only a half-step slower than I use to be. Well, maybe a full step. But here's my reasoning: there are more ole cowboys than there are ole doctors. We're a stubborn, durable lot. I've lived through drought, flood, blight, range wars, blizzards, dust storms, bank failures, lightning bolts, snake bites, stampeding cows, and some of the worst trail driving cooking imaginable. And I'm still upright and breathing. But even if this doctor-boy of mine is right, at least my sons will continue our way of life. I've passed on to them the family grit, love of nature, codes of honor, Christian morals, and my mama's manners. Tradition is big where I hail from. We uphold it.

My name is Daniel Hubbard Willis, Jr. I remember well back in '61 when a mighty Louisiana Wind threatened our way of life, even our very existence. But first let me tell ya of a happier time. Oh, yeah, it was the happiest of times! Come to think of it, it was two years ago—today.

NARRATIVE

DAY 1

March 20, 1898
The Beef Pens
Mayflower, Newton County, Texas

It had taken us five hard days to ride to Mayflower, in Newton County, Texas, to buy 2500 rangy tough Longhorn steers, cows, and heifers. I preferred those crossbred with Durham and Hereford bulls. I'd made the trip every spring since the end of the War of Northern Aggression in '65. (Weren't nothing "civil" about it.)

But, this day I needed to fulfill a promise to our Cookie, Rooster, the best cook this side of the Brazos. I agreed to buy him a chuck wagon like my friend Charlie Goodnight had rebuilt from an army surplus wagon. Now, admittedly, I was slow to change, but it was time to move forward with this modern advancement.

I would no longer need my hoodlum wagon I'd used for years to carry our food, gear, and bedrolls. Rooster wanted one with a water barrel and coffee mill attached. He also wanted me to buy enough soap, salt pork, boxes of bacon, dried fruit, flour, coffee, black-eyed peas, corn, beans, sugar, pepper, salt, onion, potatoes, lard, and sour dough starter to feed Robert E. Lee's Army of Northern Virginia.

After revising and reducing his list, I also bought assorted supplies from the general store to stock the wagon: eating irons, tin plates, bedrolls, tents, and, of course, a Dutch oven. Rooster also requested two bottles of whiskey for medicinal purposes, which I declined, knowing liniment and quinine would do. I did buy a white hat though, so everyone could locate me under the heavy longleaf pine canopy along the trail.

There was this fiddle and leather case just sitting on the store's shelf. Knowing how my youngest son Ran loved music, I bought it for him for his birthday. I also bought him three Big Chief writing tablets so we would have a record of this cattle drive. Then I hired twelve more trailers and a horse wrangler. We would need everyone of them to trail the Longhorns through the thick piney woods of Louisiana. If the weather held in our favor and we were blessed with no injuries or accidents, the return trip to the beef pens at the railroad in LeCompte would take nine days.

My four sons rode with me: Henry Elwa, the eldest, was thirty-one; Daniel Oscar was twenty-three; Robert Kenneth was twenty-one; and Randall Lee, whom we call him Ran, was only twelve. It was Ran's first cattle drive and his birthday to boot. He had read everything he could about cattle trailing and cowmen. Like me when I was his age, his dream was to be a cowboy. I'd told him he couldn't believe all that stuff about Wild Bill and about Elwa's favorite, Kit Carson. Now, Wyatt Earp, well, that was a different matter, every word of that being true. I oughta know cause I'm a lawman too. Ran would soon discover the vast difference between a dime novel cowboy and the real deal.

*   *   *

It also afforded me the opportunity to share round the campfires each night the story of our family in a land of red dirt and tall pines. For, you see, Louisiana is our home.

And if that wasn't enough, it was the 100th anniversary of my great-grandfather's swim across the mighty Mississippi, riding only a mule to settle our family in what was then known as the Louisiana Territory. Oh, no, the Cherokees and Choctaws did him no harm, not even the outlaws. The same couldn't be said of a couple of plantation owners and a few religious folks. I thought surely we wouldn't encounter as many dangers as he had. But, alas, I thought wrong. One of the things we say in the Louisiana is, pray for blessings but keep your powder dry. I was an optimist, but nobody's fool.

DAY 2

March 21, 1898
The Beef Pens
Mayflower, Newton County, Texas

After bedding down along the way in the home and barn of my old but now deceased friend Wade Mattox, who had died during the war, we arose at 3:30. Rooster had prepared biscuits in a big dough pan and coffee that would wake the dead. I preferred Arbuckle's coffee. Some called it six-shooter coffee, as it was said to be able to float a cowboy's pistol. But then, if you expect to be operational in the middle of the night, you need a jolt of liquid that can open your eyes, quicken your nerves, and put a spring in your step. Rooster's brew filled the bill in those regards.

I reminded everyone that I had an unwritten rule prohibiting any man from complaining about another's cooking. Only a fool argues with a skunk, a mule...or a cook. But woe be to the cook who didn't get our meals ready on time.

"We need to move the herd at a steady pace," I told Rooster. "I want the beef to still be on them when we get to our destination. We'll pause to let them graze now and then. Meanwhile, you drive on ahead, find a spot for us to bed down for the night at Burr's Ferry, there on the banks of the Sabine River. I'll send Robert Kenneth with you to help get things set up and arranged."

"You fellers will be hungry by the time you catch up to me," said Rooster. "You'll be plenty glad you got me this new wagon. I'll have hot grub waitin' fer all of you."

"Break out molasses," I suggested. "Something a little sweet will take out the dryness of this dusty trail."

"Got enough hand-to-mouth vittles to get you boys through the daylight hours?" asked Rooster.

"Sure enough," I said. "Canteens are full, and we've got hardtack, pemmican, parched corn, and beef jerky in our saddlebags to tide us over until we see you this evening."

"You watch out for your cowhands, I'll give you that," said Rooster. "Fair enough. I'll pack up and be on my way." He pushed back his sweat worn hat, pulled his faded bandanna to the right, and ran his fingers through his grey beard. He was as raw and feisty as a cock fighting champion, thus justifying his nickname.

I told the others we'd bring them up and spread them out along the bank, with the lead cattle headed downstream. The leads would get to drink clear water that way, and as the drags kept coming they'd get clear water, too, because they would be upstream.

We would attempt to make the first ten miles to the Sabine River by sunset. I'd brought a dozen Catahoula leopard dogs, my Jersey bell cow Ethel, a remuda of horses, and six big rawboned mules for the chuck wagon from our home in Babb's Bridge. I'd also brought my biggest covered wagon to hold the calves born on the trail. I wasn't about to leave them behind for the red wolves and coyotes, as some did. At first light we headed the herd up, took a deep seat, a faraway look, and kept our minds in the middle…the middle of that herd, that is.

We hadn't ridden but a mile or so when two young cowpokes rode up in a trail of dust. Eyeing them told me they might be brothers but they were also toting guns. I sure wasn't looking for trouble.

The older one asked, "Who's the trail boss?"

"You got him. Name's Daniel Willis, and this is my son, Elwa, our foreman."

"I'm Jeremiah Stark and this here's my brother, Jacob. Heard you were hiring back in Mayflower. We just missed ya. Sure could use the work. We've worked the drives out of the beef pens from Weeks Chapel to Toledo. We can rope, ride, and help ya with any outlaw or rustler problem. We get a tad bit more than other drovers cause we're known to be the best in these here parts with a gun."

"Is that so? How'd ya get those biblical names?"

"I reckon it was our mother, Celina Marie Stark, who named us," Jeremiah answered. "She died shortly after Jacob was born. Our sister Mary said she was one of those Bible thumpers. She should know, since she's one too."

"Boys, I've got enough help. You both look healthy, but I live by a rule…no gunslingers. Don't get me wrong, we have guns cause I'm the constable back home in Rapides Parish, and my boys carry squirrel guns and the lot, but not like those .45s on your hips."

Jacob had a look I couldn't read.

"But, Mr. Willis, you have a Colt .45 Peacemaker on your hip too," Jeremiah replied.

"The difference is, mine doesn't have a dozen notches carved into its handle."

"To each his own. We're bunking over in Burkeville. Mind if we ride along until the trail veers off?"

"It's a free country."

I decided to let them join us for those few miles. Figured they wouldn't have time to become a problem. We were doing right well, I was riding point with Ethel. She was our "lead steer." Jeremiah and Jacob rode with us. Ran was riding drag with two trailers. Elwa and the other drovers were spread out in pairs in the flank and swing positions as the cattle stretched out in a thin line for some two miles. The brothers rode tall in the saddle, but those notches still bothered me. My years as a lawman had made me a keen judge of character and a shrewd observer of strangers.

We had ridden almost to where the trail forked to Burr's Ferry and Burkeville when clouds suddenly moved in. It was an East Texas thunderstorm moving faster than a ring-tailed cat with its tail on fire. I sensed the cattle were getting restless. All of a sudden a sky fire exploded nearby. The spotted Appaloosa gelding I was riding, Augustus, almost jumped out from under me. He was barely three years old and was still a little skittish. Actually, that would be putting it mildly. I once saw him sidestep his own shadow.

Lightning shot down on the forest. The cattle spooked and started running through the tall pines at a breakneck pace. I yelled, "Stampede!" The other drovers echoed my warning. I also heard them yelling words they hadn't learned in Sunday school. My thoughts turned to my youngest son's safety. But then again that's why I had him riding drag...to appease his mama.

Jeremiah yelled to his brother, "Take cover behind those rocks and take Mr. Willis's bell cow with ya."

Jacob was headed toward a rock embankment when he called back, "Will do."

I watched him do some fancy riding on his cow pony as she dodged four-legged death. He needn't have worried about Ethel, she was already there.

The sound of those huge horns scraping the pines and knocking against each other gave me chills. The wood chips were flying faster than a hundred lumberjacks with axes.

My Catahoula hounds were trying to turn them. One had a steer by its ear and another by its tail, but they were way too outnumbered to make much difference. Jeremiah spurred his horse and was at a full gallop. He was able to slow them enough to let me move ahead while I tried to circle them to the right to get them to mill by waving my hat. Milling cattle soon become exhausted, but these were hell-bent for leather. My plan did not work.

There were moments when I was sure I'd get crushed against the trees as the ground shook with thundering hoof beats. If Augustus stumbled, it would be all over except the obligatory, "He died doing what he loved most." I asked the Lord to protect my boys cause it was now a matter of life or death. The prayer for our safety by my sweet wife before we left home echoed in my ears as loud as Ethel's copper cowbell.

The cattle stampeded through the woods and tore up the dirt like a turning plow. There was an earthy smell of pine that might have been enjoyable under other circumstances. I finally came to the conclusion that turning the herd was impossible. I assumed they'd wear themselves out. I figured wrong. Thank the Lord my Indian cow pony could run like a deer and was as sure-footed as a mule!

Then suddenly they stopped. No, it wasn't our cowboy skills. It was the Sabine River.

We'd passed Rooster with his chuck wagon. He was now about three miles back, but still intact. His six-up mule team was dilapidated looking though. Jacob had saved my bell cow, or at least that's what he told everyone. Ethel would never sleep with the herd again. From that day forward she bedded down with the horses and mules. I thought for sure my dogs had been trampled. But, nope, they were all now cooling down in the Sabine. The drovers had all made it too. But what about my sons? All were accounted for, but were pretty scratched up, bruised, and a worn out bunch.

Ran came hobbling up to me and said, "This ain't how they tell it in the dime novels. No one said anything about getting covered in cow manure, dust clouds, and flying tumbleweeds. Talk about being baptized by fire as a new cowpoke. I sure enough got mine."

I laughed, hugged him despite his wretched appearance, and said, "I'll give you a break from riding drag after all that. Ya smell bad, but I don't detect any broken bones. Hope you've got those Indian Chief notepads handy, because now you'll have one whopper of a story to put down on paper."

"Assuming my poor raw hands can hold a pencil and I can stay awake long enough tonight to make some notes," said Ran.

What a reunion we had that night as we all sat round the campfire, except for a few of the drovers who were night herding in two hour shifts. We ate plenty of Rooster's sourdough bullets and Pecos strawberries from his Dutch oven over an open fire. Those biscuits and beans, along with his beef steaks, hit the spot. And, yes, he even measured out a portion of molasses for each of us.

All that was lacking was my dear wife Julia Ann's apple pie, and, oh, yes, her Louisiana coffee made with the sweet waters of Barber Creek. I sure missed her. Everything tasted as good as a king's banquet and reminded me of our annual Willis Feast of Thanksgiving, for it was a day to be thankful—very thankful. What prompted me to share the most memorable Willis celebration I'd ever seen was Ran's comment, "Father, I thought you were a goner until I saw your white hat waving above the Longhorns."

"Not hardly, son...but almost."

NIGHT 2

March 21, 1898
Burr's Ferry
Texas side of the Sabine River
On the Middle Fork of the Beef Trail

As we sat round the campfire on the banks of the Sabine, I shared a story that has been etched into my mind with the healing hands of time. I recalled events in September of 1854. The colorful leaves had begun to fade in the mist of the autumn chilly air. I was only knee-high to a grasshopper, all of fifteen, but I remembered it as if it were yesterday. The celebration was the most glorious in our family's history.

There were songs sung and stories told. Family and friends had gathered as far as the eye could see. Some came by wagon, some by buggy, still others by way of steamboats on the Red River. Many rode horses and mules. And some even walked long distances.

I'd never seen so much love nor had I ever gotten so many hugs. It was the largest supper on the grounds that ever had been...at least in our neck of the piney woods. Fried chicken, roasted potatoes, green beans with pork, biscuits and gravy, cornbread stuffing, fresh watermelon, fried green tomatoes, okra and cabbage and corn on the cob were all added to the obvious main platter favorite of steak. When the best cooks connect with the best available fixin's, you can bet it was a feast to remember.

The dewberry pie had a special meaning that day. Although, I decided not taste it in this particular instance, for you see it was my Great-Grandfather Joseph Willis's favorite. Just five days before, on his deathbed, he had looked me straight in the eyes and said, "I've preached on Heaven many times, but I've never done it justice. There's Jim Bowie, but with no knife. I see Ruth and Naomi. Oh, my, oh, my, it's Him!"

With that Great-Grandfather smiled, closed his eyes in peace and was with the One he had so longed to see. Oh, yes, there were tears of sorrow because we would miss him. But, there were more tears of joy, for you see, he was home...*home at last*. His legacy was one that proved one man could make a major difference in this world. He had preached and traveled and witnessed. He fulfilled the calling he felt God had put upon him, and he did so with determination, fearlessness, and overflowing love for those who would allow him to share the gospel message. To that end, he left me and all others in our family with a standard to live up to. I was thoroughly convinced I would see him again one day with I joined him in Glory. That thought was comforting.

DAY 3

March 22, 1898
Burr's Ferry
Texas side of the Sabine River
On the Middle Fork of the Beef Trail

Daylight was burning in my mind cause I'd slept to 5:30.
Rooster had been up since 3:30, as always. We needed to make at
least ten miles today, and twelve would be better. The cattle were
calm, and that was a blessing considering the stampede we had
endured. Even their bellowing was music to my ears. We kept a
keen eye out for injuries. But first, we had one not-so-small task to
perform—swim the Sabine River. It wasn't exactly the swift
Neches or even the muddy Red in Alexandria, but it was dangerous
enough. The river was up two feet from the storm, maybe even
three.

We loosen up the cinches on our saddles so the horses will have
plenty of room to breathe and have more freedom in swimming.
Our bell cow Ethel took the lead to the water, the others followed.

I'd been taught to expect the unexpected on these cattle drives.
I'd expected the two dollar ferry fee for my wagons and even the
twenty-five cents for Ran and his saddle horse. The six cents a
head for my cattle was reasonable enough, but there were too
many, so that's why I felt the need to risk swimming them to the
other side. Praise the Lord, we didn't lose a single head. But we
almost did.

What I wasn't expecting is what the Stark brothers did. When I
wasn't looking, one of my thousand pound steers turned and
started to make his way down stream. Even worse, more than a
dozen head started following after him. If others followed suit, we
could have a split herd on our hands and possibly the loss of
dozens of our prize animals.

That's when something crazy happened. Those wild and
fearless Stark brothers raced into the stream, pulling off their outer
clothes as they rode. They jumped that mammoth steer, grabbed
him by his thick, sharp horns, and turned his head in the directions

of the opposite bank. Still holding on to the horns, the Starks swam with that steer until it walked up the bank, leading the other cattle right behind it. It was the dang'est feat I'd ever witnessed. In fact, I'd never even heard of such a stunt like that before, with the possible exception of the story of how my great-grandfather swam the mighty Mississippi clinging to his mule.

I rode up to the Starks and said, "I've been to rodeos where I never saw riding and steer wrestling to meet that, boys. If your offer is still open, consider yourselves working for me for the rest of this drive." They nodded and smiled. We then drove the herd some twelve more miles without incident. Those Stark brothers, notched guns or not, had proved their merit.

NIGHT 3

March 22, 1898
The Middle Fork of the Beef Trail
Caney Creek, Vernon Parish, Louisiana

After what I witnessed with that steer earlier in the day, I wanted to learn more about the Starks.

"Now, Jeremiah and Jacob, tell me where you boys were fetched up? I'd like to know more about ya."

Jeremiah jumped right in. "Mr. Willis, we never got to tell ya why we wanted to be on this cattle drive in the first place. We're from Louisiana."

"Whereabouts?"

"Branch, sir, but our sister Mary now lives in Lecompte. When we heard that's where you were trailing your herd, we figured if you hired us we could visit her. Her first husband, Charles Oliver, died in '87, leaving her with six younguns. Three years ago she married a young fellow seventeen years her junior named Arthur Allen Hanks. The age difference is a concern to us. We've heard stories about him, too, down in Branch. I told Mary don't be surprised if he runs off, but if he does he better run far—real far. They've moved to Lecompte to start a meat market. They now have a three-month-old baby girl named Lillie Gertrude. We so want to see and hold our little niece. We're hoping to live there if we can find employment."

"About finding livelihood, talk to Elwa. He's moving to Lecompte, too, to handle our cattle business. We need him there to make sure the Texas and Pacific Railway does what it promised. That's a story for another day. I'm sure we can work out something, and you boys can spoil baby Lillie all you want. And, God forbid if Hanks should ever take flight with let's say a younger filly. He'll flee Louisiana for good once he sees those notched .45's on your hips."

"We don't seek any trouble, Mr. Willis, but we don't back down either. We've found that being two of us, always together, sometimes puts things to rest without the need to clear leather. Still, any advice or help Elwa could provide us, we'd take it kindly."

"Not to worry on that account," I assured them. "Our family will always be there for you fellows. For Mary, too, and baby Lillie. Every single one us will be, from me to my sons, even young Ran. That's the cowman way. That's the Willis way."

The brothers nodded their understanding and appreciation.

"Now, one last question. Who are your father and mother?"

"John and Celina Marie Deroussel Stark."

I pushed back my hat and threw another log on the evening camp fire. "Yep, I had surmised you boys were Cajun French. I love your people. Without them what would Louisiana be? The food alone was worth trailing cows through the swamps of South Louisiana after we lost the cause."

Thinking back to earlier that day, I said, ""For Cajuns, you sure can ride those Spanish cow ponies."

Jeremiah smiled. "Mr. Willis, we call them quarter horses. They can run like deer, at least for a quarter of a mile."

"It would appear they saved your lives today."

Jacob agreed. "Yes, sir, all our family seems to stay healthy. In fact, we had to shoot one of our kin in order to start a cemetery."

Everyone laughed, but I looked at their guns again.

*   *   *

As we gathered round the campfire Ran asked me to share one of Great-Grandfather Joseph Willis's stories from days long since past. I thought of one he'd shared to father and me on a three day wagon trip in 1852.

Great-Grandfather and Miss Elvy had taken a little trip to N'Orleans on the Riverboat *Natchez* in 1828. On the voyage back home they stopped in Baton Rouge. The French explorer Sieur d'Iberville had named the city after seeing a red pole that marked the hunting boundary between the Bayougoula and Houmas Indians.

It was there that Great-Grandfather met a young man who was headed home on a flatboat from N'Orleans. He caught his eye, being so tall. His face had a determination far beyond his years. He was mighty upset after watching slaves being mistreated at a

N'Orleans' slave market.

After a spell, the young man asked his traveling companion, a Mr. Gentry, "Why doesn't someone do something?"

He then turned to Great-Grandfather. "You're from Louisiana, sir, and your wife says you're a Baptist preacher. Why doesn't the church do something?"

The young man continued to pour out his heart, "There are more slaves in N'Orleans than any other city in this country, and I hear tell that Louisiana has become very wealthy off their labors. I've seen men and woman shackled, collared, and treated like animals this week.

"I'm only nineteen, sir, and I know you cannot help the poor by destroying the rich. But something must be done to stop this. I wish I could make a difference. I'm as poor as a church mouse with little education. My heart has been crushed by my sister Sarah's death this past January while giving birth. During this trip we've had to fight off seven men who tried to rob us of our cargo. We were just trying to make a living, and then we stumbled upon a slave auction. Who am I to think that I can turn the tide in my own life, much less this scourge of human bondage? Have you ever seen a man with so many odds against him?" The young man hung his head in an expression of self-defeat. His feelings were genuine, but he saw little chance for him to correct a situation that seemed far greater than he could impact or alter.

Great-Grandfather replied, "Yes, I have, and I know it seems impossible, but with God all things are possible. I have a belief and a trust that God will raise His man when the time is right. Joseph was seven years in prison, but then he became the second most powerful man in Egypt and was able to help his family and the other Jews in his homeland. Moses wandered the wilderness for years before God told him the time was right for him to step forward and become the leader of God's chosen people. The Bible tells us that God's hand is not short and his ear is not deaf. He sees and hears and knows the evil ways of mankind. And he knows the ways to remedy it. Keep praying, young man, and never lose your sympathy for what you have observed."

He bade him farewell, but then paused and said to the young man, "I'm sorry, but I did not catch your name?"

"Abraham, sir, but most folks just call me Abe."

DAY 4

March 23, 1898
The Middle Fork of the Beef Trail
Vernon Parish, Louisiana

I'd figured we had had enough excitement for one cattle drive. What I didn't know was it had only begun. One old man and two younger ones rode up to me at the break of day. The old man had a worn leather look. The cocky younger ones rode as if they were on ten dollar horses with forty dollar saddles. I wasn't in the mood for either.

"We're interested in your cattle," the elder spoke with a wicked glee.

"They're not for sale."

"We're not here to buy."

It has never taken me long to examine a horseshoe. Especially when all three had their Winchesters out of their scabbards. Nevertheless, it would appear it was hog-killing time, and I was the hog.

"We only need a couple hundred. You'll hardly miss them. They're not worth dying for, mister," the old man said with a smirk.

I told them there were three things I couldn't abide: cold coffee, wet toilet paper, and cattle rustlers. Just when I figured it was the end of the trail for me, Jeremiah rode up and took over the conversation.

"You try to take those cows and the only thing that's going to be missed is you."

"Don't I know you?" the old man asked.

"Yep. I know you, too, Scar Bartholomew."

"Jeremiah Stark! I thought you were dead. Do you think two on three is a dogfall?"

"My friend Sam makes it even."

"Sam? Where's he?" the old man snickered.

"Samuel Colt, right here—on my hip! I heard you were a lying, thieving Jayhawker in the war. Abe Lincoln may have freed all men, but Sam Colt made them equal."

About that time Jacob rode up. Just as Scar smiled again, one of his cohorts pulled his gun, and Scar followed suit. Neither had cleared a holster when .45 caliber bullets ripped through both their hearts. The third bandit was just a trail of dust by then.

This would be eighteen-year-old Jacob's first notch on his gun. I'd hoped it would be his last. My plan was to cut them loose when I first met them, but now, as my great-grandfather always said, "You've got to dance with the one that brung ya." I reckoned I would have had my last dance without them. We stopped the herd long enough to bury the scoundrels. I didn't feel like a cross was fitting so we stacked a few rocks on them. Maybe if the coyotes got hungry enough, they might pore through the rocks and dig out the carcasses. Nature had its ways, and so did man. I had no words to say over their graves. Not any that would have mattered.

The Stark boys spoke not a word until Jacob asked me, "How do feel about all this, Mr. Willis?"

I squared my hat on my head, and got back on my mount. "There's a few men in Louisiana that need killing, but no cows that need stealing."

O   N   E

"A woman's heart should be so hidden in God
that a man has to seek Him just to find her."
—*Joseph Willis* 1785

NIGHT 4

March 23, 1898, at dusk
The Middle Fork of the Beef Trail
Castor Bayou, Leesville, Louisiana

Now Daniel Oscar was from Leesville, so as we approached the town he decided to spend the night there with his wife Ella. None of us knew that when he invited his younger brother Ken to share some of Ella's fine Louisiana cooking a plan had already been hatched. It involved Ella's friend Eulah Rosalie Hilburn. When Ken first laid eyes on Eulah the welfare of our cattle seemed to become a faded memory.

Eulah was a frontierswoman in that she had no flab on her arms, legs, or neck. Although she had a rather aristocratic heritage, she was a product of life on a farm and ranch. Her dark brown hair could fall half-way down her back, except that she kept it braided. Her teeth were straight, her eyes were a deep blue, and her smile was engaging. She wasn't perfect, however. Due to an early bout with chicken pox, she had a few small scars on her forehead and left cheek, and her right foot had a minor limp caused by a horse kick when she was a child. All things considered, however, she was an impressive specimen of womanhood, especially in parts of the country where men valued a gal's ability to cook, garden, sew, and read as much as they did their appearance.

After supper Eulah invited Ken to her father's farm just down the road to see a horse she needed advice on. Early the next morning Elwa rode back to camp and informed us Ken's saddle horse seemed to have suddenly developed a slight limp. He would catch up with us in a day or two.

Eulah's pony had a pedigree as long as her arm that was meant to impress. Ken was impressed. Not with the horse, but with Eulah. In his opinion, she was stunning, so he asked her if they could discuss the horse in more detail the next morning at the Hotel Leesville. They had an excellent café, with dark roast coffee, to start the day. He couldn't have cared less about that horse by then.

I later asked Ken, "I thought I'd taught you always to tell the truth?"

He replied, "I did, Father. I told her over coffee I would love to court her."

Ken added, "She seemed unimpressed and certainly not amused. She said she was only there for advice and was a lady that adhered to Southern traditions. She made it clear she did not wish to mislead me. I didn't have a clue what she was talking about, especially the Southern tradition part. The only Southern tradition I knew was on a horse with a rope or in a field behind a plow.

"Then she said, since she'd just met me, unfortunately, she would have to decline any overtures of friendship, especially courting. That is, until I met her mother. Lo and behold, she then invited me to join her and her mother for breakfast the next morning so she could learn more about horses, and I'm sure her mother more about me."

Well, according to Ken, her mother started asking him more questions than a Baton Rouge lawyer.

"Tell me about your education, young man. I understand you know a lot about horses, but can you read and write? Do you know Latin or any other language?"

"I trailed cattle and horses from Texas, ma'm, so I've had to learn enough Spanish to do horse tradin' and cattle swappin'. And, yes, I enjoy reading and have been blessed with a sizeable library put together by my mother. My favourites are Robert Louis Stevenson, Mark Twain, Ambrose Bierce, and Edgar Allan Poe."

Eulah was as sharp as a tack, and her English blood gave her a charm and grace such as Ken had never seen before, except when she exclaimed, "Don't ask any more questions, Mother. Cowboys love to brag about everything. How everything they do is bigger and better."

Her mother was not dissuaded and asked Ken, "Mr. Willis, just how many cows do you own?"

He told her 200. That wasn't near as many as she'd been led to believe by her Eulah Rosalie.

Ken began to sweat like General William Tecumseh Sherman in church.

"That's in my smokehouse," he explained. They both smiled, and her mother seemed to ease up on him, at least for the moment. Eulah finally told Ken, "I'd like to see those 200 cows. Maybe even the live ones, too."

"They await your inspection, Miss," said Ken, with a modest bow of the head. "And your mother is welcome to join us."

So, indeed, the proper courtship began and flourished. Before long I had another beautiful daughter-in-law. Albeit, with a lot fewer cows than Ken remembered that day. But, then again, I later learned that Eulah Rosalie knew more about horses than all of us put together.

*   *   *

Ran knew his brothers had heard my war stories on these cattle drives many times, but he hadn't, so he asked, "Father, can you tell me a story of the War of Northern Aggression?"

"Sure I will, son. I'll tell ya my favorite!" I began to unwind a story of despair, hope, redemption, and promise.

"It starts, Ran, in the winter of 1863 when a beautiful young southern belle got news that her handsome beau, a Confederate soldier for the cause, had been killed at Chickamauga. Her grief could not be abated. Each day she would read her *Red Letter Bible* and ask the Lord, 'Why?' She got no answer. Each day she would reach into her trunk and take out a photograph of him dressed in his uniform. Tears would come streaming down her checks. As the months went by she had resigned herself to living out the rest of her life as an old maid."

I paused a moment to stir the embers before us and to adjust my bedroll against my back.

"At the end of the great War Between the States she would feed the men from the Army of the Confederacy who traveled down the red dirt road in front of her father's home. Many were barefooted, all were hungry. She did this to honor her sweetheart's memory. Finally, one day, her father told her, 'Darling, we have no more to give.'

"She then would take her own supper and give it to those who traveled by on their way home to their loved ones. When her father discovered her sacrificial act of kindness, he insisted she stop for the sake of her own health. He added, 'See, it's never ending. There's yet another straggling, hungry soul.'

"As that soldier got closer, the young girl looked up, and suddenly stood, dropped her plate of food and ran down the red dirt road to the tattered soldier. She hugged him, kissed him, and practically carried him to the front porch.

"Now, Ran, that was the greatest day of the war for the beautiful young southern belle and for me, too. You see, that soldier was me, and the young girl was your mother.

"Rumors of my death had been somewhat exaggerated, as Mr. Twain once put it. Indeed, several of the men in my unit had been waylaid, scattered, and assumed to be dead. Communication was very poor in those outreach areas, so incorrect reports very often were not corrected. Once three of my companions and I finally were able to link up with another division, word had already been relayed that I was presumed dead. I never was told that such a report had been sent to my wife. Besides, we seldom were in towns with good telegraph lines. I eventually rejoined my company and suffered greatly. We were low on ammunition, food, clothes, and even water. Once we got word the fighting was over, I had to walk back home. I was dirty, exhausted, bearded, and starved. But the image of my sweet wife kept me putting one foot in front of the other. It was tortuous, but well worth it all."

*   *   *

"Father, Mother told me that story, too. I so loved it, but she didn't mention the part of her remaining an old maid forever...I don't recall the handsome beau part either."

DAY 5

March 24, 1898
The Middle Fork of the Beef Trail
Castor Bayou, Leesville, Louisiana

We saddled up while wolfing down Rooster's coffee and biscuits. The Louisiana sky was ablaze with colors. A cool wind blew across our faces as we set out for hopefully an uneventful day. And it appeared it would be until young Ran followed his favorite Catahoula cow dog, one-eyed Jack, into the thick post oak.

The chattering noise from the underbrush was unfamiliar to him, but not to Jack. Suddenly there was a loud growl as a wild boar began to charge Jack like a runaway train. Jack attacked him as if he was nothing more than a rabbit. The hog's tusk caught his belly and slit him from end to end, as he jumped.

Jack's piercing squeal echoed through the woods as Ran arrived on his mare. Rearing up, his horse fell over backward, throwing him just yards from where the boar was pawing the ground like an angry bull. He now took aim at Ran just as I rode up.

Jack, bleeding profusely, got up, and this time went for the boar's hindquarters, clamping his jaws on his tail—refusing to let go and allowing me time for one shot. I knew my handgun would not even slow him down. I took aim with my lever-action Winchester 73 and fired, hitting him in his thick skull, right between his eyes. The .44 caliber cartridge killed him, just a few feet from Ran.

Thankfully, the boar's tusk did not go deep enough to cut Jack's intestines or any vital organs. I'll tell ya, Jack has nine lives. He'd already lost an eye when he grabbed a mule by the tail. After that particular time, I had wished he would not behave with such reckless abandonment. Thank the Lord, that wish did not come true.

Daniel Oscar cleaned the wound and coated it with coal oil and Pond's Extract and then wrapped him in silver-coated bandages from Rooster's wagon. He had packed gauze with carbolic acid and wound dressings treated with iodine in his saddle bags. My future people doctor proved to be quite the veterinarian that day. He believed in Louis Pasteur's theory of germs. Others believed it was ridiculous fiction.

Ran laid Jack in the big wagon with the newborn calves with strict instructions for him to stay still. He loved that dog more than most of the people he knew. Today, he was not the only one. He then rode with the wagon and kept an ever protective eye on Jack until we camped. Fortunately, the dog would soon heal. All I could think of was, *Thank you, Lord, and thank you, Jack.* Also, I wondered what I was going to say to Julia Ann. It crossed my mind once, or maybe twice or maybe even more....

That night, Rooster prepared a rare supper of roasted pork over a fire he had kindled with wood. For some reason Ran had no appetite for pork, but he did take a slice to Jack. He refused it, too.

T W O

NIGHT 5

March 4, 1898
The Middle Fork of the Beef Trail
Burton Creek, Vernon Parish, Louisiana

Sitting around the campfire at night was a good way to unwind after a long day in the saddle. Sometimes one of the boys would pull out a harmonica and play a few ballads or hymns, and quite often we'd sing a chorus or two. Ran had his fiddle with him, and he'd serenade us occasionally with something new he was working on. A couple of the fellows would break out a deck of cards if the campfire and the stars were bright enough to make out the numbers and face cards. However, most nights were spent sharing yarns, memories of other cattle drives, stories of interesting people we'd met, sagas of the years of the war, and recollections of our family members, close friends, teachers, pastors, and neighbors.

For my own part, I was often prompted by Ran, who had a hankering for stories about the West. I never got very detailed or graphic in regard to battles I'd been in during the war, nor some of the face-offs I'd had in my role as a lawman. But one night Ran asked me to think back to my early days as a cowboy and to share some events and episodes from that period of my life. On that topic, I was open and agreeable.

"What you're about to hear, son, is a story about times not that long ago, and particularly about a circumstance that drastically altered my way of thinking about being a cowboy, and even about how to live life itself."

*   *   *

As I was being fetched up in Louisiana, I dreamed of being a cowman, so that's exactly what I set out to do after the War of Northern Aggression. Since I had no money I joined in "making the gather" in Texas. With the help of five of my younger brothers we rounded up wild and unbranded maverick Longhorns that had roamed free during the war. Before the railroads were built and busy, we drove the herds on the Opelousas Trail through the swamps to N'Orleans to be shipped north by steamboats. What we couldn't sell we kept on the open range in Rapides Parish to begin building a herd.

Many of those were later driven to shipping points at Vidalia on the Mississippi, but some were driven to Shreveport. The buffalo flies were so bad on the trail to Shreveport the cattle would run off. They hated the stinging, the buzzing, the annoyance. Who could blame 'em.

Trailing cattle to Louisiana began long before they were trailed to Kansas by those Texas cowpokes. As early as the 1830s, cattle were trailed from Stephen F. Austin's colony to N'Orleans, where they fetched twice as much as they did in Texas. Folks used to say "cotton is king," but for my money, I knew that beef was every bit as desirable to Yanks as it was to us southerners.

As the years passed I survived well, but I never seemed to be pulling in the rewards for my efforts that I had early-on envisioned would be mine. Turned out, I wasn't bringing to market the high quality steers and cows that brought in the best payments. Being stumped about his, I was eventually blessed to cross paths with someone who realigned my thinking.

Indeed, it was a grand day when I met an enterprising rancher named Charlie Goodnight who had also joined in "making the gather." We were at a Confederate Reunion in Houston. He had been a scout for the Southern cause. Before that he'd trailed cattle to Louisiana. After telling me all about it, he offered me a cigar, which I declined, and gave me advice on improving my herd through cross breeding with Hereford bulls. He convinced me, based on his experience and keen observations about cattle, weather, trails, and beef brokers, that I needed to buy more high-grade bulls to build a better herd. Weight counted. Appearance counted. Age counted. In order to raise and market prime beef, there had to be premium breeding, proper grazing, and adequate protection from varmits and storms and drought and injuries. I drank in every word of advice this gracious man was willing to share with me.

Goodnight invited me to the JA Ranch in Palo Duro Canyon, but then I got word he no longer managed it. He had a stomach ailment that almost proved fatal, too, so I figured if I ever was going to visit him I'd better do it soon. I purposed in my heart if the opportunity ever arose I would do just that.

That opportunity came in '87 when the Fort Worth and Denver City Railway was built through the Texas Panhandle. Goodnight was now ranching in Armstrong County near the Fort Worth and Denver City line.

But, first I wanted to see what the new XIT Ranch offered in the way of Longhorn bulls, maybe even a Durham. So, in 1888, I boarded the Texas and Pacific Railway at Alexandria and made my way to Channing, Texas, to visit the XIT. Surely I could find a few top-grade Longhorn bulls on their three million acres with more than 150,000 head of cattle.

If not, perhaps Goodnight would sell me one or two of his Hereford bulls. I trusted him. He was a Christian gentleman with an affable nature. I liked Longhorns because they were tough and rangy, but they were mostly long legs and long horns and not near as beefy as Herefords. Well, at least that's what Goodnight had told me. I would then sell my culls and undesirable bulls. The new town of Channing was now a major shipping point, so I had a way to ship them—my new prize bulls—back home.

*   *   *

It was a long ways from Babb's Bridge, but I finally made it to Channing. I didn't want to look like something the cat had dragged in when I first met their range foreman, so I made my way over to the barber shop. I needed a shave, haircut, and bath. I sat on an old crate waiting my turn for a nickel haircut and a dime shave. The bathhouse was outback. The quarter for the hot bath would be the most expensive I'd ever had. The soap made me smell like a flower, though. I decided to buy some for Julia Ann, even though I preferred our lye soap back home.

The old-timers were spinning tales about the weather, the scourge of the XIT's and Charlie Goodnight's barbwire fences doing away with the "real cowboys," a cattle disease called Texas Fever and many a "she done me wrong yarn." Their laughter filled the room and everybody was smiling until one ole cowboy spoke with a gravelly voice, asking, "What was that young cowpoke's name? Ya know the one that got himself thrown off a green-broke mare on the XIT. That horse was a rank one, ya know."

"I was there. His name was Jimbo. He was a praying boy," the barber said.

"Not sure that pony was green-broke though, although that's what they told young Jimbo. He came strolling out of the bunkhouse one morning when some of the cowboys started poking fun at him. He didn't have much experience, but he wanted to show them he could rope and ride."

I took it all in and spoke not a word. I was spellbound.

The barber continued, "They were daring Jimbo to ride that crazy horse brought over from a XIT line camp. They couldn't handle the pony there.

"Those cowboys were real mean to the boy. At first Jimbo did a good job of ignoring them, but they just kept making fun of him. 'Come on, ya got religion we hear tell. You can do anything with that Jewish Carpenter's help, can't ya, boy? Why don't ya wanna ride that horse? Ya scared? Maybe you're too green like that yearling cow pony. Maybe even yellow?'

"Everybody gathered 'round to see what was gonna happen. Every eye was on Jimbo. His face was beet red. He just stood there looking at that horse and didn't move. The men laughed at him, threw up their hands and started walking away. He couldn't have been more than eighteen. I watched him throw his shoulders back and begin to walk toward the corral. He grabbed a bridle and opened the gate. You could hear the whispers as most of the men came back to watch.

"He bridled her and proceeded to rub the mare all over with a saddle blanket while he whispered to her. One ole cowboy yelled, 'Bite her ear.' Another, 'Snub her to a post.' Another, 'She's got crazy eyes.'

"Jimbo ignored them all, except to say, 'She's not crazy, just afraid.'

"Didn't take long for him to get a saddle on her. He climbed on her real slow like and rode with a newfound confidence. She seemed to trust him. It beat all we'd ever seen. Left alone, Jimbo would have had that horse at his mercy in another minute or two.

"But, suddenly, someone cracked a bullwhip and yelled, 'Ride 'em, cowboy.'

"That scared pony must have jumped ten feet. And, as everyone hooped and hollered, she reared up and toppled over backward on top of Jimbo. The horse got up but not the boy. He just lay there in the dry dusty dirt. I was the first one who got to him, and he sure didn't look good. He tried to talk, so I bent close to his mouth to hear his words.

"'Please get my Book, the one that boss Jake gave me.'

"First I thought I hadn't heard him right, but he said it real clear again.

"'Please get me my Bible.'

"I sent one of the others to fetch it from his saddlebags. I tried to make him comfortable, but there wasn't much I could do. It was obvious his ribs were busted, his collar bone was broken, and his hips were crushed. His life was measured in minutes at that point, and I believe he knew it. I wondered how we'd ever explain all this to boss man Jake. When the Book arrived I show it to him. 'Here, Jimbo, here's your Bible.'

"'Lay it on my chest and open it to John 3:16, please. Put my finger on those words.'

"He spoke all raspy like. By then, blood was bubbling in his mouth from all the internal bleeding. He coughed hoarsely, but still pressed with his demand.

"'Please, do it. Please!'

"I found that verse and lifted his hand. He cried in pain cause his arm was broken, too, it turned out. I placed his finger on the verse.

"'Tell boss Jake I made that decision just like he told me I should.'

"With that he closed his eyes and was gone. No terror, no anger, no pleading. Just slipped away."

The barber had tears in his eyes as he ended the story.

*　　*　　*

I paused a minute, then said, "Boys, I made three decisions after I heard the barber's story. The first was to name the creek we now live on Barber Creek. The second was to have you boys bury me one day with my Bible opened on my chest with my finger placed on John 3:16. And the third was to give every cowboy who works with us a copy of the good Lord's Word. Your copies are in the chuck wagon. Rooster will show you where."

Jeremiah and Jacob seemed to be moved the most.

Jeremiah spoke first, "Mr. Willis, our sister Mary told us about that Carpenter. Is He for real?"

"Boys, He's as real as the skin on my bones."

"What does that verse say Mr. Willis?"

"It says that whosoever puts his trust in Jesus will have everlasting life."

"What does whosoever mean? Who's that?"

"I reckon, Jeremiah, that's you and me and every cowboy and cowgirl. Even the mavericks, the culls, and the undesirables. God swings a mighty big loop. But, there's many a cowboy who doesn't want His brand."

There was a peace in the camp as an unseasonable cool breeze blew in.

Then Jeremiah said, "I want His brand."

Jacob added, "Me, too."

DAY 6

March 25, 1898
The Middle Fork of the Beef Trail
Somewhere between Burton and Mill Creek
Vernon Parish, Louisiana

Two of our drovers from the night watch rode into camp before sunrise.

"We got a problem, Boss, and it ain't rustlers. We were doing a wide swing before coming in, and a mile back we found two steers mauled to death. Bear tracks were everywhere. We pulled our rifles and tried to follow a trail, but it was too dark. Besides, I know enough about Louisiana Black Bear to know ya don't go huntin' them solo. You want us to go back there, we will if you need our help."

"Naw, you fellers need some grub and a bit of rest. Let me ponder how to handle this."

I knew that the local Black Bears had once been sparse, but not anymore. Thanks to open range steer stragglers, these bears had had days of feasting that had allowed them to grow big, produce healthy offspring, and now even to become brazen enough to ignore the stragglers and actually attack grazing or resting herds. These bears were plentiful, dangerous, and fearless.

As a boy I learned that Black Bears were agile tree climbers, unpredictable, and bold. I'd heard their charges were pure bluff. I didn't plan on testing that theory, though. I also knew whoever had mauled our steers would be back this night, so I planned a trap. I'd used the leftover hog and a little honey as bait. A bear's sense of smell is extremely keen.

I scouted a spot where I thought Elwa and I could hide downwind.

"Stay on your mount, but don't make any noise," I cautioned, "and don't make any sudden moves. We'll need to both be pumping lead into him once he comes out in the open. Be ready."

Sure enough, half an hour later, one huge black bear came lumbering out for supper. But he stopped briefly when the wind suddenly shifted. He got a whiff of human or horseflesh, and in that instant he wasn't going to settle for a dab of honey and a slice of bacon. No, sir, he bounded forward at full throttle to do to Elwa and me what he'd done to the steers the night before.

My horse Augustus either sensed or saw him first because he must have jumped twenty feet. I had to use both hands on the saddle horn to keep from being thrown head over heels. In the process, my rifle went flying.

Just when I thought it couldn't get worse, it did. Elwa drew a bead on the beast and misfired. Here came Mr. Bear with teeth bared and claws in motion. I had no rifle, and my sidearm wouldn't even scratch a monster that size.

The only thing I had left was my lariat. Now, any man with half his wits knows that you never throw your loop around a fast moving train or a falling tree or a charging bear. But with no other options, and Elwa seconds away from being barreled over by this juggernaut, I unfurled my rope, gave it three spins for speed and landed it absolutely perfectly around that bear's head. It was beautiful…for three seconds. However, all my rope did was to annoy that brute. He swatted the rope so fiercely, he yanked me and Augustus to the side like we were rag dolls. I grabbed my knife and cut the rope. It recoiled and snapped, forming a tangled web around the bear. Baffled as to what had ensnared him, the bear tripped, rolled, came up bellowing and thrashing. His claws severed some of the rope, but it delayed him long enough for both Elwa and me and our horses to make a getaway. We looked back and saw the bear, finally free of the manmade spider web, amble off toward the hog and honey. Something, apparently, was better than nothing.

All that being said, I assured everyone that my bear roping days were over. In fact, if I ever laid eyes on that beast again, I, personally would cook him a steer and serve it to him on a silver platter–with all the fixings

At a great distance, that is.

NIGHT 6

March 25, 1898
The Middle Fork of the Beef Trail
Mill Creek, Vernon Parish, Louisiana

As we sat listening to Ran play by ear on his fiddle two tunes called "Green Grow the Lilacs" and the "Yellow Rose of Texas," I was transfixed by the popping sounds and the glow of our campfire. I also marveled at how quickly he'd learned these melodies on his fiddle. When I complemented him, he smiled and said, "Not much else to occupy my time when I'm not in the saddle. This fiddle provides me with a diversion, a challenge, and a way to keep my fingers nimble."

One of our cowpunchers by the name of Gerald Duke had taught him the tunes while they worked their shift as a night herder team. As they circled the herd from the opposite direction of the other nighthawks, Gerald would sing. His melodious voice kept the cattle calm. I suspected it was to keep themselves awake, too. Ran remembered each tune and later would practice it until he got it right on his new fiddle. (As time passed, he eventually could play anything with a string on it.)

When I first saw Gerald on his saddle horse Majestic, I knew he was a real cowboy. Oh, no, not by his clothes or such, but by his open countenance and the way he looked me straight in the eyes. He was not innocent, of course; but living next to nature was stamped on his face. His vices had left no scars that the open range had not healed. I consider myself a pretty good judge of character, and I liked Gerald from the onset.

*   *   *

As Ran finished his tunes, Ken spoke up. "Father, I have a couple of questions of my own tonight."

"Well, good then, ask them."

"I heard tell that you were part of the group that cleaned out those scoundrels on Jayhawkers Island. Some even say you had a part in Ozeme Carriere's demise?"

Ran couldn't resist chiming in. "My friends say I shouldn't even speak to one kid at school cause his papa was a Jayhawker. Were they that bad?"

"Boys, they were a bad lot, the very worst of lots. It was bad enough they were draft dodgers and deserters, but when they started stealing horses, weapons, cattle, and food from our neighbors they became my enemies.

"Then, to top it all off, when the Yankee General Nathaniel Banks invaded Alexandria in '64, he enlisted them to seek revenge on us. Banks called them scouts. I called them murderers, thieves, and conscripts. They burned our homes and even murdered civilians. They took advantage of our womenfolk while we were defending our homeland. No, I didn't shoot Carriere. I was in Alabama fighting in the Battle of Spanish Fort in May of '65 when Carriere was killed. I didn't kill him, but a friend of mine did. His name was Colonel Louis Bringier. Well, to be more precise, at least his cavalry did. They cleared out the scum down on Cocodrie Lake's Jayhawkers Island."

I paused long enough to toss a few logs onto the campfire and to let my mine drift back to those days. The memories were sharp, but telling them to my boys would take some tact.

"I reckon there are two reasons these rumors of my connection to Carriere will not die a natural death. After the war another friend, David Paul, was elected Rapides Parish Sheriff and then Mayor of Alexandria. His reputation had grown when he allowed no consideration to the Jayhawker varmints and exacted the most severe retribution. Sheriff Paul later helped me to become Constable.

"Those two friendships branded me as an enemy of the Jayhawkers. Don't get me wrong, I was, but the truth is that I was with General Randall Lee Gibson at places such as Shiloh, Chickamauga, Nashville, Badwin County, and, finally, in a Yankee prisoner-of-war stockade in Meridian courtesy of one William Tecumseh Sherman."

General Gibson is my namesake, I've heard you tell many times, Father," said Ran.

"Indeed, true. We should keep the name Randall Lee going always to honor my great commander and dear friend. You give that some careful consideration as you get older, son."

The fire crackled, and I shifted in my seat. After a brief pause, I resumed my story.

"Now William Tecumseh Sherman was another matter. His own men called him Uncle Billy because they trusted him so much, but for my money, he was ruthless, vain, and cold. Odd thing about him though, on his so-called 'March to the Sea,' he only burned Protestant churches, including one that my great-grandfather helped organize. Since Sherman himself was a Catholic, he left their places of worship unharmed. It'll be interesting to see how the Good Lord passes judgment on him for that."

There was a sardonic snicker and mild guffaw around the fire at that statement.

"Lincoln freed the slaves, and I think Sherman felt some kind of obligation to help them. So, he told his men to ignore the fields of black-eyed peas while destroying all the other crops and orchards, as the peas were a major food staple of plantation slaves. Some say that the peas were all the slaves had to celebrate with on the first day of January, in 1863...the day the *Emancipation Proclamation* went into effect. From that time on, they have always been eaten on January 1. I've never owned a slave, nor have any of my friends, neighbors, or family. Nevertheless, I don't eat black-eyed peas cause they remind me of Sherman."

*   *   *

"But getting back to the Jayhawkers, Father...."

I nodded, pushed back my hat, scratched my forehead, and said, "Right, yes. So, about Carriere. What really connected our family to him was an event your mama will not talk about to this very day. It's an event that shows God's word does not return void, as the Good Book promises. Don't tell your mother I shared this story with you, but I think it's worth hearing if for no other reason than the validity of your dear mama's testimony."

My sons, and even the fellows who worked for me, all leaned forward a bit, expecting they were about to hear an anecdote worth retaining.

"Boys, your mama was living at the Ole Willis Place down on Barber Creek during the war. One day a young man attired in the

- 322 -

uniform of a Confederate officer came riding up to our home. He had some thirty men with him. Because of his uniform your mother invited him and his men to come in for supper. She cooked for hours. After one of her famous meals, she provided them quarters in our barn.

"The next morning before breakfast she said a prayer and read a scripture to them from the Bible. The young officer then gathered his men. As they started to ride away, he turned and looked directly at your mama.

"He asked, 'Do you know who I am? I am Carriere, the notorious Jayhawker. We were going to take your horses and burn you out. Maybe even shoot you since you said your husband was a Reb.'"

Even though the campfire was not as bright as daylight, I could see that the blood had drained from the face of my boys. They had no idea their mother had come that close to getting killed and never giving birth to them.

"Why didn't he, Father? Why didn't he shoot mama?" Ran asked.

"As he and his men rode off he yelled to your mama, 'The words from your Book changed my mind. Anyhow, it would be a true shame to shoot the cook of the best meal I've ever eaten.'"

"Father, what scripture did mother read to him?"

"I know it by heart," I said. "'For what shall it profit a man, if he shall gain the whole world, and lose his own soul?'"

DAY 7

As the sun rose over the rolling hills and filtered through the trees I felt renewed and asked Elwa and Ken to ride point with me. If their intent was one day to own and manage herds of their own, they both knew they'd soon be riding point without me. Now it was time to start talking about how to carry on the business of making a living off a cow. The cattle business had changed since I had first mounted a cow pony. My boys were progressive thinkers, as most young folks are. They wanted to expand with other breeds, maybe even buy some of them muley-headed cows.

We already had crossbred with Shorthorns from England. Those Durham's were all right, but I preferred Hereford bulls to crossbreed with our Longhorn cows.

Elwa spoke first. "Father, we want to buy a couple of Brahman bulls. We've got to do something to fight this Texas Cattle Fever."

"It's a problem, all right," I admitted. "Go on, tell me more of what you're thinkin' about it."

"Well, sir, it's your own friend Shanghai Pierce who says they're resistant to ticks. He believes it's the ticks that cause the fever. They also don't get the pinkeye. They can travel long distances on very little water, too."

And here was where the experience of an older man, namely me, came to be challenged by the more modern thinking and speculation of a generation that had garnered its know-how from books and newspapers and more years in school. I stood at a fork in the road, in that I wasn't about to throw away the knowledge I'd gained by working steers across every form of terrain a man could imagine; however, I'd always been one to hear a man out, glean what I could from his experiences, and weigh the merit of what was being shared with me. In more than one instance, as I've noted with my good fortune of listening years ago to Charlie Goodnight, I've advanced myself by heeding lessons from others. So it was, then, that I gave credence to what my boys wanted to share with me.

"Father, we know you come from a generation that doesn't know much about these things. We mean no offense, sir, but formal education has come a long way. Since The Texas Agricultural Experiment Station was established 1887, there's a whole new way of looking at things. The emphasis these days in on science. You know, verifiable research. Worthwhile experiments. Progress, advances, discoveries. We understand your love of Hereford bulls, but would you at least consider a change? Ken and I have done a lot of digging into this matter."

I offered a slow grin, evidencing tolerance for their eagerness and appreciation for their respect of my position as head of the family.

"Now, grant it, boys, I'm just a hayseed cowman, but I did manage to pick up a thing or two along the way. I certainly don't know all the fancy lingo used by your generation of educated fellers. But that doesn't mean I'm no judge of beef and bone. Truth of the matter is, I'm a bit ahead of you boys in this matter. I did attempt to do my own feeble research about the breed."

The boys blinked in genuine surprise. Ken asked, "Really, Father? We didn't know. When was this? What did you find out?"

"Back in '85 I rode a train to San Antone to explore the ideas you boys have today. I stayed at the Menger Hotel because Robert E. Lee had stayed there. I was introduced to a fellow there named Richard King. I later learned he passed away in the hotel just days after our meeting. He told me of his 600,000 acre ranch with grasslands along the Santa Gertrudis Creek. I asked him about his Brahman bulls that he'd bought a decade before down in N'Orleans and explained to him that's why I wanted meet with him.

"Turns out, Mr. King had been a riverboat captain. Darn good one, for a fact. He knew that bends and eddies and channels of the Mississippi with no need of a map or compass. And he wasn't the only one. During our visit, he gave me a copy of a book written by another riverboat man that same year. The book was entitled *Adventures of Huckleberry Finn*. The author and King received a lot of their education on rivers, such as the Rio Grande and the Ole Miss. Now, don't get me wrong, I believe in formal schooling, but never forget that much of education is monkey see, monkey do. It should never be a substitute for good ole horse sense and the lessons learned on the rivers of life.

"But here I stray from my narrative. So, where was I? I first explored the possibility of buying a few Brahman bulls more than thirty years ago after Richard Barrow had four shipped by the British government to Louisiana. That was in '54. I didn't press the matter back then, but that's not to say it isn't worth revisiting these days. I appreciate your suggestions, boys, but I want you boys to make this decision. It's your call this time, not mine."

Ken became relaxed, as though something he had been dreading was now over, and it had not turned out poorly.

"Father, we've talked it over and we think we should buy ten Brahman bulls from Shanghai Pierce," Ken said. "I hope you'll respect our decision. Certainly, it is why we came to talk to you first about it."

"And I appreciate that. Your thinking is logical, and it's worth a try to see how it pans out. I just wanted to make sure you had the gumption to stick by your beliefs. Your bulls will be at the beef pens in Lecompte when we get there."

Ken wrinkled his brow, squinted his eyes and said, "But, Father, it will take weeks for us to travel to Texas, make the best deal, and have them reach Lecompte by rail," he replied.

"He's right, sir," said Elwa. "There are details to be worked out."

"Yep, that's true, isn't it? But what I held off telling you was, I bought twenty Brahman bulls two months ago. They should be in Lecompte at the beef pens by now."

The boys' mouths fell open. So, the old man wasn't as far behind the times as they might have feared. Mark a point for me.

"By the way, Richard King also told me he had an idea that he hoped his descendants would carry out someday. It was to crossbreed Brahman bulls with Beef Shorthorn cows. If they ever do, he wants them to name the breed after the Santa Gertrudis Creek on his ranch."

The boys slapped me on the shoulder, recognizing that I'd been a jump ahead of them. I laughed it off.

I said, "It never ceases to amaze me how us old folks can still have a good idea now and again. Imagine that, even an ole blind hog can find an acorn if he does some rooting."

Elwa assured me, "Father, we know you have great ideas. We use them every day!"

"That's good. You know, they say Richard King's ghost wanders the halls of the Menger Hotel! I promise not to haunt you. Well, then again, I just might if these Brahman bulls don't work out!"

NIGHT 7

March 26, 1898
The Texas Road
Big Creek, Rapides Parish, Louisiana

It had begun to rain mildly as we sat round the fire. The smell of Rooster's stew promised some relief from the chill. We pulled our ponchos over our heads and around our shoulders and leaned closer to the heat.

"Mr. Willis, Ran told me he'd lost two sisters and a brother. How did you deal with that?" Jacob Stark asked.

Jeremiah gave a stern look at his younger brother. "You don't ask questions like that."

I lifted a hand for peace. "Naw, naw, it's all right Jeremiah. I don't mind. I've spent several nights filling your heads with tales of the war and episodes as a lawman and adventures about previous cattle drives. It's only fitting that I share some insights on some of the more serious matters in life."

"I didn't mean to intrude on your privacy, Mr. Willis," Jacob said. "It's just that, like we told you before, we've got a sister named Mary and her family that we care for deeply. And life here on the trail and even on the farms just isn't all that easy. Never know when a family tragedy could befall us. I'd like to hear how you dealt with that. I hope I'll never need it, but better to be prepared than caught off guard."

I nodded my understanding. "Wise thinking, son. And I'll tell you up front that I don't have all the answers as to how one copes with loss and emotional pain and severe heartache. But I can share with you what happened in our family and how my dear wife and I came to terms with it."

Rooster distributed the vittles, and we all took a few minutes to eat the stew while it was still hot. He'd baked some sourdough biscuits that morning, and he passed the leftover ones around to each of us to mix with the beef and carrots and beans. Tasty and filling. Just what a cowboy needed at the end of a day in the saddle.

I set my bowl aside, wiped my mustache, and pulled back the

moist poncho. The rain had let up, but the fire was still very appealing.

"Our story goes back more than a decade," I began. "After Elwa was born Julia Ann and I had two beautiful girls, Carvelia and Minnie. Then we decided it was time to have another cowboy. Elwa was about four then, and we figured he needed a little brother.

"It was in January of 1872 when this new boy was born. We named him David Eugene after David in the Bible. He was tall and lanky by the time he reached eight years old. He was smart and kindhearted, a lot like his mother. Just a month after his birthday, in 1880, Julia Ann and I decided to visit my father's home. My daddy was a Baptist preacher like his own grandfather and was now pastor at Amiable Baptist Church, which Great-Grandfather Joseph had founded a half-century before.

"On the way to Amiable for church on a beautiful Sunday morning Julia Ann told me, 'Stop the buggy, Daniel, I feel something is wrong at home.' I turned the buggy round as fast as I could and kept the horse at a trot. When we arrived home David Eugene was deathly ill. How my wife sensed this, I'll never know, but I've never been one to doubt a mother's intuition. And, sure enough, when we got there we discovered that little David had a terrible pain around his bellybutton and he was running a grievous fever.

"Julia Ann was beside herself with anxiety. She knew it was a twenty mile ride to Alexandria, where the nearest doctor could be located. She turned to me and said, 'Kill your horse if need be, but get our boy some help.'

" I mounted my fastest horse and rode him into the ground with my boy crying out in pain with every leap and jump. I made the twenty mile ride to Alexandria in just a two hours, but it seemed like a year. I carried David in my arms and burst right through the doors of the doc's office. Thank goodness, he had just returned from delivering a baby on one of the nearby ranches. He had me put David on the examining table, and in five minutes he determined that David had a ruptured appendix.

"That old doc could mend broken bones, sew up wounds, bring babies into the world, and even pull bad teeth if need be. But, he was not a trained surgeon. No one in those parts was. The nearest person with those kind of skills was a hundred miles away in Shreveport. Little David overheard that old sawbones share that sad news with me, and he looked at me with sheer terror in his face, worrying that I might actually try to put him back on my horse and bounce him another hundred miles. He pleaded with me, 'No more, Papa, no more.'

The doc had some laudanum that helped reduce the pain in David's gut. I lifted the little fellow into my arms and held him and kissed him and smoothed his hair until he breathed his last. I then laid him gently back on the examining table, dropped to my knees and wept with such a deep agony, I wondered if I'd ever recover.

"The old doc had left me alone with my dying boy, and he'd gone to fetch the undertaker. When they both got back and saw that David had died, the doc told me to leave my bone-weary steed and to borrow a horse from the livery owner. He told me to ride back, tell my dear wife what had happened, and then return in a day with a buckboard to retrieve the body. It would be wrapped in linen and laid in a coffin by then.

"Over and over the doc told me that there was nothing Julia Ann or I could have done to have prevented this death. We could feel great sorrow, but there was no guilt or shame on us for what was something that just happened to folks with no rhyme or reason. It was what it was, and it was now up to us to give our boy a proper burial and then to turn our attention to rearing our other young'uns.

"That ride back was worse than anything I had ever suffered during the war, even in a prisoner of war camp. If I could have, I would have swapped places with little David, but, alas, that was not an option. As I neared the home, Julia Ann was on the porch. Amazingly, she was already dressed in black, head to toe. Again, her maternal instinct had told her that her son had passed. I dismounted, and she came into my arms, comforting me and allowing me to comfort her. We spoke no words.

"Three days later, we buried our boy in the Graham Cemetery on a hill next to Robert Graham's home, where I'd asked for David's mother's hand in marriage. How could one location have so much joy, and so quickly so much sorrow? We now knew the unimaginable pain that Great-Grandfather Joseph Willis experienced when he lost his precious twins, Ruth and Naomi."

Jacob cleared his throat. He said, "A woman carries a child for nine months, then goes through pain to bring him into the world, and then spends years feedin' him, nursin' him when he's sick, makin' clothes for him, helpin' him with his school learnin'…then, he's taken from her. I just can't imagine how anyone can recover from that, Mr. Willis."

"I don't know that you recover, Jacob, only endure. During the funeral my father spoke words of hope—*Blessed Hope.* Nevertheless, Julia Ann would later lie on David's grave and weep for hours at a time. I had hoped that maybe bringing new life into our family might help defer some of the grief. The next year we had baby Corine. She died a week after her birth. Weak heart and underdeveloped lungs, we were told. I knew I had to be strong and pray without ceasing.

"Father's Amiable Church prayed and fasted for days. I began to notice an evolution in Julia Ann. She no longer went to the cemetery and draped herself across David's grave. Instead, she sat alone, under a large elm tree, reading and studying specific passages from her Bible. I allowed her these private times of contemplation, prayer, and meditation.

"So it was, then, that a week or so after this altered behavior, Julia Ann walked into our kitchen, stood erect, and in a clear and confident voice told me that she had made a vow to the Lord that if we ever lost another child, she would never allow herself to grieve as she had for David Eugene and little Corine. She said, 'I owe that to our other children, and to you, too. Our God endured the death of His dear son. He understands the hollowness we feel. But He also has more for us to do, and I will no longer shirk that responsibility.'

"The next day we walked down to the banks of Barber Creek. I told her, 'We should have no more children. Surely it's not the Lord's will.'

"She responded, 'Daniel, I love you, but you may be wrong. The Bible says to say, "If it be the Lord's will…." and that is how we will see how this works out in His grand plan for us. He will determine if other children are to come into our family.'

"Two years later Daniel Oscar was born. When he reached twelve we told him of his brother and sister's deaths. His response was, 'We will never be without a doctor again, no, never again. I will study as long and as hard as it takes to become one.'

"Then Robert Kenneth, Ruthey Madella, Julia Coatney, and young Ran were all born. And, yes, we lost another. Precious Stella, a victim of scarlet fever, lived only four months. But Julia Ann kept her promise to the Lord, and our family too.

"Daniel Oscar is almost finished with medical school. He will be the very first medical doctor, and a surgeon at that, in Vernon Parish. A child with appendicitis now will have a fighting chance. The Lord causes all things to work together for good!"

*   *   *

"I should tell ya, Julia Ann was a Methodist, up till then. After hearing of Amiable Baptist praying and fasting for her, she insisted on joining their church."

Elwa added, "She still reads the Bible daily on the front porch while eating an orange and even its peel. We joke sometimes that she thinks there will be no one in heaven except Baptists. I told her that they may build a wall up yonder so that she won't have to know how many other folks made it into heaven, even not being Baptists."

That drew a chuckle and reminded Elwa of a funny story.

"When I asked her what religion Jesus would be in heaven, she smiled with a twinkle in her eye. 'I reckon, son, it will be like the time a Catholic, Methodist, Presbyterian, and Baptist were fishing together down on Barber Creek. They got into an argument on what denomination Jesus would be in heaven. The Catholic declared, 'No doubt He will be part of our church, since we have the Pope." The Presbyterian said, "No, oh, no. When you consider all that John Calvin did for the Christian faith, He will be one of us." The Methodist then spoke, "Nope, no way, look at all that the Wesleys did for Christianity." The Baptist looked perplexed for a few minutes and spoke, 'Gentlemen, I don't think He's going to change.'"

The Stark Brothers, my boys, Rooster, and I all had a good laugh at that one.

"Boys, you can see Jesus in your sainted mother's eyes. Through it all she still puts her confidence in the *Blessed Hope!*"

T H R E E

"The reports of my death have
been greatly exaggerated." —*Mark Twain*

DAY 8

March 27, 1898
The Texas Road
Big Creek, Rapides Parish, Louisiana

We veered off the Beef Trail onto the Texas Road to Lecompte.

As we crossed Big Creek a band of fifty or so Choctaw came riding up, hooping and hollering.

Jeremiah yelled, "Indians! Circle the wagons."

I told him, "We've only got two."

About that time they circled him. Jeremiah was as white as rice.

I had to say something. "Now, Henry, you shouldn't scare Jeremiah like that. He's mighty good with a gun. You're liable to get shot. And what would I tell your children? Better yet, my godchildren?"

"You're right, Daniel. Did you get that candy in Texas for them? They love those sugar plums."

"Sure did. Now I suppose you want the steers I promised you. Pick out the best five or so and invite me to supper sometime."

"You are a man of your word, and a good friend," said Daniel. He and his braves turned and rode out among our herd, choosing the five head they felt would serve best in feeding their families.

Later, Jeremiah asked me, "You do that often? You know, show favoritism to injuns? "

"Every year."

"Why?"

"I figure I owe it to him and his people. They were here long before us and, besides that, I'm not going to watch any child starve, godchild or not."

Jacob had listened to it all and asked me, "Mr. Willis, have you always been like this?"

"Like what?"

"A good man always doing what's right?"

I smirked and shook my head in humility. "Not hardly. I've cut a wide path at times, not always good. Glad to say I learned a few lessons along the way, but sad to say that some came with a price."

"Sir?"

"I'll tell you and Jeremiah a story of when I was a boy. Like I told you before, my father was the pastor of Amiable Baptist Church. Once a month we'd have a church conference under a huge grove of cypress trees. The old men would testify with stories of their conversions. The womenfolk would sit by a pot-bellied stove, pray, and tell stories mostly about their husbands, children, and what the Lord had done for them all.

"There was singing, and shouting, and praising the Lord. And, there was plenty of food, but there was no fishing, swimming, or games of any kind for us boys. Now, don't get me wrong, that was all fine, but I had visions of a cane pole and me on the banks of Barber Creek with brim jumping into my lap. I thought surely that would not be a sin. After all, the Lord liked to walk on water and to make sure folks had plenty of fish to eat, right?

"Anyway, these meetings could and would go on for days. Being a preacher's son I was required to sit on a log that had been cut in half on the front row. To a growing boy, it was about as exciting as watching paint dry.

"Now, my brothers offered me a quarter if I'd liven things up. Do you realize how much money that was to a boy like me? I could buy two cane polls, with the line too. I needed that quarter.

"So, I got hold of my father's Bible the night before the conference and glued some of the pages together in the front of the big Book. I knew he'd never notice, much less preach a sermon that far back in his Bible. After all, we were a New Testament church.

"When Father stood the next day to deliver his sermon, he read the text for the day, 'And in those days, Noah took unto himself a wife.'

"I thought, *Oh, no, isn't that in Genesis?* All I could think of was another sermon of Father's, something to do with your sins finding you out!

"He then turned what he thought was one page and continued, 'And she was...fifteen cubits broad and thirty-five cubits long, made out of gopher wood, and daubed on the inside with pitch.' He held up the Book and added, 'My brothers and sisters, that's the first time I've ever read that in the Word of God, but if the Bible says it, I believe it! Amen.'

"The old men all joined in with an array of amens that echoed through the trees. I should know cause I was headed up one of them.

"Father continued, 'Just goes to show, we are wonderfully and fearfully made....'

"Now, boys, trust me, my father and a piece of hickory wood convinced me my Bible tampering days were over. And, equally as bad, my brothers reneged on the payment of the quarter, saying that what I did got me a whippin', but it didn't shorten the preaching and carrying on.

"Since then, I've never roped a crippled steer nor rode a sore-backed horse nor changed a Bible verse to suit me.... In fact, every time I open a Bible, I swear I can detect a faint scent of hickory in the air."

F O U R

"To write a good love letter, you ought to begin
without knowing what you mean to say, and to
finish without knowing what you have written."
—*Jean-Jacques Rousseau*

NIGHT 8

March 27, 1898
The Texas Road
Calcasieu River, Rapides Parish, Louisiana

After supper Elwa stoked our campfire on the banks of the
Calcasieu River. He asked me to tell the story he'd requested every
year since his first cattle drive.

"Father, tell me again about your first cattle drive in '67? I
never tire of hearing it."

"And I never tire of telling about it." I'll summarize here for
you what I shared.

Just as I began trailing cattle, politics raised its ugly head. I'll
give you an example of what I mean. I was once told a story of a
woman who wanted to know what her son would become. She put
what little money she had on her kitchen table along with a bottle
of liquor and a Bible. As her son approached their home she hid in
a closet. She figured if he took the money he'd be a gambler; if he
drank the whiskey he'd be a drunkard; and if he picked up the
Bible he might just become a preacher.

When the boy saw all this he picked up the money quickly and
stuffed it into his pockets; he then drank the entire bottle of the
Devil's poison; and, finally, he put the Word of God under his
right arm and staggered out the door. The mother exclaimed, "Oh,
no, a politician."

*   *   *

I figured after the war the best way to feed my family was to be
a cowman. Robert Graham's words when I asked him for his

daughter's hand in marriage, "Can you feed her, boy?" kept haunting my mind.

Within a year my wife was with child, and my first boy was on the way. I knew I'd better get to it since the meager money I was earning from farming was not enough to feed a growing family. The woods seemed to be full of unbranded maverick cattle that had greatly multiplied during the war, but I feared some of them might have once belonged to our neighbors, so I joined in "making the gather" in Texas. There were thousands of unclaimed cows roaming free in that vast land. We were able to rope and brand 300 head on my first cattle drive. I had already registered my brand, the Bar-D-K, in Rapides Parish.

The next year Henry Warmoth became Governor of Louisiana. Now, the last thing on earth I'd do is to speak badly of that low down Yankee scoundrel. Rooster's six mules dragging me across an alligator invested swamp couldn't make me speak disparagingly of that worthless Carpetbagger. No, not me.

Where was I? Warmouth was a corrupt politician of the worst sort. He promised to help reconstruct Louisiana. It wasn't about Reconstruction, but about taking advantage of us after the war, punishing the South through fraudulent elections and outright thievery. Out of all that came The Knights of the White Camellia. They said they would defend *our way of life*. I'm not sure if they were as crazy as the Ku Kluxers, for you see our family, being part-Cherokee, never got an invitation to join either. Wouldn't matter though, I've never cared for anyone who had to hide behind masks and robes to proclaim their beliefs. And, I certainly didn't need *our way of life* defended by whippings or a lynching. I trusted them 'bout as much as I did Louisiana's double-minded scalawag politicians.

My wife's brother William Graham has a few holes in his sheets to this very day, and is proud of it. He says he's going to have his sons engrave KKK on his grave marker when his time comes. Can you imagine standing before the good Lord and explaining that, and all those burning crosses they've used to preach hate? Listening to him talk you'd think he was the One at Calvary. I told him to come down from his cross, cause someone just might need the wood.

My friend from the war, Shanghai Pierce, told me a man could have all the cows he wanted in Texas with legions of Longhorns roaming free. He'd driven a herd from Texas to N'Orleans back in '55 on The Opelousas Trail. The only problem was they weren't worth spit after the war. I got the idea that might all change, and change it did as folks decided they preferred beef over pork about the same time as Warmoth was impeached. Our beginnings were humble, but with it my wife and I fed our children.

And so at this point I launched into the tale Elwa had requested.

"All right, son, let me tell ya about that first cattle drive again. Demand began to change when a fellow named James McCoy established a cattle market in Abilene, Kansas in '67. The Chisholm and Goodnight–Loving Trails in Texas headed north, but were too far from our home to make it worth our while. Even the easternmost Shawnee Trail was not a good choice because of Texas Cattle Fever and the many drownings of livestock in the dangerous waters of the Neches River, not to mention our cattle would lose too much weight on such a long hard drive.

"There was no railroad when I chose to drive our beeves to N'Orleans on the Opelousas Trail from East Texas. We crossed the Sabine at New Columbia, Texas. I could buy cattle then in Texas at $3 a head and sell them to the U.S. Army in N'Orleans for $20 a head. I never dreamed the selling price would double one day. We trailed cattle on the Opelousas Trail until 1882 when The Texas and Pacific Railway Company built a route from New Orleans to northern railheads. The next year, when you turned fifteen, you made your first cattle drive with me."

*   *   *

I assumed Elwa would find that much jabbering about the past to be adequate, but he cajoled me into carrying on a while more. The company was enjoyable, so I resumed my narrative, but first did some oral backtracking for some important family history.

"Now, I need to step back a piece to put things into perspective for you. It was on my own very first cattle drive that I met Etienne Fontenot. He owned a *stand* for cattle drives where The Opelousas Trail crossed the Calcasieu River. He once was good friends with Great-Grandfather Joseph's friend Jim Bowie, and Jean Lafitte, too. His waystation gave drovers access to cattle pens, a soft bed, and a hot supper. I was fascinated by him, for you see Jim Bowie had introduced Fontenot to Great-Grandfather many years before. He had become one of the largest land owners in Louisiana and put the notion in my mind to buy land for our family and cattle.

"I knew much 'bout Bowie from Great-Grandfather, but I wanted to know more bout Lafitte. As a boy I'd heard many a tale about his exploits. The early inhabitants of No-Man's-Land held him in high esteem, and he reciprocated by showering them with gifts. He was considered a war hero rather than an outlaw due to his helping General Andrew Jackson during the Battle of N'Orleans.

"Fontenot had furnished his men with beef and supplies when their ships sailed up the Calcasieu River. Laffite made his Louisiana headquarters at his home. They became best friends. Once, when he admired a diamond stud Laffite was wearing in his silk shirt, Lafitte tossed it to him and said 'Here, it's yours!' I mean, that's just the kind of genuine camaraderie those fellows shared.

"Anyway, it was during this time that Lafitte fell in love with his best friend's sister, Madeline. The dark-haired, green-eyed beauty had a charm and grace that the pirate had never before encountered. He became smitten by her soft-spoken ways and fell hopelessly in love. But there was a problem, and it was a big one. She was already married. Her husband soon became jealous of Laffite, and accused his wife of having an affair with the buccaneer.

"One day when her husband returned home from a trip, he discovered she was wearing an expensive brooch given to her by the pirate. The husband went insane with both jealousy and personal insult. 'I will not permit you to be unfaithful to me,' he scolded her as he snapped a small pistol from his hand. Without allowing his wife to explain or respond, he shot her across the room. She fell flat out on the floor, and when the husband saw her limp body, he knew he would be hanged for murder if he was caught. He vamoosed, leaving her to bleed to death. Oddly enough, by the act of a guardian angel or just fool luck, it wasn't her day to die. She survived, as I'll explain in a moment.

"Murderer or not, things didn't go so well for the husband,

however. No, indeed. When the news of the shooting reached Lafitte, he vowed to kill the man. Whether he actually killed him or not will never be known, but one fact is for sure, and that is that the husband was never seen again…at least as anyone who knew him would recognize. Some folks surmised that in his hasty getaway he took a bad route and became food for the alligators. And that is very possible. But others said Lafitte found him and made him walk a plank into the turbulent waters of the Gulf of Mexico. Knowing Lafitte's reputation, there may be some validity to that story, too. However, there were some lingering tales that said the husband somehow made it to N'Oleans, grew a long beard, bought himself some silk vests and corduroy dress coats, boarded a riverboat, and spent nights at the gambling tables until he made it safely to the North. All of which goes to show you how legends are made and tall tales gain traction.

"More important to the story, however, was the amazing fact that Madeline survived and swore she'd been faithful to her husband. Farfetched as it may be to hear, the bullet hit the brooch that she was wearing, and it saved her life. When she got shot, she fainted dead away, making it seem she had been killed. They say she had a mighty bad bruise, and if her husband had not used a small caliber pistol, it would have seriously wounded her. But within a few days, she was up and virtually back to normal.

"Feeling a debt of gratitude for indirectly saving her life by gifting her with the brooch that stopped the bullet, Madeline announced that she would travel directly to Lafitte's Maison Rouge mansion in Galveston to thank him personally. She did so, and she never returned to her prior home.

"Now, as I've heard it shared by more than one old timer, one day Lafitte and Madeline sailed away with a ship loaded with treasure. What happened after that is left to speculation and rumor. They're those who believe they were lost at sea, but knowing LaFitte, I highly doubt that. Some speculated they settled on an island or found a distant port and took on new identities. Nobody has ever claimed to have found any of the gold or other treasure, nor did anyone hear any more of the life of Madeline. To this day some believe they have seen that ship on the Gulf of Mexico's horizon, not with a pirate's flag, but with one that has a pelican with three drops of blood on her chest feeding her young.

DAY 9

We crossed the Calcasieu without incident. I knew the river like the back of my hand. But in the distance was a cowpoke I thought I recognized. He was watering his horse.

I asked Jeremiah if he'd care to take a little ride with me. He agreed, and we approached the cowpoke with our Winchesters out of their scabbards. He almost started to flee until Jeremiah drew a bead on him.

Jeremiah yelled, "Do you want to end up like your padna Scar Bartholomew?"

We tied him up in the big wagon with the calves, for the nearest jail was in Alexandria. We were not far from my home in Babb's Bridge. I left Elwa in charge and rode home for the night, with the outlaw in tow. Julia Ann met me at the door of our Ole Willis Place.

How excited she was and asked, "Who's your *friend*?"

I told her that we shot this hombre's two sidewinding partners, but he made a getaway amidst all the gunplay. But, by fate, we came across him and got the drop on him.

"He will be sleeping tonight handcuffed to the foot of our iron bed cause he might get loose tied to a tree."

I told the outlaw, "I'd better not hear a sound out of you tonight. If I do, I'll do more than just tie you to a tree."

Jeremiah asked, "How'd you sleep?"

"Like a baby."

"Well, how'd your wife sleep?"

"Not a wink. I can't imagine what kept her awake."

I needed to get back to the herd so I sent a wire from Forest Hill's telegraph station to the sheriff. They would need to pick him up when we got to Lecompte. I had no time to ride to Alexandria. This skunk was just fortunate we didn't hang him on the spot.

NIGHT 9

As we approached the trails end Jeremiah asked me, "Mr. Willis, a ways back you mentioned a story about the Texas and Pacific Railway that was for another time. We're almost there. Is that a story you'd be willing to share?"

"Not only willing, but if you're going to work with us you'll need to know it. First, I want to tell ya, there are those that say there are no honest lawyers. That's simply not true. Don't you believe a word of it. Just last year I met one in Mississippi and asked him to move to Louisiana so we'd have one. Here's that story."

*   *   *

It was, indeed, one of our last nights on the trail, but the boys didn't seem to have their fill of my recollections, so I indulged them with the story about the railroad.

"In Louisiana the railroad is responsible for the health and wellbeing of our cattle once they are shipped north. That's the law, and it's a good one cause at the end of the trail we can ride home and not worry 'bout our herd again. At least, that's what I was led to believe back some time ago.

"In the spring of '83 I decided to trail 600 head of longhorn cattle from East Texas to Lecompte. Elwa was just a pup then, all of fifteen, but he'd told me he could rope and ride like one of those Mexican vaqueros he'd read 'bout. I'd read those stories, too, and told him, 'Good, cause they say they only dismount for a chance to dance with pretty girls. And since there'll be no pretty girls along the trail, you will have to sleep in your saddle."

*   *   *

The Texas and Pacific Railroad, called the T&P today, had finished a route from Shreveport to New Orleans the previous September. We would no longer need to trail cattle through the treacherous swamp country from East Texas to New Orleans. We never drove a single head on the Opelousas Trail again after the railroad came to Lecompte. From that day forward we've always driven our cattle on the Beef and Texas roads.

"That year's cattle drive went well. I'd told Elwa he could dismount anytime he wished, pretty girls or not. After we drove the longhorns into the railroad's beef pens we were eager to get home to a soft bed and the loving arms of our family.

"However, to my total shock and dismay, two weeks later I got word that sixty head of our cattle were dead. In fact, the herd was still in the railroad's beef pen cause of the large number of cattle being shipped from the railheads north of Lecompte. Or, at least that's what they claimed.

"I rode over to investigate the matter. They informed me their lawyers had said the cattle were not their responsibility until they were loaded onto the train. I gave them the most educated response I could muster for their lawyers: "Hog wash." Trust me a few other words came to mind, but discretion got the better of me.

"I rode straight from there to Alex and hired me a lawyer. He filed a lawsuit, and the judge ruled in my favor."

Jeremiah made a good point. "But, Mr. Willis, was not the judge a lawyer, too? Was he not honest?"

I stood corrected by Jeremiah. I apologized in sackcloth and ashes for falsely accusing all Louisiana lawyers of being dishonest. I was wrong. "Let me begin again. Did I ever tell ya 'bout the time I was in Mississippi and met two honest lawyers?"

DAY 10

March 29, 1898
Trail's End
The Railroad Cattle Pens
Lecompte, Louisiana

I'd made a promise the day before to the mayor when I was at the telegraph station in Forest Hill. He saw me and suggested I drive the longhorns down the main street of Forest Hill. He said the kids would love it and the not-so-young kids would, too. As we approached the town, the streets were lined with people. The longhorns were as docile as kittens as we moved through main street. Of course Ethel led the way. She looked as proud as a peacock. I asked Ran to join me as the point cowman. We could hear young boys tell their mothers, "I want to be a cowboy."

*   *   *

Now, the good mayor also suggested that we have a Willis Feast of Celebration after we drove our cattle to the beef pens in Lecompte. We were less than a day away, so I agreed. It would be a wonderful way to say thank you to our cowhands and our neighbors. No neighbor of ours had "accidently" put the wrong brand on a single head of our cows.

NIGHT 10

March 29, 1898
Trail's End
The Railroad Cattle Pens
Lecompte, Louisiana

"Father, being at the railroad again reminds me of that trip you and mama took to New Orleans," Elwa said.

"I suppose the others might want to know what you're talking 'bout. I can tell ya it was just six years ago on a hot August night in 1892. Your mother wanted to see N'Orleans. Being fetched up in Jackson Parish, N'Orleans was like a different country to her. I told her it would be that way even if she was from Baton Rouge.

"She'd never ridden a train either, so we boarded the Texas and Pacific Railway just across the tracks from here. I hid $2,000 on me just in case I was able to buy a few prized bulls at auction while we were there. I didn't trust the train's safe, and banks even less.

"After dinner in a fancy dining car we watched with amazement the abundance of wildlife along the tracks. The old plantations reminded me of a time we'd never know again. It was in the dining car that we met a school teacher named Eugene Bunch. Julia Ann told him all about our Eugene. He got tears in his eyes. He was a Southern gentleman, except maybe when he found out I was a cowman and asked, 'You must be wealthy?' Now, boys, we have always been taught not to talk about such things and never do anything that was a show of wealth, so I replied, 'Not hardly, we're just trying to feed our children and pay half the rent.'

"He laughed and excused himself so fast you'd thought the train was on fire. Julia Ann said, 'Now Daniel, that's how I hope our boys turn out. What a polite Christian gentleman.'

"Then suddenly the train came to an abrupt stop when a dozen or so men appeared on the tracks heavily armed. As they boarded, Mr. Bunch stood and introduced himself as Captain J. F. Gerard to the passengers. Your mother looked like she'd just heard a dog talk. He then politely tipped his hat to the ladies, while refusing to take their purses, and he was very polite while taking the wallets of all the men, all except mine. When he got to me, he told his gang, 'Don't waste your time here, he doesn't even have enough to pay half his rent.'

"I later heard he managed to steal $78 from the other passagers. That ended our trip, for your mother said, 'I've seen enough, take me home.' I knew I needed to find a fast horse with a buggy or a train headed in the opposite direction. I couldn't help but say, 'He was such a polite Christian gentleman. I hope our boys turn out that way.' She did not find the humor in my words, but after a brief hesitation said, 'Daniel, do you have any idea how it feels to be thrown off a moving train?' I could see that twinkle in her eyes, which always meant it's all right. Still, why press my luck?

"A few weeks later Pinkerton detectives tracked Bunch to a swamp near Franklin, Louisiana, and shot him dead along with all his gang. Hardly worth seventy-eight bucks, if you ask me.

DAY 11

March 30, 1898
The Willis Feast of Celebration
The Ole Willis Place
Daniel and Julia Ann Willis's Home on Barber Creek
Babb's Bridge, Louisiana

We had a huge bonfire to illuminate the celebration and take the chill out of the air. I also had decided to have fireworks. The kids were very excited. I was, too. You might say it was a day of *explosive excitement*, not cause of the fireworks, though. At least not the kind I lit with a piece of kindling from our bonfire.

The spark to these fireworks was kindled all the way back when I married Julia Ann. After we got married my brothers started to marry Julia Ann's sisters. Not one, not two, but three of them. Four Willis brothers, in all, married to four Graham sisters.

The problem arose when my brother Matthew decided to make it five. He set out to win Julia Ann's youngest sister Lucy Ruth Graham's affection.

However, she made it clear that someone else had declared their affection for her, and she was pleased by that. She told Matthew, "Sorry, but no. I'm in love with James Moore."

Now, that was all right with Matthew. He then got word from one of the other sisters that what she told him was not the actual reason. She confided that Lucy had told the entire Graham clan that Matthew was just too ugly to marry. That was all right with Matthew, too…until he commandeered a bottle of *Sweet Lucy*, no pun intended. The white lightning could peel the paint off Rooster's chuck wagon. If that was not enough, Lucy had asked our father if he would marry her and Mr. Moore. He had agreed!

Now the stage was set for the most exciting Willis Feast of Celebration ever. No sooner than father had said grace than here came Matthew on his horse hooping and hollering words that I've chosen to forget. I figured, *Let him ride through and sleep it off down on Barber Creek*, but he wasn't done. He had obviously noticed Lucy and James's table on his first ride through.

Here he came again! Julia Ann cried out, "Do something, Daniel."

So, I did. Now grant it I was a tad bit slower than I used to be when I could jump a four rail fence with a bail of cotton on my back. But, I wasn't thinking 'bout that as I jumped on the back of the closest horse and rode like I was eighteen again. I grabbed Matthew's horse's bridle and turned the mare in a tight circle.

The circle was too tight for Matthew. He landed face down in a chocolate cake Lucy had baked. I figured it would be the last piece of cake he'd ever have of hers, so I told him, "You might as well eat the rest." He thanked her and told her he preferred her sisters' cakes, though. She did not get the gist of his remarks.

I felt at least the fireworks were over. Then I saw father. His opinion of anything stronger than dark roast Louisiana coffee was somewhere in the vicinity of the Devil, himself, playing the *Wedding March*, on Ran's fiddle.

I walked with Matthew down to Barber Creek to wash him up a little. When he cried, my heart broke for him, but I knew he'd someday meet another who would catch his fancy, albeit I also knew it would never be one of the Graham sisters, not even a cousin, not even a distant cousin. In fact, he might consider a different Parish where there were no Grahams.

I told him, "It's just puppy love."

He responded, "It's real to this puppy!"

What the healing hands of time could not mend, eventually the arms of another did. Matthew never drank alcohol or ate chocolate cake again. At least not face down.

F I V E

"There's a Rider coming on a magnificent steed, a
white horse, I'm told. He knows all the brands and earmarks,
for you see He owns the cattle on a thousand hills. He will separate
the goats from His sheep. If you listen carefully, you might even
hear hoofbeats, for you see He's mounted even as I
speak. Not even a Louisiana Wind can change the fact that
He's coming—*coming again*!"

—*Daniel Hubbard Willis, Jr.* 1900

EPILOGUE

April 15, 1900
Easter Sunday
Babb's Bridge, Louisiana on Barber Creek
Excerpted from Randall Lee "Ran" Willis's Diary

Father had taught me much about being a cowman, and about life, too. He encouraged me to write it all down on my Big Chief writing tablets he'd bought me. He said it was so that, "Those who come after us might not make the same mistakes."

I heard tell the crappie were biting down on Cocodrie Lake. But, this being Easter they'd just have to wait to jump into my boat. Our Dominicker rooster's crowing reminded me I should start loading the wagon for church. I was truly excited, for Father had been asked to speak that day at Amiable Baptist. Father was frail but up to the task. There would be a huge supper on the grounds after church.

I'd told Mama we should have Easter eggs. A friend of mine from Spring Hill Academy told me all about them.

He said, "When my folks lived in Germany, they decorated eggs at Easter."

Mama replied, "That will never catch on here. The hens would revolt, and me, too."

"Mama, they hid them, too."

She looked puzzled and asked, "Why in the world would they do that? Were they that ugly?"

"Not to worry, Mama, a rabbit then helps them find the eggs."

"Son, I'm going down to that school tomorrow to see if they've been into the cooking sherry."

I quickly changed the conversation. "Mama, what did you bake for the supper on the grounds?"

"Apple pie, of course. And, your father has butchered a hog, so were taking a smoked ham from our smokehouse, too. You know, son, Baptists love to eat. Some I know are digging their grave with a fork."

Mother then added, "You know your Grandpa Daniel, Sr. was the pastor there for many years. He died a year and a week to the day after you were born. He was cut from the same cloth as his Grandfather Joseph Willis, and he even planted more churches than he did. He was the best man I ever knew. It was his words of wisdom from the Book that gave me strength to go on after the deaths of your brother and sisters."

As our wagon rolled down the red dirt road I could see the church steeple pointing toward Heaven. It would forever remind me of Father's words that day. As the folks gathered, father arose and slowing walked to the front of the crowd. Elwa held his arm to steady him. He spoke with a frail voice.

"Now, friends, as you know, I'm no preacher. But, I've been asked to speak a few words of my father, who is buried a few yards from here.

"But, then again, he's not there. Now, some of ya might be thinking that's not true. You might say, I was at his funeral. Others of you saw him in his open casket. A few of you helped lower his pine box in the ground, shoveled dirt on it, too.

"I can only explain why I believe that by using his own words about the loss of his Preacher. If you don't mine, I'll read them.

"'It was a sad day—the saddest day ever. For you see our Country Preacher had died. I trusted him. I'd staked my future on him. But now he was extinguished like a flickering candle in the wind. The young Preacher's enemies, and there were many, had won. Success had eluded him, for you see he didn't have enough money even for a grave, much less a marker. Fortunately, a kind soul gave him one. The womenfolk buried him on a Friday, for you see none of the men could be found, save one.

"'Oh, yes, he'd made some promises, big ones too. The kind no man could keep. But, he now had faded as the autumn colors. As victors, his enemies would surely exact revenge on his friends, so they hid like rabbits in a hole. One broke his promise and denied him. Still another betrayed him. Many others even hated him. He was rejected by the religious folk of that day.

"'The woman didn't seem to be afraid though, and three days later went to the cemetery to tend to him. But, he was not there, for you see the Country Preacher had risen, just as He said he would. One of the woman told his followers He was alive. After seeing all He'd done, one of friends even doubted that.'

"Today, many doubt that story, too, but I don't. Now, my

friends, that's why I know my father is not in that grave cross the road. Because if it could not hold that Country Preacher, it cannot hold my father, or me one day in the not so distant future. He had taken death, the grave, and even Hell captive. I have but three words to say. They're the three greatest words ever spoken: 'He is risen.'"

As father ended his words, mother stood and began to sing, "Low in the grave he lay, Jesus my Savior." We all joined in, "Up from the grave he arose; with a mighty triumph o'er his foes. He arose a victor from the dark domain, and he lives forever, with his saints to reign. He arose! He arose! Hallelujah! Christ arose!"

Yes, I was the first in line for Mama's apple pie...but first I accepted the truth of my father's words when I walked to the front of that church and knelt and asked Christ to come into my life and take over. For, you see, he arose for me, too, and you, too!

Suddenly watching paint dry was exciting to me....

Louisiana Wind's Characters

Daniel Hubbard Willis, Jr.–Great-Grandson of Reverend
Joseph Willis. Cowman, Spring Hill, Rapides Parish, Constable,
and Confederate veteran. He fought in many of the great battles of
the Civil War, including Shiloh, Bull Run, Perryville,
Murfreesboro, Missionary Ridge, and Chickamauga.

An excerpt from his obituary in the *Alexandria Town Talk*, on
June 23, 1900, stated:

"He participated in all the hard battles of that army and for
bravery, soldierly bearing, discipline and devotion to duty, he was
unexcelled in his entire Brigade. He was made Orderly Sergeant
of his Company at an early period of the war. It has always been
said by his surviving comrades that when any particularly
dangerous service was required, such as scouting parties to
ascertain the position and movements of the enemy, he was always
selected for the place, and never hesitated to go, let the danger be
what it may.

"He was for a long time connected with the famous Washington
Artillery, and at the battle of Chickamauga so many horses of the
battery to which he was attached were killed that they had to pull
the guns off the field by hand to keep them from falling in the
hands of the enemy.

"He was paroled at Meridian, Miss., in May of 1865, and
brought home with him a copy of General Gibson's farewell
address to his soldiers and of him it can be truly said that through
the remaining years of his life he followed the advice then given by
his beloved commander. His love for the Southern cause, and for
the men who wore the gray, was not dimmed by years, but he lived
and died firmly convinced of the justice of the cause for which the
South poured out so much of her best blood and treasure.

"Before death he expressed a wish that he might see his children
who were at home, especially Randall L., his baby boy, whom he
had named in honor of his beloved Brigadier General, Randall Lee
Gibson. He also requested that his Confederate badge be pinned
on his breast and buried with him."

The writer of his obituary added, "During an intimate
acquaintance, covering a period of twenty-five years, the writer

never heard a vulgar or profane word pass his lips."

*   *   *

He was the first of four Willis brothers to marry four Graham sisters. He married Julia Ann Graham on January 5, 1867. He affectingly called her Julieann.

When he asked her father, Robert Graham, for her hand in marriage, he responded, "Can you feed her?" Daniel replied, "I have a horse, a milk cow, a barrel of corn and a barrel of molasses." Robert exclaimed, "My goodness, son, you have enough to marry several of my daughters." They were married at Robert's home, near Forest Hill, Louisiana, on Barber Creek.

Just a year later, on January 16, 1868, Daniel sold Robert Graham, 119 acres, "In the fork of Barber Creek," for $350. A sum that would have been almost a year's wages at the time. When Daniel died, in 1900, he left Julia Ann $35,000 in gold (the equivalent of $980,000 today), a home, land, and the woods full of cows, hogs, and horses on Barber Creek. She lived thirty-six years after his death. She never remarried and provided for her family, even through the Great Depression. Daniel had made good his promise to "feed" Julia Ann…and then some.

After being made Constable of the Spring Hill area, in Rapides Parish, Julia Ann often spoke of the time he captured an outlaw from Texas who was hid out in the piney woods of Louisiana. She said it was too late to make the trip on horseback to the jail, in Alexandria. Therefore Daniel handcuffed the outlaw to the foot of their bed for the overnight stay. He then told the outlaw, "You better not make a sound." Julia Ann added, "Daniel slept soundly, but I didn't sleep a wink all night."

*   *   *

He was a very successful rancher. He and his sons would buy cattle in East Texas for $4 per head and then drive them to the railroad's beef pens at Lecompte. They were then shipped to the northern railheads were they would fetch $40 and more per head.

Once, on a cattle drive from Texas, in 1898, the cattle

stampeded in the woods. His youngest son Randall Lee, who was only twelve at the time and riding drag thought his father had been killed. But, then he saw his father's huge white hat waving high in the air, in front of the cattle. He was the author's great-grandfather.

Reverend Daniel Hubbard Willis, Sr.–Great-Grandson of Reverend Joseph Willis and father of Daniel Hubbard Willis, Jr. He established more churches than Joseph Willis did. He is buried, along with his wife Anna Slaughter Willis, in the Amiable Baptist Church Cemetery. He was blind the last twenty-two years of his life. His daughter would read the scriptures and he would preach. He was the author's 2nd great-grandfather.

Joseph Willis–Preached the first evangelical sermon west of the Mississippi River in 1798. He was born into slavery. His mother was Cherokee and his father a wealthy English plantation owner in Bladen County, North Carolina. Joseph swam the mighty Mississippi River at Natchez, at the peril of his own life, riding a mule! He was the author's 4th great-grandfather.

Julia Ann Graham Willis–Wife of Daniel Hubbard Willis, Jr. Daughter of Robert and Ruth Graham. She would often read her red-lettered Bible, eat an orange, including the peel. When she looked at Daniel's Civil War photo tears would come to her eyes.

When asked by her grandchildren about eating orange peels, she replied, "I don't know for sure, but I think they're good for you." She was bitten by a ground rattler, at age seventy-five, and survived with home remedies. She swam in Barber Creek twice a day until age ninety. She said that was what had prolonged her life. All her children and grandchildren loved to go swimming with her.

According to her granddaughter Ilie Close, "She always had food cooked for family and friends. There were lots of blackberries, huckleberries, and fruit of all kinds for good pies. She was reared a Methodist but later joined the Baptist Church, and was a devoted Christian. We use to joke she didn't think there would be anyone but Baptists in Heaven. Her hobby was making quilts, and she kept the family supplied with her handiwork." She was the author's great-grandmother.

Randall Lee "Ran" Willis–Youngest child of Daniel Hubbard Willis, Jr. and Julia Ann Graham Willis. Named after General Randall Lee Gibson. He married Lillie Gertrude Hanks. He learned to play the fiddle, by ear, after his father bought him one in East Texas on a cattle drive. He was known to be the very best musician in the area. He was the author's grandfather, whom he was named after.

Henry Elwa Willis–Eldest son of Daniel Hubbard Willis, Jr. and Julia Ann Graham Willis. He is buried in the Paul Cemetery in Lecompte. He named one of his eight children Kit Carson Willis after the famous dime-novel scout. He was the author's great-uncle.

Daniel Oscar Willis, M.D.–Son of Daniel Hubbard Willis, Jr. and Julia Ann Graham Willis. His father died at his home in Leesville while being treated for Bright's Disease, known as Kidney Disease today. He began his medical practice in 1904 and was the first medical doctor in Vernon Parish. He owned the first automobile in the Parish. He served in United States Army Medical Corps in World War I. He owned the Hotel Leesville. After being slandered by a young lawyer in a trial, he bodily removed the lawyer from the man's room at the Hotel Leesville and then threw him into the street. The young lawyer's name was Huey P. Long. Daniel Oscar Willis was the author's great-uncle.

Ella Willis–Wife of Daniel Oscar Willis, M.D. Born Ella Elizabeth Lamberth.

Robert Kenneth Willis–Son of Daniel Hubbard Willis, Jr. and Julia Ann Graham Willis. His wife Eulah Rosalie Hilburn died February 6, 1919, at age thirty-four, during the influenza pandemic of 1918-1919. More people died in the plague than did in World War I. His son Robert Kenneth Willis, Jr. was the first casualty from Rapides Parish in World War II. He's entombed in the *USS Arizona* at the bottom of Pearl Harbor. Robert Kenneth Willis was the author's great-uncle.

Eulah Rosalie Hilburn–Wife of Robert Kenneth Willis. Died February 6, 1919, at the age of thirty-four in the influenza pandemic of 1918-1919. She was recognized as extremely beautiful by everyone.

David Eugene Willis–Son of Daniel Hubbard Willis, Jr. and Julia Ann Graham Willis. He died of appendicitis at the age of eight. He was the author's great-uncle.

Stella and Corine Willis–Infant children of Daniel Hubbard Willis, Jr. and Julia Ann Graham Willis. Stella lived 111 days and Corine nine days They were the author's great-aunts.

Lillie Gertrude Hanks–Wife of Randall Lee "Ran" Willis. They married on January 11, 1914. She was sixteen and he was twenty-seven. They had three sons: Howard, Herman, and Julian (the author's father). She was the author's sainted grandmother and the wellspring of many of his stories.

Mary Stark Hanks–Mother of Lillie Gertrude Hanks Willis. She traveled with her parents John and Celina Marie Deroussel Stark by covered wagon to Branch, Louisiana. After the birth of six children and the premature death of her first husband Charles Oliver, she married Arthur Allen Hanks. They had five children. He abandoned her and their children. She was the author's maternal great-grandmother.

Arthur Allen Hanks–Husband of Mary Stark Hanks. He was seventeen-years younger than her and the father of Lillie Gertrude Hanks. He deserted her and their five children for a woman twenty-three years younger than him. They fled to the Indian Territory and lived near Quay and Yale, Oklahoma. He is buried in the Lawson Cemetery north of Yale, Oklahoma, in an unmarked grave. He was the author's maternal great-grandfather.

Jeremiah and Jacob Stark–Based upon Mary Stark Hank's brothers Rufus and Thomas Stark. Their stories in this book are purely fictional. Mary Stark Hank's was the author's maternal great-grandmother and the mother of Lillie Gertrude Hanks.

Matthew Willis–Brother of Daniel Hubbard Willis Jr. He fell in love with Julia Ann Graham Willis's sister Lucy Ruth Graham. She didn't feel the same way. He was the author's great-uncle.

Lucy Ruth Graham–Youngest sister of Julia Ann Graham Willis. She married James Moore. She died at age forty-two and is buried in the Moore Cemetery near Forest Hill. She was the author's great-aunt.

Boss Man Jake–Based upon Julian "Jake" Willis. He was the author's father.

Jimbo– Based upon Jimmy "Jimbo" Matheson. He is a master boot and saddle maker. He makes the gun belts for the Texas Rangers. He makes the author's boots, chaps, and belts. And he repairs his saddles. He is the author's good friend.

William Graham–Son of Robert Graham and brother of Julia Ann Graham. His gravestone, in Butters Cemetery, near Forest Hill, has KKK inscribed on it. He was the author's great-uncle.

Gerald Duke–A cowboy's cowboy. He was known as Jerry Duke. His last horse was named Majestic. As boys, Gerald and the author would work as a team, roping, branding, and herding cattle. He was the author's brother.

Jim Bowie–Famous for his knife as well as fighting to defend the Alamo. He was a slave trader and a neighbor of Joseph Willis.

Charlie Goodnight–The best known rancher in Texas history. Historian J. Frank Dobie wrote, "Goodnight approached greatness more nearly than any other cowman of history."

Richard King–Riverman, steamboat entrepreneur, livestock capitalist, and founder of the King Ranch. Some believe his ghost wanders the halls of the Menger Hotel in San Antonio.

Ozeme Carriere–Leader of the most notorious band of Jayhawkers in Louisiana during the Civil War.

General Randall Lee Gibson–Confederate general in the Civil War. He was a member of the House of Representatives and U.S. Senator from Louisiana. He was a founder of Tulane University. The author's grandfather, Randall Lee Willis, was named after him. The author was named after his grandfather.

General Nathaniel Banks–Union general in the Civil War. After occupying Alexandria he advanced up the Red River only to be halted by Confederate forces. In retreat Banks and his men burned ninety percent of Alexandria.

Shanghai Pierce–One of the most colorful cattlemen in early Texas history. He trailed cattle to Louisiana, in 1855. In 1900, Pierce lost more than $1.25 million in the Galveston hurricane. He died three months later. The Pierce estate imported Brahman cattle from India which furnished Texas with the base stock from which large herds of Brahmans have grown.

Henry Warmoth–Governor of Louisiana was widely considered a "carpetbagger," a northerner who moved to the South after the Civil War.

Jean Lafitte–French-American pirate and privateer in the Gulf of Mexico in the early 19th century. He supplied men, weapons, and his knowledge of the region during the battle of New Orleans, which helped General Andrew Jackson to secure an overwhelming victory.

Captain J. F. Gerard–School teacher in Louisiana turned bandit.

Appendix A

The Birth of the Novels and the Play
And, the real-life connections between William Prince Ford, Solomon Northup, Jim Bowie, and Joseph Willis

As a child, Randy Willis lived near Longleaf, Louisiana on Barber Creek. As a teenager, he would work cows with his family there on the open range, owned by lumber companies. Seven generations of his family have lived there, beginning with his 4th great-grandfather—Joseph Willis. Randy would often ride his horse through his family's neighboring property, which was once William Prince Ford's Wallfield Plantation, not realizing the significance of his ancestor's connection to Solomon Northup and William Prince Ford.

*　　　*　　　*

After writing the biography *The Apostle to the Opelousas*, Randy Willis got the idea for his novels *Destiny, Twice a Slave, Louisiana Wind, Three Winds Blowing, Beckoning Candle*, and the play *Twice a Slave* from his friend and fellow historian Dr. Sue Eakin. She contacted him after reading an article that mentioned he had obtained the Spring Hill Baptist Church minutes. The minutes had much information on two of its founders: Joseph Willis and William Prince Ford.

Ford bought the slave Solomon Northup on June 23, 1841, in New Orleans. He immediately brought him to his Wallfield Plantation. Just forty-six days later, Joseph Willis and William Prince Ford founded Spring Hill Baptist Church, on August 8, 1841. Ford's slaves attended the church too, which was the custom in pre-Civil War Louisiana.

The plantation was located on Hurricane Creek, a 1/4 mile east of present-day Forest Hill, Louisiana. It was also located on the crest of a hill, on the Texas Road that ran alongside a ridge.

Northup called this area, in his book *Twelve Years a Slave*, "The Great Piney Woods." Ford was also the headmaster of Spring Creek Academy located near his plantation and Spring Hill Baptist Church. It was there, in 1841, that Joseph Willis lived and entrusted his diary to his protégé William Prince Ford, according to historian W.E. Paxton.

*   *   *

Ford was not a Baptist preacher when he purchased Solomon Northup and the slave Eliza, a.k.a. Dradey, in 1841, as many books, articles, blogs, and the movie *12 Years a Slave* have portrayed.

The first part of the Spring Hill Baptist Church minutes is written in Ford's own handwriting since he was the first church secretary and also the first church clerk. The minutes reveal that on July 7, 1842, Ford was elected deacon. On December 11, 1842, Ford became the church treasurer, too. It was during the winter of 1842 that Ford sold a 60% share of Northup to John M. Tibeats. Ford's remaining 40% was later conveyed to Edwin Epps, on April 9, 1843.

It was not until February 10, 1844, that Ford was ordained as a Baptist preacher. A year later, on April 12, 1845, Ford was excommunicated for "communing with the Campbellite Church at Cheneyville." But, Ford's later writings reveal that he remained close friends with his neighbor and mentor Joseph Willis.

Dr. Eakin asked Randy Willis if he would help her with her research on William Prince Ford. He also lectured in her history classes, at Louisiana State University at Alexandria, on the subject.

Dr. Eakin wrote Randy Willis on March 7, 1984, "We had a wonderful experience dramatizing Northup, and I think there could be a musical play on Joseph Willis. It seems to me it gets the message across far more quickly than routinely written material." She added, "a fictional novel based upon Joseph Willis' life would be more interesting to the general public than a biography and would reach a greater audience."

Dr. Eakin is best known for documenting, annotating, and reviving interest in Solomon Northup's 1853 book *Twelve Years a*

Slave. She, at the age of eighteen, rediscovered a long-forgotten copy of Solomon Northup's book, on the shelves of a bookstore, near the LSU campus, in Baton Rouge. The bookstore owner sold it to her for only 25 cents. In 2013, *12 Years a Slave* won the Academy Award for Best Picture. In his acceptance speech for the honor, director Steve McQueen thanked Dr. Eakin: "I'd like to thank this amazing historian, Sue Eakin, whose life, she gave her life's work to preserving Solomon's book."

Appendix B

About Babb's Bridge near
present-day Longleaf, Louisiana

Babb's Bridge was the home of Joseph Willis, in 1828, although it was not known by any name then, other than Joseph Willis's home. It later became his great-grandson Daniel Hubbard Willis's home and then his son and the author's grandfather Randall Lee Willis's home. It was located three miles, as the crow flies, from Amiable Baptist Church (established by Joseph Willis, in 1828) and a little over a mile from present-day Longleaf, Louisiana. Longleaf is less than three miles from Forest Hill.

Babb's Bridge was a community of a few stores and homes. A pine bridge spanned Spring Creek (the headwaters to Cocodrie Lake) in the late 19th century and early 20th century. It had a post office named Lucky Hit and a schoolhouse named Spring Creek Academy (later moved and renamed Spring Hill Academy). The author's grandfather, Randall Lee Willis, attended school there.

Not long ago, the water was so clear that you could read a book at its bottom. However, later pollution became a severe problem due to sand and gravel extraction. In 1996, two Louisiana environmental groups, the Sierra Club and Louisiana Environmental Action Network filed a lawsuit, in Federal Court, against the United States Environmental Protection Agency (EPA) to stop it. They did, but the damage had been done.

Catharine Cole wrote, in 1892, in *Louisiana Voyages: The Travel Writings of Catharine Cole*, "There is a little thirty-year-old town by the name of Babb's Bridge. The bridge, Babb's Bridge you know is an affair of scented pine planks that steeply roof over a section of the lovely creek, so clear, so pure, that if one cast a newspaper on its shingly bottom I quite believe one could read its pages through the spectacles of the water." She added, "I was told of an orchard at this place where the pears weigh a pound each." And, "We put by the ponies at Babb's Bridge and I went by invitation to the schoolhouse."

The site of the long-extinct community is just off Louisiana

Highway 165. It can best be found by traveling Boy Scout Road three-fourths of a mile to a pipeline right-a-way, on the left, between Myers Road and Willis Gunter Road. The pipeline right-a-way leads directly down to the location of where the bridge once was.

The location of Daniel Hubbard Willis's home, known as the Ole Willis Place, was located on Barber Creek. There's a huge gravel pit and sand dunes next to where the house once stood. It was located on present-day Willis Gunter Road, near Boy Scout Road. Barber Creek flows into Spring Creek near the old community of Babb's Bridge and present-day Longleaf.

Appendix C

The Story of Joseph Willis
His biography by Randy Willis

Preface

My family's story in America does not begin here. It began in England in 1575. That year Nathaniel Willis was born, in Chettle, Dorsetshire, which is a county in South West England, on the English Channel coast. The county borders another county to the west that contains my deep Willis roots, Devonshire. Why would my ancestors leave their homeland, England, for an unknown land fraught with danger? The answer was religious persecution!

*   *   *

In 1620 a small group of Separatists would flee England via Plymouth Sound, situated between the mouths of the rivers Plym to the east and Tamar to the west, in the county of Devonshire. Besides fleeing religious persecution and searching for a place to worship, they wanted greater opportunities. The *Mayflower* was the aging ship that transported them. They sailed from Plymouth, on the southern coast of England, bound for the New World, seeking their new Plymouth. There were only 102 passengers and a crew of about thirty aboard the tiny 110' ship. They found their new home and named it Plymouth Colony. They became known as the Pilgrims. Five died during the voyage, and another forty-five of the 102 immigrants died the first winter. There, they signed the Mayflower Compact which established a rudimentary form of democracy.

Nathaniel later moved to London, where his son John Willis was born in 1606, only fourteen years before the historic *Mayflower* voyage. Fifteen years after that voyage, at age 29, John may have sailed for St. Christopher (a.k.a. St. Kitts) in the West Indies on April 3, 1635, on the ship *Paul* from Gravesend. But there is no record the vessel stopped in New England. Gravesend is an ancient town in northwest Kent situated on the south bank of the Thames River near London. If the *Paul* was the ship John sailed on in route to the New World and carrying the dreams that would be passed on to subsequent generations, including myself, he may have barely escaped death. The Great Colonial Hurricane was in August of 1635. It was the most intense hurricane to hit New England since European colonization. If John had sailed a month or two later, he might not have made it to America, and this story, along with his dreams, would have ended at the bottom of the Atlantic Ocean.

Nevertheless, John Willis first appears in America in Plymouth Colony, Massachusetts, in 1635, when his son John Willis, Jr. was born. He appeared again in Duxbury, in 1637, when he married Elizabeth Hodgkins Palmer, on January 2, 1637. She was the widow of William Palmer, Jr. Duxbury was first settled in 1632 by people from Plymouth Colony and set off from that town in 1637.

John Willis (a.k.a. Deacon John Willis), was later the first deacon in Plymouth Church. Reverend James Keith was the first settled minister in the area. The church parsonage, sometimes called the Keith House, was built for him. It is preserved and maintained by the Old Bridgewater Historical Society (OBHS), in West Bridgewater, Massachusetts. It is the oldest parsonage in America.

John also had brothers who were immigrants to the Plymouth Colony area. They were: Nathaniel Willis, Lawrence Willis, Jonathan Willis, and Francis Willis.

The population was about 400 in the 1630s. John Willis would have known everyone in the Plymouth Colony area, especially its Governor, William Bradford, who was the English Separatist leader of the settlers there. William was Governor of Plymouth Colony when John arrived in 1635. John Willis held offices in Duxbury in 1637 and at Bridgewater in the 1650s. Bridgewater was created on June 3, 1656, from Duxbury, in Plymouth Colony. In 1648, John was a juror at the murder trial of Alice Bishope, who was hanged for killing her daughter, Martha Clarke.

In 1623, Governor William Bradford proclaimed November 29, as a time for pilgrims, along with their Native American friends, to gather and give thanks. His proclamation contained these words: "Thanksgiving to ye Almighty God for all His blessings." It would later be known as Thanksgiving.

A century later, John Willis's direct descendant, Joseph Willis, would marry a direct descendant of William Bradford, Rachel Bradford.

I'm the 4th great-grandson of Joseph Willis and Rachel Bradford Willis.

*   *   *

John and Elizabeth Willis had nine children: Sarah, John, Nathaniel, Jonathan, Comfort, Elizabeth, Joseph (1651-1703), Hannah, and Benjamin, Sr. John died August 31, 1693, in Plymouth Colony.

Benjamin Willis, Sr. was born in 1643, in Plymouth Colony, and died there, May 12, 1696. He married Susanna Whitman in 1681 in Bridgewater. Susanna Whitman was born in Devonshire. Benjamin, Sr. and Susanna Willis had six children: Abigail, Elizabeth, Susanna, Thomas, Benjamin, Jr., and Josie. Josie married John Council.

Benjamin Willis, Jr. was born in 1690 and died in 1779 in Bridgewater. Benjamin, Jr. married Mary Leonard in 1719. Benjamin, Jr. and Mary Willis had five children: Agerton, Daniel, Benjamin, III, George, and Joanna. Joanna married James Council of Isle of Wight County, Virginia in 1751. James was the son of John Council and Josie Willis Council, and grandson of Hodges Council. Hodges emigrated from Devonshire.

Benjamin, Jr. and Mary Willis's five children would all move to North Carolina. They would become the wealthiest plantation owners in Bladen County, North Carolina, with vast land holdings, and many slaves.

One of these five children, Agerton Willis, and a Cherokee slave would have a son. He was born in 1758. He was their only son. As the son of a white man and a Cherokee, he lived as a slave on his own property. He was cheated out of his inheritance by an uncle and rejected by many in the family. He would fight for his freedom and change American history. He was my fourth great-grandfather. This is his story. His name was Joseph Willis.

His Legacy

Joseph Willis preached the first Gospel sermon by an Evangelical west of the Mississippi River.

He swam the mighty Mississippi River, riding a mule, into the Louisiana Territory before October 1, 1800, the date Napoleon secured the Louisiana Territory from Spain. The Louisiana Territory extended from the Mississippi River to the Rocky Mountains. The territory was vast and largely unexplored, with many hidden and not-so-hidden dangers.

He was born a Cherokee slave to his own father. The obstacles intensified when his family took him to court to deprive him of his inheritance, a battle that involved the state governor. Never daunted, he fought in the Revolutionary War under the most colorful of all the American generals, Francis Marion, "The Swamp Fox." He would soon cross the most hostile country and enter land under a foreign government, while the dreaded Code Noir, the "Black Code," was in effect. In this territory, he preached a message that put him in constant mortal danger. All of this was done under a cloud of racial and religious prejudice of the most dangerous kind. At first, his own denomination refused to ordain him because of his race. He lost three wives and several children in the wilderness, but he never wavered in his faith in Christ, nor in his calling to preach the Gospel of the Lord Jesus Christ.

Move to North Carolina

In the early 1750s, Joseph's father, uncles, and aunt moved to North Carolina.

The family traveled by sea and landed down the coast at New Hanover (now named Wilmington), North Carolina. New Hanover had North Carolina's most navigable seaport, and even though it was not used often for transatlantic trade, this meant the area of the state was easily accessible from all other English settlements along the coast.

Wealthy North Carolina Planters

On December 13, 1754, Agerton purchased 300 acres in New Hanover County (in what is now southeastern Pender County) "on the East Side of a Branch of Long Creek." Pender was not established until 1874. New Hanover included what is now Pender and parts of Brunswick County.

Agerton Willis was taxed on this property the next year, 1755. There were only 362 white people taxed in New Hanover that year. About twenty families owned a significant number of slaves there during that time. These families, along with others like them in southeastern North Carolina, controlled the affairs of the counties in which they lived and set the standards of morals and religion. The four Willis brothers and their sister Joanna were part of this small, socially elite group of families.

Between 1755 and 1758, Agerton moved to Bladen County, just to the northeast of Daniel, Benjamin, and Joanna. Joanna's husband James had been living there since 1753.

It was in 1758 that Agerton's only son, Joseph Willis, was born. Joseph would someday play a trailblazing role in early Louisiana Baptist history and blaze a path for the Gospel of Jesus Christ that still burns today.

Most of the early Bladen County deeds before 1784 were lost due to a series of fires; thus, we are unable to find Agerton's first purchase of land in Bladen County. Nevertheless, a description of the bulk of his lands can be gleaned from later deeds. He purchased 640 acres from his brother Daniel on May 21, 1762, on the west side of the Northwest Cape Fear River. He then bought an additional 2,560 acres between October 1766, and May 1773, on both sides of the Northwest Cape Fear River near Goodman's Swamp. Altogether, Agerton's holdings formed a vast and nearly contiguous extent of land on both sides of the Northwest Cape Fear River, near the current Cumberland County line in present-day northwest Bladen County.

Agerton, Daniel, Benjamin, James, and Joanna were neighbors on the Northwest Cape Fear River. The other brother, George Willis, went first to New Hanover, obtaining a land grant on Widow Creek in 1761 and selling out in 1767. He then moved to

Robeson County (formerly part of Bladen County), not far west of the rest of the family.

The four Willis brothers were all wealthy planters with extensive land holdings. As a planter, Agerton owned slaves, some of whom were Native American. At this time in North Carolina, many slaves were Native Americans; in fact, as late as the 1780s in North Carolina, a third of all slaves were Native Americans. Native Americans were made slaves by the white plantation owners from the very beginning.

William Moreau Goins, Ph.D., wrote in the educational *Teachers Guide South Carolina Indians* in an article entitled "The Forgotten Story of American Indian Slavery" that "When Americans think of slavery, our minds create images of Africans inhumanely crowded aboard ships plying the middle passage from Africa, or of blacks stooped to pick cotton in Southern fields. We don't conjure images of American Indians chained in coffles and marched to ports like Boston and Charleston, and then shipped to other ports in the Atlantic world. Yet Indian slavery and an Indian slave trade were ubiquitous in early America." Cherokee and other Native Americans were traded in slavery long before any arrived from Africa. The Indian slave traders of the Carolinas engaged in successful slaving among the Westo, the Tuscarora, the Yamasee, and the Cherokee.

Born a Slave

It was to a Cherokee slave of Agerton's that his only son, Joseph, was born. The relationship of Agerton and Joseph's mother can only be speculation, but under the North Carolina laws of 1741, all interracial marriages were illegal. Since Joseph's mother was a slave, he was born to a slave status. It is clear from Agerton's will, though, that he did not consider Joseph a slave but a beloved son—in fact, his only son. This fact did not sit well with some other members of the family.

Agerton's will reveals he intended to free Joseph, but this presented legal problems. "An Act Concerning Servants and Slaves," the law in North Carolina, stated, "That no Negro or Mulatto Slaves shall be set free, upon any Pretense whatsoever, except for meritorious Services, to be adjudged and allowed of by the County Court and License thereupon first had and obtained."

Joseph could not be freed solely by Agerton's wishes. In 1776, Agerton was only forty-nine but in poor health, and Joseph was still too young to prove "meritorious Services." Therefore, Agerton attempted to free him through his will written September 18, 1776, and also to bequeath to him most of his property. Just eighty days before this will was written, the Declaration of Independence had been signed, and times were very chaotic. Agerton would be dead within a year at age fifty.

The Race Card

The problem for Joseph was that the family was advised by legal counsel that this part of the will could be overturned. This was a crafty legal maneuver by Joseph's uncle, Daniel Willis, for a slave could not legally inherit real estate at this time in North Carolina. Therefore, if Joseph was not freed, he could not be a legal heir. Since Agerton had no other children, this would make his eldest brother Daniel Willis "legal heir at law" under North Carolina laws of primogeniture in effect until 1784. Agerton had intended the trustee to obtain Joseph's freedom so he could obtain his inheritance, too, but Daniel ignored these wishes, as the following letter to the governor of North Carolina reveals:

Daniel Willis Senr. To Gov. Caswell Respecting Admtn. & C.
(From MS Records in Office of Secretary of State.)
"Oct. 10th 1777.
MAY IT PLEASE YOUR EXCELLENCY
I have a small favr. [sic] to beg if your Excellency will be pleased to grant it Viz. as my Deceas'd [sic] Brother Agerton Willis gave the graitest [sic] Part of his Estate to his Molata [sic] boy Joseph and as he is a born slave & not set free Agreeable to Law my Brothers [sic] heirs are not satisfied that he shall have it. I am One of the Exectrs. [sic] and by Mr. M. Grice's Directions have the Estate in my possession as the Trustee Refused giving Security that the boy should have it when off [sic] Age If he Could Inherit it and now this seting [sic] of counsel some of them Intends to Apply for Administration as graitest [sic] Credittors [sic]. I am

my Brothers [sic] heir at Law and if Administration is to be obtained I will apply myself Before the Rise of the Counsel and begg [sic] your Excellency will not grant it to any off [sic] them Untill [sic] I Come your Excellency's Compliance will graitly [sic] Oblige your most Obedient Humble Servt [sic] to Command

DAN. WILLIS, SEN.

Pray Excuse my freedm. [sic]"

The term "Molata [sic] boy" used by Daniel might indicate his attitude toward Joseph's mixed heritage, but I suspect he used it more for a legal emphasis on the laws of North Carolina in the letter, because virtually all Native Americans of mixed blood were known as mulattos in North Carolina at that time.

Later American history graphically illustrates the intense feelings of hate and prejudice toward Native Americans. More than seventy years after Joseph was born, President Andrew Jackson persuaded Congress in 1829 to pass a bill that ordered all Native American tribes of the South to be moved west of the Mississippi River. The Cherokees appealed to the Supreme Court, and Chief Justice John Marshall upheld their claim that there was no constitutional right to remove them from their ancestral lands. Jackson called this decision "too preposterous" and ignored the Supreme Court. He then ordered the army to "get them out." The Cherokees were driven out to Oklahoma on what came to be known as the Trail of Tears. Along the way, a quarter of them died. The Cherokees were one of the so-called Five Civilized Tribes and were the most advanced of all Native Americans, with their own road system and libraries before any white person came into contact with them. They considered all men to be brothers, yet this was of little importance to many of that day. No doubt young Joseph Willis would draw from these character traits from his mother, as much as he did strength from his English father.

Daniel Willis's petition to the court also reveals that Joseph was not of legal age as of the date of the will, September 18, 1776. Legal age was then twenty-one; therefore, Joseph could not have been born before September 18, 1755, as some have supposed. It should also be pointed out that technically this case should have proceeded to the District Superior Court at Wilmington, but this court was in abeyance until 1778, following the collapse of the court law in November 1772. Therefore, Daniel was writing to the governor and council instead.

The Bladen County tax list of 1784 indicates that the case had been decided by then since Agerton's property was taxed in that year under different family members' names. Even though Agerton's will had been probated and Joseph was living as if he were free, as he had always done, he was still technically a slave.

My Cousin's Keeper

In November of 1787, Joseph's first cousin John Willis, by then a member of the General Assembly of North Carolina and the eldest son of Daniel Willis, introduced a "bill to emancipate Joseph, a Mulatto Slave, the property of the Estate of Agerton Willis, late of Bladen, deceased." The bill passed its third reading on December 6, 1787, and Joseph was a free man by law at last.

The following quotes from the settlement listed in the final act are of interest:

"Whereas, Agerton Willis, late of Bladen County…did by his last will and testament devise to the said Joseph his freedom and emancipation, and did also give unto the said Joseph a considerable property, both real and personal: And whereas the executor and next of kin to the said Joseph did in pursuance of the said will take counsel thereon, and were well advised that the same could not by any means take effect, but would be of prejudice to the said slave and subject him still as property of the said Agerton Willis; whereupon the said executor and next of kin, together with the heirs of the said Agerton Willis, deceased, did cause a fair and equal distribution of the said estate, as well as do equity and justice in the said case to the said Joseph, as in pursuance of their natural love and affection to the said Agerton, and did resolve on the freedom of the said Joseph and to give an equal proportion of the said estate…Joseph Willis shall henceforward be entitled to all the rights and privileges of a free person of mixed blood: provided nevertheless, that this act shall not extend to enable the said Joseph by himself or attorney, or any other person in trust for him, in any manner to commence or prosecute any suit or suits for any other property but such as may be given him by this act…."

There is a lot revealed in this document. First, note that they call themselves the "next of kin" to the said Joseph. The "fair and equal distribution" that is referred to turns out to be considerably less than the "graitest Part" [sic] mentioned in Daniel's letter ten years before. A later deed reveals that Joseph got 320 acres as settlement, and the above document indicates he also received some personal property as "consideration" for what "he may have acquired by his own industry."

The other real estate that Joseph should have received is described as "unbequeathed lands of Agerton" in later deeds because this part of the will was overturned. These deeds reveal that Joseph should have received at least 2,490 acres, and other deeds are no doubt lost. There was also a vast amount of personal property that Joseph did not get. There was also an additional 970 acres deeded directly to other members of the family. Sadly, Agerton's will is lost, and this information is gleaned from other recorded documents and later deeds.

Joseph Willis could undoubtedly relate to another Joseph, from the Bible, who later in his life would say, "They meant it for evil, but God meant it for good."

Slavery and Native Americans in North Carolina

According to North Carolina genealogist and historian William Perry Johnson in a letter to Greene Strother, "In North Carolina, American Indians up until the mid-1880s, were labeled Mulattos..." In her book, *North Carolina Indian Records*, Donna Spindel writes about the Native Americans of this area of the state: "The Lumbee Indians, most of whom reside in Robeson County, constitute the largest group of Indians in eastern North Carolina. Although their exact origin is a complex matter, they are undoubtedly the descendants of several tribes that occupied eastern Carolina during the earliest days of white settlement. Living along the Pee Dee and Lumber rivers in present-day Robeson and adjacent counties, these Indians of mixed blood were officially designated as Lumbees by the General Assembly in 1956. Most of the Indians have Anglo-Saxon names, and they are generally designated as 'black' or 'mulatto' in nineteenth-century documents; for example, in the U.S. Censuses of 1850-1880, the designation for Lumbee families is usually 'mulatto.'"

Joseph's mother probably was not related to the Lumbee Native Americans. She was also not a part of the indigenous peoples of this part of North Carolina since there were no Cherokees living in Bladen County at the time of Joseph's birth in 1758. Joseph's mother, therefore, would have had to have been brought to Bladen County, North Carolina, by Agerton in the early to mid-1750s or by someone else.

Tony Seybert writes in *Slavery and Native Americans in British North America and the United States: 1600 to 1865* that "Because of the higher transportation costs of bringing blacks from Africa, whites in the northern colonies sometimes preferred Indian slaves, especially Indian women and children, to blacks. Carolina actually exported as many or even more Indian slaves than it imported enslaved Africans prior to 1720."

Nothing but a Horse, Bridle and Saddle

Many years later in Louisiana, Joseph would tell his grandchildren, Polk Willis and Olive Willis, who were tending to him in his last days, that he left North Carolina "with nothing but a horse, bridle, and saddle." Polk and Olive later told their nephews, John Houston Strother and Greene Strother, this fact, and Greene Strother told me (also see Greene Strother's Unpublished Th.M. thesis *About Joseph Willis* and his book *The Kingdom Is Coming*). Different children and grandchildren also asked him from time to time about his heritage, and he would tell them his mother was Cherokee and his father was English, and that he was born in Bladen County, North Carolina. Family tradition is consistent among all the different branches of the family that I have traced and visited with starting in the 1970s. Every branch of the family, including some that have had no contact during the twentieth century, had this same family tradition handed down.

After helping to emancipate Joseph, John Willis continued to have an incredible distinguished career. He became a member of the General Assembly of North Carolina in 1782, 1787, 1789, and 1791; of the Senate in 1794; and of the House of Representatives in 1795. In the same year that he helped obtain Joseph's "legal freedom," 1787, he was appointed as one of a committee of five from North Carolina to ratify the Constitution of the United States. This was done just in time for North Carolina to enter the Union as the twelfth state and to assist in the election of George Washington as the first President of the United States.

In 1795, Governor Samuel Ashe commissioned John Willis as a Brigadier General in the 4th Brigade of the Militia Continental Army. The land that the county seat of Robeson County, North Carolina (Lumberton), is located on was a donation from John's Red Bluff Plantation. A plaque remembering General John Willis stands there today. John Willis moved to Natchez, Mississippi, in about 1800 and died there on April 3, 1802. He is buried behind the Natchez Cathedral. His son, Thomas, later ran for and was almost elected Attorney General of Louisiana.

The Swamp Fox

It was during these trying times for Joseph that the Revolutionary War began in 1775. On June 14, 1775, the Continental Congress, convening in Philadelphia, established a Continental Army under the command of George Washington. Proclaiming that "all men are created equal" and endowed with "certain unalienable Rights," the Congress adopted the Declaration of Independence, drafted primarily by Thomas Jefferson, on July 4, 1776.

Joseph and a friend of his from Bladen County, Ezekiel O'Quin, left for South Carolina to join up with General Francis Marion, the "Swamp Fox." Marion operated out of the swampy forest of the Pedee region in the lower part of South Carolina. His strategy was to surprise the enemy, cut their supply lines, kill their men, and release any American prisoners found. He and his men then retreated swiftly to the thick recesses of the deep swamps. They were very effective, and their fame was widespread.

They took great pride in themselves. Marion's orderly book states, "Every officer to provide himself with a blue coatee, faced and cuffed with scarlet cloth, and lined with scarlet; white buttons; and a white waistcoat and breeches...also, a cap and a black feather...." Joseph would later proudly tell the family and friends, "We were called Marion men." The lessons learned with Marion would serve him well his entire life. Joseph was proud of his service under Marion, for at the time in Bladen County in 1777, it was estimated that two-thirds of the people were Tories. An oath of allegiance to the state was required at that time in North Carolina, and those refusing to take it were required to leave the state within sixty days.

Joseph Willis would not take this oath of allegiance, for he was a patriot loyal to his country, the United States of America. Loyalty was a trait Joseph Willis would display throughout his life—loyalty to his country, loyalty to his family, and loyalty to his Savior, Jesus Christ.

"Patriots" was the name often used to describe the colonists of the British Thirteen United Colonies who rebelled against British control during the American Revolution. Their leading figures declared the United States of America an independent nation in July 1776.

As a group, Patriots represented an array of social, economic, ethnic, and racial backgrounds. They included college students like Alexander Hamilton, planters like Thomas Jefferson and Joseph Willis's father and uncles, lawyers like John Adams, and just people who loved freedom, like 18-year-old Joseph Willis.

South Carolina

It was in South Carolina, with the Marion men, that Joseph would befriend Richard Curtis Jr. Curtis was to play a significant role in Joseph's decision to go west. Later, in 1791, Curtis would become the first Baptist minister to establish a church in Mississippi. Ezekiel O'Quin would later follow Joseph to Louisiana as the second Baptist minister west of the Mississippi River in Louisiana. In 1786, part of Bladen County became Robeson County, and Ezekiel was listed as the head of a household there in 1790.

Early Louisiana author W. E. Paxton, in his book *A History of the Baptists of Louisiana, from the Earliest Times to the Present* (1888), would write many years later that Ezekiel was born in

1781, and every major author who followed used that date. Of course, this could not be true if he fought in the Revolutionary War and was the head of a household in 1790. Ezekiel's son John also wrote that Ezekiel "grew up in the same area as Joseph." Perhaps the Ezekiel listed in the 1790 census was his father.

Joseph Willis's wife Rachel Bradford and Her Pilgrim Ancestors

Soon after the Revolutionary War, Joseph would marry Rachel Bradford. Rachel was born in about 1762. Their first child, Agerton, named after Joseph's father, was born in about 1785. I'm a descendant of this son of Joseph Willis and Rachel Bradford Willis. Mary Willis was born next, in about 1787. Both of these children were born in North Carolina. Later Louisiana census records confirm North Carolina as their place of birth.

The last mention of Joseph in North Carolina was in the 1788 tax list of Bladen County. He was listed with 320 acres.

Taxed in the same district in 1784 was William Bradford, Rachel Bradford Willis' father. Rachel and her father descended from William Bradford (1590–1657). William Bradford had arrived in Plymouth in 1621 aboard the Mayflower, and on the death of the first governor of Plymouth, John Carver, in the same year he was chosen as the leader of the Pilgrims and served as governor for over 30 years. William Bradford is credited as the first to proclaim what popular American culture now views as the first Thanksgiving.

The Separatists' story of seeking religious freedom has become a central theme of the history and culture of the United States. At an early age, William Bradford was attracted to the "primitive" congregational church in nearby Scrooby, England. He became a committed member of what was termed a "Separatist" church since the church members wanted to separate from the Church of England. By contrast, the Puritans wanted to purify the Church of England. The Separatists instead felt the Church was beyond redemption due to unbiblical doctrines and teachings. This Separatist view would greatly influence Joseph Willis over a century later.

By 1790, Joseph was living with Rachel in Cheraws County (now named Marlboro County), South Carolina, just southwest of Bladen County, across the state line. The 1790 census lists him as the head of the household with two females and one male over 16. In South Carolina, two more children were born to Joseph and Rachel: Joseph Willis Jr., born in about 1792, and Rachel's last child, named after her, Rachel Willis, born circa 1794.

It was also here that Rachel died in about 1794. She would have only been about 32 years old. Rachel may well have died in childbirth.

Joseph was industrious and prosperous. By 1794, Joseph had moved to Greenville County (the Washington Circuit Court District), South Carolina, and bought 174 acres on the south side of the Reedy River on May 3, 1794. He purchased two adjoining tracts of 226 acres on August 16, 1794, and 200 acres on May 8, 1775, on the Reedy River. These three tracts totaled 600 acres. The 226 acres had rent houses and orchards on it. Joseph Willis, at this time, was well-to-do.

These deeds also give us the name of Joseph's second wife, "Sarah an Irish woman."

Two children were born in South Carolina to Joseph and Sarah: Jemima Willis in circa 1796, and Sarah's last child named Sarah after her, in 1798 (she later married Nathaniel West). Sarah is called Joseph's wife in a deed dated August 8, 1799, but she died after that.

Joseph lost two wives in only six years. Forty-five years old and alone with five children, he decided to venture west into a land full of uncertainty and danger. Joseph sold everything and spend it all sharing the Gospel of Jesus Christ. He would deliberately place himself in harm's way to share this message. Personal tragedies, prejudice, and rejection by his father's family would have disheartened most men from their calling to preach Jesus.

Baptist Beginnings

"Therefore, come out from them and be separate, says the Lord" (2 Corinthians 6:17).

In Greenville County, South Carolina, Joseph joined the Main Saluda Church. He also attended the Bethel Association, the most influential Baptist Association in the "Carolina Back Country." He was a delegate from 1794 to 1796. Main Saluda was declared extinct by 1797, and Joseph became a member of the Head of Enoree Baptist Church. He was a member of Head of Enoree in 1797. These churches were rooted in the Separate Baptists, which sprang from the First Great Awakening. This revival, the First Great Awakening, would be a driving force that would significantly influence Joseph Willis's determination to carry the Gospel of Jesus Christ where no preacher of the Gospel had gone before.

Head of Enoree (known as Reedy River since 1841) was also a member of the Bethel Association. Joseph was listed in the Head of Enoree chronicles, along with William Thurston, as an "outstanding member." It was this same William Thurston who would buy Joseph's 600 acres for $1,200 on August 8, 1799, after Joseph returned from a trip to Mississippi in 1798 with Richard Curtis Jr. It was also here at Head of Enoree that Joseph was first licensed to preach.

It is of interest to note that Richard Curtis Sr. was on a jury list in 1779 for the Cheraws District. This indicates that the Curtis family lived in this area for at least a short while. Other historians have also stated that the family was living in southern South Carolina at this time.

After a 1798 trip to Mississippi with Richard Curtis Jr., Joseph returned to South Carolina to move his family to the Louisiana Territory and sell his South Carolina property. Never one to squander time, he helped in incorporating the "Head of Enoree Baptist Society" in 1799 before leaving. It seems that he tarried until the spring of 1800 to depart on his second trip west, thereby avoiding the winter weather.

Joseph's Christian background was strongly influenced by the Separate Baptists in North Carolina and in South Carolina, although he came into contact with other influences in both states. The majority of Baptists who entered the South Carolina backcountry, which included Greenville County, were at first known as Separates. Another member of the Bethel Association in 1797 was William Ford. Later, in Louisiana, Joseph was closely associated with a William Prince Ford and entrusted his diary to him. But, he was born in 1803.

An interesting side note is that just a few years before Joseph became a member at Head of Enoree, its pastor, Thomas Musick, was excommunicated in 1793 for immorality. This same man later organized Fee Fee Baptist Church in Missouri in 1807 (according to the church's history) located just across the Mississippi River near St. Louis. Fee Fee Baptist Church would be the oldest Baptist church west of the Mississippi River in the entire United States. Calvary Baptist Church at Bayou Chicot was not established until 1812. Nevertheless, Musick did not preach west of the Mississippi River until at least seven years after Joseph Willis did.

Spiritual Roots and The First Great Awakening

"Will you not revive us again, that your
people may rejoice in you?" (Psalm 85:6).

As a young man, Joseph heard and accepted the call to preach the Gospel of Jesus Christ. Joseph Willis's sermons were filled with the echoes of sermons and admonitions from First Great Awakening preachers like Jonathan Edwards, George Whitefield, and Shubal Stearns.

From 1734 to about 1750, the First Great Awakening ignited a fire for revival in the hearts of men called of God to preach the Gospel. The message of rejuvenation and life in the Spirit among churches that were stagnant, dying, or dead had an impact until the nineteenth century and the start of the Second Great Awakening. The results even can be seen today. In the late colonial period, most pastors merely read their sermons, which were theologically deep but lacked emotion and the call to repentance and salvation by grace through faith in Christ. Leaders of the Awakening, such as Jonathan Edwards and George Whitefield, had little interest in merely engaging parishioners' minds; they wanted to see evidence of true repentance and spiritual conversion. Colonists soon saw a change toward more animated and passionate preaching styles, encouraging them to claim the joy of salvation and to share the love of Christ through action.

Joseph Tracy, the minister, and historian who gave this revival its name in his 1842 book *The Great Awakening*, even saw the First Great Awakening as a precursor to the American Revolution.

Whereas Jonathan Edwards sought to engage Native Americans, George Whitefield preached among the colonists. In 1745, Shubal Stearns heard Whitefield's cry for repentance and left the Congregationalist church. Stearns adopted the Great Awakening's New Light understanding of revival and conversion. This "new awareness" caused a division in the Congregational churches, into groups called Old Lights and New Lights. The New Lights claimed the religion of the Old Lights had grown soulless and formal—no longer having the light of scriptural inspiration.

The New Lights were zealous in evangelism and believed in heartfelt conversion. Sadly, by the end of the 1740s, many fervent New Lights concluded that it was impossible for them to reform established churches from within. Therefore, they felt the need to plant new churches to reach the lost and those who'd fallen away. Whitefield said, "Mere heathen morality, and not Jesus Christ, is preached in most of our churches."

In 1755, Shubal Stearns moved from Virginia to Sandy Creek, Guilford County, North Carolina, believing that the Spirit urged him to do so. Three years after Stearns's arrival and less than seventy miles from Sandy Creek, Joseph Willis made his entrance into the world.

In Paul's second letter to the Corinthian church he quoted, "Therefore go out from their midst and be separate from them, says the Lord...." As Stearns and the other New Lights left the Congregationalist church, they became known as Separatists, using 2 Corinthians 6:17 as their guide. Eighteenth-century historian Morgan Edwards wrote of Stearns, "Stearns's message was always the simple gospel," which was "easily understood even by rude frontiersmen" particularly when the preacher himself felt overwhelmed with the importance of his subject. Most of the frontier people of North Carolina had never heard such doctrine or observed such earnest preaching. The Separatists had great missionary zeal and spread at a rapid pace to the other colonies.

Stearns and his followers ministered mainly to the English settlers, and seventeen years after Stearns's arrival, forty-two churches were established from Sandy Creek. Baptist historian David Benedict wrote in 1813, "As soon as the Separtists [sic] arrived, they built them a little meetinghouse, and these 16 persons formed themselves into a church, and chose Shubal Stearns for their pastor...." Stearns remained pastor there until his death, and from this "meetinghouse" the South felt the flames of revival, the fan of which was carried west by an unlikely missionary named Joseph Willis.

In 1772, Morgan Edwards wrote that Stearns's Sandy Creek church had "spread its branches westward as far as the great river Mississippi." After courageously fighting in the American Revolution with Francis Marion, "the Swamp Fox," Joseph Willis was the first missionary and church planter to preach the Gospel of Jesus Christ West of the Mississippi River.

Mississippi Missionary

As mentioned before, Joseph was a member of Head of Enoree in 1797. Late that year or the next, he made his first trip to Mississippi with Richard Curtis Jr. This trip was made without his family, as it was the custom of the time to venture west, find a safe place, and then return for the family.

W. E. Paxton records the results of this first trip:

They sought not in vain, for soon after their return they were visited by William Thompson, who preached unto them the Gospel of our God: and on the first Saturday in October, 1798, came William Thompson, Richard Curtis, and Joseph Willis, who constituted them into a church, subject to the government of the Cole's Creek church, calling the newly constituted arm of Cole's Creek, "The Baptist Church on Buffaloe" [sic].

This church was located near Woodville, Mississippi, near the Mississippi River and due east of Bayou Chicot, Louisiana, where Joseph would organize his first church west of the Mississippi

River, Calvary Baptist. Joseph returned for his family by 1799, but it would seem likely he might have made a trip across the river into Louisiana before this date, since this is where he returned with his family.

Curtis had already made one trip to this part of the country in 1780. In that year, Richard Curtis Jr., along with his parents, half-brother, three brothers, and all their wives, together with John Courtney and John Stampley and their wives, set out for Mississippi. Mississippi Baptist historian T. C. Schilling wrote that "two brothers by the name of Daniel and William Ogden and a man by the name of Perkins, with their families, most of whom were Baptists" were also along on this first trip. The late Dr. Greene Strother, maternal great-grandson of Joseph Willis and my cousin, told me that it was a family tradition that Joseph's first trip into Louisiana was in search of a Willis Perkins. Years later in Louisiana (1833), a Willis Perkins was a member of Occupy Baptist Church while Joseph Willis was the pastor there. According to Occupy Baptist Church minutes, another member of the church during that period was Greene Strother's father, John Strother. Joseph Willis, Willis Perkins, and John Strother attended the same church meetings at the same time. Census records reveal that this Willis Perkins would have had to be a son of the latter, though.

The Curtises were originally from Virginia. W. E. Paxton wrote: "The Curtises were known to be Marion men, and when not in active service, they were not permitted to enjoy the society of their families, but they were hunted like wild beasts from their hiding places in the swamps of Pedee." They were a thorn in the side of the British and their Tory neighbors."

Paxton continued:

They left South Carolina in the spring of 1780, traveling by land to the northeastern corner of Tennessee. There they built three flat boats, and when the Holston River reached sufficient depth toward the end of that year, they set out for the Natchez country of Mississippi by way of the Holston, Tennessee, Ohio, and Mississippi Rivers. Those mentioned above traveled on the first two boats; the names of those on the last boat are not known. Those in the last boat had contracted smallpox and were required to travel a few hundred yards behind the other two boats.

Somewhere near the Clinch River, on a bend in the Tennessee River near the northwestern corner of Georgia, they were attacked by Cherokee Indians. The first two boats escaped, but the third boat was captured. The price paid for this attack was high, for the Indians contracted smallpox from them and many died.

Those on the first two boats continued on their voyage and landed safely at the mouth of Cole's Creek about 18 miles above Natchez by land. Here in this part of the state they lived. They called Richard Curtis Jr., who was licensed to preach in S. Carolina, as their preacher. He would later organize the first Baptist Church in Mississippi, in 1791, called Salem. As time passed the population increased. Some were Baptists, such as William Chaney from South Carolina and his son Bailey. A preacher from Georgia by the name of Harigail also arrived here and zealously denounced the "corruptions of Romanism." This, along with the conversion of a Spanish Catholic by the name of Stephen d'Alvoy, brought the wrath of the Spanish authorities. To make an example of d'Alvoy and Curtis, they decided to arrest them and send them to the silver mines in Mexico. Warned of this plan, d'Alvoy and Curtis and a man by the name of Bill Hamberlin fled to South Carolina, arriving in the fall of 1795. Harigail also escaped and fled this area."

Paxton said that the country between Mississippi and South Carolina was "then infested by hostile Indians." It seems likely that Joseph knew at least part of the Cherokee language, since he was half-Cherokee, an asset that could be of great help if the Cherokees were reencountered on the way to Mississippi. For this reason and, more importantly, because Joseph was a licensed Baptist preacher, that I believe Curtis brought Joseph Willis with him when he returned to Mississippi in 1798. Curtis was an ordained Baptist preacher also called to preach Jesus. In addition, Curtis knew well Joseph Willis's courage under fire, since both were Marion men together in the Revolutionary War.

After the trip with Curtis to Mississippi in 1798, Joseph returned to South Carolina for his family and to sell his property. As mentioned before, he sold all of his land to William Thurston in August of 1799, indicating his preparation to depart South Carolina.

The First Gospel Sermon Ever Preached
by an Evangelical
West of the Mississippi River

"Call to Me, and I will answer you, and show you great and mighty things, which you do not know" (Jeremiah 33:3).

When Joseph Willis crossed the mighty Mississippi River into the Louisiana Territory, the Code Noir, the "Black Code," ruled the Louisiana Territory. This decree from King Louis XIV regulated, among other things, the condition of slavery and the activities of free people of color. It also restricted religion to Roman Catholicism, forbidding the exercise of any other religion. The Black Code was in effect by law until the Louisiana Purchase on April 30, 1803. In reality, it was a hindrance to the preaching of the Gospel for many decades after the Louisiana Purchase. Joseph Willis would be hated because of his defiance of it. After crossing the mighty Mississippi, he would head first into the heartland of the Black Code, south Louisiana; that daring move would almost cost him his life.

In January 1797, the governing authorities issued regulations that made it mandatory for children of non-Catholic emigrant families to embrace Roman Catholicism and also forbade the coming of any ministers into the territory except Roman Catholics. Joseph Willis defied this most terrifying rule of law by traveling as far south as Lafayette, Louisiana, preaching the Gospel.

The exact date that Joseph preached in the Louisiana Territory west of the Mississippi River is not known, but what is known is it was almost three years before April 30, 1803, the date of the Louisiana Purchase, and in fact even before October 1, 1800, the date Napoleon secured Louisiana from Spain.

There are three facts that confirm the above statements. First, Joseph sold all his property in South Carolina in 1799 and is not found there in the 1800 census. Second, in 1813, historian David Benedict wrote in his book *A General History of the Baptist Denomination in America and Other Parts of the World*, "Joseph Willis... has done much for the cause, and spent a large fortune while engaged in the ministry, often at the hazard of his life, while the State belonged to the Spanish government." That would place Joseph Willis in Louisiana before October 1, 1800. Third, in 1854, the Louisiana Baptist Associational Committee wrote in Joseph Willis's obituary, "The Gospel was proclaimed by him in these regions before the American flag was hoisted here." That would have been before April 30, 1803. David Benedict was a contemporary of Joseph Willis and wrote his book only thirteen years after Joseph Willis preached west of the Mississippi River.

In violation of the Code Noir and at the risk of his life, Joseph Willis preached the Gospel west of the Mississippi even before Lewis and Clark began their historic journey by traveling up the Missouri River in May of 1804. He preached Jesus west of the Mississippi almost a decade before Abraham Lincoln was born. This would qualify as the first sermon ever preached by an evangelical minister west of the Mississippi River.

The Fiery Furnace

Joseph settled at Bayou Chicot between 1800 and 1805. In 1806, the Mississippi Baptist Association was organized. Though he was a licensed minister, a church had never ordained him. It was his belief that he should be ordained by the church. Some have questioned this and have asked why he did not just organize churches without his ordination. The answer is clear that he believed in the authority of the church and that it was important to him to be accountable to that authority, as he had been in both North Carolina and South Carolina.

He also knew well the importance of banding together with other believers, but there had been no need for ordination before because the population at that time in Louisiana was very sparse— he had only six members in 1812 when he organized Calvary Baptist Church.

However, Louisiana was growing at a rapid pace. In 1812, the state population was slightly over 80,000. Eight years later, it was over 200,000, yet this section of the state was still thinly populated with churches twenty to fifty miles apart and having little communication with each other.

Therefore, in 1810, Joseph left for Mississippi to seek

ordination. His son, Joseph Jr., would later often speak of Joseph Willis crossing the Mississippi River at Natchez and how dangerous it was. Joseph Jr. said that his father would swim the mighty river riding a mule to take a shortcut and save time to preach Jesus.

After he reached Mississippi, once again the race card would be played. Joseph took his letter to a local church stating that he was a member in good standing while in South Carolina. The custom then as now among Baptists was to transfer church membership by a letter. The church to which he gave his letter objected to his ordination "lest the cause of Christ should suffer reproach from the humble social position of his servant." Paxton wrote, "Such obstacles would have daunted the zeal of any man engaged in a less holy cause." The "humble social position" of Joseph was certainly not his wealth but the fact that his skin was swarthy. I'm often reminded when I think of Joseph Willis at this point in his life of the statement that "the test of a man's character is what it takes to discourage him."

Once again, we see an important personality trait of Joseph's that is recorded over and over again. He was longsuffering and willing to pay whatever price was necessary to proclaim the Gospel. After being betrayed by his father's family, losing two wives, and being rejected by his own denomination, he never became embittered. In Joseph's mind and heart, no price was too high for the cause of Christ. His focus was not on the fiery furnace but on the Fourth Man in the fire; he knew the safest place in life to be was in the fiery furnace because that was where the Fourth Man was—his Savior and Lord Jesus.

Paxton wrote, "he was a simple-hearted Christian, glowing with the love of Jesus and an effective speaker." His youngest son Aimuewell Willis said before his own death in 1937, "the secret of my father's success was personal work." He said that as a boy he saw his father go to a man in the field, hold his hand, and witness to him until he surrendered to Christ. Today, many generations later, his influence can still be seen. One grandchild said Joseph would be reading the Bible and talking to them as a few of them would slip away, and he would say, "Children, you can slip away from me, but not from God."

According to Paxton, "Joseph was never 'daunted,' for his was a high calling, a single-mindedness of purpose."

The Churches

After Joseph's rejection in Mississippi, a friendly minister advised him to obtain a recommendation from the people he worked among. This he did, and he presented it to the Mississippi Association. The association accepted the recommendation, ordained Joseph, and constituted a church called Calvary Baptist Church at Bayou Chicot, Louisiana, on November 13, 1812. Calvary Baptist Church is still active today and celebrated its 200th anniversary in 2012.

Louisiana had been a state barely seven months when Calvary Baptist was founded and was in a state of turmoil. Great Britain did not consider the Louisiana Purchase legally valid, and Congress had declared war on Great Britain the past June—The War of 1812.

Just a month and a day earlier on the Boque Chitto River, in what is now Washington Parish, Half Moon Bluff Baptist Church was organized. Located approximately eight miles from the Mississippi border, Half Moon Bluff was the first Baptist church organized in what is now Louisiana but was east of the Mississippi River. Some fifteen to twenty miles southwest of Half Moon Bluff Church, Mount Nebo Baptist Church was organized on January 31, 1813. Half Moon Bluff is extinct, but Mount Nebo is still active.

The Methodists had established a church even before these dates near Branch, Louisiana, but the first non-Catholic church in Louisiana was Christ Church in New Orleans. Its first service was held November 17, 1805, in the Cabildo, and it was predominantly Episcopal.

Paxton wrote, "The zeal of Father Willis, as he came to be called by the affectionate people among whom he labored, could not be bounded by the narrow limits of his own home, but he traveled far and wide." Once when he was traveling and preaching, he stayed at an Inn.

Several other men were staying there. One of these men was sick, and Joseph read the Bible to him, prayed with him, and witnessed to him about Christ. The next morning all of the men were gone very early, except for the man who was sick. He told Joseph that the night before he had overheard the men talking about Joseph and that they had gone ahead to ambush him. He told him about another road to take, and Joseph's life was spared. Joseph would receive warnings other times, too, just in time to avoid harm's way.

Paxton said those who loved Joseph called him the "Apostle to the Opelousas" and "Father Willis." According to family tradition, strong determination and profound faith were his shields. He would often walk great distances to visit and preach to small groups. He rode logs in order to cross streams or travel downstream. He would sometimes return home from a mission tour as late as one o'clock in the morning and awaken his wife to prepare clothes so that he might leave again a few hours later.

By 1818, when Joseph and others founded the Louisiana Baptist Association at Cheneyville, he had been instrumental in founding all five charter member churches. They were Calvary, 1812; Beulah, 1816; Vermillion, 1817; Aimwell, 1817 (also called Debourn); and Plaquemine, 1817. Calvary was at Bayou Chicot, Beulah at Cheneyville, Vermillion at Lafayette, Aimwell about five miles southeast of Oberlin, and Plaquemine near Branch. In 1824, he helped establish Zion Hill Church at Beaver Dam along with William Wilbourn and Isham Nettles. He went far and wide, establishing Antioch Primitive Baptist Church on October 21, 1827, just seventeen miles from Orange, Texas, and the Texas State line near Edgerly, Louisiana.

Joseph kept a diary. William Prince Ford arranged these notes in 1841, and Paxton copied them in 1858. Paxton admits most of his facts concerning Central Louisiana Baptists are from Joseph Willis's manuscript, which is lost today, and Louisiana Association Minutes. Ford also made remarks in this manuscript. Paxton records one of Ford's observations made in 1834, and it is very revealing concerning Joseph's heart:

Nearly all the churches now left in the association were gathered either directly or indirectly by the labors of Mr. Willis. Mr. Ford remarks of this effort: "It was truly affecting to hear him speak of them as his children and with all the affection of a father allude to some schisms and divisions that had arisen in the past and to warn them against the occurrence of anything of the kind in the future. But when he spoke of the fact that two or three of them had already become extinct, his voice failed and he was compelled to give utterance to his feelings by his tears; and surely the heart must have been hard that could not be melted by the manifestation of so much affection, for he wept not alone."

No church ever split while Joseph was its pastor. Baptist historian John T. Christian remarks in his book *A History of Baptists of Louisiana* (1923), "It must steadily be borne in mind that in no other state of the Union have Baptists been compelled to face such overwhelming odds; and such long and sustained opposition... The wonder is not that at first the Baptists made slow progress, but that they made any at all."

Louisiana Property and Slaves

The Opelousas Court House records that Joseph first bought land in Bayou Chicot in 1805. In Bayou Chicot, on June 29, 1809, he sold a slave to Hilaire Bordelon for $500.00. Again in June of 1810, he sold another slave for $480.00 to Godefrey Soileau. On January 5, 1816, he sold a slave for $200.00 to Cesar Hanchett, with the provision that this slave would be freed at the age of 32. On March 10, 1818, Joseph sold 411 acres for $2,000 to John Montgomery "in the neighborhood of Bayou Chicot." The deed reveals that Joseph had initially purchased this land from John Haye on September 21, 1809. This property had a lot of improvements on it. On the same day, Joseph bought a slave from John Montgomery for $800.00.

Other deeds refer to property that Joseph bought while there, such as 148 acres he sold for $351.00 to James Murdock on January 6, 1824. This land was part of a tract Joseph originally purchased from Silas Fletcher on April 20, 1818. He sold the balance of these lands to Thomas Insall on October 31, 1827, for $500.

Joseph's last sale at Bayou Chicot was the sale of three slaves on August 17, 1829, to James Groves for $1,500.00. Thomas Insall paid off a note he owed Joseph on October 11, 1833. These are but a few of Joseph's business transactions while at Bayou Chicot. They confirm historian Benedict's statement in 1813 that Joseph "spent a large fortune while engaged in the ministry," for all of this money was gone in his later years.

It was at Bayou Chicot that most of his children were born to his third wife. The late Bayou Chicot historian Ms. Mabel Thompson of Ville Platte wrote me that she had in her possession the diary of her great-grandfather, who was the schoolteacher in that area. In his diary, he listed the patrons of the children who attended school. Ms. Thompson later mailed me a copy. Joseph Willis is listed as a patron on July 12, 1814.

According to Miss. Thompson in another letter to me, "Chicot's chief attraction was it had an abundance of natural resources, such as timber, good water, wild game, good soil and friendly Indians...Chicot became a trading center for a large territory extending as far west as the Sabine River, serving Indians, trappers, frontiersmen, homesteaders, as well as plantation owners."

Third and Fourth Wives

Between 1799 and 1802, Joseph's second wife Sarah died. Joseph married a third time. This third wife was probably a Johnson and was born in South Carolina, but it would seem that Joseph met and married her in Mississippi or Louisiana. A son was born on January 6, 1804. He was named William Willis and is buried at Humble (formerly called Willis Flats) Cemetery next to the Bethel Baptist Church in Elizabeth, Louisiana.

Other children born to this union were Lemuel Willis, born circa 1812 (died 1862); John Willis, born circa 1814; Martha Willis, born April 9, 1825 (four females were listed in the 1830 census between the ages of five and twenty). There was also a Sally Willis listed in the 1850 Rapides Parish census as age forty-eight and living near William Willis.

The last two known children of Joseph were born to his fourth wife, Elvy Sweat. They were Samuel Willis, born circa 1836; and Aimuewell Willis, born May 1, 1837, and died September 9, 1937, at age 100. Joseph would have been about 79 years old when Aimuewell was born. The 1850 Rapides Parish Census also list an additional four males in Joseph Willis's household: James, born circa 1841; William, born circa 1845; Timothy, born circa 1847;

and Bernard, born circa 1848. It would be unlikely that Joseph would have a second son named William. Aimuewell Willis always said he was Joseph Willis's youngest son. These last four males are most likely Joseph's grandchildren. Historian Ivan Wise wrote in *Footsteps of the Flock: or Origins of Louisiana Baptists* (1910) that two sons of Joseph died, "poisoned on honey and were buried a half mile from the present town of Oakdale, Louisiana."

Joseph's third wife died and is buried at Bayou Chicot. The location of her unmarked grave is unknown, but I suspect she is buried next to the site of the original Calvary Baptist Church, in Vandenburg Cemetery.

One historian wrote that Joseph Willis had 19 children. Joseph's children who were still living would follow him when he would later move to Rapides Parish. Many were neighbors with him as late as 1850, as the census reveals, as well as several grandchildren, who were grown by then.

Joseph's eldest child Agerton married Sophie Story, an Irish orphan brought from Tennessee by a Mr. Park, who then lived near Holmesville below Bunkie, Louisiana. Agerton's son, Daniel Hubbard Willis Sr., was the first of many descendants to follow Joseph into the ministry. Paxton calls Daniel "one of the most respected ministers in the Louisiana Association." He established many churches himself and was blind in his later years. His daughter would read the Scriptures for him as he would preach. He was pastor of Amiable and Spring Hill Baptist Churches for many years. He was my great-great-grandfather. He settled on Spring Creek, near Glenmora, at a community called Babb's Bridge. Many of my cousins still live in that area today.

Joseph's daughter Jemima Willis married William Dyer, and they lived on the Calcasieu River near Master's Creek. Mary married Thomas Dial (her first husband was a Johnson) from South Carolina, and they both were living in Rapides Parish in 1850. Joseph Willis Jr. married Jennie Coker at Bayou Chicot and later moved to Rapides Parish and settled near Tenmile Creek. Lemuel Willis married Emeline Perkins from Tenmile Creek and settled near Glenmora in Blanche, Louisiana; the late Dr. Greene Strother, Southern Baptist missionary emeritus to China and Malaysia, was his grandson. William married Rhoda Strother on the "Darbourn" on the upper reaches of the Calcasieu. Aimuewell married twice and settled in Leesville. His first wife was Marguerite Leuemche, and his second wife was Lucy Foshee.

Many of the descendants of these children live in these same areas today. At least eight generations have lived in the Forest Hill area, including Joseph himself. Oakdale, Louisiana, probably has more descendants of Joseph than any other region.

I visited with Aimuewell's daughter, Pearl, in Denver, Colorado, in December of 1980, and a short time later with Aimuewell's son Elzie Willis near Leesville, Louisiana. It was a strange feeling to talk with someone whose grandfather was born in 1758. Joseph was about 79 when their father was born, and Aimuewell was in his eighties when they were born.

No photograph exists of Joseph Willis. The photograph in Durham and Ramond's book, *Baptist Builders in Louisiana* (1934), is of Aimuewell, listed as Joseph in error.

In Service of America

Not surprisingly, many descendants of Joseph Willis are Baptists, but far from all are. Many have fought in the major wars and served America faithfully. Joseph fought in the Revolutionary War. Daniel Willis Jr., Aimuewell Willis, William Willis, Crawford Willis (killed at Shiloh), and Lemuel Willis served in the Civil War for the South. Dr. Daniel Oscar Willis and Dr. Greene Strother served in World War I. Dr. Greene Strother, Joseph's great-grandson, captured more Germans than any other soldier, besides the famed Sgt. York, in World War I. He was awarded the French *Croix de Guerre*, the Distinguished Service Cross, and the Purple Heart.

Greene Strother also served as chaplain to General Claire Chennault's Flying Tigers while in China as a missionary. Like Strother, Chennault was reared in the Louisiana towns of Gilbert and Waterproof. A host of descendants of Joseph Willis fought in World War II, including Robert (Bobby) Kenneth Willis Jr, who was the first soldier killed in action in World War II from Rapides Parish, Louisiana. Louisiana's Pineville American Legion post was named in his honor (the post no longer exists). The Japanese killed him on December 7, 1941, during the surprise attack on Pearl

Harbor. His body is entombed at the bottom of Pearl Harbor, aboard the *USS Arizona*. I have visited the *USS Arizona* memorial twice and have marveled at his sacrifice and the others as I viewed their names carved in marble at the memorial.

Pioneer Church Life

After moving to Spring Creek, east of the Calcasieu River near Glenmora, Louisiana around 1828-1829, Joseph began to establish churches in that area as well. The first established was Amiable Baptist Church on September 6, 1828, near Glenmora. He next established Occupy Baptist Church in 1833 near Pitkin, and then he established Spring Hill Baptist Church in 1841, near Forest Hill.

Joseph was about 83 when Spring Hill was established. The Baptist churches of that day did not necessarily meet weekly. Preachers would have to travel long distances. Those who met weekly might have a preacher only once a month or every other month. Discipline was stern, with members being excluded (fellowship being withdrawn by the church) for gossiping, drinking too much, quarreling, dancing, using bad language, and in one case at Amiable, for "having abused her mother." But, the churches were also forgiving, if you admitted you were wrong and promised not to do it again. Repentance along with salvation was emphasized.

A good example is found in the Spring Hill Church minutes. After twice promising not to "partake of ardent spirits" anymore, Robert Snoddy had the fellowship of the church withdrawn from him on May 31, 1851. A month later, Snoddy sent this letter to the church explaining his actions:

Dear Brethren, Having been overtaken in an error I set down to confess it. I did use liquor too freely, but did not say anything or do anything out of the way. In as much as I do expect to be at the conference I send you my thoughts. I did promise you that I would refrain from using the poison, but I having broken my promise I have therefore rendered myself unworthy of your fellowship and cannot murmur if you exclude me. I suppose it is no use to tell you that I have been sincerely punished for my crime in as much as I have confessed the same to you before, but I make this last request of you for forgiveness, or is your forgiveness exhausted towards me. It is necessary that I say to you that I sorely repented for my guilt, but my brethren if you have in your wisdom supposed that my life brings too much reproach on that most respectful of all causes, exclude me, exclude me, oh exclude me. But I do love the cause so well that I will try to be at the door of the temple of the Lord. Brethren, whilst you are dealing with me, do it mercifully, prayerfully, and candidly. I was presented by a beloved brother with a temperance pledge to which I replied I would think about it, but if I could have obtained enough of my heart's blood to fill my pen to write my name I would have done it. It is my determination to join it yet – and never taste another drop of the deathly cup whilst I live, at the peril of my life. Nothing more, but I request your prayers, dear brethren – Robert Snoddy

Robert Snoddy was restored to membership. Four months later, he was once again reported drinking and once again excluded.

The Amiable Baptist Church minutes in 1879 declared their position in no uncertain terms: "On motion be it resolved that we as a church are willing to look over and forgive the past, and we as a church for the time to come allow no more playing or dancing among our church members. If they do, they may expect to be dealt with." The Amiable minutes record that one dear member was admonished at a church service for dancing. He then stood in the church aisle, did a jig, and walked out.

Pastors were usually called to preach by the church for a one-year period. In 1857, Amiable voted to give Pastor D. H. Willis $100.00 "to sustain him for the next twelve months...it being the amount stated by him."

In 1833, Joseph became pastor of Occupy Baptist Church near Pitkin, Louisiana. The church is presently located next to Tenmile Creek. He served as pastor there for about 16 years. There he married Elvy Sweat, who was many years younger than he. She is listed as age 30 in the 1850 census; Joseph is listed as 98 in the same census. He was actually only a mere 92. I suspect her age is listed wrong too. Joseph's son Lemuel and others said she was not good to him. As a result of this and Joseph's failing health, his son Lemuel and two men went and got him. They took him to Lemuel's home in Blanche, Louisiana, where he lived the remainder of his life.

On a bed in an ox wagon used for an ambulance, he sang as the wagon rolled along to Lemuel's home. Joseph witnessed to the two men while lying in the back of the wagon. He preached to his last breath, either from a chair in the church or from his bed at home.

It was during this time that a man named John Phillips, from the government, came by taking affidavits as to the population's race. Joseph signed this affidavit and stated that his mother was Cherokee and his father was English. This was registered at the courthouse in Alexandria, Louisiana.

Homecoming in Heaven

Joseph Willis died on September 14, 1854, in Blanche, Louisiana, about three miles south of Glenmora. He is buried in the Occupy Baptist Church cemetery. Twenty years after he began his ministry in Louisiana in 1800, there were only ten preachers and eight Baptist churches with a membership of 150 in the entire state. On January 18, 1955, just over 100 years after his death, 250 people, among them 16 ministers, gathered in freezing weather to unveil a monument in his memory at his grave.

The Louisiana Association published the following estimate of his work:

Before the church began to send missionaries into destitute regions, he at his own expense, and frequently at the risk of his life, came to these parts, preaching the gospel of the Redeemer. For fifty years he was instant in season and out of season, preaching, exhorting, and instructing regarding not his property, his health or even his life, if he might be the means of turning sinners to Christ.

Louisiana Baptist historian Glen Lee Greene wrote in *House Upon A Rock* (1973), "In all the history of Louisiana Baptists it would be difficult, if not impossible, to find a man who suffered more reverses, who enjoyed fewer rewards, or who single-handedly achieved more enduring results for the denomination than did Joseph Willis."

*   *   *

Author's Note

The Road Not Taken

One of my favorite poems is *The Road Not Taken*, written a century ago by Robert Frost. The last stanza contains my favorite words in the poem: "Two roads diverged in a wood, and I–I took the one less traveled by, And that has made all the difference."

My life began on a Louisiana red dirt road. We didn't have much money, but I never noticed it because no one else did either—at least those whom my family knew.

As a boy, we lived near Willis Gunter Road, on Barber Creek, near Longleaf, Louisiana. Barber Creek was as cold as ice.

One day, when I was just a pup of barely four, I decided to venture up the narrow red dirt road lined with longleaf pines to my Grandma's house. Her home was just a mile up Willis Gunter Road and overlooked Barber Creek. I remember stopping to pick some wild dewberries. Perhaps Grandma would be so happy to see me she'd bake me a pie, while I swam in Barber Creek. No sooner had I arrived than Mama drove up in our Oldsmobile.

Now, Mama didn't seem to be happy with me. Visions of her making a switch by slowly cutting it from a tree—I mean very slowly—and removing the twigs one by one flooded my mind. The drama of her cutting the switch was always worse than her use of it. But that did not occur that day, although I later wished it had. She looked up and pointed to an old man driving a wagon down Willis Gunter Road. She then explained, "Ran, that old man drives up and down these red dirt roads looking for little boys. He then puts them in a gunnysack and hauls them off." She did not say where he took them. I did not want to know. To this day, I've never run away from home again.

When I first shared this story with my eldest son Aaron, his response was, "He was driving a wagon? Who'd you vote for Dad, Lincoln or Douglas?"

I seldom get to walk those red dirt roads anymore.

Yet, there is another road, perhaps even less traveled than the red dirt road I trod as a boy in Louisiana or even the one Frost wrote about.

Travel this road if you will. It will change your life. It will change your destiny.

*   *   *

In 1829, a man named George Wilson was found guilty of six charges and was given the death sentence. However, Wilson had influential friends who petitioned President Andrew Jackson for a pardon. Jackson granted the pardon, and it was brought to prison and given to Wilson.

To everyone's surprise, Wilson said, "I am going to hang." There had never been a refusal to a pardon, so the courts didn't know what to do. The case went all the way to the Supreme Court, and Chief Justice John Marshall gave the ruling, saying, "A pardon is a piece of paper, the value of which depends upon the acceptance by the person implicated. If he does not accept the pardon, then he must be executed."

God loves you and, yes, He has provided a pardon for you and me, paid for with Christ's own life-blood, but you have the right to refuse the pardon. Jesus was crucified between two thieves. One thief said yes to Jesus, but the other said no to Him. One accepted the pardon, and the other refused it.

The question to you and me today is the same as it was 2,000 years ago. Which thief on the cross are you? The one who said yes to God's pardon or the one who said no to His pardon? I have chosen to say yes.

You have the same choice.

Come

The last invitation in the Word of God is found in Revelation 22:17: "And the Spirit and the bride say, 'Come!' And let him who hears say, 'Come!' And let him who thirsts come. Whoever desires, let him take the water of life freely."

Are you thirsty? Then come. Let him who hears come. And, whosoever will, come.

That invitation is to you…it is to me…it is to everyone!

Bring your disappointments, bring your failures, bring your fears, bring your heartaches. The Holy Spirit says come to Jesus.

He loves you. He wants to save you. He *will* save you. Come to Jesus, and drink the water of life freely.

He suffered, He bled, He died, because He loves you. Listen to the still small voice, of the Holy Spirit, bidding you to come to Jesus. Don't wait—come!

Look

"Look to Me, and be saved, All you ends of the earth! For I am God, and there is no other." (Isaiah 45:22)

"All you ends of the earth" includes the Aboriginal people of the Central Australian desert. "All you ends of the earth" are those in darkest Africa. "All you ends of the earth" are the isolated tribes in the Amazon rainforest in Brazil. "All you ends of the earth" is presidents, world leaders, and kings. "All you ends of the earth" is the polished lawyer, the gifted doctor, and the brilliant college professor. "All you ends of the earth" is the prostitute, and the drug dealer, and the rapist, and the thief, and the murderer. "All you ends of the earth" is you...and me.

God's Word, the Bible, states, "So Moses made a bronze serpent, and put it on a pole; and so it was, if a serpent had bitten anyone, when he looked at the bronze serpent, he lived." Those who looked lived. Those who looked were healed. Those who looked were made whole. Those who looked were saved. They didn't wait until they were better people. They just looked.

Jesus tells us that this is a picture of Him being lifted up on the cross. "And as Moses lifted up the serpent in the wilderness, even so must the Son of Man be lifted up, that whoever believes in Him should not perish but have eternal life." (John 3:14-15)

That serpent represented the sin of the people. Christ was made sin for us. Will you look to Jesus—will you put your trust in Him—the One who died for your sins. Will you put your faith in Jesus—the One who shed His life-blood for you...and for me?

*   *   *

Some years ago my eldest son, Aaron, was in an automobile accident. His back was broken so severely that the doctors said he might not ever walk again. After fusing several vertebrae in his lower back he was able to begin the long task of healing from the spinal fusion surgery. He was encased in a rigid plastic back brace from his neck to his waist. Later, his doctor finally agreed to let him briefly remove the brace to take a shower, as long as someone was with him.

As I was driving to pick him and his brothers up for the weekend, unbeknownst to me, his brother, Josh, and he removed the brace so he could take a hot shower, in his shorts. Josh was with him but was much smaller than him at that time.

I decided to stop at the post office in Austin, when a still small voice spoke to me saying, "You need to go now." I passed the post office and drove as fast as I could to Wimberley, an hour away, wondering what that warning was about. There were no cell phones then. As I entered the house, I asked his mother where he was. She said in the shower. I ran to it and as soon as I entered the bathroom, he said, "Dad, I'm dizzy." I stepped into the shower and placed my arms under his arms from his back. He immediately passed out. I told his younger brother to help me move him to a bed while their mother called 911. His dead weight was more than I could have ever imagined. We got him onto the bed without reinjuring his back. I knew if he had fallen he probably would have been paralyzed.

As I prayed, following the ambulance to the hospital's emergency room, I noticed the symbol on the back of the ambulance. It was the American Medical Association's (AMA) logo of a serpent wrapped around a staff. The sign of healing medicine reminded me of the bronze serpent on the staff lifted up by Moses. Many Christians believe that's where it originated from. But, more importantly, it reminded me of Jesus being lifted up on a cross for my son. God's son suffered in place of my son. I can't fathom love that great. To this day I cannot see that symbol without giving thanks to the Lord for that warning, and the shed blood of Christ lifted high upon a cross for my sins, for your sins, for the sins of the entire world. Surely, there can be no greater love than God giving His Son's life-blood for us.

When we arrived at the hospital, the doctors gave him

intravenous (IV) fluids and two bottles of Gatorade for dehydration. The hot shower, along with pain medication and dehydration, had caused his blood to rush to his feet and thereby causing him to faint.

Will you look to the One who was lifted up on a cross for you? Will you look to the Great Physician—Jesus—to heal you of all your pain? Will you look to Jesus, who took your place on a cross and died for your sins?

Choose

As I said before, Jesus hung between two thieves on a cross. One of them rejected Him, but the other one put his faith in Him. "Will You remember me when You enter Your kingdom?" Jesus replied, "Assuredly, I say to you, today you will be with Me in Paradise." (Luke 23:43) Both of those men were guilty. One put his trust in Jesus, and the other chose not to. Again, the question is, which thief on the cross are you?

Now, there was a third cross that day. It was for another criminal named Barabbas, and he represents us. Jesus was crucified on a cross meant for Barabbas—it was your cross, too—it was my cross, also. Jesus bore your cross and my cross. He took our place on that cross. The just for the unjust. The Righteous for the unrighteous. The sinless Lamb of God for the sinner.

Self-improvement will not qualify you for salvation, for God's Word says, "There is none righteous, no, not one." (Romans 3:10) Comparing yourself to others will not work either, "for all have sinned and fall short of the glory of God." (Romans 3:23) Doing your best cannot save you, for the Scriptures record, "But we are all like an unclean thing, And all our righteousnesses are like filthy rags." (Isaiah 64:6)

Ask yourself, if you could be good enough to pay for your sins, then why did Jesus have to die for you? The answer is you can't be good enough.

Come—come just as you are. Will you say yes to Jesus—today?

There's a Scripture that I love, and it explains things very simply.

It says, "If thou shalt confess with thy mouth the Lord Jesus, and shalt believe in thine heart that God hath raised him from the dead, thou shalt be saved. For with the heart man believeth unto righteousness; and with the mouth confession is made unto salvation." (Romans 10:9-10)

You can settle this question right now in heaven and on earth by saying yes to Jesus—accepting His pardon, just as that one thief did on the cross.

There are no prescriptive or mandated words. Praying is just talking to the Lord.

If these words are how you feel in your heart, then pray:

"Heavenly Father,

I come to You in prayer, asking for the forgiveness of my sins.

I confess with my mouth and believe with my heart that Jesus is Your Son, and that He died on the cross at Calvary that I might be forgiven.

Father, I believe that Jesus rose from the dead, and I ask You right now to come into my life and be my personal Lord and Savior.

I repent of my sins and will surrender to You all the days of my life.

Because Your word is truth, I confess with my mouth that I am born again and cleansed by the blood of Jesus!

In Jesus' name, I pray. Amen!"

The most famous words ever spoken:

"For God so loved the world that He gave His only begotten Son, that whoever believes in Him should not perish but have everlasting life." (John 3:16)

"Whoever" is you…it's me…it's everyone. Come to Jesus. Look to Jesus. Choose Jesus.

Today!

*   *   *

Yes

We moved to Clute, Texas, from Longleaf, Louisiana, when I was four-years-old.

All I remember of the trip was stopping at the Stateline in Deweyville, Texas. The pouring rain awoke my sister Marjorie, and she awoke me crying because her paper dolls had gotten wet.

Daddy had gotten a job at Dow Chemical in Freeport, Texas. A.J. Jeffers was the first from the Longleaf area to leave for a job at Dow. He returned and encouraged Daddy and others to do the same. A. J.'s brother Jimmy Jeffers and Daddy's brother Herman Willis soon followed. We all were close friends in Texas.

We also kept our home in Longleaf and often visited to work cows with my Uncle Howard Willis and his sons. I was always happy to return. I still am to this day.

Every Sunday morning, Sunday night, and Wednesday night we were at Temple Baptist Church in Clute. It seemed to me that everyone attended church in those days.

One Wednesday night mother was unable to attend, so I walked to church with my twelve-year-old sister Marjorie. I was only eight-years-old. I had no intention of that night being any different from any other.

I cannot recall a single word Pastor Bill Campbell said in his sermon. But I do remember vividly another voice that spoke to my mind—to my heart. It was not an audible voice. It was a still gentle voice, tender but ever so clear telling me to go forward and accept Christ as my Savior.

I recall my response to the Holy Spirit as if it was five minutes ago. "Lord, I'm too shy. I would if my mother was here to go with me."

I felt someone touch my arm. It was my sister Marjorie who was sitting on the back row with her friends. She could not have seen my face for I was seated near the front.

She said, "I'll go with you if you want me to." I immediately walked with her to the front of the church and made my decision public.

I know you do not have to have an experience like that to be saved. Nevertheless, I'm so grateful for that experience for it has never left my mind or my heart.

Oh, that I would today be more still and listen for that still soft voice. Oh, that I would speak less and listen more.

Listen, He is speaking. Look, He has manifested Himself. Choose—say yes to Jesus—today. You will never regret that decision.

—*Randy Willis*

*   *   *

"He is no fool who gives what he cannot keep to gain what he cannot lose." – *Jim Elliot*

In Appreciation

I'm thankful to the many people that encouraged me to write our family's history. My first-cousin, Donnie Willis, planted the first seed in my mind to write about our 4th Great-Grandfather, Joseph Willis. Donnie has been pastor of Fenton Baptist Church in Fenton, Louisiana, for 50 years.

I'm also thankful to my sainted grandmother, Lillie Hanks Willis. She had a treasure chest of stories about Joseph Willis and insisted I write them down.

My Uncle Howard Willis was our family's master storyteller when I was younger. I sat for many hours mesmerized by him. His granddaughter and my cousin Kimberly Willis Holt was inspired by him too. She is a National Book Award Winner, author of *When Zachary Beaver Came to Town*, *My Louisiana Sky*, and the *Piper Reed* series. *When Zachary Beaver Came to Town* and *My Louisiana Sky* were adapted as films of the same names.

I'm thankful to my late cousin, and the maternal great-grandson of Joseph Willis, Dr. Greene Wallace Strother. His Uncle Polk Willis and Aunt Olive Willis tended to Joseph Willis in his final years, and they shared all that Joseph told them. Dr. Strother gave his vast research to me in 1980. He served as chaplain to General Claire Chennault's "Flying Tigers" while in China as a missionary. He was a Southern Baptist missionary emeritus to China and Malaysia.

Karon McCartney, Archivist at the Louisiana Baptist Convention, has provided much help in organizing, cataloging, and protecting my research for decades, at the Louisiana Baptist Building in Alexandria.

My fellow historian and friend, the late Dr. Sue Eakin asks me if I would help her with her research on William Prince Ford. I learned much about William Prince Ford and Solomon Northup and their relationship to Joseph Willis from her. She encouraged me to have my research adapted into a play. The play is entitled *Twice a Slave* and is based upon my novel of the same name. My novel *Three Winds Blowing* is partly based on the relationship of Joseph Willis with William Prince Ford and Solomon Northup.

Dr. Eakin is best known for documenting, annotating, and reviving interest in Solomon Northup's 1853 book *Twelve Years a Slave*. She, at the age of eighteen, rediscovered a long-forgotten copy of Solomon Northup's book, on the shelves of a bookstore, near the LSU campus, in Baton Rouge. The bookstore owner sold it to her for only 25 cents. In 2013, *12 Years a Slave* won the Academy Award for Best Picture. In his acceptance speech for the honor, director Steve McQueen thanked Dr. Eakin: "I'd like to thank this amazing historian, Sue Eakin, whose life, she gave her life's work to preserving Solomon's book."

And above all, I am thankful to the Good Lord. He has given me wells I did not dig, and vineyards I did not plant.

—*Randy Willis*

"Preach Christ at all times. When necessary, use words."
–*St. Francis of Assisi*

About the Author

Randy Willis is as much at home in the saddle as he is in front of the computer where he composes his family sagas. Drawing on his family heritage of explorers, settlers, soldiers, cowboys, and pastors, Randy carries on the tradition of loving the outdoors and sharing it in the adventures he creates for readers of his novels.

He is the author of *Destiny, Beckoning Candle, Twice a Slave, Three Winds Blowing, Louisiana Wind, The Apostle to the Opelousas, The Story of Joseph Willis,* and many articles.

Twice a Slave has been chosen as a Jerry B. Jenkins Select Book, along with four bestselling authors. Jerry Jenkins is the author of more than 180 books with sales of more than 70 million copies, including the best-selling *Left Behind* series.

Twice a Slave has been adapted into a dramatic play at Louisiana College, by Dr. D. "Pete" Richardson (Associate Professor of Theater with Louisiana College).

Randy Willis owns Randy Willis Music Publishing (an ASCAP-affiliated music publishing company) and Town Lake Music Publishing, LLC (a BMI-affiliated music publishing company). He is an ASCAP-affiliated songwriter.

He is the founder of Operation Warm Heart, which feeds and clothes the homeless, and is a member of the Board of Directors of Our Mission Possible (empowering at-risk teens to discover their greatness) in Austin, Texas. He was a charter member of the Board of Trustees of the Joseph Willis Institute for Great Awakening Studies at Louisiana College.

Randy Willis was born in Oakdale, Louisiana, and lived as a boy, near Longleaf, Louisiana and Barber Creek. He currently resides in the Texas Hill Country.

He graduated from Angleton High School in Angleton, Texas, and Texas State University in San Marcos, Texas. He was a graduate student at Texas State University for six years. He is the father of three sons and has four grandchildren.

Randy Willis is the fourth great-grandson of Joseph Willis and his foremost historian.

*   *   *

To learn more about the author and
the characters in this book visit:
www.threewindsblowing.com
www.randy-willis-novelist.com

Randy Willis
PO Box 111
Wimberley, Texas 78676

512-565-0161
randywillis@twc.com

Made in the USA
Columbia, SC
05 February 2019